Michael Robotham started his career as a journalist but then became a ghostwriter, writing many bestselling autobiographies in collaboration with politicians, pop stars, psychologists, adventurers and showbusiness personalities. His thrillers have been translated into twenty-two languages and he has twice won Australia's Ned Kelly Award for best crime novel. He was shortlisted for the CWA Steel Dagger in 2007 and 2008 and was also shortlisted for the inaugural ITV3 Thriller Awards.

MICHAEL ROBOTHAM

CLOSE YOUR EYES

sphere

SPHERE

First published in Great Britain in 2015 by Sphere

1 3 5 7 9 10 8 6 4 2

A CIP catalogue record for this book is available from the British Library.

Hardback ISBN 978-0-7515-5287-4
Trade Paperback ISBN 978-0-7515-5288-1

Typeset by Palimpsest Book Production Ltd, Falkirk, Stirlingshire
Printed and bound in Great Britain by Clays Ltd, St Ives plc

Papers used by Sphere are from well-managed forests
and other responsible sources.

MIX
Paper from
responsible sources
FSC® C104740

Sphere
An imprint of
Little, Brown Book Group
Carmelite House
50 Victoria Embankment
London EC4Y 0DZ

An Hachette UK Company
www.hachette.co.uk

www.littlebrown.co.uk

For all those victims of domestic violence –
may we *never* close our eyes.

Acknowledgements

Thanks to all at Little Brown Book Group UK, Mulholland in the US, Hachette Australia, Goldmann in Germany, de Bezige Bij in the Netherlands and all of my international publishers and translators. In particular I wish to thank Mark Lucas, Richard Pine, Ursula Mackenzie, Georg Reuchlein, David Shelley, Lucy Malagoni, Josh Kendall, Melissa van der Wagt, Louise Sherwin Stark, Justin Ratcliffe, Nicki Kennedy and Sam Edenborough.

A year ago, on July 2nd, 2014, I lost one of my great champions, my Australian publisher Matt Richell, who was killed in a surfing accident at Bronte Beach in Sydney. Matt was not just a brilliant publisher but a wonderful friend, father, son, brother and husband. This book is for him.

Finally, as always, I wish to thank my three daughters, Alex, Charlotte and Bella, along with my long-suffering wife, Vivien, who has been my designated reader, sounding board, whipping post, life coach, publicist, cajoler, flatterer, confidante and true love. Should there be a Heaven it will have a special place for the husbands, wives, partners and children of writers.

My mother died with her head in another man's lap. The car collided head-on with a milk tanker, which in turn crashed into an oak tree, sending acorns pinging and bouncing off the bodywork like hailstones. Mr Shearer lost an appendage. I lost my mother. Fate laughs at probabilities.

The car was a bright red Fiesta that my mother called her 'sexy little beast'. She bought it second-hand and had it resprayed at some back-street cutting shop my father knew about. I watched her leave that day. I stood at the upstairs window as she reversed out of the driveway and drove past the Tinklers' house and Mrs Evans who was pruning her rose bushes and Millicent Jackson who lives on the corner with her twelve cats. I didn't realise that my world was coming apart until later. It was as though she had taken hold of a loose thread and the further she drove away from me the more the thread unravelled like a cheap sweater, first the sleeve, then the shoulder, then the front and back until I was standing naked at the window.

My Aunt Kate told me what happened — not the whole story, of course — nobody tells a seven-year-old that his mother died with a penis in her mouth. Those details tend to be glossed over like plot holes in a shitty movie or questions about how Santa Claus squeezes down all those chimneys in a single night. Everybody at my school knew before I did (about my mother, not Santa Claus). Some of the older boys couldn't wait to tell me, while the girls giggled behind their hands.

My father said nothing, not that first day or the next or any of the subsequent ones. Instead he sat in his armchair, mouthing words as though conducting some unfinished argument. One day I asked him if Mum was in Heaven.

'No.'

'Where is she?'

1

'Rotting in Hell.'

'But Hell is for bad people.'

'It's what she deserves.'

I had always assumed that Mr Shearer also went to Hell, but discovered later that he survived the crash. I don't know if they re-attached his penis. I don't expect they cremated it with my mother. Maybe they had to make him a prosthetic one – a bionic penis – but that sounds like something from a cheap porno.

Details like this have stayed with me while most of my other childhood memories disappeared into the long grass. My mother's final day, in particular, is fixed in my mind, flickering against my closed eyelids, light and dark, playing on a continuous loop like an old home movie. I have protected and preserved these scenes because so little remained of my mother after my father had finished expunging her from his life and mine.

I cling to them still, these fragments of my childhood, some real, others imagined, polished like gems and as tangible and definite to me as the world I walk through now, as solid as the trees and as cool as the sea breeze. I stand on the brow of a hill and look at the spired town, shimmering beneath shades of darkening blue. Thin wisps of cloud are like chalk marks on the cold upper air. Beyond the rooftops, past the headlands and rocky beaches and sandstone cliffs, I can make out the distant shore where fallen boulders resemble sculptures, carved and smoothed by the weather.

I am not a fast walker. I take my time, stopping and pointing out things. Sheep. Cows. Birds. Horses. I make the sounds. Sheep are such passive, apathetic creatures, don't you think? There is no intelligence in their eyes – not like dogs or horses. Sheep are just blobs of wool, blindly obedient, ignorant, as gullible as lemmings.

The footpath reaches a blind bend, hidden by the trees. This is a good place to wait. I sit with my back braced against a trunk and take an apple from my pocket, along with a blade.

'Would you like a piece?' I ask. 'No? Suit yourself. You keep walking.'

I don't mind waiting. Patience is not an absence of action – it is *about timing. We wait to be born, we wait to grow up and we wait to grow old . . . Some days, most days, I go home disappointed, but not unhappy. There will always be other opportunities. I have the patience of a fisherman. I have the patience of Job. I know all about the saints, how Satan destroyed Job's family and his livestock and turned him from a rich man to a childless pauper overnight, yet Job refused to condemn God for his suffering.*

The breeze moves through the branches of the trees and I can smell the salt and the seaweed drying on the shingle. A sharper gust of wind blows leaves against my legs and somewhere above me a dove coos monotonously. Then a dog barks, setting off a conversation with others, back and forth, bantering or grandstanding.

I get up and put on my mask. I slip my hand into my trousers and cup my scrotum. My penis doesn't seem to belong to me. It looks incongruous, like a strange worm that doesn't know if it wants to be a tail or a talisman.

Withdrawing my hand, I sniff my fingers and lean against the tree, watching the path. This is the right place. This is where I want to be. She will be along soon, if not today then perhaps tomorrow.

My father liked to fish. He had so little patience with most things in life, yet could spend hours staring at the tip of his rod or the float bobbing on the surface of the water, humming to himself.

'Thou shall have a fishy on a little dishy,
Thou shall have a fishy when the boat comes in.'

1

'You can't lie on the grass,' says a voice.

'Pardon?'

'You're on the grass.'

A figure stands over me, blocking the sun. I can only see his outline until he moves his head and then I'm blinded by the glare.

'I didn't see a sign,' I say, shielding my eyes, my hand glowing pinkly around the edges.

'Someone stole it,' says the university porter, who is wearing a bowler hat, blue blazer and the requisite college tie. He's in his sixties with grey hair trimmed everywhere except his eyebrows, which resemble twin caterpillars chasing each other across his forehead.

'I didn't think Oxford suffered petty crime,' I say.

'Student high jinks,' explains the porter. 'Some of 'em are too bloody clever for their own good, if you'll pardon my language, sir.'

He offers his hand and helps me to stand. As if by magic, he produces a lint roller from his coat pocket and runs it over my shoulders and the back of my shirt, collecting the grass clippings. He takes my sports jacket and holds it open. I feel as though I'm Bertie Wooster being dressed by Jeeves.

'Were you a gownie, sir?'

'No. I went to university in London.'

The porter nods. 'It was Durham for me. More an open prison than a place of higher learning.'

I find it hard to imagine this man ever being a student. No, that's not true. I can picture him as an overbearing prefect at some minor boarding school in Hertfordshire in the 1960s, where he had an unfortunate nickname like Fishy Rowe or Crappy Cox.

'Why can't people lie on the grass?' I ask. 'It's a lovely day – the sun is shining, the birds are singing.'

'Tradition,' he says, as though this should explain everything. 'No walking on the grass, no sitting on the grass, no dancing on the grass.'

'Or the Empire will crumble.'

'Bit late for that,' he admits. 'Are you sure we haven't met, sir? I'm pretty good with faces.'

'Positive.'

He snaps his fingers exultantly. 'You're that psychologist. I've seen you on the news.' He's wagging his finger now. 'Professor Joseph O'Loughlin, isn't it? You helped find that missing girl. What was her name? Don't tell me. It's on the tip of . . . the tip of . . . Piper, that's it. Piper Hadley.' He beams as though waiting to be congratulated. 'What brings you here? Are you going to be lecturing?'

'No.'

I glance across the college lawn where coloured flags flutter above the entrances and balloons hang from windows. The university Open Day is in full swing and students are manning tables and stalls, handing out brochures to prospective under-graduates, publicising the various courses, clubs and activities. There is a Real Ale Society and a Rock Music Society and a C. S. Lewis Society; and the Lesbian, Gay, Bisexual, Transgender and Queer/Questioning Society – a mouthful whichever way you swing.

'My daughter is looking over the colleges,' I say. 'She and her mother are inside.'

'Excellent,' says the porter. 'Has she been offered a place?'

'I'm not sure,' I say, trying to sound informed. 'I mean, I think so, or she might still take a gap year.' In truth, I have no idea. The porter frowns and his eyebrows begin to crawl, dipping and bowing above his eyes.

My body chooses that moment to freeze and I'm caught in a classic James Bond crouch, without the gun of course, my face rigid and body locked in place like I'm a playing a game of musical statues.

'Everything all right?' asks the porter when I jerk back into motion. 'You went all stiff and scary.'

'I have Parkinson's.'

'Tough break. I have gout,' he says, as though the two conditions are somehow comparable. 'My doctor says I drink too much and my eyesight is getting worse. I have trouble distinguishing between a pub sign and a house fire.'

Two teenagers are chasing each other across the grass. The porter yells at them to stop. He touches his bowler hat and wishes me the best of luck before he takes off in pursuit, swinging his arms as though doing a quick march on a parade ground.

The midday tour of the college is finishing. I look around for Charlie and Julianne among the crowds of people spilling from the doors and wandering along the paths. I hope I haven't missed them.

There they are! Charlie is chatting to a student – a boy, who points to something over her shoulder, giving her directions. He tosses a non-existent fringe out of his eyes and types her number into his mobile phone. Another boy leans down and whispers in his ear. They're checking my daughter out.

'She's not even a fresher yet,' I mutter to myself.

Julianne is picking up brochures from a table. She's wearing white linen trousers and a silk blouse, with a pair of red sunglasses perched on her head. She doesn't look so different from when we first met almost thirty years ago – tall and dark-haired, a little more muscular, athletic although curvaceous. Estranged wives shouldn't look this good; they should be unappealing and sexless, with belly fat and drooping breasts. I'm not being sexist. Ex-husbands should be the same – overweight, balding, going to seed . . .

Charlie has chosen a loose-fitting dress and Doc Martens, a combination that doesn't come as a surprise. Mother and daughter are almost the same height, with the same full lips, thick eyelashes and a widow's peak on their foreheads. My daughter has the more inquisitive face and is prone to sarcasm and occasional profanities, which I can live with unless she utters them in front of Emma, her younger sister.

Eleven weeks from now, Charlie will be leaving home for university. She was interviewed for a place at Oxford last December – as well as at three other universities – and I know she received offers in January, but she hasn't revealed which one she accepted or what she might study. Lately I have caught myself hoping that she's flunked her A-levels exams and will have to retake them. I know that's a terrible thing for a father to wish, although I suspect I'm not the first.

Charlie spots me and waves. She breaks into a trot like a pedigree dog at Crufts. Likening my teenage daughter to a dog is not very PC or paternal, but Charlie has many other fine canine traits, not least of them loyalty, intelligence and sorrowful brown eyes.

Julianne puts her arm through mine. She walks slightly up on her toes, resembling a ballet dancer. Always has done.

'So what have you been up to?' she asks.

'Chatting to the locals.'

'Was that a college porter?'

'It was.'

7

'It's nice to see you making friends.'

'I'm that sort of guy.'

'Normally you appraise people rather than befriend them.'

'What does that mean?'

'You remind me of a mechanic who can't look at the car without wondering what's under the bonnet.'

Julianne smiles and I marvel at how she can make a criticism sound remarkably similar to a compliment. I was married to this woman for twenty-two years and we've been separated for six. Not divorced. They say hope springs eternal, but I sense that I may have excavated that particular well and found it to be bone dry.

'So what do you think?' I ask Charlie.

'It's like Hogwarts for grown-ups,' she replies. 'They even wear gowns to dinner.'

'What about a sorting hat and floating candles?'

She rolls her eyes.

I don't know what's more out-of-date, Harry Potter or my jokes.

'There's a band playing down by the river,' says Charlie. 'Can I go?'

'Don't you want to have lunch?'

'I'm not hungry.'

'We should talk about university,' I say.

'Later,' she replies.

'Have you accepted an offer?'

'Yes.'

'Where?'

She holds out her arms. 'I'll give you one guess.'

'But what are you going to study?'

'Good question.'

Charlie is teasing me. Keeping her own counsel. I will be the last to know unless fatherly advice or money is needed, when suddenly I will become the fount of all wisdom and master of the wallet.

'Where are we going to meet?' asks Julianne.

8

'I'll call you,' replies Charlie, holding out her open palm towards me. I pretend to look elsewhere. Her fingers make a curling gesture. I take out my wallet and, before I can count the notes, she has plucked a twenty from my fingers and kissed me on the cheek. 'Thanks, Daddy.'

She turns to Julianne. 'Did you ask him?' she whispers.

'Shush.'

'Ask me what?'

'It doesn't matter.'

They're obviously planning something. Charlie has been particularly attentive all day, holding my hand – the left one, of course – and matching stride with me.

What is it that I'm not being told?

When I look back from Julianne, Charlie has already gone, her dress billowing in the breeze, pushed down by her hands.

It's almost lunchtime. I need food or my medication will likely go haywire and I'll begin twerking like Miley Cyrus.

'Where do you want to eat?' I ask.

'The pub,' says Julianne, making it sound obvious. We walk through the arched stone gate and turn along St Aldate's where the pavements are crowded with parents, prospective students, tourists and shoppers. Chinese and Japanese tour groups in matching T-shirts are following brightly coloured umbrellas.

'It's all very *Brideshead Revisited*, isn't it? Sometimes I wonder if it's more a theme park than a university.'

'Has Charlie told you what she's going to study?' I ask.

'Not a word,' says Julianne, sounding unconcerned.

'Surely there must be some rule against that. No walking on the grass – or keeping secrets from your parents.'

'She'll tell us when she's ready.'

Despite my reservations about her leaving home, I love the idea of Charlie going to university. I envy her the friends she'll make and the fresh ideas she'll hear, the discussions and debates, the subsidised alcohol, the parties, the bands and romances.

As we approach the intersection, I hear a commotion. A

protest march is converging on the high street. People are chanting and carrying placards. Pedestrians have been stopped at the corner by several police officers. Someone is beating a snare drum next to a girl playing 'Yankee Doodle' on a flute. A boy with pink streaks in his hair thrusts a leaflet into my hand.

'What are they protesting about?' asks Julianne.

'Starbucks.'

'For serving lousy coffee?'

'For not paying UK tax.'

Further along the street, I notice the Starbucks logo. One of the posters bobs past, reading, *Too little, too latte*.

'We used to march against apartheid,' I say.

'It's a different world.'

The march moves on. They're a harmless-looking bunch. I can't imagine any of them blowing up parliament or piloting the tumbrils to the guillotines. Most of them are probably heirs to family fortunes or ancestral titles. They'll be running the country in thirty years. God help us!

Julianne chooses a pub by the river, which is decorated with hanging baskets of flowers and has an outside courtyard with tables overlooking the water. There are couples punting on the river, negotiating the wilting branches of willow trees and the swifter current on the outside of each bend. A rogue balloon skitters across the rippled surface and gets caught in the reeds.

After ordering a mezze plate to share, I go to the bar and get a large glass of wine for Julianne and a soft drink for myself. We toast and clink and make small talk, which is relaxed and natural. Ever since the separation we've continued to communicate, phoning each other twice a week to discuss the girls. Julianne is always bright and cheerful – happier now that she's not with me.

As exes go, she's one of the better ones – from all reports. Maybe it would be easier if she were a harridan or a poisonous shrew. I could have put our marriage behind me and found someone else. Instead I hang on, forever hopeful of a second

10

chance or extra time. I'd happily go to penalties if the scores are still level.

'Are you sure Charlie has a plan?' I ask.

'Did you have a plan at eighteen?'

'I wanted to sleep with lots of girls.'

'How did that work out?'

'It was going fine until *you* came along.'

'So I should apologise for cramping your style.'

'You dented my average.'

'You were a complete tail-ender. A number eleven batsman if ever I saw one.'

'I managed to bowl *you* over.'

'Now you're mixing metaphors.'

'No, I'm not – I'm an all-rounder.'

She laughs and waves me away. It feels good to make her happy. I met Julianne at London University. I'd spent three years doing medicine despite fainting at the first sight of blood, and Julianne was a fresher in her first year studying languages. I changed direction and transferred to psychology – much to my father's disgust. He'd expected me to become a surgeon and carry on four generations of family history. They say a chain always breaks at the weakest link.

Our food has arrived. Julianne scoops hummus on to crusty bread and chews thoughtfully. 'Are you seeing anyone?' she asks, sounding nervous.

'Not really, how about you?'

She shakes her head.

'What about that lawyer? I can't remember his name.'

'Yes, you can.'

She's right. Marcus Bryant. Handsome, successful, painfully worthy – a suitor from central casting, if such an agency existed. I once made the mistake of looking him up on Google, but didn't get past his four-year stint working for the International War Crimes Tribunal in The Hague and his pro-bono work with death row inmates in Texas.

There is another long silence. Julianne speaks first.

'If I had my life over again, I don't think I would have married so young.'

'Why?'

'I wish I'd done more travelling.'

'I didn't stop you travelling.'

'I'm not criticising you, Joe,' she says, 'I'm just making an observation.'

'What else do you wish you'd done – had more lovers?'

'That would have been nice.'

I try to share her laugh, but instead feel melancholy.

She responds, reaching across the table. 'Oh, I've hurt you now. Don't get sad. You were great in the sack.'

'I'm not sad. It's the medication.'

She smiles, not believing me. 'There must be something you'd change.'

'No.'

'Really?'

'Maybe one thing.'

'What?'

'I wouldn't have slept with Elisa.'

The admission creates a sudden vacuum and Julianne withdraws her hand, half turning away. Her gaze slips across the river to a boathouse on the far bank. For the briefest of moments her eyes seem to glisten but the sheen has gone when she turns back.

Almost ten years ago, on the day I was diagnosed with Parkinson's disease I didn't go straight home. I didn't buy a red Ferrari or book a world cruise or draw up a bucket list. Nor did I purchase a case of Glenfiddich and crawl into bed for a month. Instead I slept with a woman who wasn't my wife. It was a stupid, stupid, stupid mistake that I have tried to rationalise ever since, but my excuses don't measure up to the damage I caused.

A single, random, foolish event can often change a life – a

chance meeting, or an accident or a moment of madness. But more often it happens by increments like a creeping tide, so slowly that we barely notice. My life was altered by a diagnosis. It was never going to be a death sentence, but it has robbed me by degrees.

'I apologise for prying,' says Julianne, toying with the stem of her wine glass.

'You're allowed.'

'Why?'

'I guess technically we're still married.'

She sips her wine, not responding. Silence again.

'So what are your plans for the summer?' she asks. 'Going anywhere nice?'

'I haven't decided. I might pick up one of those late package deals to Florida. Palm trees. Pouting girls. Bikinis. Surgically enhanced bodies.'

'You hate the beach.'

'Salsa. Mambo. Cuban cigars.'

'You don't smoke and you can't dance.'

'There you go – spoiling my fun.'

Julianne leans forward, putting her elbows on the table. 'I have something important to ask you.'

'OK.'

'Perhaps I should have asked sooner. I've thought about it for a long time, but I guess I'm a little scared of what you might say.'

This is it! She wants a divorce. No more tiptoeing around the subject or beating around the bush. Maybe she's going to marry Marcus and join him in America. Or she's decided to sell the last of her father's paintings and take a round-the-world cruise. But she hates cruises. An African safari – she's always talked about going to Africa.

'Joe?'

'Huh?'

'Have you been listening?'

'Sorry.'

'I was telling you a story.'

'You know I love stories.'

Her eyes darken, warning me to take this seriously.

'It was in the newspaper. An old woman in Glasgow lay dead inside her house for eight years. No one came to visit. Nobody raised the alarm. Her gas and electricity were cut off. Windows were broken in a storm. Mail piled up on the floor inside. But nobody came. They found her skeleton lying next to her bed. They think she fell and broke her hip and could have lived for days before she died, crying out for help, but nobody heard her. And now her family are fighting over her house. They all want a slice of her money. Makes you wonder . . . '

'What about?'

'How terrible it must be to die alone.'

'We all die alone,' I say, but regret it immediately because it sounds too flippant and dismissive. It's my turn to reach across the table and touch her hand. She raises her fingertips and our fingers interlock. 'We're not responsible for other people's mistakes. Isn't that what you're always telling me?'

She nods.

'You're a good father, Joe.'

'Thank you.'

'You're too soft on the girls.'

'Someone has to be the good cop.'

'I'm being serious.'

'So am I.'

'You're a kind man.'

I've always been a kind man. I was a kind man six years ago when you left me.

Is this leading up to some sort of apology, I wonder. Maybe she wants to give me another chance. A pearl of sweat slides from my hairline, down my spine to the small of my back.

'I know we can't have our time over again,' says Julianne, 'and we can't make amends for all of our mistakes . . . '

'You're beginning to frighten me,' I say.

'It's nothing that dramatic,' she replies, solemn again. 'What I wanted to ask is whether you'd like to spend the summer with us?'

'Pardon?'

'Emma and Charlie are willing to share, which means you'll have a room to yourself.'

'At the cottage?'

'You said you were going to take a few weeks off. You could commute to London if you have to work. The girls really want to see more of you.'

'You want me to move back in . . . as a guest.'

'You're not a guest. You're their father.'

'And you and I . . . ?'

Her head tilts slightly to one side. 'Don't read too much into it, Joe, I just thought it might be nice to spend the summer together.' She withdraws her hand and looks away. Breathes out. Breathes big. 'I know it's short notice. You don't have to say yes.'

'No.'

'Oh.'

'No, I mean, I know there's no pressure. It sounds perfect, it really does . . . it's just . . . '

'What?'

'I guess I'm scared that if I spend so much time with the girls, it's going to be hard to say goodbye again.'

She nods.

'And I might fall madly in love with you again.'

'Restrain yourself.'

I hope I'm smiling. A young couple at a nearby table laugh loudly. The girl's voice is light and sweet and happy. I take a deep breath and hold it in my lungs.

Saying nothing is the wrong choice. I must make a declaration or meet her halfway. She has thrown me a lifeline. I should grab it with both hands, but I'm not sure if the lifeline is tied on to anything.

'You don't have to let me know straight away,' she says defensively. Hurt.

'No, I think I'll come.'

Even as I utter the statement, I can hear a small alarm pinging in my head, as though I haven't fastened the seat belt or I've left my keys in the ignition. It's not much of a plan. There are bound to be repercussions. Tears.

Julianne's lips stretch into a wide smile, showing off her teeth, wrinkling her eyes. We continue to eat, but the conversation isn't as easy as before, the questions or the answers.

Charlie calls and arranges to meet us. She's not far away. Outside the pub, Julianne fishes for her car keys in her soft leather shoulder bag.

'You do understand that this is just for the summer?'

'Of course.'

'I don't want you getting your hopes up.'

'My hopes are exactly where you want them to be.'

Julianne turns her back to me as though she's retrieving something secret from her bag, but she's carrying nothing when she turns. 'So when would you like to come?'

'How about at the weekend?'

'Excellent,' she answers. 'I guess I don't have to give you directions.'

'No.'

She pauses. 'Do you feel all right, Joe?'

'I do.'

'There are lots of things we haven't talked about.'

'True.'

'Maybe we will.'

She leans closer to kiss me. I am tempted to go for the lips, but she turns her cheek and I make do with the warm, soap-scented smell of her and the weight of her head when it rests for a moment on my shoulder.

Take heart, I tell myself, as she slips on her sunglasses.

My phone is vibrating. I fish it out of my pocket and glance at the screen. Veronica Cray is calling me. I put the phone away.

'You should get that,' says Julianne.

'It can wait.'

My phone vibrates again. Same caller ID. It won't be good news. It never is when it comes from a detective chief superintendent in charge of a serious crime squad. She won't be calling to say I've inherited a fortune or picked a six-horse accumulator or won the Nobel Peace Prize.

Julianne is watching me. Waiting. I smile at her apologetically and hold up a finger, mouthing the words 'one minute'.

'Chief Superintendent.'

'Professor.'

'Can I call you back?'

'No.'

'It's just that I'm—'

'Busy, yeah, I know, so am I. I'm busier than a one-legged Riverdancer and you won't call me back because you don't want to talk to me. You never do because you think I want something. But just stop for a moment and consider that this could be a social call. I might be calling as a friend. I might want to chew the fat.'

'*Are* you calling as a friend?'

'Of course.'

'So you want to chew the fat?'

'Absolutely, but since we've run out of things to talk about, I want you to look at something for me.'

'I've retired from profiling.'

'I'm not asking for a profile. I want your opinion.'

'On a crime?'

'Yes.'

'A murder.'

'Two of them.'

I wait, picturing the detective, who is built like a barrel with spiky, short-cropped hair and a penchant for wearing men's

17

shoes. She spells her surname with a 'C' not a 'K' because she doesn't want anyone to know that she's related to a pair of psychotic brothers, twins who terrorised London's East End in the sixties.

I've known Ronnie Cray for almost seven years, ever since she watched me vomit by a roadside after a naked woman jumped to her death from the Clifton Suspension Bridge. I was supposed to talk the woman down. I failed. The events that followed cost me my marriage. Ronnie Cray was in charge of that investigation. I think she blames herself for not protecting my family, but it was nobody's fault except mine. Since then the DCS has stayed in touch, sometimes asking for my advice on a particular case or dropping details like breadcrumbs, hoping that I might follow the trail. Now she's a friend, although I'm never quite sure when to call someone a friend. I have so few of them.

'Find another psychologist,' I tell her.

'I did. He calls himself "the Mindhunter". Advertises his services. You must have heard of him.'

'No.'

'That's odd. He says you taught him everything he knows.'

'What!'

'Even used your name as a reference.'

I pause. Julianne and Charlie are waiting to say goodbye.

'Where do you want to meet?'

'I'll give you the address.'

2

The West Country roads are choked with caravans and tourist coaches that look like jammed logs on a flooded river. Already I wish I hadn't let Cray talk me into this. She piqued my professional interest. No, she dangled the bait and sank the hook, reeling me in like a fat trout.

Someone has been using my name to open doors and gain the trust of the police. He could be a charlatan or a glory-hound or an ambulance chaser. I hate psychologists who strut around crime scenes and pontificate on TV shows, profiting from other people's misery. Either that or they write books about particular murders, explaining how and why – which is easy in hindsight. I can't understand how someone could gain pleasure from such work. This is not some sort of intellectual puzzle or parlour game. Someone is dead, defiled or missing. They had a family and friends and were part of a community.

My left arm is jerking on my lap. I grip the steering wheel and fight the temptation to turn the car around. I could be in London in a few hours. I could pack a suitcase and arrive at the cottage early. Show my enthusiasm.

On the outskirts of Portishead I stop and ask directions at a pub called the Albion. The door, heavy and wide, resists me and I have to lean my weight to pull it open. I see a notice pinned to the frosted glass.

Police Appeal For Assistance

DID YOU SEE ANYTHING?
Mother and daughter Elizabeth and Harper Crowe were murdered in their farmhouse near Clevedon on or about midnight Saturday 6 June.
Were you in the vicinity of Windy Hill Farm between 10 p.m. on Saturday to early Sunday morning?
Did you see anyone acting suspiciously?
Please call Crimestoppers on 0800 555111

The publican is a round, short-armed Bob Hoskins type with booze-flushed cheeks and a boxer's nose. The place is almost empty and he's reading a newspaper between his elbows. 'Customer,' he yells. A woman emerges from the cellar, her copper-coloured hair bunched high on her head with several strands plastered to her neck.

'What can I get you, love?'

'I'm looking for Windy Hill Farm?'

Her smile fades. 'Are you a reporter?'

'No.'

'You don't look like a copper,' says the publican, folding the *Daily Mirror*. 'Maybe you're another rubbernecker. We've had 'em all in here. Grief tourists, amateur detectives, true-crime nutters . . .'

'I'm none of those,' I say.

'Maybe he's looking to buy the place,' says the woman.

The man scoffs. 'I wouldn't spend a single night in that house.'

'Since when were you so squeamish?'

'As if you'd live there! You jump at your own shadow.'

I've triggered an argument and they seem to have forgotten me. I clear my throat. 'Windy Hill Farm?'

They stop bickering and immediately begin again, this time disagreeing over the directions. She says it's two miles, he says three.

'Look for the flowers,' she says definitively. 'You can't miss them.'

I drive on, following the coast road, crossing rolling hills and descending into swales, past white-painted cottages, farmhouses and livestock yards. Stunted trees are clinging to the ridges, bent arthritically as though crouching in expectation of future storms.

As predicted, I come to a mound of flowers and soft toys that has obscured the fence beneath. There are cards, candles and hand-painted signs. One of them reads: *Justice for Elizabeth and Harper*. Crime scene tape has been threaded between the gateposts and torn by previous vehicles. Faded and fraying, it flaps like leftover party decorations.

Turning off the road, I cross a cattle grate and drive along a rutted track with six-foot-high hedges on either side. I see nothing until I turn the next corner and a whitewashed two-storey farmhouse comes into view, tucked hard against the ridge, protected from the worst of the prevailing winds.

An unmarked police car is parked near the front gate. Ronnie Cray gets out of the passenger seat and rocks her neck from side to side, hoisting her trousers high on her waist. For some reason her spiky hair is never dyed the same colour as her eyebrows and creates the impression that she's wearing a wig. With Cray I'm never sure if I should hug her or slap her on the back. She holds out her hand, takes my fist and pulls me into an embrace that's brief enough to be a chest bump.

She's accompanied by another familiar face, Colin Abbott, better known as 'Monk', a black Londoner who is a foot taller than his boss. Monk has been promoted since I saw him last

– he's now a detective inspector – and his tight curls are starting to grey, clinging to his scalp like iron filings on a magnet.

'How are the boys?' I ask. He's got three of them.

'They're good,' he says, crushing my hand. 'The eldest is up to here –' Monk touches his shoulder.

'Sign him up for basketball.'

'I would, except he inherited his mother's hand-eye.'

'Can't catch?'

'Not even a cold.'

Other pleasantries are exchanged and exhausted. Cray grows impatient. 'Afternoon tea is over, ladies, you can gossip later.'

'So who has been using my name as a reference?' I ask.

'Emilio Coleman.'

'Never heard of him.'

'Late twenties, good-looking, fancies himself. He says he studied under you.'

I think again. Emilio Coleman? Emilio? I mentored an older student called Milo through his thesis at the University of Bath. That was four, maybe five years ago. Milo was clever but lazy. He spent more time using his skills to bed undergrad students than passing his exams. I remember his first suggestion for a thesis was 'Do loud music and excess alcohol make women more likely to have sex on a first date?'

'So he *is* one of yours,' says Cray, making it sound as though I'm personally responsible.

'What did he do?' I ask.

'Mr Coleman offered his services to the previous SCO, using your name as a reference. He was allowed to look at statements and photographs. He then went straight to the media.'

My heart sinks. Cray continues. 'By revealing details that were deliberately withheld from the public such as the position of the bodies, injuries and markings on the wall, he has allowed potential suspects to claim they read about the case in the papers. We also have fewer ways of weeding out the timewasters and false confessions.' She lowers her voice. 'This is what happens when you don't return my calls, Professor. We get amateur fucking hour.'

'This is hardly my fault.'

'Yeah, well, you taught this clown.'

'I saw him once or twice a semester.'

'I'm not here to argue with you. I want you to make this better.'

'How?'

'Review the case. Look at the statements and decision-making. Tell us what we've missed.'

'Are there any suspects?'

'Too many,' she grunts. 'The local community thinks we've cocked this up. Tempers are starting to fray. There's a public meeting tonight. I want you to be there.'

'Why me?'

'Let's call it a show of friendship.'

'That's not my definition of friendship.'

Cray rolls back her shoulders and smiles, her eyes twinkling. 'That's the thing about us, Professor, we can agree to disagree and it doesn't affect our deep and abiding bond. Come on, I'll show you the scene.'

3

Detectives have a way of talking that condenses information into bullet points and dispenses with a lot of prepositions. It's a sort of verbal shorthand that colleagues understand instinctively. Ronnie Cray launches into it now.

'Two victims, mother and daughter, Elizabeth and Harper Crowe, aged forty-three and seventeen or possibly eighteen . . . '

'Possibly?'

'It was Harper's birthday on the Sunday. We don't know if she died before or after midnight.'

A gust of wind blows through the trees, making me feel restless. I study the farmhouse, which is seventeenth-century, Grade II listed, with mullioned windows and flowerboxes on the sills. It's set on sixteen acres, with an orchard, walled garden, old granary, stables, milking shed and chicken-coop.

'Looks like a bed and breakfast.'

'Funny you should say that,' says Cray, running fingers over her scalp. 'Three months ago Elizabeth Crowe applied for a licence to set up a B&B. A council inspector gave her a list of work that had to be done – installing fire doors, emergency lighting, new bathrooms and proper signage. She had tradesmen coming in and out of this place for the past month.'

'How was she funding it?'

'Bank loan and her divorce settlement.'

I notice the splintered wooden panel on the front door. Someone punched a hole big enough to reach through and turn the latch. Cray keys open the padlock. The door swings inward. Duckboards are arranged like stepping stones down the length of the hallway. I look at my shoes.

'Don't bother,' she says, reading my thoughts. 'Forensics have been over the place twice.' We step inside. My eyes fall upon a pockmarked mirror in a gilt frame and an assortment of walking sticks in an umbrella stand.

'The bodies were discovered at 7.33 a.m. Sunday the seventh of June. Harper was upstairs and Elizabeth in the sitting room.'

'Who found them?'

'A neighbour, Tommy Garrett, lives with his grandmother. They have a farm just beyond those trees.' She points across a field.

'What was he doing here?' I ask.

'Says he heard the burglar alarm when he got up to start milking. Doreen made him finish his chores before he came across. He jumped the fence and went to the back door first. Then he walked around to the front and saw the busted door. He came inside and found Mrs Crowe.'

'Did he go upstairs?'

'Says not. The first responders found him raving, kicking at the fence and screaming.'

'Is he a suspect?'

'Top of the list.' Cray looks at Monk. 'How would you describe Tommy Garrett?'

'Slow,' is the reply, 'although he didn't waste any time selling his story to the tabloids.'

'That was probably the grandmother,' says Cray, 'but I'm not underestimating the kid's potential.'

I look at a rectangle of sandy sunlight on the worn floor-boards. 'You said Elizabeth was divorced.'

'Eight months ago,' replies Cray.

'Her ex?'

'Dominic Crowe is a local builder. They were married twenty-four years. About a decade ago Crowe set up a development company with his best friend, an architect called Jeremy Egan, but Dominic had to sell his stake during the GFC. Elizabeth bought him out. She had family money. Insisted the company be put in her name. Then she divorced him and took the lot.'

'That must have been galling.'

'He's suspect number two,' says Monk.

At the far end of the hallway I can see a large open plan kitchen. Immediately to my left is a dining room with a polished mahogany table and matching chairs. The mantelpiece has framed photographs and a bronze statue of a fox. Several watercolours are hanging on the wall: landscapes and coastal scenes.

Cray hands me two photographs. The first shows an attractive blonde of middle years with hair just brushing her shoulders. She has a slightly crooked smile and blue eyes beneath thinly plucked eyebrows. The second image is of her daughter, Harper, whose eyes are more grey than blue and her darker hair is pulled into a ponytail. Pretty and athletic, her smile exposes a narrow gap between her two front teeth.

'Harper was found upstairs in bed, suffocated, most likely with a pillow. No sign of sexual assault. Minimal disturbance. The mother was found here.'

Turning right, I step into the sitting room. The atmosphere suddenly changes. It's as though someone has opened a door or window, subtly altering the air pressure or temperature. My eyes are drawn to the smeared reddish brown symbol above the fireplace – a five-pointed star framed by a circle – whose lower edges seem to be seeping out of the plasterwork as if the wall were bleeding.

Certain symbols evoke a visceral response – triggering reactions before we even have thoughts. The pentagram is one of them. Regarded as a pagan sign, it dates back much further, to ancient Mesopotamia. Over the millennia it has been an emblem of Freemasonry, a knight's insignia, a protection against evil, a badge of royalty and a Christian symbol representing the five wounds of Christ. I don't know what it represents in this context – something twisted and vile, a calling card or statement of intent.

Elsewhere in the room the furniture has been pushed back. The sofa is against the main wall and twin armchairs are on either side of the window. Candles have been placed around the room and I notice a Bible open on the coffee table. The pages are covered in fingerprint dust.

'I took the liberty,' says Cray, opening a folder of crime scene photographs. Despite the markings on the wall, I'm not prepared for the visual impact of the images. At first glance they look like staged publicity shots from some Hollywood B-grade horror movie where buckets of blood have been thrown around. A woman's body is lying on the floor, her arms and legs outspread, her palms facing upwards in supplication. Her semi-naked body has been butchered. Violated. Insulted. Defiled.

I have seen death before. I have seen autopsies and accident victims and the remains of children, yet nothing can desensitise a person to a scene such as this – the sheer horror, sadness, disbelief, puzzlement and anger, the senseless brutality and the sick display of artistry.

'She was stabbed thirty-six times,' says Cray, 'most of them after death. You can see he focused on her genitals, but the post mortem found no evidence of a sexual assault either before or after.'

Another image shows the victim's face. Her eyes are open, but there is no evidence of pain or horror on her face. I hope she died quickly. I hope she didn't suffer.

'I don't think I can help you,' I whisper.

'Why not?'

'I'm a clinical psychologist. You need someone who handles cases like this – someone who understands them. Call Broadmoor or Rampton.' I'm already turning away, walking along the hallway, seeking fresh air.

'I don't want anyone else,' says Cray, an edge to her voice now. 'Trust me, Professor, I don't want you here, but this goes beyond friendship or whether you have the stomach to look at those photographs. I don't understand it either. It's beyond my comprehension. But I've seen you do this. I've seen you piece together a crime. You can read minds—'

'I *can't* read minds.'

'Motivations then, stimulus, impulses, whatever you want to call it – I need your help.'

I don't respond. I can't find any words. Cray is waiting. She suddenly looks much older than when I saw her last. Exhaustion has pouched the skin below her eyes and deepened the wrinkles on her forehead.

Every fibre of my being is screaming at me to walk away. Just go. Get in the car. Don't look back. Today has been a good day for me. Julianne has asked me to come home. She would hate me even being here. She'll blame me. Yet almost without thinking, I am collecting details and picturing events.

Taking the photographs from Cray, I stand in front of the fireplace, holding up individual images, positioning myself where the photographer did, looking through his lens and trying to recreate that morning. Elizabeth was naked except for a light dressing gown. Urine stained the front. How is that possible? The first stab wound severed her carotid artery. Arterial blood sprayed the armchair nearest her head. She lost control of her bladder. He laid her down gently, before going berserk.

This is what I do – I look at the scene and imagine the act, replaying it in my mind, identifying the psychological markers that underpin each element of human behaviour. I have seen and heard many disturbing things in my consulting room. I

28

have treated the sad, the lonely, the disconnected, the angry, the anxious, the jealous, the suicidal and the murderous. I have plumbed the depths of human misery yet I know that there is always another layer, darker and more dangerous.

'Were there traces of blood in any of the bathrooms?' I ask.

'In the laundry,' says Cray.

'What about upstairs?'

'No.'

'Latent prints?'

'Forty-eight full or partial prints from the house – most of them match with the family. A concentration of blood was found inside the front door, along with a smeared shoe print.'

I walk along the hallway into the kitchen. There are twin cups draining beside the sink next to a single wine glass. Rubber gloves are hanging on the tap. The Aga stove is cold.

Cray is still talking. 'Forensic services collected fibres from the rug. There were old semen stains on the daughter's bedding. The DNA results match her boyfriend. The mother had multiple semen stains on the front seat of her car, but none on her sheets. We've run the DNA through the database. Nothing yet.'

'Was the mother seeing someone?' I ask.

'Not exclusively,' says Cray, grimacing slightly.

'Meaning?'

'Do you know what dogging is, Professor?'

'I have come across the term, but maybe you should enlighten me.'

Cray lowers her eyes, uncomfortable with the topic. 'Some people get off on committing sexual acts outdoors in semi-public places. There's a whole subculture around it – rules of engagement, etiquette, websites . . . '

'And Elizabeth Crowe was into this?'

'That's our belief. We have at least one statement that puts her at a dogging site performing a sexual act in public and we have the semen stains in her car.'

'So her killer could have met her or watched her?'

29

'Yes.'

'That makes it more difficult.'

'Tell me about it.'

Cray runs through the hours preceding the murders. 'Elizabeth had told her sister she was staying in for the evening, but a mobile phone trace shows she left the farmhouse just after eight-thirty. We tracked her movements to Clevedon Court Woods on Tickenham Road. It's a known dogging site. Secluded. Private.'

'Did anyone see her there?'

'We set up a mobile incident room and tried to talk to drivers, but word spread pretty quickly. Nobody bothered turning up.'

'Could she have arranged to meet someone?'

'Nothing has showed up on her text messages, phone records or emails, but she could have planned it earlier.' Cray rubs at her eyes, which are puffy from lack of sleep. 'There's another complication. We know that Mrs Crowe joined an online dating agency six months ago. She went on two dates – both with local men.'

'Did she have sex with them?'

'They denied it at first. One of them was married. His semen stains were found in Elizabeth's car. The other is a widower. He had sex with her at a flat in Bristol. The widower has an alibi for the night of the murders. The married man is still on our radar.'

A dripping tap makes a dull plinking sound like someone plucking on a single harp string. Standing at the kitchen sink, I gaze out the window where the shadows are lengthening and trees are etched against the ridgeline. Something catches my eye – a movement near the stables. A ginger-and-black tabby cat is sniffing at the rubbish bins.

'Did they have any pets?' I ask.

'A cat,' says Monk. 'She's missing.'

'I think she's come home.'

He opens the back door and walks through the garden. I watch him crouch and call softly to the tabby, holding out his hand. The cat looks at him suspiciously. He moves closer. With a flick of her tail, she's gone, disappearing into the long weeds that brush the curved belly of the diesel tank.

'She's probably starving,' he says, returning to the kitchen and opening cupboards. He finds a can of cat food and looks for an opener. Cray is impatient to continue.

'There is an adopted son – Elliot – aged twenty-six, lives in Bristol. Has a history of substance abuse, two minor convictions. He was fostered at age eight and adopted soon afterwards. Elizabeth had been told she couldn't have children but fell pregnant with Harper almost immediately. Isn't that often the way?'

'Does Elliot have an alibi?'

'Claims he spent the night with a stripper in Bristol, but can't remember her name or address.'

'Convenient.'

'Exactly.'

'How did he and his mother get on?'

'Elliot sided with the father during the divorce. Wouldn't talk to Elizabeth. That didn't stop him putting his hand out for money.'

'Does he inherit the house?'

'As far as we know.'

I pour myself a glass of water. My left hand shakes as I raise it to my lips. I brush water from the front of my shirt.

'So this Tommy Garrett – the neighbour – discovered the bodies. Apart from being found at the scene is there any reason to suspect him?'

'The kid does a lot of work around the farm – mowing the grass and cutting firewood. About six months ago Mrs Crowe lodged a complaint that someone was stealing underwear from her clothesline. She blamed Tommy but had no proof. The local police gave him a lecture and that seemed to resolve matters.'

31

'Does he have a key?'

'No.'

'What about an alibi?'

'Says he was watching TV until late.'

'Anyone confirm it?'

'His grandmother won't hear a bad word said about him.'

Cray is ready to show me Harper's room. At the top of the narrow staircase we turn back on ourselves and follow a landing through the length of the house. There are bedrooms on either side. Some of them have en-suite bathrooms, which are naked shells, half-finished, awaiting tiles and fittings. There are drop sheets on the floors where tools and bags of tiling grout await the return of tradesmen.

We reach an attic room with a single bed tucked beneath the sloping roof. It is a typical teenager's room. Messy. Cluttered. Characterful. Clothes are hanging on radiators and spilling from drawers and wicker baskets. A bra hangs from the doorknob. Dirty clothes have missed the hamper. Photographs are stuck on the walls, along with posters and pennants and banners. It reminds me of Charlie's room at the cottage, only her posters feature hipsters with heavy beards or effeminate-looking boys with fine-boned faces.

'She was lying in bed,' says Cray. 'Didn't have a mark on her.'

'Were the blinds up or down?'

'Down.'

I pull the cord and a fabric blind concertinas upwards, revealing the window, which is cracked open. The sill is deco-rated with soft toys, knick-knacks, pet rocks, crystals and a snow dome of the Eiffel Tower. I notice a small missing square of glass in one corner.

'It was broken from the outside,' says Cray. 'We found shards of glass on the floor.'

I slide open the window and look outside. The slate tiles are etched with dried moss. The drop to the ground is about twenty feet. I guess someone could have shimmied up or down a drainpipe, but the broken pane of glass is too low for anyone to reach the latch.

The room is messy, but nothing has been upset or knocked over by bodies in motion.

I look at the sketches and unframed watercolours.

'Who did these?'

'Harper,' says Cray. 'She was going to study art.'

There are books on painting and photography on a floating shelf above Harper's desk and the sloping ceiling above her bed is dotted with Polaroid photographs. She must have liked the whole retro look – using film instead of a digital SLR. Maybe it was the sound of the pictures spitting out of the camera, or watching how the chemicals formed images on the blank paper.

'Did you find her camera?' I ask, glancing along the shelves.

Cray is still standing at the bedroom door. 'It was on the back seat of her car.'

I cross the landing to Elizabeth's bedroom where an antique cast-iron bed holds a sagging mattress as if an invisible corpse were still lying in the centre. The sheets are gone. Forensics will be searching for fibres, sweat, semen or flakes of skin.

A walk-in wardrobe leads to the en-suite. Standing amid the hanging racks of clothes, I run my fingers over the garments, feeling the fabrics. Size 12. Name brands. Most of the styles belong to past years. These are clothes being made to last by a woman once accustomed to having money, who discovered that she might not have enough.

When I pull open a drawer, lingerie spills out: G-strings and camisoles and matching bra and panties, some of them almost lighter than air. Were they gifts or did she buy these things for herself?

I slip my hand into her coat pockets, pulling out a sweet wrapper, a dry-cleaning stub, loose change, half a cinema ticket, a petrol receipt and a business card for a plumbing company.

I step into the en suite. The toilet seat is down. A single towel is hanging neatly on the rails outside the shower/bath.

Cray is waiting in the bedroom. I try to put the events in order. A panel on the front door was broken. The burglar alarm was triggered. It would have woken Elizabeth. She would have called the police. Instead she put on her dressing gown and went downstairs.

Pausing at the window, I look across the small rectangular front garden to where a railing fence separates it from a field that drops away in a gentle slope to the hedgerows that line the coast road.

'Were these curtains open?' I ask.

'Yes.'

'What about the bedside lamp?'

'It was on.'

A book is resting on the side table beneath the light: *Life after Life* by Kate Atkinson. A bookmark pokes from between the pages, halfway through. She will not finish the story. Not unless she finds another life.

Psychologists view crime scenes differently from detectives. Physical clues and witnesses are important when it comes to *making* a case against a known suspect, but have little benefit unless they have a context. The farmhouse contains tens of thousands of pieces of information. It tells me how Elizabeth and Harper lived, what they ate, wore, drank, shared, read, listened to and watched on TV. Open any drawer, or book, or photo album and I will learn something about mother or daughter. But what good is all this information if I can't tell which of these details are important and which are white noise?

Did Elizabeth arrange for someone to come? Did she leave her curtains open that night as a signal or out of habit?

'I want you to do something for me,' I say to Cray. 'Ask DI Abbott to drive down to the front gate, turn around and drive back again.'

The DCS doesn't ask me why. Moments later I watch from the bedroom window as Monk negotiates the farm track in the unmarked police car. It disappears between the hedgerows and I imagine him doing a three-point turn when he reaches the road. In the meantime, I stretch out on the bare mattress and pat the bed.

'Come on, lie down.'

Cray raises an eyebrow. 'I don't bat for your team.'

'Maybe you haven't met the right man.'

'Are you seriously going to run that line on me?'

'Shut up and lie down.'

'What are we doing?'

'Listening.'

We both remain still, staring at the white-painted ceiling, until I hear the sound of the car labouring up the track and crunching over gravel. It pulls up outside the stables. A vehicle door opens and closes.

'Could you sleep through that?' I ask.

'Depends how much wine I'd consumed.'

'You'd certainly hear someone break through the front door.'

'True.'

Retracing my steps, I descend the stairs and walk along the hallway to the kitchen and then outside to the rear gate where the lawn needs cutting and weeds have commandeered the flowerbeds. The sun is dropping quickly, etching one horizon against a fiery sky. I turn back to look at the house, which is now bathed in an orange glow. My gaze sweeps over the windows and the French doors. I watch for a long time without stirring, hearing only the slow beat of my own blood and the hoarse cry of gulls.

DCS Cray has followed me outside.

'Was anything taken?' I ask.

'Mrs Crowe sometimes kept cash in the house to pay tradesmen and some of her jewellery is missing, according to her sister. We're searching pawn shops and online dealers.'

'What about the murder weapon?'

'A seven-inch single-sided kitchen knife – also missing.'

'He didn't come prepared.'

'Is that important?'

'Maybe.'

I go back over the details, trying to fix the timeline in my mind. If someone broke into the farmhouse through the front door, it would have woken Elizabeth and Harper, who would have called the police. Instead the mother put on her dressing gown and went downstairs. She opened the door, had a conversation and invited the killer inside. Perhaps they argued . . . ? No, Harper would have woken. Elizabeth must have been attacked so suddenly that she didn't have time to cry out.

Why stage a break-in and trip the alarm? It was never going to look like a robbery – not after what he did to Elizabeth. And if someone did want to break into the farmhouse – there are at least a dozen easier places. They could have shattered one of the sash windows or jemmied the patio doors.

'What about the pentagram and the Bible?' asks Cray. 'Are we dealing with some sort of ritual killing?'

'I honestly don't know.'

'So you're going to help us?'

'I need time to think,' I say.

She looks pleased with herself.

'On one condition,' I add. 'You don't call me again or seek my advice.'

'Agreed.'

'I mean it.'

'Understood.'

Monk asks if he should lock up the farmhouse. DCS Cray nods and we wait as he threads a chain and padlock on the door.

'I can give you an office in the incident room,' says Cray, rolling down her sleeves and buttoning the cuffs.

'What's happening to this place?'

'Officially it's still classed as a crime scene.'

'I'd like to come back here. It could help me understand more.'

'I'll get you a set of keys.'

'I also want copies of statements and photographs.'

'We have a 3D scan of the crime scene – the latest technology – it creates a computer-generated model of the farmhouse. You can move from room to room in a virtual sense.'

'I'll have that too.'

The DCS looks at her watch. 'The public meeting is at eight-thirty. We'll have to hurry.'

'What are you going to tell them?'

'As little as possible.'

4

Clevedon is one of those sleepy English seaside towns that seem to burst into life for a few months every summer and then hibernate for the rest of the year. Quaint. Historic. Swept clean. The locals cling to their traditions and complain about the rich interlopers who blow in from London or Bristol and buy up the best houses with the best views. These outsiders arrive at weekends in their Range Rovers and four-wheel-drive BMWs, bringing children, dogs, quinoa, rocket, coffee machines and bottles of Tanqueray.

I once brought the family to Clevedon for a bank holiday weekend. Charlie must have been about ten and Emma a toddler. We stayed in a lovely old Victorian hotel with creaking stairs and gloomy hallways and baths with clawed feet. It overlooked the town's historic pier, which juts ornately into the Severn Estuary. I remember carrying Emma on my shoulders and buying ice cream cones at a kiosk near the Old Toll House, which had historic photographs of the bathhouses and bathing huts. The tourists still come in the summer, but only the young, the old and the brave seem to swim any more.

The community centre is already crowded with every seat

taken and the overspill lined along the walls. I estimate more than two hundred people, an even spread of men and women, mums and dads, professional types, solicitors, teachers, accountants, whiskery farmers and retirees. Two North Somerset council members from opposite sides of the political divide are moving through the auditorium, glad-handing and nodding sagely, letting people know that these are troubling times but the right people are in charge.

The only other person I recognise is Terry Bannerman, a morning radio presenter who is known for his confrontational broadcasting style. During phone-ins he likes to hang up on callers he disagrees with, or who are too slow to make their point. He also likes to pick on particular groups, depending upon his mood, targeting bankers, union officials, immigrants, Muslims, welfare cheats, single mothers, gays, politicians, out-of-touch judges or health tourists, which proves that his prejudices run wide and deep, even if his listeners come from the shallowest of gene pools.

'This could get ugly,' whispers Monk, as he watches DCS Cray walk to the side of the stage, flanked by two constables. People notice her arrival, nudging each other and whispering. Cray nods to a local Police and Community Support Officer, a young woman in navy trousers and a vest over a blue short-sleeved shirt.

A local TV news crew has turned up plus several stringers for national newspapers, hoping to get a story. The meeting is called to order by a woman with a single swath of white running down one side of her dark hair as though a road-marking machine has run over her.

'Ladies and gentlemen, thank you for coming. My name is Patricia Collier and I run the North Somerset Women's Refuge. I'm also the coordinator of the Avon and Somerset Rape Crisis Support Centre. You'll find our leaflets on a table near the door. Please take one.'

A man next to me turns to his mate and whispers, 'Dyke.'

He catches me staring at him but his eyes don't manage to hold mine. Perhaps it's the Parkinson's mask that intimidates him – the blankness of my face can look almost spectral.

'Tonight's meeting is about getting answers,' continues Miss Collier, speaking with a whistling lisp featuring the sibilant s-sound. 'But before we start I want to introduce some special guests. We have two local councillors, Geoff Fryer and Janelle Spencer. Also I'd like to welcome someone who I'm sure needs no introduction – radio personality Terry Bannerman, who has been a tremendous advocate for our community.'

There is a smattering of applause.

'Elizabeth and Harper Crowe were part of this town and were much loved. We have some of their family members with us this evening, including Elizabeth's sister Becca and her husband Francis. Thank you for coming.' The young couple are sitting in the front row of chairs on either side of a baby capsule with a sleeping infant.

'I also welcome Elizabeth's son, Elliot, and want to say that our hearts go out to him.'

She points to a young man dressed in a heavy winter coat, who is leaning against the wall, hands in his pockets. He stands upright, raising his chin.

'Two of Harper's best friends are also here, Sophie and Juliet, along with her boyfriend Blake.'

The girls look to be about Harper's age, dressed in frayed denim shorts and sleeveless puffy jackets. They're sitting on each side of a man in his twenties with wire-framed glasses and wavy hair that he's tried to tame with too much gel. One of the girls is holding his hand. The other is red-eyed from crying, clutching a ball of soggy tissues in her fist. All three stand up and face the crowd, revealing matching T-shirts with the slogan: *Justice for Harper*.

Miss Collier continues: 'Many people in this room knew Elizabeth and Harper – and even if you didn't I'm sure you are just as shocked and horrified by what happened. It has been twenty-five days since that night. There have been no arrests. This community is in shock. We're frightened. We invited the Chief Constable of Avon and Somerset Police to address the community tonight, but he had another engagement.'

There are boos and catcalls. Patricia Collier waits for silence. 'The Chief Constable has sent along Detective Chief Superintendent Veronica Cray, who is heading the investigation.'

'When are you gonna do your job?' someone yells.

'Hear, hear,' echoes another.

'We're not safe in our own homes,' shouts someone else.

DCS Cray has been sitting on stage next to Terry Bannerman and the councillors. She gets to her feet and takes the microphone, waiting for the noise to abate.

'Ladies and gentlemen, I have come here this evening to brief you on the ongoing investigation into the murders of Elizabeth and Harper Crowe. There are forty-four detectives working full-time on this case and every one of them is totally committed to catching the perpetrator of this terrible crime. My task force has so far interviewed more than three hundred people and taken over two hundred statements from family, friends, neighbours, visitors, tradesmen and persons of interest. Detectives have gone door to door in the local area and forensics teams have collected fibres, fingerprints and DNA samples.'

A man yells from the crowd, 'How about telling us what you haven't done – such as arrest anyone!'

Cray ignores the outburst. 'I didn't come here to give you a running commentary on our investigation, but I do want to—'

'Why *did* you come here?' shouts a faceless man.

'Not one suspect!' echoes another voice.

There are more jeers and catcalls. Monk is watching the DCS, waiting for a signal. Cray continues, trying to quell their anger. 'Too much has already been made public,' she says. 'It does not help us when theories are postulated in the media or

41

when suspects are named before we've had an opportunity to interview them.'

'What are you doing to protect us?' someone yells from the back.

'I got three kiddies,' says another. 'Their summer holidays begin next week. How am I going to keep them safe?'

A woman in front of me leans towards her husband, whispering: 'Everyone knows it's her ex-husband. He used to beat her up.' She glances over her shoulder. Seeing me, she stiffens and her lips tighten into lines, as though challenging me to disagree with her.

Another woman comments, 'I taught Harper at primary school – such a sweet thing – now I'm scared for my own children.'

There are more shouts and jeers. The undecided are being swayed. Terry Bannerman raises his arms. On the wrong side of obese, he has one of those deep, baritone radio voices that don't require a microphone to reach the back of a room.

'Calm down, people, we're all friends here.'

I find myself cringing at his choice of words. The phrase annoys me – the fake bonhomie of it, the implied bond: how does he know we're all friends? The killer could be in the crowd.

Bannerman lowers his arms. 'Let's allow this little lady to say her piece and then we'll hear from someone who *knows* what they're talking about.'

Cray gives him a 'fuck you' glance. Bannerman responds with a half smile.

The DCS begins again, trying a different approach. 'Catching this killer is a job for all of us, not just the police. We need public support. You have to be our eyes and ears.'

'Oh, we'll catch him,' says a man at the front. 'And we'll string him up.'

'I'm not talking about vigilantism,' replies Cray. 'Look around you. Someone has likely given this killer an alibi. It could be a misguided wife, or disbelieving girlfriend, or a well-meaning mother or friend. If you have any suspicions, I urge you to call the Crimestoppers number. Your information will be treated with the utmost sensitivity and your identity will be protected.'

'What about the attack on the coastal path?' a woman yells.

I glance at Monk and give him a questioning look. He leans closer and whispers. 'A woman was attacked on the outskirts of Clevedon, same day as the murders.'

'Is it linked?'

'Not that we can tell.'

Bannerman has grown impatient for his turn. 'All I've heard so far are lots of fighting words and feeble excuses from the police,' he says in a grandiose rumble. 'Seems to me the DCS is feeding us a load of BS.' The crowd laughs and heads nod appreciatively. 'Now we have the police telling us that somehow *we're* responsible for this. It's *our* fault that nobody has been arrested.'

'That's not what I said,' protests Cray.

Bannerman ignores her. 'Do you know how long it took the police to catch Peter Sutcliffe, the Yorkshire Ripper? Five years. In that time he killed thirteen women and attempted to murder another seven. Later we discovered they could have caught him much earlier, but the police failed to put the clues together. Sutcliffe bashed a prostitute six years before he ever killed one – but nobody thought he might be a suspect until it was too late. And do you know what the police told the community back then? "We're doing everything we can. It's under control. Trust us." Sound familiar?'

Cray interrupts him. 'You cannot equate this case with the Yorkshire Ripper.'

'I don't see why not,' says Bannerman. 'There's a ripper on the loose. How many more women have to be attacked or murdered before you do your job? How many nights do these good, law-abiding citizens have to be prisoners in their own homes?'

'We are doing everything possible to—'

'You're doing everything possible to protect your arse,' says Bannerman. 'You had your turn, DCS Cray. Let someone else have a say. We have our own expert – the man who blew the whistle on your incompetence – the psychologist who resigned from the investigation because the police were misinforming the public and putting us in danger. I want to welcome to the stage Emilio Coleman – better known as the Mindhunter.'

That's when I see Milo. Dressed in skinny jeans, open-necked shirt and blue blazer, he's not the same callow youth I remember from university. The cheap haircuts and math-nerd glasses have been replaced by designer stubble and blue contact lenses. Although always an assertive figure, he now seems to have refined his body language and become more than the sum of his parts.

Leaping on to the stage, he shakes hands with Bannerman and extends the same hand to DCS Cray, who ignores the gesture. Milo raises his eyebrows to the crowd and gives them a cheeky smile, getting the laughter he wanted. Then he walks to the edge of the stage and turns slowly, surveying every corner of the auditorium. I notice that he's clenching and unclenching his left fist at five-second intervals. It's more than a nervous mannerism.

Milo doesn't speak until he has the room's attention, starting quietly so that people lean forward to catch every word.

'Elizabeth Crowe was stabbed more than thirty-six times with a seven-inch kitchen knife, with the killer focusing on her genitals,' he says bluntly, aiming to shock.

I hear a collective intake of breath.

'Even after she was dead, he kept stabbing her,' says Milo. 'It was an act of butchery worthy of Jack the Ripper.'

DCS Cray has jumped to her feet. 'You have no right to reveal details of the investigation. You don't work for the police. I could have you arrested—'

'For what?' asks Milo. 'Telling people the truth?'

'For hindering a murder investigation.'

'Go on, then.' Milo holds out his hands, wrists together. The DCS has been painted into a corner. Milo turns back to the crowd, knowing the audience is now 'his'. 'I think that proves my point,' he says. 'The police wish to keep these details from you. That's why I withdrew from the investigation and that's why I am here tonight – risking arrest – to tell you the truth.'

Terry Bannerman pipes up. 'What else don't we know?'

'A pentagram was painted in blood on the wall and candles were found arranged around Elizabeth Crowe's body, which leads me to believe there were ritualistic elements to these murders.'

'Are you saying these were satanic killings?' asks Bannermen, his voice rising.

'There were certainly features normally associated with pagan sacrifice,' replies Milo, 'and a Bible was found with bloodstained pages. I can also reveal that Harper Crowe had an encyclopaedia of witchcraft and occult philosophy in her bedroom. She was also known to wear heavy eyeliner and dress in black.'

'You think Harper Crowe was into the occult?' asks Bannerman.

'She clearly had an interest.'

'That's not true,' yells a female voice, close to tears. Elizabeth's sister, Becca, has leapt to her feet. 'My niece was not a Goth or a witch.' She jabs her finger at Milo. 'Harper was a sweet girl. She did nothing wrong.'

Milo is momentarily shaken. 'Of course, I understand, I'm simply pointing out how the police have failed to investigate this particular angle.'

Becca's husband tugs at her hand asking her to sit down, but she ignores him. 'You shouldn't make accusations like that, Mr Coleman, not when people aren't around to defend their reputations.'

Milo holds his right hand against his heart. 'Please accept my sincerest apologies. I do not wish to cause offence or add to your grief.'

Becca is coaxed back to her seat and Milo continues. A part of me is appalled by his performance, but another part is mesmerised. He reminds me of a Pentecostal preacher on a US religious channel – a man who can cry as easily as he can summon a miracle and play a crowd like a cheap fiddle.

'I have prepared a psychological profile of the killer, which I will release tonight in the hope that it will keep people safe and trigger memories that might help close this case and put a psychopath behind bars.'

Milo reads from the screen of his phone. 'This was a targeted killing. He chose the farmhouse because it was isolated. He could well have been watching Elizabeth and Harper for weeks. He may have befriended them. He clearly had knowledge of the house, which suggests he may have visited it before.'

DCS Cray is still on stage but seems lost. If she arrests Milo there will be headlines all over tomorrow's papers.

'We also know that Elizabeth Crowe had been using a website to meet sexual partners,' says Milo. 'There is evidence that she took part in orgies in public places with random strangers.'

The information causes a buzz in the crowd. Becca jumps to her feet again. Tearful. Angry. 'Liar! You're calling my sister a . . . a . . . ' She can't bring herself to use the word.

Francis joins in this time. 'How dare you insult our family! We didn't come here to listen to gossip and innuendo.'

'Why did you come here?' asks Milo, dismissing him with a sad-eyed smile. 'You want answers, the same as everyone else. I'm not judging Mrs Crowe, but I cannot ignore the possibility that she met the killer at one of those locations where people gather to have sex or watch others.

'What isn't in doubt is that someone attacked and overpowered Elizabeth. The assault was frenzied, yet efficient, carried out by someone with forensic awareness. He took care to clean up afterwards. This man is ruthless, confident and able to carry out his plans with precision. This suggests he may have a military background or be involved in a job that requires organisational skills.

'I believe the killer is most likely aged between twenty-five and fifty-five. He was strong enough to have overpowered a fit and healthy woman and suffocate her teenage daughter. He will have a fascination with violent pornography and also the occult.'

Cray has heard enough. She leaves the stage, flanked by the two constables. Monk turns to me. 'Are you coming?'

'I'll stay.'

'Suit yourself.'

On stage, Milo seems to be growing in stature, his face lit with evangelical zeal. This is his moment in the spotlight. 'I don't want to antagonise the police,' he explains. 'They do an important and difficult job, but sometimes detectives lose sight of the salient points of an investigation. They stare at the murder map for so long they are blind to its elements – unable to see the wood for the trees.

'Now I want you all to remember back to the night of Saturday June sixth, and the early hours of the following morning. The killer would have been covered in blood – his clothes, his face, his hands and his shoes. Do you know of anyone who came home that night in a different set of clothes; someone who acted suspiciously or who has taken an unhealthy interest in the coverage of the murders? It could be a neighbour, a friend, or somebody who lives under your roof, or drinks at your local pub or works in your office. He might even be here tonight.'

The audience has fallen silent, shifting uncomfortably in their seats, some purposely avoiding eye contact while others focus upon me – a stranger in the room.

'This is not about living in fear or being paranoid,' Milo says. 'It's about searching your memories.' He glances towards the door. 'It's a shame that DCS Cray has gone because I do not blame the police. They are still our best hope for solving this shocking crime. So if you do have information, feel free to come to me. I will treat it confidentially and pass it on to the right people. Thank you.'

Milo steps down from the stage. He makes a point of going straight to Becca and Francis, offering his condolences and apologising. Becca refuses to shake his hand. Francis seems more protective than angry, telling Milo to leave them alone.

Meanwhile people are pushing past me as they leave the hall. I can hear snatches of their conversations.

'Sex in public . . . who'd have thought . . .'

'I always said there was something odd about her.'

'Some of those clothes she wore . . .'

'I didn't like the way she looked at my husband.'

'Did she flirt with him?'

'All the time.'

'Divorce can do that to some women.'

'Well, I feel sorry for her daughter.'

'She's dead!'

'But apart from that, you know.'

5

Milo is surrounded by people who want to shake his hand, pose for photographs or ask him questions.

'That was quite a performance,' I say.

'I just tell it as I see it,' replies Milo, smiling for another camera. He turns and recognises me. 'Professor O'Loughlin! Long time no see.'

'Hello, Milo.'

My left arm trembles.

'So how's it shaking?' he asks.

'Rattling and rolling.'

'Good to hear. You caught the show?'

'I thought it was a public meeting.'

'Whatever.'

Harper's two girlfriends pass nearby and Milo seems to drink in their curves as though committing every detail to memory.

'So what brings you to Clevedon?' he asks.

'Same thing as you.'

'I thought you'd retired.'

'Not yet.'

Milo signs an autograph for a middle-aged woman whose

daughter is waiting at the door. 'We really appreciate what you're doing,' she says. 'You're an angel.'

He bows. 'You give me far too much credit.'

'They treat you like a rock star,' I say, when the woman has gone.

'Just doing my bit,' Milo replies. 'I have my own business now.' He hands me a black, gilt-edged business card with the word *MINDHUNTER* written in cursive script. On the next line is his name, followed by several initials, most of which mean nothing. The smaller print details his services: *Criminal profiler, police consultant, employee vetting and psychological testing.*

'How's business?'

'Booming! Crime is a growth industry. You were really on to something with this profiling gig.'

'It's not a gig,' I say, trying to hide the harshness in my tone.

Milo hears it anyway. 'You're right. It doesn't pay very well, but the publicity is priceless. I'm thinking books, maybe my own crime TV show. I could look at cold cases or reinvestigate old crimes.'

'Like a modern-day Sherlock Holmes.'

'Yeah,' he replies, ignoring my sarcasm.

'You used my name,' I say.

He shrugs. 'I told people that I studied under you.'

'I want you to stop.'

'Why? You're getting some of the credit. You taught me everything I know.'

'I taught you nothing.'

He sighs. 'Listen, Professor – can I call you Joe?'

'No.'

Amusement sparks in his eyes. 'OK, Professor, I hope you don't feel as though I'm muscling in on your territory. I mean, it's not as if you have a monopoly on this business. Murder is the second oldest profession – or is that politics? – I can never remember. Anyway, there's plenty of room for healthy competition.'

'I'm not competing with you.'

'Exactly. I'm a forensic psychologist. You're a clinical psychologist. You stick to treating phobias and OCD and I'll handle the sharp end.'

'You have no idea what you're doing.'

'Sure I do. I'm making money out of something you couldn't. I'm a professional profiler. You're an amateur. Have you ever been paid for profiling?'

'That's not the point.'

'I think it is. I think you're jealous. I also think you're old. Go home. Take a pill. Leave this to me.'

I should ignore him, I should walk away, but stiff-upper-lip stoicism and turning the other cheek won't put Milo back in his box. He is dangerous and delusional and he has jeopardised a murder hunt by treating it like some sort of intellectual parlour game or Agatha Christie puzzle. In the same breath I realise that Milo won't listen to reason or be convinced of his failings because he doesn't admit to any. And he can't be motivated to moderate his behaviour or tone down his message because such subtleties are lost on him. Where does this leave me?

'Hey, Milo, remember that term we studied personality disorders and you chose to write your assignment on narcissism?'

He nods.

'That was the finest paper you ever penned. I mean, you nailed it, Milo. It was almost autobiographical.'

He smiles at me serenely. 'Is that the best you can do?'

I feel something small and fragile break in my mouth, as though a tiny glass vial has cracked between my teeth, leaking poison into my bloodstream. 'How often are you seeing a therapist?' I ask.

Milo's mouth opens but he doesn't speak.

'That little thing you do – clenching and unclenching your fist – you were counting to five and telling yourself to breathe.

Someone taught you to do that to relieve stress – a therapist or a psychologist. What makes you anxious, Milo? Is it the crowd or your own doubts? You're not the type to worry about what other people think of you. You're brighter than they are. You're brilliant. There must have been someone else here that you were trying to impress – a woman, standing near the back. She was filming you. You wanted a record of tonight so you can replay it later. Watch yourself. Pick up any mistakes. Or maybe you get a sexual charge out of seeing yourself on stage.'

Milo's eyes slightly glaze over and colour flushes into his cheeks. He wants to hit me. Maybe I'm the bully.

Terry Bannerman has dragged himself away from a cluster of fans. He slaps Milo on the back, congratulating him. He looks right past me, almost dismissively, and then refocuses on my face.

'You're that professor,' he says, excitedly. 'You must be very proud of your protégé.'

'Yes, he's come a long way,' I reply. 'Let's hope he finds his way back.'

6

Halfway down Mill Hill Lane, opposite the cottage, there is a huge chestnut tree that is famous among local children for the size and strength of its conkers. I am parked beneath the lowest branches. The dashboard clock reads 9.45. There are lights on upstairs. Charlie is still awake but Emma will be asleep by now, curled up under a small mountain of stuffed rabbits, bears and dogs arranged in a specific order, smallest to largest, or alphabetically, or by colour, depending upon her whim.

Downstairs a soft light glows from behind the curtains. Julianne must be watching TV or curled up on the sofa with a novel. Her book club meets every month, more for the wine than any literary discussion, she says.

I shouldn't have come. I should have booked into to a bed and breakfast or a hotel. I should have called ahead. But here I am, sitting opposite the cottage, replaying my conversation with Julianne, trying to read between the lines of her invitation to come home for the summer.

In my mind the cottage has always been 'home'. We moved out of London nine years ago, looking for better schools, more space and cleaner air – the usual arguments, along with the unspoken one – less stress. All that fresh country air, organic food and slow talking was going to make me a new man who could arm-wrestle Mr Parkinson and pin his skinny trembling limb to any table.

I took a job lecturing at Bath University, teaching an introductory course in behavioural psychology and mentoring PhD students like Milo Coleman. We stumbled upon Wellow almost by accident when I drove along a narrow road looking for somewhere to turn around. The village is full of stone cottages and pretty terraces with brightly painted front doors and windowsills lined with flower boxes. Picturesque. Postcard-worthy. There is a pub, the Fox and Badger, and a village shop, a primary school and a church with a graveyard where the headstones are so weathered that most of them can't be read.

When Julianne and I separated I rented a smaller place around the corner where the girls could come and visit me after school. Emma would play hide and seek in a house that had four hiding places. She still managed to squeal whenever I found her. Meanwhile, Charlie would waltz in, make a sandwich, accept help with her homework and then both my daughters would go back to the cottage and their mother.

Two years ago I moved back to London because I needed the work. Since then I've seen less of the girls, but once a month they come to London or I come to Wellow. Occasionally, Julianne has let me sleep on the sofa. Once she let me sleep in her bed. That's what scares me most about her invitation – the false sense of hope that keeps ballooning in my chest no matter how hard I try to dampen my expectations.

I am not the same person I was a decade ago. Existence has become infinitely more complex and less joyful. Mr Parkinson has become my cellmate and we're serving 'life' together. Middle age is taking hold. I'm thinner, more stooped and less well dressed without Julianne's input. Old age is no longer a foreign country that I hope to visit one day. It's over the horizon but on the itinerary.

During the past six years we've each dated other people and dipped our toes in the shrinking pond of possible partners, but I was never fishing with any bait. I can't speak for Julianne. She hasn't moved on. Maybe that's the best I can hope for.

Looking at the cottage now, I have a fierce urge to get my old life back. Julianne asked me what I would change if I could go back and do things again. My answer should have been nothing. By changing the smallest detail I might alter how Charlie and Emma have turned out. It would be like going back to prehistoric times and accidentally stepping on a butterfly – setting in train a sequence of events that could subtly alter the present.

Even so, given a time machine, it would be so tempting to return to that rainy day at Bath University when a policeman asked me to talk a woman down from the Clifton Suspension Bridge. I could say no. He could find someone else. And that seemingly random tragedy of a woman jumping to her death would no longer trigger the series of events that cost me my marriage. And yet . . . yet . . . we are the sum total of our experiences. We are who we are because of what happened – Julianne, Charlie, Emma and even me. How could I want to change that?

There is a small Fiat hatchback parked outside the cottage next to Julianne's car. Maybe she has a visitor. I should have called. I should have found somewhere else to stay.

The door of the cottage opens suddenly and Charlie emerges. She's wearing track pants and a baggy sweater, talking to someone on her mobile. The locks trigger and lights flash on the hatchback. Charlie opens the passenger door and retrieves a folder. I slide down below the level of the steering wheel.

Charlie is still talking. She laughs. I can't hear what she's saying. Her head turns. She stares at me. Crosses the road. Ends her call.

'Hi, Daddy.'

'Hi.'

'What are you doing out here?'

'Nothing.'

'Really?'

'I just arrived — I was about to knock.'

There are several beats of silence. I can hear crickets chirruping in the grass and water splashing over the weir at the bottom of the hill.

'Does Mummy know you're coming?'

'I was going to call her.'

'But you're here already.'

'I know. Does she have a visitor?'

'No.'

'Who owns the hatch?'

'Oh, that's mine.'

'Yours?'

'Mummy bought it for me.'

'Really. Why didn't you tell me?'

'It was going to be a surprise.' Charlie is holding the folder against her chest. Her cotton sweater has her name embroidered above the school crest. It was personalised to celebrate her last year at school.

'Are you staying the night?' she asks.

'No, I mean. I don't think . . . I should go . . . but I have to be here in Somerset tomorrow.'

'Mummy won't mind. Come on.'

Charlie opens the car door and drags me through the gate and towards the front door. 'Look who I found!' she yells, making me feel as though I'm a treasured artefact uncovered at a jumble sale.

Julianne is in her dressing gown. She frowns and looks from face to face. 'Is everything all right? What's wrong?'

'Nothing.'

We're standing in the living room. The TV is casting flickering shadows.

'I was just passing by.'

'Nobody just passes by this house unless they're driving a tractor.'

'Or riding a horse,' adds Charlie.

'I needed somewhere to crash for the night. Is the sofa-bed available?'

Julianne looks at me dubiously, wondering if Charlie and I have cooked this up together.

'I'll get some blankets and bedding,' she says, and then to Charlie. 'I thought you were going out?'

'Change of plan.'

'Well, I need to talk to your father, so scram.'

Later when the sofa is made up and the house is quiet, Julianne makes herself a mug of peppermint tea and sits cross-legged in the armchair opposite, prepared to listen. 'Were you sitting outside again?' she asks. 'I hoped that you'd grown out of that.'

'I was about to call. It's been a strange day.'

'What happened?'

'Do you remember Ronnie Cray?'

Julianne stiffens and goes quiet. I am used to such silences. They come with separation.

'She wants me to look at a case.'

'You told me you'd stopped doing that.'

'I have. This is different. Someone has used my name to inveigle his way into an investigation. A former student, Milo Coleman, has set himself up as a criminal profiler.'

'Let him do it.'

'He's compromised the investigation. Leaked confidential details.'

'Which has nothing to do with you.'

'He used my name. He's telling everyone that he trained under me.'

'Tell him to stop.'

'I did. I don't think he was listening.'

She narrows her eyes. 'You're going to do this, aren't you?'

'I'm going to review the investigation – to see if anything has been missed.'

There is a long pause. The cottage seems to creak as it settles down for the night. Julianne slides her legs from under her and cinches her dressing gown tighter around her narrow waist. 'Is this about that mother and daughter who were killed in North Somerset?'

'Yes.'

'Do the police know who did it?'

'Not yet.'

She has stopped at the door, leaning her hand on the frame. 'Do you have any pyjamas?'

'No.'

'What about a clean shirt for tomorrow?'

I shake my head.

'Give me your shirt. If I wash it now it will be dry by morning.'

'You really don't have to—'

'Off.'

I stand and try to unbutton the shirt, but my left hand is shaking. Julianne steps closer and finishes the job. She also unbuckles my belt.

'I've been here fifteen minutes and you're trying to get into my pants.'

'In your dreams.'

If she only knew . . .

Some days I wake and feel as though my life doesn't fit me any more. It pinches like a pair of shoes that are a size too small or rides up the crack of my arse like ill-fitting underwear. Is it possible to outgrow a life? I've heard people say it of a job or a relationship. And it's one of those excuses people use when they're cheating on their partners. 'I've outgrown you,' they say. 'I need more space.'

I have heard all of these pathetic self-justifications and glib explanations. I feel trapped. It's not you — it's me. Things aren't like they used to be. You deserve better. I feel suffocated. You've changed. You left me before I left you. You work too much. You don't listen to me. I'm tired of having to do everything around here. You've grown fat. I don't fancy you any more. Sex isn't fun. You were never there for me when I needed you.

Some men will tell you that adultery is about meeting a need. It's not really their fault. It's biological. Monogamy is easier for a woman. The male sex drive is greater. Men eat when they're hungry, sleep when they're tired, fuck when they're frisky — simple needs for simple minds.

'It didn't mean anything,' they'll say. 'It was nothing — a one-night stand. Over before it started. I was drunk. We didn't kiss. I don't love her like I love you . . .'

Particular men will try to redefine the word 'affair' or say that sex and love are two different things because one is physical and the other emotional.

Pathetic, self-serving bullshit! Nothing absolves. Nothing exonerates. My father taught me that. He beat it into me, cursing my mother's name.

'Put your hands through the stair railings,' he'd say. 'Hold your elbows.' He unbuckled his belt and pulled it from his trouser loops. Doubling the leather in his fist, he swung it from behind his back in the widest possible arc so that it whistled through the air before it landed.

If you saw my father now you wouldn't recognise the monster that once lived behind his watery blue eyes, not when you see him flirting with the nurses, making cheeky comments about their sex-lives, acting as though he's in with a chance.

He shows them his old tattoos, which seem to be melting and leaking down his arms. He used to works as docker for the Bristol Port Company at Avonmouth. Tough work. Man's work. But most of his thirty-five years were spent as a union rep, avoiding each round of redundancies and telling his 'comrades' that he had fought the good fight, but now it was about 'limiting the losses' and 'protecting as many jobs as possible' — most notably his own.

Meanwhile he propped up the bar of the Three Kings on the waterfront, preaching about the evils of capitalism and Margaret Thatcher, who he called the wicked witch and vowed he would 'piss on her grave'. Now he's doesn't even know she's dead. How ironic! My old man and Margaret Thatcher, both afflicted by dementia — a disease with no regard for class or fairness or old hatreds.

Most days he doesn't recognise me. He calls me Stevie and thinks I'm his best mate from fifty years ago. He keeps telling me the same story — how he and Stevie stowed away on a ship to America, but it was only going as far as Glasgow.

I visit him after work and take him out of the nursing home for long walks. He can power along for miles, following the coastal footpath with his odd, shuffling gait, until I tell him to turn back. Sometimes I think I might let him keep going. He'd walk all the way to John O'Groats if nobody stopped him. Some dementia patients get anxious, but my old man's emotions are blunted and stultified. Children fascinate him — they're like mini-people — and tears are just water leaking from a person's eyes.

I should hate him. I should want to punish him, but he wouldn't understand why. Instead I feel a peculiar kind of loneliness — as though someone who should love me has forgotten my birthday.

Sometimes I write letters to him in my head — not the man he is now but the one he was then. I tell him that I've tried to understand why he did those things and quite honestly, given what's happened since, I think I do. He was an alcoholic, but his addiction wasn't an addiction — it was a hobby or a pastime. He was being sociable. He was being a man. He couldn't let his mates drink alone, could he?

Many of these same mates also drank too much and beat their wives, but didn't see their behaviour as a compulsion or something beyond their control. Drinking was just drinking, never addiction.

It wasn't until my mother died that my father lost himself completely in the bottle – and it wasn't her dying so much as the circumstances of her death. And it wasn't the car accident so much as the man behind the wheel. And it wasn't so much the man driving as the fact that his severed penis was found in my mother's mouth.

That's tough to swallow (and I use that sentence with no pun intended). The Sunday Sport ran the story on the front page. You can imagine the quips. My father didn't go to the pub so much after that. He drank at home, lecturing his children just as he once lectured his mates. A new sort of anger burned in him, a cold hard gemlike flame, and it felt as though a line had been crossed and he'd lost even the faintest spark of paternal love.

When he wasn't drinking, he pumped iron. He made himself a weight bench in the garage, welding a cradle to take the bar. He made me spot for him. I was only eight and couldn't have lifted the bar off him had it slipped. All I could do was steer it to the cradle when it rose on his rubbery ink-stained arms, his eyes bulging and veins popping. I know what he was doing – punishing himself, enjoying the pain.

Afterwards he would make me lift. 'See if you can beat your old man,' he'd say, grinning maliciously.

I couldn't hope to lift the same weight. It crushed my chest and he bleated in my ear about being a pansy and a 'nancy boy'. Twice he cracked my ribs, which was before my broken arm and dislocated elbow; before I was taken into care.

The first few drinks seemed to mellow him and clear his head, but soon he'd be looking to pick a fight with someone – usually my brother, or sister, or me. The slightest thing would set him off: a knife scraping on a plate or a tap left dripping. I felt sorriest for Agatha, my sister. She didn't get physically abused. I didn't see my father touch her once – to hug her or hit her – but he punished her in hundreds of other ways.

'Are you on the rag?' he'd say. 'I can smell you. Have another shower . . . You get any fatter I'll have to widen the doors . . . If that skirt was any shorter you'd be arrested for selling crack.'

My father believed that women were to blame for the first sin and all that followed. With shaking hands and drool drying on his chin, he would lecture me about adultery, sitting in his armchair, his penis resembling a turtle's head, poking from his yellowing Y-fronts. Women were sluts and witches and devious betrayers. A vagina was like a Venus flytrap that could snap shut and trap a man.

The first time I sat next to a girl at school I was surprised at how sweet she smelled. Her shampoo. Her breath. Her skin. Her name was Sandra Martin and I followed her home that day because she made me feel light-headed and strange. Sandra was one of the popular girls who knew she was pretty and didn't need to try hard to make friends or turn heads. Other girls who were less attractive seemed to crave affection almost as much as I did. One of them, Karen Basing, who had greasy hair and a runny nose, would pull her knickers down and show boys her slot, but only if they bought her a Mars Bar. That's what it reminded me of, her vagina, the pink slot in a piggybank.

We were caught one day by one of the nuns. Nothing happened to Karen Basing, but I was sent to the priest, who said he was very disappointed. 'How would you feel if that was your mother?' he said. 'Or your sister?'

I wanted to tell him that my mother died with a penis in her mouth and that my sister had left home by then and could do what she damn well pleased. They could all go to hell. My family. The Church. Karen Basing.

Normally when children go missing people rally around and search, fanning out across the fields and vacant ground from where the bicycle or schoolbag was found. Emotionally they adopt the child, saying prayers for his safe return and wondering what sort of sick pervert would snatch an innocent from their midst. Meanwhile, they eye their neighbours suspiciously, the drifters and single men and midlife pensioners.

That didn't happen to me. Nobody bothered to search or to pray for me because I'd been taken by one of my own. I'd gone missing in my own family.

7

Awake. Bleary. Trembling. For a moment I wonder if I'm dreaming. Emma has climbed on to the sofa bed next to me, dressed in her pyjamas, which are covered in cartoon polar bears.

'When did you come?' she asks excitedly. 'Why didn't you wake me? Did you bring me something? Are you staying? Can we go to the cinema? Will you make me pancakes for breakfast? Do you like my new pyjamas? Mummy bought them when we went to London. We saw *Matilda*. The little girl who played *Matilda* was the spitting image of Maddie Hayes, a girl in my class, only Maddie has darker hair and she can't sing. Not even a note. You should take your pills. Your arm has gone all jerky.'

This is how Emma talks, barely pausing to inhale. Sometimes I think she must cycle breathe like a didgeridoo player. Either that or she streams her thoughts directly from her brain without any filter. I take my medication and wait for the tremors to stop. Emma flits around me, a skinny little thing with a mop of curly hair and an oversized mouth with two rabbit-like front teeth.

'I'll stay home today,' she says.

'But you have school.'

'It's my last day. We can go for a bike ride. You'll have to pump up my tyres and fix my bell. Justin Barclay broke it when he rode my bike into the river.'

'Why did he do that?'

'I dared him.'

She makes it sound so obvious.

'I have work today. You should go to school.'

'OK, but you'll be here when I get home. Mummy said you weren't coming till the weekend. You're sleeping in my room, so don't make any bad smells. You'll have to look after Oscar.'

'Who's Oscar?'

'My goldfish. Charlie doesn't want him in her room because he sucks rocks and spits them out, but he's a goldfish, right, he's supposed to suck rocks.'

'Right.'

Julianne rescues me and tells Emma to get ready for school. Grudgingly she obeys, stomping noisily up the stairs. She yells over the banister, 'I know you're talking about me.'

Julianne rolls her eyes. 'Tell me she's not a narcissist.'

'What ten-year-old isn't?'

My wife – *can I call her my wife?* – is wearing a two-piece business suit and heels, with her hair pinned up. She looks great, like some fashion editor's idea of a career woman. She speaks four languages and works part-time as a court-appointed interpreter in Bristol.

'Do you have a trial today?' I ask.

'No.'

'Meetings?' I ask.

'A doctor's appointment.'

'Is everything all right?'

'Under control.'

What sort of answer is that? I want to press her on the details, but she hates me meddling. That privilege was lost to me when we separated. She's already gone to collect two bottles of milk from the doorstep, along with the local newspaper, the *Somerset Guardian* – an august organ of record for locals interested in births, deaths, marriages and bicycle thefts.

Charlie is the last to arrive downstairs, her hair wet and half-brushed, wearing black jeans and her Doc Martens. She grabs the newspaper and begins turning pages.

'You're up early,' I say.

'Job hunting.'

'What sort of thing?'

'Part-time. Pays a fortune. No experience necessary.'

'Good luck with that.'

'Thanks.'

'How about some cereal?' Julianne asks.

'Not hungry,' says Charlie.

'At least take a banana.'

Emma interrupts. 'Can Daddy walk me to school?'

'You can walk to school by yourself,' says Julianne.

'I can do it,' I say.

Charlie has stopped turning pages. 'Hey, that's you!'

The headline reads: RIPPER WILL KILL AGAIN. Underneath is a sub-heading: *Profiler Accuses Police of Incompetence.*

The photograph shows Milo on stage, arms spread, face raised to the lights, looking every inch the evangelist. I'm visible in the background at the side of the stage.

'So he's your competition,' says Julianne. 'He's rather handsome.'

'Very tasty,' choruses Charlie. 'Who is he?'

'One of your father's old students,' replies Julianne.

Charlie bites into a banana. 'I'm going to enjoy university.'

'You have to be careful of the good-looking ones,' says Julianne.

'Why?'

'Other girls will try to steal them away.'

'What about Daddy? Did girls try to steal him?'

'I had to beat them off with a stick.'

Emma looks up from her cereal bowl. 'Who did you hit with a stick?'

'Nobody.'

'But you said you beat someone with a stick.'

'It's just a turn of phrase,' explains Julianne, but Emma has already launched into another story.

'Casey Finster hit Beau Pringle with a stick and knocked out his tooth and Mrs Herbert made him write a letter to Beau's parents, who said Casey had to pay for the orthodontist, but Casey's father said Beau started the fight by throwing a rock, only it wasn't a rock, it was a clod of dirt with a rock inside it but Casey didn't know that so it wasn't really his fault.'

The entire sentence is delivered without her drawing breath.

Charlie rolls her eyes and grabs her car keys. 'Will you be here tonight?'

'That depends,' I say, glancing at Julianne. 'Would that be OK?'

'Sure.'

Charlie kisses us both on the cheek. 'Later, losers.' And then she's gone, throwing open the front door with a flourish and confronting the day like an actor walking on to a stage.

Emma takes my hand as we climb Mill Hill Lane, heading for St Julian's Primary School, which is opposite the church. Her questions, observations and statements become the background noise, which I occasionally punctuate with 'uh-huh' and 'really' to make her think I'm listening. Emma knows this but seems happy to leave her thoughts drifting like dandelion seeds, perhaps hoping one might germinate into a conversation. From somewhere in the hum and whirr I hear the words 'hospital' and 'mummy'.

'Pardon?'

'Will you be looking after us?'

'When?'

'When Mummy goes to hospital.'

'Why would Mummy be going into hospital?'

'For her historicalectomy.'

'Do you mean hysterectomy?'

'That's what I said.'

I don't argue with her. 'When is she going into hospital?'

Emma shrugs. 'Nobody tells me anything.'

8

The windscreen wipers pause between each sweep across the glass. Rain, a summer shower, warm rather than cold, makes the villages blur and streak. Having passed through the southern outskirts of Bristol, I reach the coast road and follow the shoreline where the trees are stunted and bent by the prevailing winds.

Across the Severn Estuary I can make out the mauve mountains of the Brecon Beacons. I grew up on the border of Snowdonia, a very similar landscape to this, where low islands, cliffs and shingle beaches were punctuated by wetlands. It was an idyllic childhood until I was sent away to boarding school at the age of twelve. I missed my sisters. I missed my mother. I even missed my father – God's personal physician-in-waiting – an imposing yet compelling presence, quick to criticise and slow to praise. Every summer I would ride my bike to Abersoch and watch the teenage girls run shrieking into the waves, imagining that one day I might have the courage to sit down beside one of them. I fell in love with a girl called Carise who had a friend called Tessa; they would rub coconut oil on each other's backs and lie on their stomachs, casually lifting their legs to kick at the sunshine.

My mobile is sitting in a cradle on the dashboard. I have tried to call Julianne twice and left messages. She's not answering. Avoiding me. Pulling over to the side of the road, I try again, typing the words: Emma told me you needed an operation. Please explain. Call me.

I wait. A message pings back: Can't talk now.

I type: When?

Later.

I try to call her. She doesn't answer. Why is she so bloody infuriating!

All this time I've been worrying that there was someone else – another man, a new lover, my replacement – and now I discover that she's sick. That's why she invited me to live at the cottage.

She needs a hysterectomy. I studied medicine for three years and I know enough to be worried. It could be bleeding, or fibroids, or a prolapse. She could have cancer. My stomach lurches. I'm the one who's supposed to be sick and crumbling, jiggling my way through each day. Julianne never gets sick. Hardly ever. She's the healthy one.

I feel as though someone has played a tasteless practical joke on me, tricked me into believing that happiness is a possibility before snatching it away. Now I'm sulking, touching at the truth with the barest tips of my thoughts, frightened of what I might find. When was she going to tell me? Did I have to wait until she went into hospital?

I'm angry at her secrecy, but at the same time I feel guilty. I have wished for something like this to happen – some event that I imagined would send her hurtling back into my arms. Now that it's transpired I blame myself for contemplating such a terrible thing. Nobody can know. *Please, please let her be OK.*

Just after ten o'clock I pull through the farm gates, splashing through puddles before parking in the cobblestone yard. Monk is waiting. He almost seems to unfold as he gets out of the car and pulls on a rain jacket.

'Could be wetter,' he says sarcastically, carrying a box to the front door and keying open the padlock. He brushes raindrops from his hair and hands me a USB stick. 'The statements are on this.'

'What about the post-mortem report?'

'That too.' He hangs up his jacket. 'You'll also find the 3D scan of the farmhouse, maps, timelines, phone records, financial statements and receipts. The statements are colour-coded – red for high priority, then orange, then yellow. The boss thought you might want hard copies of the photographs.' He points to the box.

'I might also need a printer.'

'Colour?'

'Yes.'

'I'll see what I can do.'

We walk past the open sitting room door. I don't look inside.

'You going to be OK out here?' asks Monk, as we reach the kitchen. He opens the curtains.

'I'll be fine.'

He tests the lights and turns on a tap, checking that I have water.

'What do you think happened?' I ask.

Monk flexes his nostrils and rubs the grained skin of his jaw with one finger. 'I think Mrs Crowe met some random stranger for sex, or someone watched her having sex, and followed her home.'

'She chose the wrong one.'

'It happens.' Monk's face is elongated, almost jug-shaped. 'I don't like speaking ill of the dead, but by most accounts Mrs Crowe was the sort of woman who liked all flavours of ice cream except the one she had in the freezer.'

'Care to explain that?'

'You see it often enough – a middle-aged woman goes searching for a little excitement or to recapture her youth – a Mrs Robinson type, who reaches her sexual peak and then sees

70

her beauty starting to fade. I'm not being sexist – men do it as well: buy a Porsche or run off with their secretary. I got a feeling that Mrs Crowe was never going to settle for slippers and a cat.'

'You sound as though you're speaking from experience.'

Monk grins sheepishly, 'I used to have women hitting on me all the time when I was young and single. Some of them wanted to sleep with a black man. Try it once. See if the stories were true.'

'And now?'

'I'm a happily married man,' he says, 'and my Trisha would snip Little Monk with garden shears if she caught me bumping nasty with another woman.'

'Tell me about Elizabeth's ex-husband.'

'Dominic Crowe. Nice guy. Bitter.'

'Why?'

'She took him to the cleaners. Hired a head-kicking lawyer from London – the same brief who looked after Nigella Lawson when she split with Charles Saatchi.'

'He lost the house.'

'And his share of the company. You want to know the worst part? Dominic's best friend and business partner had been shagging Elizabeth Crowe for years.'

'Jeremy Egan?'

'Yeah. Dominic had no idea. Poor schmuck.'

Monk circles the kitchen counter, running his finger over the bench top.

'What do other people say about Mrs Crowe?' I ask.

'Depends who you talk to. I interviewed some of the tradesmen who were fitting out the bathrooms. None of them liked her. She screwed them on costs and kept changing her mind.'

'Did any of them have keys to the farmhouse?'

'The architect.'

'Egan?'

'Yep.'

'What's going to happen to this place?'

Monk shrugs his shoulders. 'Elliot Crowe will most likely inherit . . . unless we find that he's responsible.'

'You think he could have killed them?'

'He's a junkie, not a genius, but yeah, he's in the mix.' Monk looks at his watch. 'I got to get back to headquarters. I'll try to get you that printer.'

After he's gone, I boot up my laptop and plug in the USB. The files are indexed and dated. Within two hours I realise the size of my task. There are hundreds of statements and thousands of other pieces of information that have to be collated and cross-matched to reveal any inconsistencies or anomalies.

Opening a new file, I hit 'play' and the 3D scan starts to run. Time-coded at the bottom of the screen, it begins on the morning after the murders. An overview of the farmhouse shows the floor-plan and the relationships of the different buildings. There are two cars parked in front of the barn. One of them is a Volvo estate and the other a small hatchback, which belonged to Harper. A sticker in the rear window reads: *Horn Broken, Watch For Finger.*

By moving my cursor I can circle the farmhouse, entering doors, moving along corridors and turning 360 degrees. The detail is extraordinary. It's as though I'm standing in each room exactly as it was that morning. I can see coffee cups on the shelves, a spoon beside the sink, condiments on the table. There is a coat-rack on the wall. Matching Barbour jackets. An umbrella stand. Walking sticks.

The front door has a splintered wooden panel above the deadlock. Shards of wood were found scattered on the doormat. Elsewhere there are no obvious signs of a struggle.

Moving the cursor, I enter the sitting room. Elizabeth is lying on her back, her legs splayed, her head turned to one side, arms outspread, one hand seeming to point towards the door. Opening an album of crime scene photographs, I see an attractive woman, not beautiful but well preserved, her stomach sagging slightly in a paunch and a caesarean scar the only blemish on her white skin.

I change the point of view until I see the candle holders coated in wax. He left them burning. Why light them at all? Amid the speckles of blood on the sofa there are larger smears on the front of the cushions. He sat down after he finished. He needed to rest. I can also see where he knelt to clean the knife on a cushion. A partial shoeprint was found inside the front door and further bloodstains in the hallway. Did he remove his shoes?

Traces of blood show his progress through the house, into the kitchen, then the laundry. He cleaned up using a cake of soap and a hand towel. Perhaps he took off his clothes. *Did he bring a spare set, or borrow something?*

Closing the computer, I walk to the sitting room and take a seat on the solitary armchair. Opening an album of the crime scene photographs, I leaf through the pages. Elizabeth is lying on her back, her dressing gown open. She's naked underneath. One breast is visible. The blood and urine stains suggest that she had been standing when the fatal blow was delivered. He held the knife in his right hand. He raised the blade above his shoulder and drove it into her neck below her left ear, angling down to her spine. He let her fall. She lay on her back.

The second phase of her injuries then began. He stabbed her thirty-five more times, most of the blows delivered after death, some so violent and deep they damaged the rug beneath her body. He focused on her genitals. The knife rose and fell in an uncontrolled frenzy. There was anger in this act. Hatred. Perhaps revenge. Likewise exploration. He wanted to punish Elizabeth, but also to test his own boundaries.

I open my eyes. The dark stain on the floor is like a shadow without a light source. Crossing the room, I crouch down, propping on my haunches, and study the speckled pattern of blood on the floor. Something must have been covering the floor when Elizabeth was first stabbed. The object had one straight edge and one obvious corner, slightly curved. *A plant? A table? A lamp?* Nothing in the photographs or the 3D scan reveals the source. Perhaps the forensic team took it away for analysis. I cross-check with the evidence log and find no record of the item. Either a mistake has been made or the killer took something away with him.

Leaving the sitting room, I climb the narrow stairs, pausing involuntarily as my left leg freezes mid-step. Focus. Move. Obey.

Entering Harper's room, I see a publicity poster for *Game of Thrones* fixed to one wall. Opposite are two large photographs of a wind farm and a coal-fired power station. *Which is the greater blight on the countryside?* reads the caption.

The ceiling slopes above the bed, following the roofline. Harper has used the space to display dozens of Polaroid images, mostly artistic shots of abandoned buildings, railway goods yard.,warehouses and stretches of stark coastline. Elsewhere in the room there are charcoal and pencil portraits, given depth by the delicate cross-hatching and shading. Some of the drawings still have notes in the margins from her art teacher: *Tone does not follow form . . . flattens it . . . Don't use cross-hatching for foliage . . . You lose perspective in the foreground . . .*

Opening the relevant album of crime scene photographs, I follow as each shot moves closer to the single bed where the duvet has been pulled up, shielding the occupant from immediate view. I can only see the top of a head with sleep-tousled hair. The duvet is pulled back for the next series of images. Harper looks as though she's sleeping. I half expect her to groan in protest and roll over, telling me to go away.

She is lying on her back with her hands folded on her chest, her right thumb hooked into the silken bow tied at the front of her pale yellow nightdress. Her hair is spread in a halo across her pillow, perfectly framing her face, except for a few strands that have come to rest on her cheek.

A fuzzy-looking brown teddy bear is tucked between her arm and her side. Her nightdress extends to her thighs, pulled down. Her legs are slightly apart. Her feet splayed at forty-five degrees. Her toenails painted.

She has been left like this. Arranged. Someone came to this room and suffocated her. Afterwards he rearranged her body, pulling down her nightdress, placing her hands on her chest as though she's Sleeping Beauty waiting for her prince.

Questions are forming. This wasn't sexual. Harper wasn't raped or violated or defiled with stab wounds. It was almost the opposite. He tried to safeguard her modesty or protect her innocence. He created an idealised fairy-tale resting place. Why? What did Harper represent that Elizabeth didn't?

The teddy bear strikes a strangely paternal note. This small gesture is the act of someone who loves children. Perhaps the toy had special significance to Harper – every child seems to favour one above the others. A father would know. A father would care.

According to the post-mortem report, Harper had two broken fingernails. She fought back as the pillow was pressed upon her face and may have scratched her attacker. Afterwards, he dipped her fingers in bleach to remove any possible evidence.

Going back over the details, I try to understand the sequence of events.

If the killer had broken through the front door, Elizabeth and Harper would have heard him. One of them would have phoned the police. Instead Elizabeth put on her dressing gown and went downstairs. More likely she knew this man. She opened the door, perhaps expecting him. She poured a glass of wine – a nightcap, just the one – her prints were found on the glass.

The police assume that Elizabeth was murdered first and didn't have time to cry out or to warn Harper. The killer must have been covered in her blood – his clothes, his hands – yet no traces of blood were found on the stairs or in Harper's room. He must have cleaned up, changing out of his clothes, washing his face and hands.

Unless . . . unless . . .

What if there was more than one killer? Two perpetrators. One went upstairs, the other stayed with Elizabeth. No, a mother would have warned her daughter of the danger. She would have fought. Harper would have barricaded herself in her room, phoned the police or gone to help her mother.

I look at the window and the small corner pane of broken glass. A desperate teenage girl might have tried to climb out and shimmy down the rainwater pipe, but the window was broken from outside rather than within.

Whatever the sequence of events, the break-in was staged afterwards to make it look like . . . like . . . like what? It was never going to be confused with a robbery. Instead the killer was laying a false trail, trying to complicate or obfuscate or muddy the water.

I have no way of knowing what happened unless I learn more about Elizabeth and Harper. I have to explore their lives, discovering their likes and dislikes, fears and dreams. Were they risk-takers? Did they draw attention? Make enemies? Attract admirers? By understanding them I will learn more about their killer. I will see the world through his eyes and then hold up a mirror to his face.

There is someone at the farmhouse. Not a detective – he doesn't have the bovine walk or cheap haircut. Maybe he's from one of those specialist companies that clean up crime scenes; or he could be a tradesman or a valuation agent. He's walking around the house, peering through windows, studying the building from every angle, as though examining a work of art and deciding how it makes him feel. Why does art have to make us 'feel' anything? Why can't art be art for art's sake?

I keep being drawn back here by fear and regret. Once I thought I glimpsed Harper in the window upstairs, but it was just a trick of the light or wishful thinking or remorse. That's what happens when you kill someone you love – the guilt grows inside you, bloated and parasitic, curling around your heart like a poisonous jellyfish.

I want to know what the stranger is doing. I don't appreciate it when things change . . . not unless I change them. That's why I have reconstructed my history – dug it up and reburied it, deeper than before. Not forgotten. Never that.

People often misjudge me. It's something I have spent a lifetime perfecting. The trick is not to set the bar too high. Never be too clever. Never volunteer. Never raise your voice or put up your hand or take a step forward. Never be first or last. Be average, be ordinary, be invisible in the crowd . . .

My father didn't have that philosophy. He believed in making a noise. 'If you don't show people you're the boss they'll walk all over you,' he'd say. 'Blaze a trail or be roadkill.' These were lessons I learned before my mother died, as I'd watch my father get ready to go out on important 'union business'. A clean shirt lying ready for him on the bed, his trousers hung on the radiator. My mother banging pots in the kitchen, unable to look at him.

Sometimes he would forget to wipe the remnants of shaving foam off his face. It would stick to the bottom of his ears or to his neck.

77

My mother never said anything. She'd sit at the kitchen table, her fingers around the cup of tea, staring at the steaming liquid. She wouldn't raise it to her lips. It was as though the cup had become too heavy. Instead she'd dip her nose, blow a breath and sip from the rim.

At closing time my father would come home, searching for his keys as he stumbled up the steps. Entering the house he would trip over, cursing and kicking at whatever object had attacked him in the dark. Feigning sleep, my muscles aching with the tension, I would strain to hear him as he climbed the stairs, ricocheting off the walls.

Lying still. Barely breathing. My fists clenched around the bedding. I wanted my mother to be asleep. 'Please be quiet. Please be quiet,' I prayed. But she wouldn't or she couldn't hold her tongue. Instead she accused him of smelling of beer and curry and whatever whore had sucked his 'pencil dick'. Even with his reflexes dulled by alcohol he could still knock her across the room with the back of his hand, making her crumple to the floor.

'Such a big man, hitting a woman – does it make you feel proud? Hit me again, you'll feel even bigger.'

'You want more. I'll give you more.'

'Please be quiet. Please be quiet,' I whispered.

I covered my ears, but could not shut out the sound of his fists hitting her flesh, or her cries of pain. Afterwards, I would cry myself to sleep and dream of murder.

In the morning my father would be a changed man, gentle, pitiful, wheedling, begging her forgiveness, calling her pet and sweetheart and darling. She ignored his performance. She served his breakfast. She cleaned the house. She went to work. She did not speak. Why now, I wondered. Why couldn't she have been quiet last night?

But it was her silence that hurt him most. 'You're killing me,' he'd say. 'Call me names. Hit me. Throw something. Don't send me to Coventry.'

I hoped it meant she was sending him away, but he never went to Coventry or anywhere else.

He was a weak man, a coward, a hypocrite and a cheat, but I craved his affection. I hung on his every word and treasured those moments of closeness when he ruffled my hair or threw me a wink or bought me a Coca-Cola as I waited outside the pub. How can you hate someone yet crave their affection? Love and hate are not the same emotion turned upside down. One is an illusion of the heart and the other is love betrayed. Apathy lies in between.

I can see the stranger walking from room to room, as though looking for something. He has a twitching hand and a stooped walk and he seems to peer right through walls, seeing shadows and shapes that others cannot.

Perhaps he's looking for the loose ends. There are still so many of them. No matter how hard I concentrate, I cannot think of every contingency. I cannot make myself completely safe.

9

At midday I take a break and make a coffee, eating a chocolate digestive over the sink to avoid spilling crumbs on the floor. The rain has gone and the air is sharp and clean. I walk outside and stand in the overgrown kitchen garden, which is neatly laid out with gravel paths and box hedges. I quite fancy myself living in a place like this, playing the gentleman farmer, tending vegetables and animals, watching the seasons pass.

I check my watch and swallow another pill. It takes a few minutes for the tremors to slow. They never completely disappear any more. My left thumb and index finger will rub together in a pill-rolling motion as though I'm asking someone to 'show me the money'.

Returning to the kitchen table, I begin to concentrate on the timelines, starting with Harper. She finished her last A-level exam in May and had enrolled in a foundation course in art and design at Falmouth University which was due to begin on 8 September. In the meantime she'd been working part-time as a waitress at a local pub, the Moon and Sixpence. She had a lunchtime shift on that Saturday from ten until three. Afterwards she drove to the home of a friend, Sophie Baxter, and the two of them spent an hour watching music videos. They arranged to meet later that evening to celebrate Harper's birthday.

Harper was home at 7.30 p.m. when she called her father from the landline. It was her birthday the next day and he planned to take her to lunch. She left the farmhouse at 8 p.m. and met Sophie at the Salthouse, a landmark pub west of the pier.

Harper didn't have her mobile phone. She had spent the previous night with her boyfriend, Blake Lehmann, and had left her phone charging at his flat. I remember Blake from the public meeting. He was six years ahead of Harper at school but had left at sixteen to take up an apprenticeship as a mechanic. On that Saturday he went dirtbike-riding with friends, but had arranged to meet Harper that evening to return her phone.

Blake showed up an hour late at the Salthouse, still dressed in his muddy leathers. He returned Harper's phone, which began pinging the nearest phone tower just after 9.15. She picked up her voicemail messages, including one from Aunt Becca asking her to babysit. Harper returned the call and they spoke for about four and a half minutes.

At 10.30 p.m. Blake Lehmann and Harper were seen arguing in the pub car park. An employee at a funfair in Salthouse Field witnessed the confrontation, describing how Blake grabbed Harper by the shoulders and shook her. She retaliated, slapping his face. Blake returned to the pub alone.

Harper sent a text message to her mother at 10.42 p.m. saying she was coming home. Her mobile signal shows she was at the farmhouse by 11.08 p.m. She died before midnight or in the two hours that followed.

I write a question on a notepad: *What was Harper doing between four and seven that afternoon?* It might not be important, but these are the only missing hours in her timeline.

Climbing to the first floor, I go into Harper's bedroom and stand for a long while at the end of her bed. Her drawings are pinned to the corkboard and stuck on the wardrobe doors. A watercolour is framed above her bed. She painted Clevedon Pier under a stormy sky with a shaft of sunlight bursting through the clouds like a heavenly intervention.

At the window I lean against the frame and look out at the distant sea. A fly is buzzing itself to death on the sill, spinning on its back in small, spiralling circles. A movement catches my eye. A figure has paused at the entrance to the stable block. He seems to take a deep breath, as though daunted by the dark of the interior, before slipping through the door.

Descending the stairs, I go through the laundry and emerge outside, crossing the flagged yard. I step into the cool gloom of the stables and wait for my eyes to adjust. He is moving between the empty horse stalls, a man in his mid-twenties, dressed in greasy jeans and a flannelette shirt, buttoned down to his wrists. I watch him as he fills a small ceramic bowl with water from a tap.

'Afternoon.'

His first reaction is to cringe as though expecting a punch. Light from the door falls on his pale face but doesn't soften the dark shadows that swallow his eyes.

'My name is Joe.'

He doesn't look at me. I notice the can of cat food in his hand, along with a penknife. 'Are you looking for the cat?' I ask.

He licks his lips.

'It's Tommy, isn't it?'

He nods.

'You live next door.'

Another nod. He has a face that seems to be constantly moving, first a fidget, then a wince, a tic, a grimace, an eye-roll, as though a swarm of bees is buzzing behind his eyelids. He's six foot tall, on the cusp of obesity, but trying to hide the fact by cinching his belt tight and low on his hips, causing flesh to spill over the waistband.

In the silence I hear a faint feline mewl.

'Show me what you've found.'

Tommy leads me past the stalls into a corner of the barn where empty oil barrels and paint tins are stored on rough wooden shelves. I notice a packing crate full of straw and torn newspapers. The ginger-and-black tabby is lying on her side while four – no, five kittens are suckling against her abdomen. Tiny, helpless, their eyes just open, the kittens are being moved by their mother's rough tongue as she cleans them.

Tommy picks up the biggest of the litter. The kitten sits in the palm of his hand, squirming and trying to stand. He strokes his thumb over its fragile head and under its chin.

'How old are they?' I ask.

He raises his spare hand, opening his fingers twice.

'Ten days.'

He nods.

'You've been feeding the mother?'

'Uh-huh.'

'Why didn't you tell anyone?'

He opens his mouth, but no sound comes out. He's not ducking the question. He's trying to find the answer.

'Nan don't like me c-c-coming over here.'

The words are hesitant yet overly articulated as though he's trying to disguise a lisp or cure a stammer. He swaps kittens, letting each of them become accustomed to being handled. I get a better look at him now. Built large in the hips and thighs, he has acne scars on his cheeks and scruffy hair spotted with paint that looks like bird-shit. His jeans are stained with grease and oil and the dark hollow of his right eye turns out to be a bruise.

'What happened?' I ask.

'Rugby.'

'It's not rugby season.'

He cups a kitten in both his hands, holding it against his cheek. For a fleeting moment I recognise a boy rather than a man, lonely, isolated, lacking in confidence, but then I see something else spark in his irises – not intelligence so much as a certain animalistic cunning.

'You found Mrs Crowe and Harper.'

He nods.

'Why did you come here that Sunday morning?'

'I 'eard the alarm.'

'Were you friends with Harper?'

He doesn't answer, but I can see him struggle with the question. I pull up an empty old drum and take a seat, holding my left arm to stop it trembling.

'How long have you lived next door?'

'All me life.'

'You did work around the place – looking after the garden?'

He nods.

'Where were you that Saturday night? You know the one I mean.'

'H-h-home.'

'All night?'

'Aye.'

'When did you last see Harper?'

'Saturday.'

'What time?'

'Early evening.'

'You saw her go out?'

'Saw her car.'

'What time?'

'Must have been about eight.'

'Where were you when you saw her?'

'With the cows.'

'Was Harper alone?'

He nods.

'What about Mrs Crowe – did you see her go out that night?'

'I were watching TV.'

'What were you watching?'

'Don't remember.'

'Did you see her come home?'

He shakes his head. Dropping to his haunches, he opens the tin of cat food with his penknife, scooping out the contents with the blade. The tabby rises from her bed and kittens tumble in her wake, blindly kneading and suckling at the air. She eats hungrily and cleans herself.

Tommy wipes his hands on his jeans.

I pick up a kitten. Its eyes open, bluer than blue.

'They're lovely.'

He nods.

'What are you going to do with them?'

'Drown 'em most likely.'

'Why?'

'Nan won't let me keep 'em. We got too many animals to feed.'

'I'll make a deal with you. I'll help you find homes for them, but first you have to tell me the truth. Did you see Mrs Crowe come home that night?'

Tommy seems to contemplate lying, but then looks at the kittens. 'I saw her.'

'What time was that?'

'It were dark.'

Sunset on that Saturday was at 9.30 p.m.

'You were outside?'

Another nod.

'Show me.'

Tommy puts the penknife in his jeans and tosses the empty can of cat food in an old water trough. He leads me across the yard and shows me a spot near the water tank where the grass is worn away and earth compacted. Facing the house, I scan the windows. I can see Elizabeth's bedroom. Her curtains are open. I can also see Harper's room and the broken pane of glass.

'When did you first find this spot?'

He shrugs.

'Did you ever watch Mrs Crowe get undressed?'

'N–n–n–no.'

'What about Harper?'

He shakes his head more strenuously. I probe him gently, using a tone that carries no hint of censure or criticism. 'I'm not the police, Tommy. I can't get you into trouble. I'm just trying to understand what happened.'

He picks at a patch of flaking paint on his thumbnail. 'It were h–h–her fault.'

'Mrs Crowe?'

'She d–d–d–don't . . . ' He stops. Starts again. 'She d–d–d–don't close her curtains.'

His stutter gets worse when he's under pressure.

'Did you masturbate while you watched her?'

'N–n–n–n–no.'

'Is that why you stole her underwear from the clothesline?'

His fists are clenched and shoulders hunched. I can't see his eyes. 'She called me a p–pervert. She's the one t–t–to talk.'

'What does that mean?'

'I seen her d–do–doing stuff.'

'You saw her with men?'

He nods.

'Was she with anyone that night?'

'Yeah,' he says defiantly.

'In the bedroom?'

'D–d–downstairs. He was lighting candles.'

'Did you see his face?'

'I saw his shadow.'

'Did he have a car?'

Tommy hesitates. 'Aye, I guess.' He can't remember.

'How long did you stay watching?'

He shrugs.

'What time was this?'

'Don't have a watch.'

'Were you still here when Harper came home?'

He shakes his head. A strong gust of wind shakes the trees and a leaf spins and falls, landing on Tommy's shoulder. He brushes it away. On the rooftop a weathervane spins back and forth.

'Tell me, Tommy, did you ever try to get into the house?'

He looks at me, puzzled.

'Did you ever try to open a window or test if the doors were unlocked?'

He gives me a slow shake of the head.

'Did you imagine going inside?'

He doesn't answer.

'Did you watch Harper?'

'No!'

'Why not?'

He lowers his gaze, his cheeks colouring. It's more than just embarrassment.

'Did you love her, Tommy?'

His face twists in embarrassment.

'Did you ever tell Harper how you felt?'

'N-n-no.'

'Why not?'

'Sh-sh-she'd laugh at me.'

'What makes you say that?'

'They always do.'

10

Veronica Cray is pacing her office, her eyes electric with excitement. 'It's him,' she says elatedly. 'Rule number bloody two! If it's not family it's the neighbour.'

'It wasn't a confession,' I remind her.

'He lied to us.'

'That doesn't make him guilty.'

'He had the motive and the opportunity.'

'But not the intellect.'

'How bright do you have to be to stab a woman thirty-six times?'

'He barely left a trace.'

'He left DNA in the house.'

'He *found* the bodies.'

Her temporary office is small and windowless with a filing cabinet, a desk and computer. One wall is covered in press clippings about the farmhouse murders and a satellite map showing the various buildings and surrounding fields.

The incident room is visible through the vertical blinds. Detectives are cradling phones and peering at screens. The abiding atmosphere is one of anxiety, stress and fatigue.

The longer the investigation goes on, the higher the mountain of detail and the harder it becomes to check and cross-check. Things get overlooked. Missed.

One entire wall contains cardboard box-files with hard copies of every interview, statement, telephone record and tip-off – twelve thousand documents in all.

Cray is still arguing. 'Garrett has a history of sexual deviance.'

'Not a long history.'

'Folks have complained about him for years. He prowls the streets, jumping out at women . . . stealing underwear.'

'He's antisocial and degenerate, but that doesn't make him a killer.'

'You've said it before, Professor, killers rarely emerge from nothing; there's a progression. They peep through windows. They steal underwear. They flash their bits at schoolchildren. They practise. They train. And eventually they graduate from sexual deviancy to the Premier League.'

'This was too sophisticated a crime, too shrewd, too smart—'

'He hacked her to death.'

'Look at the aftermath – the way he cleaned up. The killer didn't panic. He took his time. What about the candles and Bible? Tommy Garrett wouldn't know a pentagram from a mammogram.'

Cray grunts dismissively. 'People only think he's slow. Tommy Garrett is rat-cunning. At sixteen he was knocked off his bike. Got an insurance settlement. Claimed he couldn't even shower by himself. Now he's milking cows and mowing lawns.'

'What about his alibi?'

'His grandmother always lies for him.'

'He mentioned seeing a visitor – someone lighting candles.'

'Yeah, very convenient.'

'We know Elizabeth let the killer into the farmhouse. That's not going to be Tommy, is it?'

Cray sighs and rubs her mouth. 'You may be right, Professor, but we've spent almost a month chasing our tails. I want to make an arrest. I want to show these good people that we're doing something.'

'By scapegoating Tommy Garrett.'

'By holding him for forty-eight hours and getting a warrant to search his house. And I'll bet you a pound to a pinch of shit that we find the murder weapon or something else that incriminates him.'

I can't talk to Cray when she's like this. Psychological profiling isn't an exact science and cannot be presented in court in the same way as fingerprint evidence or DNA analysis. I remember once seeing a series of photos of the everlasting shadows of Hiroshima caused by the atomic blast. When the heat from the detonation hit a person standing close to a wall, they were vaporised instantly and a 'shadow' was left behind, as though printed in two dimensions against the wall. That's what it feels like when I look at a murder scene. I see the shadows.

DCS Cray is already on the phone, making a request for a search warrant. She seems happier than before. Some people have to keep moving forward because standing still feels as though they're being left behind.

She finishes the call and checks some of her phone messages. 'The coroner just released the bodies. Elizabeth and Harper are going to be cremated on Tuesday.'

'Is that a problem?'

'Yes. No. Maybe. I'm always concerned the pathologist will have screwed things up, or they'll discover some new technology and we won't have the right samples.'

'It's been almost a month.'

'I know.' She stares at her cluttered desk and the stack of papers waiting to be signed. Budgets. Overtime. Requisition forms.

'Are you sure you want me reviewing this investigation?' I ask. 'What if I identify failings?'

'I can handle criticism.'

'So long as it's not public.'

She eyeballs me angrily. 'Terry Bannerman is an obnoxious blowhard whose opinions I couldn't value less. If we've missed something, I'll take responsibility for that.'

'I'm going to need help.'

'I can't spare anyone.'

'Can I bring someone in?'

'Who did you have in mind?'

'Vincent Ruiz.'

Wrinkles concertina around her eyes. Cray and Ruiz have a mutual loathing. I once put this down to professional rivalry, but it's more a clash of personalities. They're like sumo wrestlers stomping around a ring, slapping their thighs and throwing salt.

'He *was* a detective,' I say.

'*Was*. Past tense. Old. Retired. Gone to seed. Pain in the arse.'

'He speaks very highly of you.'

'Very funny.'

'I need his help.'

She mutters something under her breath. 'Keep him away from me.'

'Yes, guv.'

'I'm not your guv.'

She waves me away as a woman constable appears at the door, raising her hand to knock.

'What is it?' Cray barks.

'A call, guv.'

The telephone console has been blinking unanswered on the desk. Cray punches the lighted button and picks up the receiver.

'Are you sure it's her? . . . No, don't arrest her. Bannerman would have a field day. Yeah, OK. I'm coming.'

She hangs up and grabs her coat. 'You're coming with me.'

'What's happened?'

'Elizabeth Crowe's sister is stopping traffic on Walton Road.'

'Why?'

'She's trying to find the killer.'

11

'No sirens,' Cray says to her driver – the same young constable who delivered the message. She's in her late twenties with her hair pinned up beneath her cap and freckles that look as though they've been pencilled on to her nose.

'This is Bennie,' says Cray, introducing us. The female officer makes eye contact with me in the rear-view mirror, smiling nervously.

'The Professor is a psychologist,' says Cray, 'so be careful what you say around him. He claims to be a Freudian, but I think he's Jung at heart.'

The DCS thinks she's hilarious. Bennie smiles at me in the mirror, sympathetically this time.

Within minutes we're out of Clevedon, heading east along narrow roads through a patchwork of fields. The next village is barely a speck on the map, with a few dozen buildings clinging to the road and a church steeple rising above the trees. Traffic has banked up. The police car pulls over.

Ahead of us I notice a woman standing in the middle of the road, waving down cars. She steps in front of each vehicle and holds up her hands as though physically bringing them to a halt. Tapping on the driver's side window, she waits for it to be lowered.

I recognise her from the public meeting. Blonde, medium build, denim skirt, white blouse, Becca Washburn is holding a framed photograph of Elizabeth and Harper, which she shows to each driver.

'This is one for you,' says Cray.

'I don't know her.'

'Does it make a difference?'

I step out of the car and weave between the stationary vehicles until I reach the head of the queue.

'What are you doing, Becca?' I ask.

She glances up and blinks, searching her memory. Everything about her is curiously indistinct, as though she's fading away. Dismissing me with a flick of her head, she goes back to the cars, knocking on the next window. The driver lowers it a few inches.

'This is my sister and niece. They were murdered a month ago. Do you know who did it?' she asks.

The driver shakes his head.

'Are you sure? Have you seen them before?'

'No.'

She moves on, ignoring my presence, determined to finish what she started. A horn bleats, answered by others. She doesn't seem to hear them.

I glance back at Cray, who gestures impatiently.

'My name is Joe. Maybe I can help.'

Becca turns suddenly and holds up the photograph. 'Do you recognise them?'

'I know who they are.'

'Do you know who killed them?'

'No.'

She turns away and continues walking.

'I'd like to talk to you about Elizabeth and Harper,' I say. 'We could have a cup of tea.'

Becca ignores me.

'You can't just stop traffic – you'll get yourself arrested.'

'Wouldn't that be ironic?' she says bitterly. 'For a month we've had someone living in our house, answering the phone, opening the mail, dealing with reporters. Now they've gone. The police have given up. Nobody talks to us any more.'

'I'm sure that's not true.'

'How would you know?'

'I'm helping the police . . . reviewing the case.'

'You're a detective?'

'A psychologist.'

Mistrust clouds her eyes. 'The last one was a moron.'

'I agree.'

Some of the drivers are out of their vehicles. A bald guy yells at me to 'move the stupid bitch'. It triggers something inside me. I take a dozen paces towards him and shove him hard in the chest, telling him to get back in his car. He mutters something under his breath.

Meanwhile, Becca wipes perspiration off her top lip and glances down the road. Twenty cars are waiting. I can see her thinking – what if one of them contains the killer? How will she know? Her eyes are shining and her hand stops halfway to her face as though interrupted. There is an expression on her face that I haven't seen before – a sense of permanent sadness, or a question about whether she will ever stand on this spot again and have an opportunity to discover the truth about her sister and niece.

'What was Elizabeth like?' I ask.

'I don't have time for this,' she replies wearily.

'I know she came from a loving family. She was strong. Independent. You could help me get to know her.'

'Why?'

'That's what I do. I try to understand what happened and why. It's not easy when they've gone. People can be like those Magic Eye pictures – you know the ones I mean? Sometimes you have to look right through them and pull back again to see the secret figure hidden inside the picture. You can help me to see the *real* Elizabeth and Harper. Let's have a cup of tea.'

She casts a thoughtful, sideways glance. 'And Earl Grey will solve everything?'

'No, but I'm thirsty and it always makes me feel better.'

Becca lets me take her hand and we walk to the side of the road. Traffic begins moving.

'Where's your husband?' I ask.

'Working.'

'What about your baby?'

She brushes damp hair from her eyes, searching her memory. I try again. 'What's your baby's name?'

'George.'

'Where is he?'

'Sleeping.'

'Did you leave him sleeping somewhere?'

She shakes her head.

'Who's looking after George?'

'Francis took him to work.'

In the same instant, out of the corner of my eye, I see someone running towards us from the opposite direction. He's wearing belted trousers and a pale blue shirt, carrying a baby in his arms. Becca lets out a hiccuping sob and collapses into his embrace, hugging the baby between them.

'It's OK, pet,' whispers Francis. 'I'm here now.'

They're standing in the middle of the road, ignoring the blasting horns and gawking motorists.

Francis looks at me as though I'm responsible. He's about my height and maybe half a stone heavier, with his brown hair shaved close to his scalp, accentuating his ears.

'Your wife needs help,' I say. 'She should see a grief counsellor.'

'My wife is fine,' he answers, clenching his teeth and flexing the cartilage behind his jawline.

'Can't you see she's struggling?'

'Leave my family alone.'

The DCS is walking towards us. Francis stabs a finger in her direction. 'This is your fault!' he yells. 'Do your job.'

12

It's amazing how easily I slip back into the rhythms and routines of the cottage, practices that are embossed upon my memory like Braille – rinsing plates, packing the dishwasher, wiping benches and discussing the day's events. Julianne is making small talk and acting as though nothing is wrong. Meanwhile, my mind is conjuring up every worst-case scenario.

I keep trying to get her alone, but she finds excuses to slip away. Even now, when Emma is watching TV in the sitting room and Charlie is upstairs, she avoids the subject.

'You can't keep fobbing me off,' I say.

'I'm not fobbing you off.'

'We have to talk.'

She surveys the kitchen. 'When are you going back to London?'

'First thing in the morning.'

'But you're coming back, right?'

'I'll pack a suitcase and make sure my neighbour waters the plants.'

'You have plants?'

'I have two.'

'I'm impressed.'

'Don't do that.'

'What?'

'You're changing the subject. I'm not leaving until you tell me what's going on.'

'OK, let's talk. Take me to the pub.'

She wants to be somewhere public. Not a good sign.

It's still light outside. I hear shouts of young children playing in a paddling pool and the sound of canned laughter from open windows. At the Fox and Badger the heavy door eases shut behind us. The publican, Hector, nods and asks if I've been on holiday. Hector still thinks I live in the village even after two years away. I'm one of the founding members of the Divorced Men's Club in Wellow, which includes Hector. Our numbers are dwindling. Two of the lads have remarried and a third has come out and is living with his former best man. Who says romance is dead?

I order Julianne a glass of wine. We take a table in the quietest corner, away from the kitchen and the busy end of the bar. I recognise most of the regulars – lumpy-faced locals who nod and say 'aye' even when disagreeing; and 'no, no, no, aye' when agreeing.

Julianne centres her wine on her coaster. Not satisfied, she picks up the glass and places it down again.

'I have ovarian cancer,' she says, not looking at my face. 'They did an ultrasound a week ago. The mass is about seven centimetres. They want to do a CT scan next Wednesday and then I'll have surgery.'

I struggle to swallow and feel the sweat prickle beneath my hairline. 'What exactly did they say?'

'My doctor is hopeful it might only be stage one. He said that ninety per cent of patients are still alive after five years. That seems pretty positive. The CT scan should tell us more. I'm refusing to worry until I know exactly what I'm dealing with.'

The silence is filled with a kind of temporal static and I have the sharpest, almost visceral sense that Julianne is going to die. My lips unglue. 'How long have you known?'

'A week.'

'Why didn't you tell me?'

'I'm telling you now.'

'What are the options?'

'A hysterectomy is pretty standard, then chemotherapy.'

'When?'

'As soon as possible.'

The gold flecks in her eyes seem to swim, or maybe they're floating in mine. I almost put my arms around her. I almost touch her hair. The moment is lost. Questions spill out of me. When is she seeing the doctor again? Is her oncologist any good? Has she researched the surgeon? Who has she told? We can go private. No waiting.

'We need to get a second opinion.'

'This *is* the second opinion.'

'When are these other tests?'

'Wednesday at four.'

'I'll come with you.'

'You don't have to.'

'I'm coming. Have you told your mother?'

'I didn't want to bother anyone until I was sure. It's not as though it's anyone's business except mine.'

'Do the girls know?'

'I talked to Charlie a few days ago. I told her about the ultrasound. Emma must have been listening.' Her voice almost breaks. She picks up her wine. Two hands. Unsteady. Sips.

Up until this moment, Julianne and I have had a nice, cosy system worked out – living separate lives in separate houses, sharing our daughters. We have had flings, woes, laughs and a Heinz-like variety of irritations, but fundamentally we're still the same two people in slightly different orbits. Now she is trying to dismiss this as nothing – a mere trifle, another hiccup – but this *is* something. This is life-changing. This is epochal.

When I was diagnosed with Parkinson's I couldn't go home and tell Julianne. Instead I slept with a woman who wasn't my wife. It was a one-night stand that will *always* stand – the low point of our marriage, the low point of my life. My diagnosis had devastated me. I was dumbfounded. Distraught. How could I tell Julianne and pull the pin on our perfect life and golden future? I should have had more faith in her. Instead I went to see Elisa – an old friend and a former patient – a woman who had spent years listening to unhappy men, not as a therapist but as a prostitute.

We think we know ourselves. We imagine our reaction to such a diagnosis. We've seen enough movies about cancer sufferers or read anything by Nicholas Sparks. We're supposed to pound the walls, howl at the moon, buy a Porsche, take a world cruise, write to everyone we've ever wronged and then sit in the dark, watching old Bob Hope and Bing Crosby movies, drinking ourselves into oblivion.

The weird thing is I slept fine after my diagnosis. No nightmares. It was only during the day that I remembered. How could I forget? Now someone I love is going to experience this. I hear myself talking to Julianne, sounding like a veteran campaigner, but I've never had cancer or had to endure surgery.

She grows pensive again. 'You don't have to stay – I feel as though I've tricked you into coming.'

'You didn't trick me.'

'It's just until I get out of hospital.'

'I'm here until you ask me to leave.'

Acorns snap and pop under our feet as we walk down Mill Hill Lane to the cottage. Julianne hooks her arm into mine and we match strides.

'I know what you're going to do,' she says. 'You'll spend all night on the Internet, trying to Google up a cure.'

'Might do.'

'This feels a little strange.'

'In a good way?'

'Like uncharted territory.'

'That can be good.'

'I'm glad that we're friends.'

'Me too.'

That night, lying alone in Emma's bed, I hold out my hand, reaching into the darkness, and I trace Julianne's curves in my mind, feeling her breath against my face, her heart against mine. I know her body better than my own: her knees, her elbows, her belly button and the spot behind her ear that produces a sigh when kissed. I imagine it's my secret place that nobody else knows about, but I wonder who else has discovered it or gone looking. It doesn't matter any more. I'm here.

13

Just before dawn, when mist hangs in the valleys like spilled milk and the air is cool and clear, four police cars arrive at a farm in the Gordano Valley, less than six hundred yards from the murder house. Tommy Garrett and his grandmother are already awake, working beneath the dangling yellow light bulbs in the milking shed. Tommy is quickly handcuffed and led to a waiting car. Doreen slaps her grandson on the back of the head and yells, 'What did you do?'

'N-n-nothing.'

'Must have been something.'

While the police search the house, Tommy is taken to Clevedon Police Station on Tickenham Road. Doreen stays at the farm, complaining about the search and demanding to know who is going to clean up the mess.

I'm in London by this time. The outskirts of the capital are interminable, but once I see the dense green of Hyde Park and Kensington Gardens I feel a little more well disposed towards the city, with its stone arches, soaring domes and storybook qualities with place names that belonged to Dickens and Woolf and Keats.

Stopping at my flat, I drag a suitcase from beneath the bed

and hurriedly pack some things. When I was young my mother insisted on picking out my clothes and hanging them on the doorknob while I slept. She dressed me like Little Lord Fauntleroy in a waistcoat and tie, while my sisters looked like Hayley Mills in *Pollyanna*. Ever since then I've struggled to make choices about what I should wear, which is why my wardrobe is full of chinos and long-sleeved cotton shirts and blue blazers. I have become a creature of habit in middle-aged camouflage.

After emptying the fridge of perishables, I leave a note for Henry, downstairs, asking him to water my indoor plants and keep an eye on the place. Stowing the suitcase in the car, I drive south to Fulham, parking outside a pastel-coloured terrace house in Rainville Road less than eighty yards from the Thames. Nobody answers the doorbell. I call Ruiz on his mobile and leave a message.

The pub over the road isn't his regular boozer. The Crabtree is far too bright and welcoming. Ruiz prefers to drink in places where punters shield their eyes when the door opens and guard their drinks as though the Chancellor of the Exchequer has rationed them. I don't understand the attraction, but Ruiz says the cleanliness of the pipes and quality of the ales are more important than buxom barmaids and sparkling conversation. Vincent is a man of simple tastes and complex humanity, who has never tried to shake his past, because he knows that it cannot be altered. Instead he reminds me of a punch-drunk boxer who hears a bell and charges out of his corner, head down and arms swinging. The footwork has slowed, but he can still deliver a punch that will stop a tram.

I see him now, standing at the entrance to the beer garden, searching for me. I wave. He nods. Gesticulates. Do I want a drink? I shake my head. He gets himself a Guinness.

'A little early,' I say, as he centres the foaming pint glass on a coaster.

'It's a pub not a coffee shop.'

He takes a small sip and then a bigger one. Satisfied, he

drains half the glass. Dressed in loose-fitting jeans, a T-shirt and a scuffed leather jacket, he has the physique of a rugby prop, straight up and down, with thinning hair and battered ears. Half his left ring finger is missing, amputated by a high-velocity bullet; and he walks with a limp because the second bullet came even closer to killing him.

We sit at a table overlooking the river. It's low tide and gulls are fighting for scraps on the exposed mud.

'How's the Parkinson's?' he asks.

'Like I'm always on vibrate.'

He smiles. 'You've been saving that up.'

I notice a black band on his wrist. 'What's that?'

'Miranda bought it for me,' he replies.

'What does it do?'

'Tells me how far I've walked.'

'You're exercising?'

'I prefer to think I'm earning my daily alcohol intake.'

Miranda is Ruiz's ex-wife − his third − but they seem to have more sex and fewer arguments since they divorced.

'She says I'm getting fat,' he explains. 'I have to do ten thousand steps a day.'

'Ten thousand!'

'If I walk to her house, I get a treat.'

'Are you a man or a dog?'

'Good question.'

'So what's the treat?'

'I get to sleep over.'

'She lives in Bayswater.'

'Exactly.'

'You could always catch the bus.'

'Yeah, well, that's the problem. This thing has a GPS-style widget, which means Miranda can look at her computer and see exactly how far I've walked. Last week I paid the kid next door to go jogging but he went too far. Miranda smelled a rat. It cost me a hundred-quid dinner to make it up to her.'

'And you think *I'm* hung up on a woman!'

'At least I'm getting laid.'

I contemplate telling him that I'm staying at the cottage for a few weeks with Julianne, but it no longer seems like something to celebrate. Ruiz swallows the rest of his Guinness, pausing to belch quietly into his fist.

'So why are you here?' he asks.

'This could be a social visit.'

'We both know that's not true.'

I've known Ruiz for nearly ten years – ever since he arrested me as a murder suspect. Since then we've become friends and sometimes help each other out – although I suspect the ledger favours him.

'I'm working on a case,' I say, explaining the reasons, trying not to sound as though I'm justifying them.

'And where do I come into this?'

'I need your help.'

Ruiz clears his throat, his voice gravelly. 'Let me consult my diary.' He licks the tip of his index finger and holds it up to the breeze. 'I appear to be free.'

I buy him another Guinness before outlining the details of the case. On 6 June, between 11 p.m. and 2 a.m., a mother and daughter were killed in a farmhouse on the outskirts of Clevedon – one stabbed, the other suffocated. There are six prime suspects: an ex-husband, his business partner, a stepson, the daughter's boyfriend, a neighbour and one of the men who Elizabeth met through a dating agency. A second list compiled by the task force includes the names of all the registered sex offenders in the area with no alibi for the murders. A third list records everyone who had contact with Elizabeth and Harper in the preceding days – tradesmen, friends and visitors.

'There's another complication,' I say. 'Elizabeth may have invited a stranger home. She was known to frequent local dogging sites. You know what dogging is?'

'I'm retired, not expired, Professor, but I don't claim

first-hand experience.' Ruiz's eyes are smiling. 'Who's in charge of the investigation?'

'Ronnie Cray.'

'How is the Fat Controller?'

'She's a chief superintendent now.'

'All that hot air – she floated right to the top.'

'Don't be harsh.'

'Does she know I'm coming on board?'

'She suggested I call you.'

Ruiz knows I'm lying. 'So what's the brief?'

'We go over the statements, review the investigation, see if there's anything the police might have missed.'

'The two of us?'

'We're reviewing it – not solving it.'

Ruiz drains his glass and contemplates getting another. 'In my opinion, which I know you'll ignore,' he says, 'you may have allowed your personal feelings to cloud your judgement on this one.'

'How so?'

'You're pissed off that your former student is treading on your territory.'

'It's not my territory. He's compromised an investigation.'

'And trashed your name?'

'I don't care about Milo Coleman. I want to make sure the killer gets caught.'

'If you say so.'

14

Early afternoon and the high-altitude clouds in the western sky have formed a pale wash that grows lighter as the sun reaches its zenith. I'm driving west along the M4 through rolling hills that are swathed in vibrant yellow. When did the wheat, barley and corn of my youth become usurped by rapeseed?

Snatches of my conversation with Julianne keep replaying in my mind. Mostly I remember the look of uncertainty in her eyes. I have known this woman for more than half my life. I have seen her frightened for a missing child or an unborn baby or a husband bleeding to death in her arms – but never for herself. This time her body testified to it and her doubts were written on her face: the reality of her mortality and fear of what lies ahead.

Passing Bristol, I glimpse the Severn Bridge with its twin pyramids of wire, spanning the estuary. Ruiz is going to join me on Monday. The following day will be the funerals of Elizabeth and Harper. Ronnie Cray has suggested I be there. Family dynamics are on display at weddings and funerals – the subtle alliances and factions and old hatreds, patched up for the

day, but never far below the surface. My mother barely acknowledges her sister-in-law, who she accuses of stealing a shortbread
recipe thirty-five years ago, and my father hasn't talked to his
younger brother since 1986 because of an unpaid bet on a Cup
Final.

My mobile chirrups. Emma thinks it's funny to keep changing
my ringtone. Charlie's voice echoes through the car speakers.
'I want the truth about Mummy.'

'I thought she talked to you.'

'She gave me some rainbow-and-dolphins speech about
everything being fine and it's no big deal.'

'She *is* going to be fine.'

'Don't treat me like I'm a child,' she says angrily, and I can
picture the twin frown marks etched deeply above the bridge
of her nose. 'You're a doctor, you know about this stuff.'

'I'm a psychologist.'

'But you studied medicine.'

'I didn't finish.'

'Stop making excuses! Ovarian cancer – that's serious, isn't
it? I mean, it can spread. It can be . . . you know . . . it can
be . . .'

'She might need an operation.'

'A hysterectomy?'

'We won't know until she sees the oncologist on Wednesday.
They might have to take out her ovaries or uterus. Then she'll
probably need a few rounds of chemotherapy.'

'Oh, crap!'

'What?'

'Freya's dad had chemo. He had a brain tumour.'

'A lot of people have chemo.'

'He died.'

'That's not going to happen to Mum.'

'How do you know? You're not a doctor!' Her voice is
breaking. 'That's why she asked you to come back, isn't it? She's
afraid she's going to die.'

'No.'

'Why then?'

'She knew she might need an operation.'

'Well, it's not fair,' says Charlie. 'It's not fair on you and it's not fair on us.'

'It's not fair on *her*,' I say.

Charlie sniffles.

'We have to be strong,' I tell her.

'I'm scared.'

'She's scared too.' There is a long silence. I can hear her chewing on her bottom lip. 'Are we good?'

She sighs, and blows her nose. 'Yep, we're good.'

The minicab office takes up the front room of a pebble-dashed terrace in Old Street, Clevedon. A banner sign hangs from the first-floor windows, drooping at one corner. The waiting room has two plastic chairs and a low table where a dozen glossy magazines are curling with age. The dispatcher is sitting at a desk that is pushed up against a doorway to form a makeshift counter. She has ketchup-coloured hair and a mole on her top lip that seems to lift off like a fly and settle again every time she talks.

'You want a car, love?'

'I'm looking for one of your drivers – Dominic Crowe.'

'He's on the road.'

'When is he due back?'

'Unless you book him, I can't be certain.'

The sign above her head says: *Anywhere in Clevedon for £3.50*.

'I'll book him.'

'Where do you want to go?'

'I'll tell him when he gets here.'

She flicks on the radio. *'Hey, Nic, got a fare waiting at the office.'* She meets my gaze and keeps talking. *'He asked for you by name? . . . Didn't say . . . Skinny, my age, curly hair . . . doesn't look like one . . . You want me to ask? . . . OK, I'll tell him . . .'*

109

She turns to me. 'He'll be ten minutes. Are you a reporter?'

'No.'

'We've had lots of reporters in here. Some of them lie.'

'I'm not a reporter.'

I can see her finger hovering over the button of the two-way, itching to spread the latest bit of news. Smiling politely, I pick up a magazine and read about how Kate Middleton is losing her baby weight and getting back into shape. Who'd be a princess?

A few minutes later a car pulls up outside.

'That's your ride,' says the woman.

Dominic Crowe gets out and opens the rear door. Tall and loose-limbed with a shock of dark hair, he has Harper's high forehead and sharp cheekbones beneath a five o'clock shadow.

'I'll sit up front,' I tell him.

He shuts one door and opens another. 'Where do you want to go?'

'Show me the sights.'

'That's not how it works. I drop you somewhere and you pay me.'

'How far will twenty quid get me?'

'I'm not giving you a blow job, if that's what you mean. So what's this about?'

I tell him the truth. He doesn't get annoyed or try to avoid the subject. If anything he seems grimly accepting. 'I've been interviewed three times already. Surely you can find some better use for your time.'

'I'm a psychologist – I ask different questions.'

He smiles wryly. 'Yeah, well, I probably need my head read; I was married to that woman for twenty-four years.'

He gets behind the wheel and we drive down Chapel Hill and along Lindon Road until we reach Clevedon Pier. He pulls into an angled parking space overlooking the rocky beach where swaths of mud and shingle have been exposed by the outgoing tide. I can see people walking along the pier, stopping to read the name plaques on the benches.

'It falls forty-seven feet,' he says.

'What does?'

'The tide – they say it's the second highest in the world.' He lowers the window and rests his elbow outside, before motioning to the pier. 'About forty years ago the outward spans collapsed when the legs failed. It took years of haggling, but eventually it was rebuilt.'

'You'd make a good tour guide,' I say.

'It's where I grew up.'

We sit in silence for a while, pretending to listen to noise that isn't there. His long, tapered fingers are sliding over the steering wheel.

'Did they tell you I had a nervous breakdown?' he asks.

'No.'

'I beat up my former business partner and set fire to his car.'

'For sleeping with your wife.'

He makes an imaginary gun and shoots himself in the temple. 'Not very clever, huh?'

'It shows you have a temper.'

'I wanted to wipe the smug look off his face.'

'And what did you want to do to Elizabeth?'

He grows more circumspect. 'I know people think I killed her. I mean, I hated her guts and maybe I said a few things I regret, but . . . '

'But what?'

'I didn't want her dead.' He looks at me sorrowfully. 'You have to understand what she did to me. I worked seven days a week, keeping our heads above water, but that bitch was never going to drown. Instead she sailed off into the sunset with my fucking money. I lost everything.'

'Your wife took out a restraining order against you.'

'I lost my temper. I shouted. I didn't hit her.'

'That's not what her mother and sister told police.'

He makes a *pfffft* sound. 'Have you met them? They're like a coven – the witches of Clevedon. I blame her mother. She

111

thinks all men are destined to disappoint her sooner rather than later. Elizabeth's father walked out on the family just after Becca was born. Ever since, the mother has been predisposed to hate men. You know she once told Elizabeth that whatever happened she should marry a man who worshipped her, so that she'd never be dumped or abandoned. Don't you think that's horrible advice to give a daughter? Forget about love. Go for security.'

His eyes drift across the beach where seagulls are hovering against the breeze like tethered kites. The shadow sweeps across the water, changing the colours, and I can imagine some ancient sea monster swimming just below the surface.

'You left an abusive message on Elizabeth's voicemail the day she died.'

'I regret that, but I was provoked. Elizabeth told Harper that I'd cancelled our lunch on her birthday.'

'Why would she do that?'

'She was always trying to turn Harper against me. I think she worried that our daughter might love me more.'

'Was Elizabeth really that insecure?'

'No, but she held grudges.'

'How did you and Harper get on?'

'Great, you know, we've always been tight, but after the divorce it got harder.'

'Did you resent that?'

'Sure. Look I know I put the police offside by acting tough and being uncooperative, but I would never have hurt my daughter.'

He unbuttons the cuff of his shirt and pulls it upwards. Harper's name is tattooed on his left forearm in a swirling script. His Adam's apple rises and falls as he swallows. He pulls the sleeve down again.

'Did your wife have more than one affair?'

He shrugs. 'I don't know.'

'She must have loved you once.'

'I hope so.'

The words seem to turn to dust in his mouth. I ask whether Harper had a favourite toy when she was little.

'A brown teddy bear with chewed ears,' he replies. 'She once left it on a train to London. It took me three days to get it back. Cost a fortune in couriers.'

'Who else knew about the bear?'

He rocks his head from side to side. 'I have no idea. Her friends. Family.'

'Where were you the night they died?'

'Working. Driving.'

'You finished at midnight.'

'Yeah.'

'Why did you turn your mobile off?'

'I was tired. I didn't want the dispatcher calling with any more jobs. Any fare at that hour is usually drunk or bleeding.'

'Which means you don't have an alibi.'

'I don't need one. I'm innocent.'

Running his hands over the steering wheel, he watches a child being carried on her father's shoulders along the seafront. Something inside him seems to shred.

'Who do you think killed your ex-wife and daughter?' I ask.

His voice grows thick. 'Elizabeth invited the wrong man home.'

15

Jeremy Egan works out of an office on Portishead docks, over-looking the harbour where the flotilla of moored yachts and launches is so white it hurts my eyes. One corner of his office has a table displaying his latest project – a scale model of a grand old Victorian hotel that he's redeveloping into luxury apartments. I recognise the building – the Regency. It's where I stayed with Julianne and the girls when we spent a weekend in Clevedon.

Egan notices my interest. 'Looking to buy?' he asks. 'We still have a two-bedroom available.'

'How much?'

'Three hundred and fifty thousand.'

'A tad rich for me.'

He smiles knowingly and suggests I take a seat. Tall and good-looking with shoulder-length hair and a foppish fringe combed down over his forehead, Egan reminds me of an over-grown schoolboy home on holidays from Eton. The accent completes the picture. Not good or bad. I went to a boarding school and hated every moment. Other boys seemed to flourish in these all-male domains, the fittest surviving in a Darwinian sense, or perhaps I mean *Lord of the Flies*.

His desk is completely empty except for his mobile phone and a framed photograph of a pretty dark-haired woman and two dark-haired boys. Teenagers. Strapping lads in Bath Rugby kit.

'Nice family,' I say.

'Thank you.' He doesn't look at the picture. 'You said you were helping the police.'

'Reviewing the case.'

'Well, I've given a statement. There's nothing I can add.'

'When did you stop sleeping with Elizabeth Crowe?'

The bluntness of the question seems to offend his sensibilities. He recovers and straightens, patting his fringe.

'My relationship with Elizabeth ended more than a year ago.'

'Did your wife know about the affair?'

'I don't see how that's relevant.'

'She forgave you. Some would say you got off easily.'

'What is it you want to know, Professor? You seem intent on antagonising me.'

'When did the affair start?'

'Six or seven years ago, I can't remember the exact date. We'd just completed a project and went out to celebrate. Dominic got drunk. I helped him get home, put him to bed, Elizabeth offered me a nightcap. One thing led to another . . . '

'You screwed your best friend's wife while he was sleeping in the next room?'

'Snoring. Elizabeth seemed to get off on that.' He smiles. 'The look on your face is priceless.'

'Most people would make an excuse.'

'I don't need an excuse,' he says. 'You're not my wife or my priest or my bartender. I don't have to justify or explain my actions. Shit happens. People fall in love and out of love. They fuck whom they want to fuck. Honour is for knights and virgins and Muslim fathers who murder their daughters.'

'Charming.'

He touches his fringe again. It's almost a nervous tic.

'How did you and Elizabeth keep the affair secret for so long?'

'I'm an architect. I'm good with details,' he replies. 'I'd tell my wife I was golfing with some old university buddies. Elizabeth would tell Dominic that she had a medical conference. We'd meet up and spend the weekend in Scotland or Portugal or some local hotel.'

'Dominic didn't suspect?'

'We paid cash for everything. Never sent text messages or emails. I gave Elizabeth a mobile phone – my own personal hotline.'

'Was there ever any question of her leaving her husband or you leaving your wife?'

This time he laughs.

'What's so funny?' I ask.

'The thought of me setting up house with Elizabeth is hilarious. We were fuck buddies, Professor. I think that's the term for it. No strings attached. If anything, it made our marriages stronger.'

'I wonder if Mrs Egan would agree.'

'Please leave my wife out of this.'

'You seem to have done that already.'

The comment seems to light a flame behind his eyes. Perhaps he does *feel* something for someone other than himself. Then again, Egan doesn't strike me as a man who spends a great deal of time regretting his mistakes or doubting himself. Instead he has all the swaggering self-possession of a high-functioning narcissist, incapable of introspection or second thoughts. Bertrand Russell once said that the problem with the world is that fools and fanatics are always so certain of themselves, and wiser people so full of doubts.

'Tell me about the business partnership with Dominic Crowe,' I ask.

Egan recounts how the two of them met fifteen years ago – an architect and a builder – and decided to team up, borrow money, develop properties and ride the building boom.

'How did it work out?'

'We struggled early, but were doing pretty well until the

GFC ripped the guts out of the economy. Demand fell. Credit dried up. We had half-finished projects and no buyers. Suppliers were demanding payment. We needed to put more money into the business but Dominic couldn't raise his share. I offered to buy him out but he wasn't interested. He hit up Elizabeth's mother. She loaned him the money, but insisted that Dominic sign over his half of the business to Elizabeth.'

'And you did a deal with her to get the whole company?'

'I had first option to buy it.'

'When did Dominic realise?'

'When we were drawing up the papers, he saw the contract and knew that I had the power to push him out. He hired a private detective. He followed Elizabeth and photographed us together. Dominic filed for divorce. His share of the company was in Elizabeth's name, but the loan meant her mother was the real owner. Dominic got nothing.'

'Did you and Elizabeth plan this?'

'No, not really, but it suited both of us.'

'What happened after the divorce?'

'Elizabeth wouldn't sell to me.'

'She double-crossed you.'

'I think she liked the idea of having me on a leash.'

'How did you feel about that?'

'Fine and dandy,' he says sarcastically. 'I got rid of one deadweight partner and inherited another, who was even less use to me. Once we started making money again, Elizabeth wanted to take the profits out and I wanted to reinvest.'

'You fought?'

'We disagreed.'

'Were you still sleeping with her?'

'I wouldn't have touched her with a fifty-foot pole.'

'You phoned on the afternoon she died. What did you talk about?'

'I can't remember. It was probably something to do with the business.'

'On a weekend?'

He shrugs his shoulders.

'Did you arrange to meet her that evening?'

'No.'

'You had sex with her.'

'No.'

'Your semen stains were found in her car.'

'Along with how many others?'

'Where were you on that Saturday night?'

'Home with my wife.'

His secretary knocks on the door. Pretty and leggy, she's almost a younger, slimmer version of the woman in the photograph. She has brought him a coffee.

'I'm sorry. I didn't know you were here,' she says, adding, 'I would have offered you something.'

'That's OK, Emily, Professor O'Loughlin won't be staying.'

The secretary's eyes widen just a fraction, but she looks at her boss warmly. She's wearing a flared skirt that billows slightly as she turns. Egan notices. The door closes.

'Do you know what dogging is, Mr Egan?' I ask.

'Sex with random strangers in public places.'

'Is that something you enjoy?'

'Sounds like a recipe for an STD.'

'I'd appreciate an answer to my question.'

He sighs and glances out of the window where cranes are lifting another girder into place. 'My private life is none of your concern.'

'Did you introduce Elizabeth to dogging?'

'She was a very adventurous and highly sexed woman. Once she identified what she wanted she always found a way of getting it.'

'She didn't get you.'

'She didn't *want* me . . . not to keep, just to borrow occasionally.'

'For sex?'

He smiles. 'Good a reason as any.'

'How is the dogging scene around Clevedon?'

Egan stands and stretches. 'I get the impression you enjoy asking these questions. Maybe that's how you get your jollies.' He grins. 'Or do you prefer to watch? That little shake of yours makes you look like a dirty old man.'

I glance again at the photograph on his desk, feeling desperately sorry for his wife. Rarely do I lose my temper because it's unprofessional, but this man's self-absorption and arrogance have fed 'the wrong wolf'. As a young boy I had a book of fables and myths. One of my favourites was an old Cherokee legend about a grandfather who tells his grandson about the two wolves that are fighting inside each of us. One wolf is full of anger, envy, sorrow, regret, greed, arrogance, false pride and ego. The other is full of joy, peace, love, hope, humility, kindness, truth and compassion. The grandson asks, 'Which wolf will win?' And his grandfather answers, 'The one you feed.'

'I've met a lot of people like you,' I say, getting to my feet, meeting Egan eye to eye.

'I doubt that,' he replies.

'No, I have. You believe you're better than everyone else and feel you have some special right or privilege that allows you to forgo the rules or moral sensibilities that govern the rest of us.'

'You don't know me.'

'You play golf. Right-handed. You wear a fingerless glove on your left hand. You pulled a muscle in your neck and can't rotate it fully, which makes it hard on the follow-through and also means you wince slightly when you turn your head to the left.

'Your wife bought you that sweater. Cashmere. It's what she buys you every birthday, which is one of the reasons you think she's boring. She's also fat, gone to seed and turning into her mother, which is why you sleep in separate bedrooms. No, I'm wrong. You have a flat here in town. She stays at the big house with the boys.

'I noticed your Range Rover parked downstairs. New. Personalised plates. Mud on the wheels. You don't hunt or ride – I checked your profile on LinkedIn – but you've been out in the countryside. Have you introduced your secretary to the dogging scene? No, she's too young. She worships you. You can't risk scaring her away.'

Egan's composure disintegrates and he looks ready to reach across the desk and put his hands around my throat. His mobile begins chirruping on his desk. Momentarily distracted, he glances at the screen, not recognising the number. By then I'm at the door, one hand in my pocket, pressing a button to end the call.

16

Tommy Garrett has been interviewed since early morning by two teams of detectives working in shifts, allowing him ten-minute breaks every hour, giving him soft drinks and sandwiches when he's hungry. He's still dressed in his work clothes – cowboy boots, jeans and a heavy-cotton shirt with only one sleeve rolled up, the other buttoned down.

Whenever they ask Tommy a question that he cannot answer he hunches a little more and stares at the back of his hands. Either that or he closes his eyes, as though trying to think through the confusion the questions are causing.

Watching on the CCTV feed, I notice that one detective moves around the room while the other stays seated. Tommy struggles to follow both and has to twist back and forth in his chair. There is a mirror in the room. Occasionally he looks at his reflection, raising his hand to make sure it's him. It's almost as if he's watching a TV show or movie rather than experiencing a real-life interrogation.

I have seen a lot of lonely, socially inept young men in my consulting room. Almost always they were the slow kid, the dumb kid, the fat kid from school – the last one picked for teams, who changes behind a towel or chain-puffs on an asthma inhaler, or stutters his way through classes never raising his hand to answer a question; the one everyone seems to forget when they send out class birthday invitations. Most of them grow up to overcome their awkwardness and low self-esteem. They find a friend or a decent role model or a girl who recognises their potential. But a few suffer depression and ongoing social anxiety. They slide into alcohol and drug abuse or develop a pathological perfectionism because they hate their former selves.

Cray is standing beside me, watching the screen.

'He should have a lawyer,' I tell her.

'We gave him the opportunity.'

'He's vulnerable. Impressionable. You mustn't put words in his mouth.'

'Don't tell me how to do my job, Professor.'

There is a sharp edge to her voice. Our friendship has boundaries and I have to be careful what I say.

'What do you know about him?' I ask.

'Father walked out on him. Mother is dead. Raised by his grandmother from the age of eight. Below-average intelligence. Arrested twice for public nuisance. No charges.'

'What did you find at the house?'

'Plenty of porn on his computer.'

'What sort of porn?'

'We're still going through the hard drive.'

'The killer may have rape fantasies. You should be looking at anything that involves violence and coercion. What about the murder weapon?'

'Nothing yet, but we found bloodstains on one of his shirts – the lab has it now. There was also a stash of women's under-wear. Looks like he's been collecting for a while.'

Tommy is gazing at the mirror. He seems to be studying the detectives. Counting them. Wondering how two became four.

Cray pinches her eyes with her thumb and forefinger. 'He

denies being at the farmhouse that night. He says you tricked him into saying that.'

'Can I talk to him?'

'That's not such a good idea.'

'He talked to me once.'

I follow her along the corridor to the interview room. She knocks twice. The door opens. Tommy looks up, cocking his head to one side, reminding me of a bird in a cage. Cray tells the interview team to take a break and checks her watch before announcing the time, date and names of those present for the recording.

Taking a seat directly in front of Tommy, I wait until he looks at me . . . and then longer.

'How are the k-k-kittens?' he asks.

'They're good. I'm going to feed the mother later.'

'You have to change her water.'

'I will.'

My eyes wander over his face. There are tiny black specks in the brown of his irises like ants trapped in honey. 'When I talked to you at the farmhouse, you told me that you watched Elizabeth and Harper.'

He shakes his head.

'I'm not judging you, Tommy. We all have secret desires. Sometimes we do things that we know aren't right. It's as though we have another voice in our heads. I know you want a girlfriend. Someone to love. Someone to hold. You're not sick. We don't choose who we fall in love with. And sometimes we do things that we regret later. We hurt people we love. Did you hurt Elizabeth or Harper?'

'I w-w-wasn't there.'

'You told me you were watching.'

He frowns and moistens his lips with the tip of his tongue. Hair is plastered to his forehead and he looks feverish and pale.

'I can help you, Tommy, but I need the truth. You told me that you saw someone else at the farmhouse that night. You said he was lighting candles.'

123

Tommy sniffles and wipes his nose on his sleeve.

Cray opens a manila folder and shows Tommy a photograph of Dominic Crowe.

'Do you know who that is?' she asks.

'Harper's dad.'

The next photograph is of Jeremy Egan.

Tommy nods.

'Have you ever seen him at the house?' asks Cray.

'Uh-huh.'

'In Elizabeth's bedroom?'

He nods.

'What about that Saturday night?'

'I d–d–didn't see him. The man was behind the c–c–curtains.'

'What about this person?' Cray shows him a photograph of Blake Lehmann.

'That's Harper's boyfriend.'

'Was he at the house that night?'

Tommy frowns in concentration. 'I heard his m–m–motorbike.'

'How do you know it was him?'

'Dunno.'

I decide to take him back to earlier in the day, asking him to remember what he was doing. He talks about fixing a fence, changing the oil on the tractor, cleaning the milking machines. He grows more confident with his answers because I'm not accusing him of anything. His stutter disappears.

'You told me that you saw Mrs Crowe come home. It had just got dark. There was someone lighting candles behind the curtains.'

Tommy hunches his shoulders, not looking at me.

'Did you hear his voice?'

'He were singing.'

'What do you mean?'

'No, not singing . . . chanting.'

'Did you hear the words?'

'No.'

'Did you see Mrs Crowe?'

'No.'

'Did you hear her voice?'

'Yeah.'

'What happened then?'

'I went home.'

I nod to Cray, who reaches beneath the table and produces a plastic bag. 'We found this under your mattress, Tommy. Do you wear women's underwear?'

'N-n-n-nah.'

'Who do they belong to?'

Tommy shakes his head.

'Are they Harper's?'

'N-n-no!'

'Do they belong to Mrs Crowe?'

Tommy stares at his hands, looking miserable.

Cray leans over the table. 'We're going to find out, Tommy. We'll do DNA tests and find out exactly who they belong to. You know about DNA, don't you? It can tell if you've been wanking into these.'

Tommy looks horrified. Disgusted. 'I w-w-wouldn't.'

'Who owns the underwear?'

'M-m-my m-m-a.'

'Who?'

'Ma.'

'Your mother is dead.'

'I kept 'em.'

'Why?'

Tommy squirms in his chair.

Cray demands an answer. 'Why do you have your mother's underwear?'

'Cos I miss her,' cries Tommy. 'It's all I have left that smells of her.'

Cray starts to speak and stops herself. Instead she picks up a blue folder and slides a sheet into view, running her finger down several paragraphs and then tapping it thoughtfully with her index finger. She's overreached and has to rethink.

Tommy's chest heaves and a bubble of spit forms on his lips, bursting with a tiny plop. He wipes his eyes with the back of his hand.

'Tell us about the blood,' says Cray.

He blinks at her.

'There must have been a lot of it . . . on your hands . . . your clothes. Do you see it when you close your eyes?'

Tommy's mouth gapes open like a thick-lipped fish, but no sound emerges. He turns slowly, searching my eyes for sympathy. Then he launches himself from the chair, aiming for the door. Covering the distance in four strides, he beats his right fist against the metal.

'You seem to think you can leave,' says Cray. 'You're here for another forty hours, Tommy. That's nearly two days. Two nights. Then I can apply for more time.'

'I want to go home.'

'Tell us about the blood.'

'Don't shout at me.'

'I'm not shouting.'

'Yes, you are.'

Tommy squeezes his eyes shut and seems to wish the walls would melt away. He returns to his chair and slumps down, cradling his left arm in his lap.

'How did you get blood on your shirt?' I ask, more gently than the DCS.

'The fence.'

'What fence?'

'Barbed wire c–c–cut me. Tried to clean it up. Nan was angry.'

Cray glances at me, again derailed.

'Show me your arm,' I ask Tommy. 'The one you're holding.'

'Don't touch it.'

'I won't touch it.'

Gingerly, he pulls up his left sleeve, edging it higher, revealing a bandage wrapped around his forearm. Blood is leaking through the soiled fabric, yellowed by pus at the edges.

That's why he looks so feverish. He's burning up. Cray has opened the interview room door and yells for a doctor. I hear other voices from further away, getting nearer.

'I demand to see my client,' says a grey-suited man with a squeaky voice. 'My client is represented,' he bleats, his pale blue eyes divided by bifocal lenses.

Cray looks ready to rip his head off. 'And who might you be?'

'My name is Thomas Archer. I'm Mr Garrett's lawyer.' He holds up his business card as though it's a police badge. 'My client has been interviewed illegally. Anything he has said is inadmissible.'

'He was read his rights,' says Cray.

'I'm not talking about today. I'm referring to yesterday at Windy Hill Farm.'

'I don't have to caution people,' I say. 'I'm not a police officer.'

'You're working for them.'

Tommy's grandmother, Doreen Garrett, is with him. A tall, spare figure with a ravaged-looking face, her hair is pulled back so severely that her eyebrows look like French accents painted on her forehead. She points her finger at me. 'You put words in his mouth.'

Mr Archer has noticed Tommy's bandaged forearm. 'Have you seen a doctor?' he asks.

Tommy shakes his head.

'My client has been denied medical attention. I'm taking him to hospital.'

'He's still under arrest,' says Cray.

'You have tortured Mr Garrett. I will be recommending that he sue Avon and Somerset Constabulary for cruel and sadistic treatment.'

'That's not what happened,' says Cray.

'Explain that to the judge.'

Tommy lumbers down the corridor with his squeaking shoes,

sallow skin and wheezing breaths. At the last possible moment he turns and I'm expecting one of those pleading, kicked-dog looks. Instead he rubs his chin with the ball of his thumb and his lips curl into a smile.

'You're a bully and bullies never win.'

A crowd has gathered outside the police station, drawn by rumours of an arrest. Some of them are reporters, but most are stragglers and hangers-on, standing in the early evening light, hoping to catch a glimpse of a killer.

'When did they arrive?' asks Cray.

'About an hour ago,' replies Monk. 'Bannerman broadcast the story.'

'How did he know?'

'No idea, guv.'

'Christ! That's all I need.'

Tommy and his grandmother are just exiting the doors. The crowd has something to focus upon.

'That's him,' someone yells. 'They're letting him go!'

They surge forward. Doreen Garrett clings to her grandson. The two constables on crowd control duty are outnumbered. Cray tells Bennie to get backup. Meanwhile, the DCS steps in front of the mob, calling for calm. 'This man has been not been charged. You must let him pass.'

Someone breaks free from the crowd and hurls himself at Tommy, driving his shoulder into his stomach. Together they fall down three steps and I can hear the air being forced from their lungs. Dominic Crowe has his hands around Tommy's throat. Monk reaches them first. He drives his fist beneath Crowe's ribs. He rolls aside, clutching his stomach and fighting for breath. Spilling tears.

Meanwhile a dozen uniformed officers appear, clearing a path to the solicitor's Mercedes.

'This man is going to the hospital,' yells DCS Cray. 'You will let him pass or I will have all of you arrested.'

Tommy and Doreen get into the back seat and the doors close. Mr Archer blinks from behind the wheel, his face startled and bloodless, as the Mercedes pulls away from the kerb, ghosting into the traffic.

Dominic Crowe is still hanging from Monk's fist. He touches his bloody nose and stares at his fingers as though he's discovered something remarkable about himself while cameras record his every gesture.

Last night I dreamt that a mouse crawled into my mouth and I crunched it up between my teeth until the fur and blood and broken bones started to choke me. I retched and retched but nothing came up.

I didn't close my eyes after that. I stared at the ceiling and pretended to be dead, picturing them finding me cold and stiff in my bed. I imagined the funeral and what they would say about me. Will they blame me for how I turned out? I am my father's son. He cannot wash his hands of me, or this, even if his mind has been scoured by dementia and he cannot remember my name.

If my father was a monster, my mother was complicit in her compliance. How many times could she have avoided violence if she had simply gone to bed and let him sleep it off? No, she cannot escape her share of the responsibility. Even in death she is still an elemental force. What a pair they make, my parents. I have their DNA and cell by cell, gene for gene, chromosome for chromosome, they are still fighting inside me, battling to see who can fuck me up the most.

I remember my mother's last day. The phone rang. She laughed. Blushed. 'Stop that,' she said, but didn't sound as though she meant it. She disappeared into the bathroom where I heard the sound of sprays and lip-popping.

'Why do you put that gunk on?' I asked.

'So I can be a different person,' she replied.

Afterwards I watched her dress, her back to me, her buttocks smooth and perfect, her waist firm.

'Where are you going?'

'Out.'

'Can I come?'

'Not this time.'

She crushed my head against her breasts, which felt like soft feather pillows except for the underwire of her bra cutting into my ear.

'Your da will be home soon. You watch TV.'

I stood at the front window as she drove away in her bright red Fiesta, never to return. In hindsight, it's easy to think that I had some sort of premonition about what was going to happen, but no child could possibly foresee that a front-seat blow job would rob him of a mother. I had never heard of oral sex. How does the joke go? I thought fellatio was a famous Italian footballer or a character from Hamlet.

In the days that followed the accident (that's what people called it – 'the accident') friends and neighbours fluttered around our family, leaving casseroles on the doorstep and trays of lasagne in the freezer.

Aunt Kate took me to the funeral home to view the body before they closed the coffin. They had put so much make-up on my mother's face she looked like an over-painted fairy at a little girl's birthday party. I looked at her lipstick-painted mouth and remembered the lip-popping sounds from the bathroom.

I sat between Patrick and Agatha at the funeral. The coffin was only a few feet away. I remember wanting to open it up – just to make sure that my mother was still inside.

Aunt Kate gave the eulogy and afterwards we went back to our house. There were more handshakes and powdered hugs and ruffling of my hair. People I barely knew would crouch to talk to me, telling me that I was being very brave, or that I should 'let it out', as though I had a cat inside me.

Agatha and Patrick stayed in the back garden, smoking and talking to our cousins and younger aunts and uncles. Nobody mentioned the accident, but it was there, hovering in the background like an uninvited guest.

My father played the role of the grieving husband and most people genuinely felt sorry for him. It was only later that the nudges, sly winks and asides began to eat away at his guts. By then people had retrieved their Tupperware and their Crock-Pots, leaving an empty fridge and the loudness of silence. We were left with our father and his anger. He watched TV. He drank. He slept in the armchair, refusing to climb the stairs and sleep in a bed that 'stinks of her'.

When we were hungry he would send us to the neighbours for pity meals, or to borrow bread, or plaster our cuts or get our clothes washed. Agatha suffered the worst of it. He wouldn't let her wear make-up or get her ears pierced and he collected her clothes from charity shops and second-hand dump bins. Although still at school, she took over the cooking and cleaning, trying too hard to please him.

'What's this?' he'd ask, his fists clenched on either of the side of the plate.

'Steak and onions.'

'What did you do with the gravy?'

'Nothing.'

'It's got lumps.'

'I'm sorry.'

'What did you put in it? Are you trying to poison me?'

'No. I'm not good at making gravy.'

'I wouldn't feed this slop to a pig. Do you think I'm a pig?'

'No, Daddy.'

Oinking, he forced her back to the kitchen, demanding that she make him something else.

I don't blame Agatha for running away. My father took her name off the answering machine and didn't mention her again. She wasn't hated like my mother . . . simply forgotten. I have seen Agatha twice since then, the last time when Aunt Kate died. Occasionally, she sends me a cheque to help look after Dad – 'spending money that he never spent on us', she says.

When Patrick left home I was the last one standing, so to speak, alone in the house with my father. It didn't help that I looked so much like my mother – the same eyes and nose and mouth. (The mouth! Is that why he wouldn't look at me?)

Over time I came to enjoy that perverse fact – the idea that my mother tormented him through me, asleep and awake, drunk or sober, but there was no balancing of the scales. She died. He lived. We lost.

17

Sunday morning in Wellow and we feast on open bagels with grilled ham, tomato and Swiss cheese, requested and highly praised. Nobody makes them the way I do. The girls tell me this and I believe them.

'Why do fathers think that making a simple breakfast is worthy of a Michelin star, whereas a mother does it every day without seeking compliments?' asks Julianne as she scrubs the melted cheese off the grill.

'That's one of life's great mysteries.'

She throws the scouring pad at me. I duck just in time.

Afterwards she suggests a walk. Emma wants to fly her kite. I don't think there's enough wind, but we'll take it anyway. Dressed in light clothing, we climb Mill Hill Lane and walk past the church and down the main road to the old viaduct. Turning left up a tarmac footpath, we cross a stile where the track turns to grass and drops downhill through an avenue of field maples. Flax and corn poppies and ox-eye daisies are poking through the grasses and flying insects buzz in the hedges.

There is a natural spring called St Julian's Well where they draw the water for christenings at the church. According to local legend, this is where Hungerford family ghosts appear, foretelling calamity for the Lords of the Manor.

We walk in silence for a while. Julianne buries her hands deep in the khaki pockets of her shorts. There are other ramblers on the path. Some of the men pause to glance at Julianne, looking with admiration or envy.

'I read a story the other day,' she says, balancing one foot on a fence to retie her shoe. 'It was about a woman who tried to talk a suicidal boy down from a rooftop. He jumped and she reached out and grabbed him by the belt, just in time. They were dangling off the side of the building until bystanders pulled them up. Afterwards, a reporter asked her whether she feared for her life and she said, "We're all going to die. Why be frightened of it?"'

'I wonder if she *was* dying,' I reply.

'What do you mean?'

'People who are diagnosed with a terminal illness tend to show less regard for their personal safety. They know they're living on borrowed time.'

'So you're saying her sacrifice wasn't so great?'

'No, I'm saying that expecting to die isn't the same thing as expecting to live.'

We walk past a family picking raspberries to fill a big white enamel bowl. 'Can I ask you a question?' asks Julianne.

'Sure.'

'You've had to deal with Parkinson's for ten years. How did you stop thinking about it?'

'You try to think of other things.'

'Such as?'

'Do I have enough milk to get me through until Monday? What time does the dry cleaner close? Which of the Marx brothers pretended to be mute?'

'Important stuff?'

'Yeah.'

'So I just ignore this?'

'No.'

'What then?'

'Don't make it everything. Don't let it define who you are.'

Julianne glances along the path to the stream where Emma is searching for tadpoles. 'It does rather concentrate the mind – having cancer. Up until now I've never really thought about dying.'

'You're not going to die.'

'Don't patronise me, Joe.'

'I'm not patronising you. Lots of people have cancer. It's almost like a stage of life these days.'

'Just let me talk?'

'Sorry.'

'And stop apologising.'

'OK.'

She takes a deep uncertain breath, lip bitten, mouth intent. I don't know what I'm supposed to do, except not make things worse. She steps to me, taking hold of my left hand, toying with my fingers as a teenager might – one who had briefly, many years ago, been in love with me.

'I'm not mad at you. I don't know what I am. I don't think there's a word for it.'

She begins to pull away.

'I wish I could help you find the word,' I say.

'You can't do everything.'

Charlie has gone to a party at a country house which has twelve bedrooms and an orangery that automatically turns to follow the sun across the sky. She seems to have a lot of glamorous young friends with rich or artistic parents. I don't know why I think of them as glamorous; perhaps because they're so much more self-assured than I was at the same age. Would-be doctors, lawyers, scientists, playwrights and artists – all going off to university or art college or taking gap years to travel to Cambodia and Vietnam.

Julianne is reading and Emma is watching *Frozen* for the umpteenth time. I open my laptop and go back to the statements, trying to piece together Elizabeth Crowe's last day. The images of her defiled body keep polluting my thoughts. I have to force them away and concentrate on the other details.

Academics refer to something called the 'half-life of facts'. Over time half of what we know now will become untrue. New research, better technology and greater understanding will make a mockery of the current truth, or a better version will be accepted as correct, which in turn will begin to grow obsolete. Smoking was once doctor-recommended. Pluto was once a planet. The Earth was once flat.

Based on this hypothesis, half of what I know about this crime will be proven to be wrong. The longer the time frame, the greater the change. But which half will it be? I can only base my assumptions on the available evidence.

Sherlock Holmes had a maxim: 'When you have eliminated the impossible, whatever remains, however improbable, must be the truth.' That's bollocks, by the way. The impossible cannot be defined or quantified or labelled or listed, so how can it be eliminated?

As I read the statements, I take notes, underlining certain details and putting question marks next to others. Elizabeth wasn't some bland, almost anonymous divorcee, living quietly with her teenage daughter. She was university-educated, gregarious and sexually confident. She spoke French and a little Spanish. She began working as a medical researcher for a pharmaceutical company in Bristol, but quit her job when Harper was born. Later she worked three days a week as a sales rep selling medical supplies to GPs and surgeries.

Friends and colleagues have described her as feisty, opinionated, intelligent, warm and generous, but these are empty descriptions, platitudes and generalities. Nobody likes to speak ill of the dead. Not publicly. Yet behind the veneer of middle-aged respectability, Elizabeth led another life. She took risks.

She joined an online dating agency. She went on Internet chat rooms. She engaged in intimate acts in public places. She was a strong, vibrant, sexual being, who fought against the mundane and the ordinary.

On that Saturday morning she had her hair done, a regular appointment at a salon in Clevedon. Afterwards she met up with a friend for coffee and went looking at linen and furnishings for the bed and breakfast. The police tracked her movements by triangulating the signals that bounced between her mobile and local phone towers. Her ex-husband called her at midday. According to Dominic Crowe they argued about his plan to take Harper for lunch for her birthday.

Elizabeth arrived home just after four. She took a call from Jeremy Egan an hour later. Her sister, Becca, called shortly after six and Elizabeth told her that she was spending a quiet night at home. Harper showed up, showered, changed and went out again. At 8.37 p.m. Elizabeth left the farmhouse. For the next hour her mobile signal placed her at a popular lover's lane known Clevedon Court Woods. More than thirty mobile phones had been identified in the immediate vicinity, but most had been linked to local residents. Five numbers were still being traced.

One of the curious truths about small towns is that rivalries and intrigue are just as common as in cities, although harder to hide. People fall in love and out of love. Men cheat on their wives and wives cheat on their husbands. There are exhibitionists, paedophiles, voyeurs, sadists, masochists and transvestites — the full box of chocolates — none of them confined to a particular demographic or social class.

Since her divorce Elizabeth had been on two dates — both organised through a matchmaking website. The first was with Mark Sherwin, an antique dealer from Taunton. Widowed. Alibied. They had a drink and went to his flat. He didn't contact her again.

The second date was with Dion Ferguson, a sales rep for a

fitness equipment company. Married. Four children. He lied on his web profile, giving a false name and saying he was divorced. He has no alibi for the night of the murders.

Elizabeth arrived home by 10.20 p.m. She showered and got ready for bed. She had a drawer full of sexy lingerie, but chose to sleep naked. She checked her emails and looked at a website for bathroom fittings.

At 10.42 Harper sent her a text message: Got my phone back. Had a fight with Blake. Coming home.

By 11.08 p.m. she was back at the farmhouse. Mother and daughter were together. Tommy Garrett mentioned seeing a silhouette behind the curtains, but that was closer to 9.30. Perhaps the killer had been in the house all along.

18

Monday morning. Traffic crawls along the coast road, banked up behind convoys of caravans and campers. I have never understood why some people take their holidays in the same place every year, parking their caravan next to the same families, eating at the same cafés and restaurants, listening to the same stories, as though their lives are trapped on a continuous loop. There are all kinds of ghettos in the world and some are built afresh every holiday season.

Ruiz is driving. He picked me up from the cottage first thing, flirting with Julianne and promising he'd come for dinner one night. We reach the western edge of Portishead where the streets are lined with pebble-dashed houses with net curtains and flat façades. These are the sorts of places Margaret Thatcher sold off in the eighties because she had a vision of a home-owning democracy where everybody could owe money to a bank.

Three redheaded boys are playing in the front garden of a tired-looking house. The oldest boy is riding a bike with training wheels that buckle under his weight. The other two are whacking everything in sight – a tree, a rose bush, a garden gnome and a compost bin. Small boys are a mystery to me. They gain such joy from destroying things.

'Is your daddy home?' I ask.

The eldest looks at me sullenly and wipes his nose, smearing a silver trail along his sleeve.

'Can you tell him he has visitors?'

The boy jumps off his bike, letting it fall, and runs up the front steps, wailing as though he's about to be kidnapped. A second boy follows him, mimicking his performance. The last one stares at me and picks at a scab on his elbow, telling me how it happened.

A man steps outside. Dion Ferguson has a broad, jovial face and the same colour hair as his children.

I introduce Ruiz and myself. Ferguson doesn't shake our hands. A new face appears at the window, a girl this time. The redheaded children seem to be multiplying.

'We were hoping to talk to you about Elizabeth Crowe,' I say.

Ferguson's mouth drops open and he looks panic-stricken. 'You can't come here! They promised me. They said my wife wouldn't have to know.'

'She doesn't,' says Ruiz.

'She's inside now,' he whispers. 'You have to leave.'

'Say we're Seventh Day Adventists,' says Ruiz. 'It won't be the first time you've lied to her.'

All four children are now outside in the yard – three boys and a girl, all of them under six. The oldest boy has a spoon covered in peanut butter. The girl tries to take it off him, but he holds it above his head, out of reach.

'Mine. Mine. Mine,' she says, over and over.

Ferguson ignores them. 'You shouldn't have come here. It's not fair.'

'You went on a date with Elizabeth Crowe,' I say.

'Yeah, OK. I'm not proud of it, but I can't unmake that particular omelette.'

He glances over his shoulder again. A woman appears at the

door. She's wearing a pink housecoat and resting a laundry basket on her hip. Matronly. Pear-shaped. Harried. 'Did you get Marcie breakfast?'

'I'm just talking to these two gentlemen from the council,' says Ferguson.

She studies Ruiz and me. 'Is this about them dogs barking? It's about bloody time. I must have called a dozen times.'

'Yeah, it's about the dogs,' says her husband.

'Tell 'em they bark all bloody night,' she says.

'I'm telling 'em now.'

'Maybe I should talk to 'em.'

'I got this.'

Marcie is still trying to get the peanut-buttered spoon, but her voice is growing more strident. 'Mine. Mine. Mine.'

'Just give her the bloody spoon,' says Ferguson, cuffing the boy behind the ear.

'But tha' was mine.'

'We share in this house.'

'When does *she* share?'

'You'll get nothing if you don't shut up and leave me be. I'm talking here.'

His wife has gone from the doorway. I can see along the hallway where clothes are drying on the radiators and the rug is littered with toys.

Ferguson looks at us, exasperated. 'One date, one lousy date.'

'Why did you sign up?'

'I wish I'd never heard of that website.'

'You gave a fake name. You lied about your age, about being married . . .'

'Yeah, yeah, OK, I've been over this.'

'You wanted to have an affair,' says Ruiz.

'No. Yes. No.' He scratches under his armpit. 'I just wanted to go out on a date, have a conversation about something other than my kids and barking dogs and unpaid bills.' He glances at the house. 'I'm suffocating here.'

141

'You slept with Elizabeth Crowe?' I say.

'I didn't expect that.' He looks from face to face. 'Honestly. I mean, I didn't think I'd even get to buy her a drink when I saw her. I was shocked. Everybody lies on those websites, don't they? They tell porkies about their weight or their age or they find their most flattering photograph. But she didn't tell any lies. She was drop-dead gorgeous . . . I mean, way out of my league.'

'Where did you meet her?'

'At a pub in Bridgewater.'

'Somewhere away from home.'

He nods.

'What did you talk about?'

'I honestly can't remember. I was too busy staring at her. I thought any moment she was going to make some excuse and leave. I mean, look at me.' He opens his arms showing the pot belly and sloping shoulders. 'I'm a sales rep. I sell gym equipment.'

'A walking advertisement,' says Ruiz.

Ferguson sucks in his stomach. His two older boys are shooting at each other with pretend guns. One of them is using the trigger attachment from the hose. The other has found an old pump-action water pistol.

'We had a few drinks and she was very sweet. She'd been a sales rep, she said, so she knew all about dealing with retailers and suppliers. It got to about nine o'clock and she didn't want another drink. I thought she was going to say goodbye, but then she said she wanted to crawl under the table and blow me. Right there! In the bar! Said she'd done it before – and I believed her.'

'So what did you do?'

'I suggested we take a drive. We took her car. I didn't want her seeing mine – it's full of booster seats, toys and other crap.'

'You knew what she was suggesting?'

'I'm ugly, not stupid.'

'Where did you go?'

'Trinity Waters – near one of the fish farms.'

'Had you been there before?'

'Never. She pulled up and walked around to my side, opened my door and unbuckled my belt and went down on me. It was the most exciting and terrifying thing that had ever happened to me. When my eyes uncrossed, I looked up and noticed two people watching us while they, you know – did their thing. This other woman had her skirt rucked up and was lying on the front of a car while this bloke was between her legs, banging away. They were doing it right in front of us. I tried to tell Elizabeth, but she didn't stop.' He wipes his top lip, wide-eyed like a schoolboy telling his mates what he'd discovered about girls. 'I'd never had sex in public. I'd never heard of dogging.'

'What happened then?'

'Nothing. I mean, I freaked out. I mean, I enjoy it as much as the next guy, but indoors, you know, and not as a spectator sport.'

'Your semen was found in her car.'

His face reddens. 'Yeah, well, that was an accident. I mean, I sort of came to the party a little early. And I couldn't get up again – not with people watching. She called me a few names, which I probably deserved. Then she drove me back to the pub and said goodbye. I didn't see her again.'

'But you tried to contact her?'

'No, she contacted me.'

'Why?'

'She said she knew that I was married and that she'd tell my wife if I didn't give her a thousand quid.'

'Did you give her the money?'

'Never,' he says, shaking his head adamantly. 'A woman like that gets her claws into you and she doesn't let go.'

'You're talking about someone who was murdered,' admonishes Ruiz.

Dion looks shame-faced and apologises. His wife yells from the house.

'Is there a problem, Dion?'

'No problem,' he replies.

'Did Marcie get breakfast?'

'Yeah.'

The little girl has peanut butter smeared all over her face. She wraps her arms around Ferguson's leg.

'You used a fake name on the dating site. How did Elizabeth contact you if she didn't know your real name?' Ruiz asks.

'Once we made contact through the website, we swapped details. She had my mobile number.'

'That was risky,' says Ruiz.

'I guess.'

Marcie is tugging at her daddy's sleeve. He picks her up and puts her on his shoulders.

'Did you tell your wife?' asks Ruiz.

'Are you kidding me?'

'Where were you that Saturday night they were killed?'

'I was coming back from Stansted. It's where my company has its head office.'

'So you don't have an alibi.'

'I don't need one. I barely knew the woman. We went on one date . . . had one drink.'

'You're leaving out the blow job,' says Ruiz.

'You're right,' says Ferguson. 'That's not easy to forget.'

19

The motorcycle workshop has a dozen bikes parked in the fore-court, a mixture of new and second-hand, all of them washed and gleaming. The display window is plastered with glossy colour posters that promise a life of freedom, speed and semi-clad women, but only if you buy a particular brand of tyre or engine oil.

A buzzer sounds as we step inside. The man behind the counter is eating a sandwich, picking fallen lettuce from the pages of a magazine between his elbows. Straightening up, he adjusts his crotch, not looking at me. Instead he studies Ruiz as though weighing his potential for trouble, or estimating his correct fighting weight.

'How can I help you, gentlemen?' he asks, wiping his hands on his thighs. 'You want to buy a bike? Got some new machines just delivered. Got a Harley. You want to ride a hog?'

'Does it make a lot of noise?' asks Ruiz.

'Yeah.'

'Why?'

The man looks at him quizzically.

'I always wanted to ask someone,' says Ruiz, 'what sort of middle-aged shovelhead buys a bike that turns petrol into decibels? Then he rides around in a piss-pot helmet, jeans, lace-up boots and reflective sunglasses, looking like a complete tool. Is it a penis issue?'

The man blinks at him. 'Maybe you don't want the Harley.'

'Is Blake Lehmann around?' I ask.

'He's busy.'

'We won't keep him long.'

The boss motions us out back. We walk through the side door into a workshop where a dozen bikes are in various states of disassembly. Floor-to-ceiling shelves are stacked with spare parts and one wall is covered in pictures of Page 3 girls whose breasts are yellowing rather than sagging. A Pirelli calendar hangs from a nail – well out of date unless Miss November 2011 is a workshop favourite.

The rear door is open. It leads to the lane, where Blake Lehmann is locked in a passionate kiss with a girl, who is pressed hard up against a brick wall, her tight black skirt bunched on her thighs and her white blouse unbuttoned where his hand disappears. She breaks the kiss long enough to tell him not to get her blouse dirty. They lock lips again. She pushes at his hand. 'I got to go. I'll be late.'

She catches sight of me and her eyes go wide. She fights a little harder. 'Someone's watching.'

'Let 'em,' says Blake.

'No, no, not now.'

She pushes him away and tugs down her skirt, before adjusting the pair of glasses on the bridge of her nose, which look more like a fashion statement than vision-related. I recognise her now: Sophie Baxter, Harper's best friend.

Blake is dressed in skinny jeans, motorbike boots and an oil-stained T-shirt. He probably thinks he looks like James Dean or Dennis Hopper, a rebel without a cause. On second thoughts I doubt if he's heard of either of them.

'What do you want?' he asks, his face full of angles and sharp edges.

'Let's talk about Harper Crowe.'

'Are you the police?'

'No.'

'Then fuck off.'

Sophie lets out an embarrassed squeak as though she's stepped on a bath toy. 'Maybe I should go.'

'I also have questions for you,' I say.

'I'm late for my shift.'

I notice the badge on her blouse for the Moon and Sixpence pub. It's where Harper used to work.

'I'll catch up with you later,' I say.

'I'm pretty busy.'

'It won't take long.'

She leaves in a hurry, her heels wobbling on the cobblestones.

Ruiz focuses on Blake Lehmann. 'It's nice to see that you've moved on. How long did you wait?'

The question causes barely a ripple on Blake's pond. Turning on a tap, he begins filling a tin tub, adding a squirt of washing-up detergent that foams in the spray. Dunking bike parts into the soapy water, he begins cleaning them with a wire brush.

'What did you and Harper fight about on the night she died?' I ask.

'She thought I'd forgotten her birthday.'

'Had you?'

'No,' he says defensively. 'It wasn't until the next day. What is it with women – their birthdays are like festivals.'

'Fact of life,' says Ruiz. 'You don't question it.'

Blake relaxes a little. Water sloshes from one side of the tub to the other, splashing his jeans. I ask him about that Saturday.

'I was dirt-biking all day. Didn't get home until late. Mechanical problems.'

'You ride motocross?'

'Nothing professional, but I got plans.'

He holds up a dripping chrome sprocket and dunks it in the water again. 'I turned up late – still muddy. Harper was all

147

dolled up. She said I was taking her for granted. It's no big deal.'

'Why didn't you go home first?'

'I did. I picked up her phone.'

'Why didn't you have a shower?'

'Like I said – I was running late.' He takes a seat on a drum, rolling himself a cigarette with quiet concentration. He has small neat hands that move surely, spreading the tobacco evenly along the paper and pressing it into a cradle and then a tube. He licks it closed.

'How long had you and Harper been seeing each other?' I ask.

'We hooked up on New Year's Eve.'

'Weren't you a bit old for her?' asks Ruiz.

'Six years.'

'Prefer 'em young?'

His top lip curls. 'Yeah, I'm a cradle-snatcher.'

'Was it serious?' I ask.

He gives me another shrug from his repertoire and examines the cigarette from every angle.

'Did you meet her mother?'

'Course.'

'How did you get on with her?'

He flicks at a cheap disposable lighter. Many clicks. Flame. Cupping his hands, he belches smoke and picks a strand of tobacco from the tip of his tongue. 'You don't want the mothers to like you.'

'Why's that?'

'If the mother likes you, the daughter won't . . . in my experience.'

'He's right,' says Ruiz, not being helpful.

'Mrs Crowe didn't think I was good enough for Harper,' says Blake. 'She wanted her princess to be stepping out with a budding lawyer, or a doctor. I was beneath her. You know what she said to Harper when she first started seeing me?'

I shake my head.

148

'She said, "Fuck him, sweetheart, but don't think of marrying him." She was a snob. Thought she was better than the rest of us, the way she talked, putting on a posh accent.'

Blake forms his lips into a puckered 'O' and blows three perfect smoke rings, watching them with satisfaction. 'She was two-faced, you know. She didn't want anyone touching Harper, but she didn't mind putting it out herself.'

'Meaning?'

'Mrs Crowe could be a right cougar, coming on to me like, you know. I mean, she treated me like shit most of the time, but then she'd brush up against me, flirting her arse off.'

'Elizabeth Crowe?'

'Yeah. This one day I came to the house and she answered the door. She said Harper was upstairs but she didn't step out of the way. When I tried to get past her, I swear she leaned into me and got this look on her face like she was the queen of MILFdom.'

'Maybe it was accidental,' says Ruiz.

Blake grunts dismissively, 'Whatever.'

'Why didn't you tell the police any of this?' I ask.

'Didn't seem right — bad-mouthing Mrs Crowe.'

'Tell us about the fight with Harper.'

'It weren't no fight. We had a disagreement. That's all. I turned up late. I was dirty. She was proper vexed.'

'She hit you.'

'No.'

'A witness says you had a scratch on your face.'

'That was from earlier — when I was on the bike.'

'According to the phone records, you tried to call Harper later that night.'

'I wanted to apologise.'

'Is that why you went to the farmhouse?'

'I didn't.'

'Police found fresh motorcycle tracks on the drive.'

'They checked my bike.'

I glance through the open door into the workshop. A handful of motorbikes are propped on stands. Others were parked out front. The office had a rack of keys. 'Did they check all of these?' I ask.

He blinks at me.

'I think you borrowed a bike and rode out to the farmhouse.'

Blake discards the cigarette and stands, unfolding in a casual way, as though every limb knows where it should be. Once upright, he puts one foot at a slight angle behind the other. It is a classic position for a martial arts fighter. 'Are you calling me a liar?'

'Oh, no, son,' says Ruiz, stepping forward. 'I'm the one calling you a liar.'

They eyeball each other for a few seconds and the moment passes. Blake sits again.

'I didn't do anything wrong . . . you're saying I did something—'

'You lied to the police about being at the farmhouse.'

'I didn't kill anyone.'

'That's good to know,' says Ruiz. 'But you might want to come up with something a little stronger before you next talk to the police. Flesh out an excuse. Make it sound a little more plausible and a lot less whiney. You know what plausible means? Truthful.'

'It *is* the truth.'

'That'll be a novelty for them.'

One corner of his mouth curls upward, making him look surly rather than tough. 'I tried to call Harper — to say I was sorry — but she wouldn't answer. My bike had engine problems — water in the carburettor — so I borrowed a bike and we rode out there.'

'We?'

'No, I meant me!'

'What time was that?' I ask.

'Eleven-thirty maybe.'

'What happened at the farmhouse?'

'Mrs Crowe wouldn't answer the door. I knew she was in there.'

'How?'

'The lights were on downstairs and I could hear her breathing behind the door.'

'Did you see any candles?'

'Candles? No.'

'You broke Harper's window.'

'I was trying to wake her by tossing gravel, but she wouldn't come to the window.'

'Was her light on?'

'No. I figured she was still angry. I had Harper's birthday present. I left it on the front step.'

'What did you buy her?'

'This limestone oil burner, I think it was Balinese. You put different oils in a little bowl and heat them with a candle. Makes the place smell nice. Harper liked that sort of stuff.'

'The police didn't find any present on the doorstep.'

'I wrote a note with it, saying I was sorry.' He looks aggrieved. 'Some bastard must have stolen it.'

20

'The kid lied,' says Ruiz, smearing a layer of English mustard on a pork pie – enough to blow the head off any normal person. He bites into the pastry, holding a cupped hand underneath to catch the crumbs. His eyes don't even water.

We're sitting beneath an umbrella outside the Salthouse pub, where the tables are full of families, who are watching their pink-nosed children play on the grassy bank.

'When are you going to tell the Fat Controller?' asks Ruiz.

I don't answer straight away. He takes another bite of his pie.

'He didn't see any candles burning,' I say quietly.

'Huh?'

'Blake Lehmann said there was a light on downstairs but no candles.'

'So?'

'Nobody answered the door.'

'I don't understand.'

'Lehmann was convinced he heard somebody inside. Forensics found blood pooled in the hallway near the front door. The killer must have been standing there.'

Ruiz puts down his half-eaten pie. 'You think Elizabeth and Harper were already dead.'

'The killer could have been interrupted as he was cleaning up.'

'Only if you believe Lehmann's story,' says Ruiz.

'You're right – it's not a good look. Did you notice how he said "we" when he mentioned riding out to the farmhouse?'

'Slip of the tongue.'

'Or he's covering for someone.'

'Could be Sophie Baxter.' Ruiz pushes the pie away as though no longer hungry. 'Cases like this give me the shits.'

'Why?'

'Most murders are mundane. Tragic. Boring. Predictable. Drug addicts fight over a fix, Criminals fall out over money. Drunks argue in a bar. A wife hits her husband over the head with a frying pan. Crimes like that are usually solved within a matter of hours because the killing is unplanned. But this one – this is a rare bird. Multiple suspects, all of them with the motive and the opportunity – the ex-husband, the ex-lover, the boyfriend, the stepson, the random men she dated . . . it could be any of them. Then there's something else that bugs me. Elizabeth Crowe could have had just about anyone, but she signed up to an online dating agency and was shagging strangers in parked cars.'

'Sex in public is a pretty common fantasy.'

'Yeah, OK, I accept that, and there was a time when I would have had sex in the middle of Wembley Stadium at half time if I could have found a willing partner, but that was before I discovered hotel porn and feather beds.'

I try to explain the psychology of voyeurism and exhibitionism, describing how our two core instincts are survival and reproduction. We can be aroused by danger and aroused by sex and sometimes the brain doesn't know the difference or confuses the two, and we get excited by acts of rebellion, or exhibitionism, or the fear of being caught.

'What's the strangest place you've ever had sex?' he asks.

'A beach in Turkey, how about you?'

'A VW Beetle on the vehicle deck of a ferry to Calais.'

'Tight fit.'

'That's what she said.' He grins and picks up the pie, hungry again. 'What about this dogging scene? Aside from STDs, aren't people worried they'll finish up with someone ugly.'

'Orgies reduce people to their genitals and erogenous zones. Bodies are mere props.'

I can see Ruiz struggling with the idea. Having grown up in an age when girls played hard to get and boys worked hard to woo them, he's quite old-fashioned in his views on sex and marriage.

'So you're back with Julianne,' he says, changing the subject.

'We're under the same roof.'

'Sharing a bed?'

'Not quite.'

'Same room?'

'Same floor.'

'You're on the floor?'

'We're on the *first* floor. Separate rooms. We're going on a date Thursday night.'

'Aren't you a bit old for dates?'

'What would you call it?'

'Foreplay.'

'Very funny.'

Ruiz chuckles and his eyes fold closed and I feel genuine relief for his friendship and humour. After a while I notice that his eyes are open again, watching me.

'Is everything all right?' he asks.

'What do you mean?'

'There must be a reason that she's asked you to come back.'

'Everything is fine,' I say, aware of how hollow the statement sounds. I collect his plate and empty pint glass and stack them for the waitress. Then I check my phone for messages, aware that the silence is weighing more heavily on me than on Ruiz.

Minutes pass. I frame a question in my head. I reword it silently, trying to make it sound casual and conversational. It still comes out badly.

'When your first wife had cancer did they do any surgery?'

'A double mastectomy and chemo,' Ruiz replies.

'How long afterwards – I mean, how long did she live?'

'Five years from the diagnosis – the twins were twelve.'

The silence stretches out. Ruiz is studying me, but I know he won't ask the obvious question.

'Julianne has ovarian cancer,' I say, relieved to get it out.

'What stage?'

'They're still doing the tests.'

'How is she holding up?'

'OK, I guess. She's scared.'

'How about you?'

'I spent the weekend researching online and talking to cancer victims from all over the place. Helsinki. Chicago. Sydney. I discovered a whole community of people who were happy to talk about their surgery, the aftermath, the percentages, the life expectancy.'

'Did it help?

'Maybe. I don't know. The doctors are talking about Julianne having a hysterectomy.'

'Good! They should cut it all out. Laura waited too long. She tried all these herbal cures and alternative medicines and macrobiotic diets. They should have just cut it out. Maybe things would have been . . . ' He doesn't finish the statement. 'Do the girls know?'

'Some of it.'

'Want my advice?'

I nod.

'Tell them everything. Don't keep them in the dark. That's the mistake I made with the twins. Help them understand.'

'I don't want to frighten them.'

'At least tell Charlie. It helps to have someone to share it with.'

'I'm sharing it with you.'

'That's good,' he says. 'Any time.'

We sit opposite each other, saying nothing because words aren't necessary. Meanwhile I imagine the cancer cells multiplying inside Julianne. She must fight them. She must prevail. I cannot bear the thought of my life without her. The one small mercy of having Parkinson's was the knowledge that I was likely to go first. I still hope that's the case, because Julianne is a better person than I am. More deserving.

Today it is too hot to walk. I take my father to the beach and he paddles back and forth in the shallows with his trousers rolled up to his knees and his shirt unbuttoned and flapping around his pigeon chest. He stares at a little boy who is playing with a plastic truck. The boy's mother smiles at me and I try to remember if my mother ever took me to the beach.

What do I recall about her? Her hoarse voice and husky laugh, her softness, her hugs, her dressing table with its gull-winged mirror, littered with cosmetics and hairbrushes, pins and bands and clips and ribbons. Her favourite winter coat made her look like a Russian Cossack. Her favourite film was To Catch a Thief. She loved Elvis Presley, Frankie Valli, Bobby Darin and Tom Jones. She knew how to jitterbug and do the samba, or maybe it was the rumba. I'm not good with dances.

I have only one photograph of her. I hid it from my father. It shows her at eighteen – the age she married – already pregnant with Patrick, but not showing. She's dancing with a group of friends at a Beatles concert in Liverpool, laughing at the camera. Young. Carefree. She has no idea of what's coming. Death saved her from growing old.

In the months that followed the accident I would ride my pushbike to the crematorium to visit her grave. I didn't imagine her as a pile of ashes in a marble urn. Instead I pictured her in the dress she wore in the photograph – the one with the floral sleeves and the black drop skirt that she bought when Aunt Kate got married.

People used to smile at me sadly when they saw me at the cemetery. Some of them were regulars, like the bald man in wellingtons, who had a family plot and spent hours pulling weeds and deadheading flowers. His mother and father and sister were already in residence, which left just enough room for him, he said, 'when the time comes'.

'How do you know when the time comes?' I asked him.

'You don't. It just does.'

A young married couple would visit their daughter's grave. She died at age three. I don't know what happened to her. I was too nervous to ask. Another regular visitor was an ancient woman who arrived in a big shiny black car with a driver who opened the door for her and carried her flowers. He would set up a chair and she would sit while he arranged the vase. She talked all the time, as though delivering a lecture to someone who should have listened the first time around.

I didn't tell my father about visiting the cemetery. I kept it a secret, just like the photograph. And I tried not to listen when he railed against my mother, calling her a painted whore and a scheming witch. He accused her of always flirting and showing off her breasts and brushing her hand down other men's backs and leaning her hip against their groins. He was a hypocrite, of course. I saw the way he looked at other men's wives and at Agatha's friends on those few occasions she risked inviting someone home.

I quit school at sixteen and got a job on the rigs, first as a dishwasher and later as a rigger. I worked in Africa, Australia and the Gulf of Mexico and didn't see my father for eight years. I brought a girlfriend home with me from Miami. We hired a car at Heathrow Airport and drove to Bristol. My father was living in the same house but he'd rented out two rooms upstairs to an Afghan family, whom he despised. I remember knocking on the door for ten minutes before he answered.

'So it's you,' he said, turning back into the house. He was pale and his hands were shaking. Sitting in a grubby armchair, he knocked back four quick beers and then he came to life, telling my girlfriend stories that belittled me.

We had booked into a hotel. He called me 'Mr Moneybags' and made me out to be a class traitor. We arranged to meet him later for dinner, but he didn't show up. A week later his house burned down, killing the tenants upstairs. My father would have died too if a fireman hadn't pulled him out. The coroner couldn't decide how the fire started and my father refused to give evidence.

The sky is clouding over and the air growing cooler. I tell my father it's time to go back. He sits on a rock while I lace his trainers, noticing *the purple veins on the back of his ankles and the bony spurs on his heels.*

He doesn't say a word when I drop him back at the nursing home. He doesn't acknowledge my leaving. 'I'll see you next week,' I say. 'Do you want me to bring you anything?'

Apropos of nothing at all, he begins telling me how he lost his virginity to a prostitute who had a tattoo of a butterfly on her shoulder and would turn tricks at the Avon Docks. The dockers and stevedores called her the Clifton Butterfly and she worked the streets dressed in a short skirt and fishnet stockings, in all weathers, unable to go home until she'd earned ten shillings.

'I felt sorry for her and gave her a charity fuck. She gave me the clap. There's a lesson in that. Never donate to charity.' He gives me a wink.

I leave him lying on his bed, arms at his sides, as though waiting for the undertaker. Trembling with rage, I walk along a corridor, angry that he can remember the Clifton Butterfly, but he can't remember my name. My conscious mind hates what I've become. Nature has not triumphed over nurture. Both are equally at fault.

I notice an open door, an empty room, a bed and a handful of banknotes on a side table. The occupant is in the en suite bathroom or somewhere else.

I slip inside and take the money, pushing it deep into my pocket.
'Can I help you?'

Mrs Addison, the supervisor, is standing in the doorway. She normally works in the office upstairs and I only hear from her when the nursing home fees are owed.

'What are you doing in this room?'
'I got lost.'
She knows I'm lying.
'This isn't your father's room.'
'I realise that now.'
I feel a bead of sweat roll over my vertebrae at the base of my spine.

Fuck you, bitch! *I want to scream.* You shut your mouth or I'll . . . I'll . . .

21

The balloons make the biggest impression. Hundreds of them are tied to the railings and the iron gates and bobbing from people's wrists as they gather outside the Church of the Immaculate Conception. Harper's schoolfriends are carrying large clown-like clusters, all of them purple and mauve, handing them out to mourners and passers-by.

'Take two,' says a pretty girl in a short black dress. She ties one to each of my wrists, while explaining that purple was Harper's favourite colour.

She turns to Ruiz. 'You want a balloon?'

'I'm a bit old for that.'

'You're not old,' she says, winking at him. He holds out his hand.

'Did you see that?' he asks.

'What?'

'She flirted with me.'

'It's "Be Nice to Pensioners Week".'

'Fuck off.'

'Language. Remember where you are.'

Posters are displayed at the entrance to the church, each

featuring a photograph of Elizabeth and Harper. The message above reads: 'Celebration of Life Service'. There are more photographs in the printed 'order of service': Harper on her first day of school, or with a bucket and spade, or riding a donkey, or bouncing on a trampoline, or posing with her friends . . . Elizabeth has her own photographs that show her changing hairstyles and colours and fashions. Sometimes it's difficult to tell mother and daughter apart.

On the edge of the churchyard, TV crews and photographers have taken up positions on a footpath, spilling on to the narrow road where a police constable is directing traffic.

Dominic Crowe arrives alone, wearing a black suit and tie, his eyes hidden behind dark glasses. In contrast, Elizabeth's mother has worn bright colours – a mauve blouse and voluminous white skirt. Becca walks through the gates with Francis, who is carrying the baby in a car seat. People stop, bend and smile at little George. Someone ties a purple balloon to the handle of his carrier.

Inside the church they take a seat in the front row. An organ is playing. Becca turns and makes eye contact with Dominic Crowe, holding his gaze for a several seconds, long enough for something to pass between them.

I've been to my share of funerals but this one seems wrong. Most of the mourners are young and won't have lost someone close to them before. Standing in clusters, unsure of what to say or do, they talk in whispers and hug each newcomer. Harper's boyfriend is with Sophie Baxter and another girl I recognise from the public meeting. Blake is wearing a purple satin jacket that makes him look like a member of a boy band. He's sitting on the aisle, occasionally glancing over his shoulder as though expecting the drinks trolley to be along at any moment.

Harper's brother Elliot is being shepherded by other family members. Dressed for the occasion in a black overcoat, dark grey suit and thin black tie, he looks emaciated and strung out, his face shiny with sweat.

The service begins with a jazzy hymn. The priest opens his arms.

'The grace and peace of God our Father and the Lord Jesus Christ be with you,' he says.

'And with you,' is the murmured reply.

'My name of Father Abermain,' he says. 'There are many people still outside. I know it might not seem like an occasion for making new friends, but what better way to celebrate these two lives than to embrace each other. So squeeze up, people, let others sit down.'

The funeral is a simple, sombre affair with gospel readings, communion and prayers before words of remembrance. A friend from school talks of Harper's artistic talent – her eye for beauty and composition. 'She was lively, lovely and smart. She was going to change the world.'

Elizabeth's oldest friend recounts their first meeting. 'The moment Elizabeth walked into a room she commanded attention. Nobody could ignore her energy, the sparkle in her eye, the spirit that said, "I am here and I will not be ignored."'

Dominic Crowe is the last to speak, breaking down as he tries to read from a prepared speech. Someone steps up to the microphone and helps him finish.

'I am overwhelmed by the support we have received. I drove past the farm on my way here and I saw all the ribbons and the flowers and the cards on the gate. And I thought how much people must have loved Elizabeth and Harper.'

After a final hymn, the coffins are carried outside and I can hear broken sobs from the pews behind me. Those who couldn't make it inside the church are still waiting, lined up along the driveway and the road. The coffins are slid into the hearses and wreathes are arranged. The cars pull away, flanked by police motorcyclists. Most of the town seems to have come out. Some are holding posters. One of them reads: *Harper We Love You. You Won't Be Forgotten.*

I drift to the edge of the mourners and notice Jeremy Egan trying to slip away as quietly as he must have arrived.

'I didn't expect to see you here,' I say.

Egan stiffens and stands awkwardly. 'Elizabeth was my friend before any of the rest happened,' he says defensively. Rocking back and forth on his polished shoes, he pats at his fringe. 'I'm sorry about the other day – the things I said about your, ah, shaking . . . '

'I was also out of line,' I admit.

'That was very clever, how you summed up my life. How did you do it?'

'Observation. Research.'

'I thought you must have been reading my mail.'

'Hardly.'

Egan takes off his sunglasses. 'You might not believe me, but I regret what happened between Elizabeth and me. It should never have started. Maybe I wanted to punish Dominic for holding back the company and costing me money. I know that's no excuse. Elizabeth had a way of getting her hooks into someone.'

'She was needy?'

'I'd say greedy.' He glances at me apologetically. 'I guess that's not a very nice thing to say – in the circumstances.'

'No. Did your wife blame you or Elizabeth for the affair?'

'You should ask her.'

'Is she here?'

'Afraid not. I did invite her, but we don't do a lot together. Familiarity breeds contempt – isn't that what they say? It's my fault. I'm your classic example of someone who marries up and screws down. My wife is the youngest daughter of a baronet. I still love her. I just don't fancy her.'

We don't shake hands when he leaves. Mourners are milling outside the church. Someone touches my shoulder. My arm twitches strongly.

'I'm sorry,' says Francis Washburn, thinking he's caused the reaction.

'It's not you,' I explain. 'I get spasms like that.'

163

He nods, not understanding, but he's too polite to ask. His face tilts at an angle and his eyes seem to focus on my mouth. 'I wanted to apologise for Friday. Becca said you were very kind to her and I was extremely rude.'

'Don't give it another thought,' I say.

He smiles gratefully. 'I don't usually lose my temper. Becca says I'm old-fashioned. Stiff upper lip and all that.'

We stand for a moment, sharing the view, until he talks to cover his awkwardness. 'You're welcome to come back to the house. We're serving refreshments. My mother-in-law particularly wants to meet you. She seems to think you're famous.'

'I'm not.'

'Well, she wants you to come. Please say yes or she'll blame me.'

'Blame you?'

He laughs. 'My mother-in-law is a force of nature. I love her to bits, but it sometimes feels as though we have another child in the house.'

'She lives with you?'

'It's a big house. She has her own wing.' He gives me the address on a printed card. 'You were right about Becca – she does need help. I keep hoping the police will make an arrest and things will settle down.'

Francis hears his name being called. Cars are leaving for the crematorium.

'Two o'clock,' he shouts behind him.

The last of the mourners are making their way to their cars. Some are still carrying purple balloons. Others have released them, watching them float away on the breeze, as though it symbolises something they can't put into words.

A new one rises. Dominic Crowe is beneath it. The balloon swirls sideways in the gusty breeze and is caught in the branches of a tree. After a moment it pops and suddenly denotes something different. Dominic lowers his head and leaves quickly, walking in his own reality.

Before he can reach the gate a scrum of reporters surrounds him. I see Bannerman among them. Shouldering people aside, he shoves a microphone under Crowe's nose. 'Did you kill your wife and daughter?'

The bluntness of the question shocks everyone else into silence.

'What did you say?'

'I asked you if you killed your wife and daughter.'

Dominic finds the strength to ignore him and pushes through the crowd. Cameras chase him across the road and into a side street where he dodges between cars, trying to shield his face with his coat.

Meanwhile, Milo Coleman has materialised with a camera crew. He confronts Ronnie Cray. 'Why haven't the police made an arrest?'

'What are you doing here?' asks the DCS.

'I'm filming a documentary about the murders,' replies Milo. 'We're calling it *Manhunt*.'

Cray pushes the camera out of her face.

'Are you trying to avoid my questions?' asks Milo, his left hand opening and closing at his side. 'Do you admit that mistakes have been made?'

'I have no comment to make.'

'What are you trying to hide?'

For a moment it appears as though Cray might ignore him completely but then she stops and turns, staring straight into the barrel of the camera. 'Is that thing turned on?'

The cameraman nods.

Cray looks into the lens. 'Today we have said goodbye to and celebrated the lives of two people who were the victims of a violent unsolved crime. Unfortunately some members of the media have shown they have no respect for the dead or the law. Even worse, certain individuals have actively sought to sabotage a double murder investigation. I *did* make a mistake. I allowed a pseudo-psychologist, Milo Coleman, to volunteer his services and gain access to confidential information. This man has jeopardised any future prosecution by releasing those details to the public. He has compounded this by trading on people's fears and turning them against each other.'

'I'm keeping them safe,' says Milo.

'You're a pariah and a fraud.'

'You can't say that.'

'I just did, Mr Coleman. I have sent a file to the CPS seeking to have you charged with perverting the course of justice.'

She turns and leaves. Mourners step aside. Momentarily robbed of speech, Milo looks from face to face. The camera is still recording. He pushes it away. In the same breath he spies me on the edge of the crowd. Dropping his shoulder as he passes, he tries to knock me down, but Ruiz has seen it coming. He intercepts Milo and braces for the inevitable contact. The younger man goes down like a felled tree, holding his face.

'You saw that,' he yells. 'He hit me. That's assault.'

Ruiz looks disgusted rather than surprised.

'Get on your feet,' he says, and then to the crew, 'Show's over, lads.'

Milo is still complaining, but his colleagues ignore him.

'That was some dive,' I tell Ruiz.

'I scored it an eight.'

22

The double-fronted house has a gabled roof with chimney pots
at either end giving it a pleasant symmetry and illusions of
grandeur. I grew up in a place similar to this – a large Victorian
home with strange internal angles, creaking corridors and dodgy
plumbing, which left behind an impression on my consciousness like a pen pressed too hard into a sheet of paper.

Becca Washburn greets me at the front door. She is still
wearing her funeral attire – a simple black dress, which clings
to her heavy breasts. She smiles at me nervously and turns to
the next group of mourners. I navigate along the crowded
hallway and reach the rear garden where people have clustered
beneath a white marquee and the shade of a large jacaranda
tree.

Trestle tables are laden with food – party pies, sausage rolls,
spinach triangles and samosas. Trays of sandwiches, curling in
the heat, are being protected from flies beneath muslin. Two
young men are operating a makeshift bar, serving wine and
beer from barrels full of ice.

A matronly woman wields an oversized teapot, offering me
a cup. Pancake make-up pools in the hollows of her cheeks.

'That strong enough for you, pet?' she asks, as liquid creeps up the inside of the mug.

'The man don't wanna be drinking that,' says her husband, looking over her shoulder. 'Might as well be water.'

'There's nothing wrong with my tea.'

'It's so weak it can barely crawl out the spout.'

I leave them bickering and carry my cup into the garden. Father Abermain has a group of women around him. Like an island in a sea of black, he cuts an impressive figure in his laundered white shirt with twin golden crosses on the starched collar. Handsome, steady and a good listener, if he weren't sworn to celibacy I can imagine a lot of middle-aged women queuing to catch his eye.

Francis Washburn leaves another group and crosses the lawn to greet me. 'I'm glad you came. We men are rather outnumbered. Can I get you something stronger to drink?'

'No, I'm fine; you mentioned Elizabeth's mother . . . '

'Right, yes, I'll try to find her.'

In the meantime he introduces me to a clutch of distant relatives who have travelled from Ireland for the funerals. They include an Uncle Ira who is so deaf he shouts at everyone, and a cousin with macular degeneration, who is showing off a much younger husband. I hover on the edge of their conversation, nodding and smiling. I am not a lover of small talk. I don't feel equipped. One of the problems is that I discover too much about people. It's not a conscious thing. I don't set out to unpick their psyches or explore their motivations. The information comes to me almost instinctively. I see their clothes, how they're groomed, where they stand, whom they speak to, where they look and the thousands of almost imperceptible tics, gestures, shrugs and mannerisms that clutter human behaviour and reveal hidden truths about them. It is not mindreading, but it feels just as intrusive – knowing so much about someone I've barely met.

Leaving the group, I walk across the lawn to the house in

search of the bathroom. It's occupied. I wait. Most of Harper's friends have gathered in the adjoining dining room. I don't see Blake Lehmann or Sophie Baxter among them. Elliot Crowe is swigging beer from an oversized can. Pale and perspiring, his eyes and lips are darkened like an actor in a silent movie. There is a strange disconnectedness between the neatness of his clothes and how his body looks ready to fall apart.

'I fucking hate funerals,' he announces too loudly.

'You shouldn't say that,' whispers a girl with a pink streak in her hair.

'Why not? I wanted to miss this one. Bad form, I suppose, to be a no-show at dear Mummy's funeral, but I keep asking myself – are they sure she's really dead? Did the killer use a wooden stake?'

The girl hushes him and stifles a giggle.

The bathroom is free. When I'm finished, I wash my hands with a tiny square of newly unwrapped soap – the sort you find in hotels. There are dozens of miniature bottles of shampoo and conditioner and shower gel on a shelf above the sink and more on the windowsill. It must have been a job lot, I think, as I swallow one of my pills and scoop water into my mouth.

As I leave the bathroom something cold and wet touches my fingers. A golden retriever with a grey muzzle has risen slowly from under the hallway table so he can lick my hand.

'He's a dear old thing,' says Becca, watching me from the first-floor landing. She's holding baby George in her arms. I can only see the top of his head, which is covered in hair as fine as corn silk.

'You have a beautiful baby,' I say.

She smiles and says thank you, cradling his head, which fits neatly into the palm of her hand. She comes down the stairs. 'He's just woken . . . hungry, as usual.'

I follow her into the kitchen, where she takes a seat and rests George on her lap while she unbuttons her blouse, revealing a nursing bra. I avert my eyes.

'Am I embarrassing you?' she asks.

'Not at all.'

When I turn back she has lifted George to her breast and he has latched on, his mouth stretched wide and his lips barely seeming to move, but I can see him swallowing. Becca half closes her eyes. 'I wanted to apologise to you for the other day.'

'There's no need.'

'I don't know what happened to me. One minute I was at home and the next . . . '

'What's the last thing you remember?'

'I was taking a nap. I lay down upstairs and fell asleep. I had a nightmare. I dreamed about going to the mortuary to identify Elizabeth and Harper. They showed me Elizabeth first. I couldn't look at Harper . . . ' She shudders and the sentence trails off. 'Francis says you're helping the police.'

'Yes.'

'Why do you do it? I mean – do you enjoy investigating crimes?'

'No.'

'Why, then?'

'I have trouble saying no to people.'

Becca doesn't seem convinced by my altruism.

'How old is George?' I ask.

'Five months.'

'Are you back at work?'

'I'm on nights this week.'

'You're a nurse.'

'Yes.'

'What does Francis do?'

'He's a property manager. He looks after holiday houses and rentals. We have to juggle the babysitting. My mum helps.'

'She lives with you?'

'Yes.'

Becca glances through the window at the people in the garden. 'Everybody has been so nice, calling and dropping by, but I think I'm ready for them to go home now.' She uses two fingers to brush hair from her face. 'Is it true that Tommy Garrett was released?'

'The police didn't have enough evidence to hold him.'

Two children run into the room and out again, their faces pooled with colour. Becca puts a finger on her lips. They see her breastfeeding and spin away, giggling as they run outside.

'Were you and Elizabeth close?' I ask.

'Not always. Maybe it was the age difference – ten years. I idolised Lizzie when we were growing up. She was the pretty one, the bright one, the popular one, but as the youngest everybody doted on me.' She smiles serenely. 'Ever since George was born we'd grown a lot closer. She was a wonderful aunt. Harper was our babysitter.'

'Was Elizabeth religious?'

'Not especially. She didn't go to church every Sunday if that's what you mean.'

'Would she have read the Bible?'

'I'd be surprised. She was superstitious rather than religious. I know she thought the farmhouse was haunted and talked about having an exorcism.'

'She believed in ghosts?'

'And palm readers and fortune tellers and tarot cards.'

'Do you have any thoughts on who might have wanted to harm them?'

Becca's shoulders rise and fall. 'We're a very ordinary family. We don't have enemies.'

'What about Dominic Crowe?'

'What about him?'

'You've stayed in touch.'

She stares past me as though distracted by something outside. 'Dominic likes to sing. We're in a choir together. We practise twice a week at the community centre. He has a lovely voice. Elizabeth used to laugh at him.'

'You know he's a suspect.'

171

'He would never hurt Harper.'

'He hit your sister. She took out a restraining order.'

'It's true that he and Lizzie fought like cat and dog. She knew how to press his buttons.'

The phone rings. I give Becca the handset. She listens and then covers the receiver. 'Can you excuse me, Professor? I have to take this.'

Stepping into the dining room, still holding George, she kicks at the door, which only partially closes. I hear her voice rising in concern and then irritation. 'You haven't received it? That's strange. I paid last week . . . '

A woman appears in the kitchen, asking for Becca.

'She's on the phone,' I explain. 'Is something wrong?'

'Somebody shouldn't be here.' She motions through the window and I see Milo Coleman standing beneath the jacaranda tree, carrying his jacket over his shoulder, hooked on his finger.

'Where's Francis?' I ask.

'I can't find him.'

'I'll handle it.'

Milo is chatting to some of Harper's friends. Dressed in pleated trousers and an open-necked shirt, he seems to have recovered completely from his meltdown at the church.

'Professor, we keep bumping into each other,' he says, rolling a toothpick from one side of his mouth to the other.

I grab him by the forearm and pull him away from the crowd.

'Are you the bouncer?' he jokes.

'You're not welcome here.'

'I thought it was a general invitation.'

'You have to leave.'

'But I could have important information for the family.'

'Do you?'

'I'd be willing to share it with you. We could work together, just like the old days.'

'There were no *old days*.'

He grins cheekily. 'So how is the investigation going? I hear they arrested the neighbour. Was it your idea? Garrett is an imbecile. I'm a more likely killer than he is.'

'Is that a confession?'

He flashes another smile. 'You're playing catch-up, Professor. I've been following this case from the beginning and I'm going to get the credit when it's over.'

'Leave now, Milo, or I'll call the police.'

'Don't get your knickers in a twist. I just came here to pass on an observation. You should look more closely at Elliot Crowe. He's a junkie and he can't provide an alibi for the night of the murders. He also inherits the farmhouse. Motive. Means. Knowledge. Addiction. Ticks all the boxes.'

Over Milo's shoulder, I see Francis emerge from the house, his eyes fizzing with anger. He's searching the garden. Milo has seen him now.

'Well, it's been fun talking to you, Professor, but I have to places to be, people to meet.' He shrugs on his jacket. 'How's that lovely daughter of yours?' he asks. 'I met her years ago. She was waiting outside your office at the university. Quite the looker, even then — must take after her mother.'

He vaults athletically over the gate and is gone by the time Francis comes around the side of the house.

'What did that creep want?' he asks.

'Nothing. Milo is a human horsefly — he bites and flies away.'

Francis looks over the gate to make sure. 'I don't want him coming here.'

'I told him.'

Sunlight flickers through the trees and I notice something dangling from his hand — a small handgun.

'What are you doing with that?'

Francis looks surprised to have the weapon in his hand, before clumsily pushing it into his pocket.

'I'm taking precautions,' he mumbles defensively.

'You think you're in danger?'

'Someone killed my sister-in-law and niece. Until I know why . . . ' He doesn't finish.

At that moment I hear Becca calling his name. Francis turns back along the path and rounds the corner of the house. Becca meets us in the shade of the jacaranda. She looks at Francis. 'Is everything all right?'

'Hunky-dory,' he replies, keeping his hands in his pockets.

'My mother wants to meet you,' says Becca. 'I hope you don't mind.'

'Of course.'

She leads me across the lawn to a corner of the garden where a large wicker chair has been positioned beneath a trellis of lilac blossoms. Shaped like a snowman with steel-wool hair and heavy jewellery, Becca's mother looks every inch the family matriarch, surrounded by a semicircle of women of a similar age, giving her cake and cups of tea.

'Please don't stand,' I tell her, but she insists on getting to her feet with the aid of a polished wooden cane. 'I'm very sorry for your loss,' I say, introducing myself. My left arm jerks but she looks amused rather than frightened.

'Sit down. Sit down. Call me Betty.' She turns to one of her friends. 'This is the psychologist I was telling you about – the famous one.'

'You have an odd definition of fame.'

'Don't be modest. I read about your wife and wee girl being kidnapped.'

'That was a long time ago.'

'Oh, but I bet it seems like only yesterday. Do you still think about it?'

Every day, but I don't tell her that.

'I was hoping I might talk to you about Elizabeth.'

'Of course,' she says.

'Perhaps somewhere more private.'

She reaches behind her for the polished cane walking stick and a packet of cigarettes. 'It's time I moved my arse.' I help

174

her stand. She holds my forearm. We walk along a path beneath a vine-covered arch and down three steps on to a lower lawn.

'Should I offer you one?'

'No.'

Lighting up, she exhales, waving her hands at the smoke. 'I couldn't wait for that funeral to end,' she says.

'I thought it was very moving.'

'Yes, well, some people sob louder than others.'

'Anyone in particular?'

'Her ex-husband.'

'You don't like him.'

The old woman rolls her eyes and doesn't answer me directly. 'I think society tolerates aggression in men. They are seen as being fragile, unhappy creatures, no longer in control, no longer having the same privileges or power as in the past, so we are supposed to forgive them if they swing a fist.'

'He denies that he hit Elizabeth.'

'I saw the bruises.'

'Did you see him hit her?'

She doesn't answer.

'The problem with men,' she says, 'is they don't understand their own gender. You're not a man until you've broken a heart, or had your heart broken, or beaten the shit out of someone or had the shit kicked out of you. How does that sound?'

'You just summed up the last thirty years of my life.'

She laughs. 'Congratulations, you're a man.' We're standing next to the fishpond, where several carp are doing lazy circles and mouthing at the surface of the water. A gust of wind swishes the foliage and a serviette goes flying across the lawn.

'Does Becca feel the same way as you do?'

'About men?'

'About Dominic Crowe.'

She places her hands on the railing fence. 'Becca is a bit soft in the head when it comes to men. She married Francis.'

175

'What's wrong with Francis?'

'Oh, he's all right, I suppose. Doesn't have an ambitious bone in his body, but he's harmless enough.'

'He seems to be a good father.'

She mellows. 'You're right. He's very good with George and tries hard to keep Becca happy.'

Pinching the half-finished cigarette, she tears off the burning tip and pockets the unused portion, saving it for later. Everything she does seems to be the act of a survivor. Rationing words. Keeping her own counsel. She reminds me of an old-school Fabian and suffragette who has not mellowed with age.

'Are you going to catch whoever killed my daughter and granddaughter?'

'I'm going to try.'

'And what can you do that the police haven't done?'

'I look at things in different ways. I study the victims. I discover how they'd react under stress. What they'd do if confronted by someone late at night.'

Betty sticks out her chin. Lipstick has smudged her teeth. 'Blame it on the victim – isn't that what you're saying?'

'No.'

'I hear what people are saying about Elizabeth.'

'What are they saying?'

'She was divorced. She was good-looking. She took care of herself. She had a shitty marriage and wanted to enjoy life. What's wrong with that? She was her own woman. She was liberated and self-sufficient. She did not believe that her marriage should define her.'

It feels like a speech that she's made before – the homily of a woman with a great capacity to defend her own and hate outsiders – the skivers, shirkers, puritans, hypocrites and small-town gossips.

'What's going to happen to Windy Hill Farm?' I ask.

'We'll sell it.'

'And Elliot gets the money.'

176

She breathes in, breathes out. Something rattles in her chest. 'That depends upon what Elizabeth wanted. Her will is being read next week.'

'You think she left the farmhouse to someone else?'

'I don't know. But I'll tell you one thing for certain – Lady Muck next door won't get the place. Not if I can help it.'

'Doreen Garrett?'

'She's been trying to buy the farmhouse for years. Her family used to own Windy Hill, but had to break it up in the seventies. Ever since she's been trying to buy it back. That's a motive for murder, isn't it?'

'You think Doreen Garrett is the killer?'

'Maybe she put her grandson up to it. He's an odd creature. Elizabeth caught him stealing her underwear.'

'*Did* she catch him?'

'Stuff went missing.'

'That's not the same.'

She looks at me directly, her jaw working. 'Are you married, Professor?'

'Separated.'

'Thought so. You have that look on your face – like someone just pinched the last biscuit.'

I find myself laughing at the line. She also smiles, but her eyes don't show any amusement. She reminds me of a child born into poverty who watches all her friends queue up at the local 'chippy', seeing them unwrap the greasy parcels while she cringes inside from the embarrassment of wanting.

Across the garden, I can see Becca showing off the baby. It's amazing how the mood of the gathering seems to lift at the sight of the infant. Betty is no longer focused on me. Her grandchild is more important.

23

Death is supposed to be the final act, yet so much is left unfinished when someone dies suddenly or unexpectedly. It's as though they've walked offstage in the middle of the performance, hoping to come back later to explain the plot and tie up any loose ends. This is what I contemplate as I sit in my car, watching people drift away from Francis and Becca's house. Up until now I've had some vague notion that I might stumble upon the key that unlocks this crime – a cache of family papers, or a diary, or a bundle of love letters – but nothing is going to arrive in the post or fall into my lap.

Putting the car into gear, I pull away and drive into Clevedon, parking on the seafront, opposite the Moon and Sixpence. The pub is one of those places that look bigger on the outside than on the inside, with exposed beams and riotously patterned carpets and Toby jugs on a shelf above the beer taps. Still too early for the dinner crowd, the restaurant is empty and most of the patrons are downstairs at the bar. I take a table on the terrace, overlooking the seafront and pier.

Sophie Baxter is setting tables. She has a dense shock of brown hair, walnut-coloured eyes and the traces of a fake tan unevenly applied to her legs. At some time in her past she suffered a facial injury, which has left her with a small feather-shaped scar on her left cheek.

'Do you have a few moments?' I ask, as she nears my table.

Nervously she drops her head. 'I'm working.'

'It won't take long.'

She glances over her shoulder at her manager and moves closer, wiping down my table.

'You weren't at the wake,' I say.

'I had a shift.'

'Tell me about you and Blake.'

'We're just friends.'

'Oh, I see, so the other day – the kiss – you were checking his fillings with your tongue?'

She gives me a heavenward flick of her nose. 'That's a shitty thing to say. We've been helping each other grieve.'

'Touching.'

'You are a horrible man.' She takes a small packet of tissues from the edge of her bra. 'I actually met Blake first. Harper said she didn't even like him, but then she changed her mind.'

'Did you two fight over him?'

'No, not really.' She blows her nose. 'Harper tended to get what she wanted. I mean – look at me compared to her.'

Sophie is looking for sympathy, but I don't sense any lack of self-esteem. The manager has wandered outside. 'Is there a problem?' he asks.

'Not at all,' I reply. 'Sophie is just explaining the specials.'

'The restaurant isn't open yet.'

'I'm planning ahead.'

He nods, unconvinced, and moves away. Sophie whispers, 'You're going to get me in trouble.'

'Oh, I'm the least of your problems.'

'What does that mean?'

'It's a criminal offence to impede a murder investigation.'

'I done no such thing,' she says, more anxious than affronted.

'Harper worked on the Saturday she died. She came to your house after she finished her shift. What did you do?'

'Watched music videos and tried on clothes.'

'When Harper left you – where was she going?'

'She had her sketchbook.'

'What was she going to sketch?'

She gives me a pantomime shrug. 'I don't know – the usual stuff. She drew a lot of buildings and people's faces. I'm hopeless at drawing, but she didn't mind stopping some random and asking if she could draw them.'

'Random?'

'Stranger.'

'When you met up with her that evening, how did she seem?'

'OK, I guess – excited about her birthday.'

'What did you talk about?'

'I can't remember.'

'You don't normally forget the last moments you spend with your best friend.'

'How would you know?'

'Personal experience.'

Sophie flinches, annoyed with herself.

'Did you talk to anyone at the pub?'

'A couple of older guys tried to chat us up. They were business types, trying to act like they were hipsters.'

'When you say older . . . ?'

'Thirtyish.'

Ancient.

'Did you recognise any of them?'

'Harper knew one guy. I think he was a family friend . . . an architect.'

'Jeremy Egan?'

'That might have been his name. He couldn't keep his eyes off Harper – a real D.O.M.'

'What's a "D.O.M."?'

'Dirty Old Man.'

I make a mental note to check out Jeremy Egan's statement. According to his wife he was home at the time of the murders, but Egan didn't mention seeing Harper earlier in the evening.

'Did anything happen that night that was unusual or out-of-the-ordinary?' I ask.

'What do you mean?'

'Anything strange or surprising?'

Sophie screws up her face. 'You're talking about Clevedon, right?'

Ignoring her sarcasm, I ask her to think back and try to picture the scene at the pub. Where were they were standing. Who else was there? Was anyone watching?

Her tongue peeps out from between her teeth. 'Harper saw something on the TV. She wanted the barman to turn up the sound, but he was too busy serving drinks.'

'Why was she so interested?'

'It was something about a woman being attacked on a footpath.'

'Did she know this woman?'

'No.'

'Where was the footpath?'

'She didn't say.'

'And you didn't ask?'

'No. That's when Blake arrived. He hadn't bothered having a shower or getting changed. Harper was narked.'

'They argued.'

'I guess.'

'Did you see the fight?'

'It wasn't a fight. Harper left in a huff. Blake followed her.'

'She scratched his face.'

'He had the scratch when he arrived.'

'Did he tell you to say that?'

'No.'

'You must like Blake a lot to risk lying for him.'

'I'm not lying.'

'I know you went to the farmhouse that night.'

Sophie's eyes shoot up to mine. She shakes her head. 'I don't know what you're talking about.'

'You see – right there – that little pause before you responded tells me that you're lying. I know you were at the farmhouse that night. Blake said it was your idea.'

'What! No! It was him – he wanted to give Harper her present.'

'And you volunteered to go with him. That's sweet. There's a theory that two people killed Harper and her mother.'

Sophie chokes on her response. Her head pivots from side to side. 'You can't be serious – I would never – I mean . . . that's just crazy.'

'You ever heard of Bonnie and Clyde?' She shakes her head. 'They were young lovers who went a killing spree in Texas in the 1930s. They got off on murdering people until the police shot them. Bonnie Parker was twenty-three, Clyde Barrow twenty-five.'

Sophie scratches at her wrists. 'We didn't do anything wrong.'

'Why didn't you tell the police?'

'Blake told me to keep my mouth shut. He was scared people might think we were involved. But we didn't do anything wrong. I swear. Mrs Crowe wouldn't let us in. Blake broke a window but that was an accident.'

She's shouting the words. The manager has reached the table. Sophie pushes past him and disappears into the kitchen. Everything about her persona reminds me of an actress in a bad play, who wants to rush off the stage and disappear, but there are still two more acts to come and the script doesn't get any better.

Tuesday afternoon and I thread my way along the crowded footpath where tourists are lunching at cafés or queuing for gelato at the Italian restaurant. On the seafront children are paddling in the shallows, watched over by mothers wearing wide-brimmed hats and sunglasses. Teenage girls are lying on their bellies, chatting and texting, ignoring the boys who are sitting on the steps checking them out. Meanwhile, joggers jog and old people amble and the waves sigh upon the shingles.

Catching the bus I take a seat halfway down, watching the driver's forearms knot and bulge as he turns the wheel. People get on. Fewer get off. A trio of girls laughs at some private joke. An old woman sags under the weight of her age. A little girl looks at me from the folds of her mother's dress. I offer the mother a seat. She doesn't smile or thank me.

Eventually the bus is a crowded, rackety sweating box, reeking of diesel fumes and deodorant. People bump against me, touching my knees, and I tense up. Light and shade tick over my eyelids. I am physically aware of the woman I seek, even though I can only see the back of her head and her shoulders. A man is sitting next to her, sneaking glances when she turns her gaze out the window. She is clutching a bag on her lap.

When I last saw her she was dolled up in a cocktail frock, twirling stilettos on her finger. Now she's dressed in a blouse and simple skirt, sitting near the back of the bus, head down, noodling on her phone.

It has taken me weeks to learn her routines – where she lives, where she works, what bus she catches, who she's really married to . . . I knew she was married. I saw the tell-tale white band of skin where she had taken off her wedding ring.

Fields roll past the windows of the bus. Narrow lanes. Small villages. I get off the bus first and walk quickly away along the narrow country lane, knowing the woman is behind me.

I pass the church and turn into the graveyard, where I squat on my haunches, bracing my back against the cool stone, listening for her footsteps. I can hear them now, getting closer. Does she speed up a little? Perhaps she has some sense of foreboding, that funny fluttering sensation in the pit of her stomach.

Let her pass.

— Take her now.

It's too open. Just watch her.

— I'm sick of watching.

Let her pass.

— No. No.

What if she runs? What if she screams? The last one spoke to the police. I made her promise, but she lied to me. They all lie. I won't trust this one.

I step out suddenly. She doesn't scream. People rarely do what TV cop shows and movies say they should. Instead she opens her lips and makes a small noise, almost a hiccup, before my hand covers her mouth. I can feel her heartbeat. Smell her hair. Picture her nerves prickling on her skin. I can feel the energy beneath her shoulders and the tightness of her bladder and the smell of her sweat.

'Are you frightened?' I whisper.

She nods, muttering something beneath my hand.

'Some people say that we should embrace our fears and that fear makes us feel our own humanity. Others think we fear what we want the most, but that's not true, is it? You see, fear cannot be defined or enclosed. It has no confines and shows no mercy and respects no laws. Fear doesn't begin in the mind. It goes deeper. It is wired into muscle fibres and nerve-endings, our very DNA. That's why the body reacts faster than the mind. We fight or flee or freeze before we ever know why. Unconsciously. Innately.'

Her tears and snot are wetting my fingers, oily and warm. She's trying to fathom what's coming — considering the possibilities from rape to death and the infinite landscape that lies between. She's trying to think of a way out, but her mind is her enemy, not her last hope.

I have felt a soul leave a body. I have felt a soul struggling to escape. Every one of them cries out for one more chance to see, smell, touch, hear and taste. This one is doing the same.

I take my hand from her mouth and place my forearm around her throat, pressing my mouth close to her ear.

'Please let me go,' she croaks.

'You must try harder than that.'

'Why?'

'It's more fun that way.'

The blade touches her skin. Her flesh opens. Three lines: Adam's initial. Her body heaves as blood leaks over her eyelids and sprinkles her white blouse like garnets.

24

That night at the cottage I spread my notes across the bed and begin writing a report for DCS Cray. In the morning Ruiz will talk to the tradesmen who worked at the farmhouse, going over their statements, looking for any inconsistencies.

I've interviewed most of the major suspects, studied the crime scene photographs and footage, and talked to family and friends. No gaping holes or anomalies have emerged apart from the obvious one – the killer's identity.

Blake Lehmann lied to police. He didn't mention visiting the farmhouse or throwing rocks at Harper's bedroom window. Sophie Baxter also lied. It's possible the two of them killed Harper and Elizabeth, with Blake as the dominant personality and Sophie being manipulated to follow.

Dominic Crowe has no alibi and seems caught between grieving for his daughter and feeling sorry for himself. Jeremy Egan has a long-suffering wife to back up his story and is safe from prosecution unless smugness becomes a criminal offence. Dion Ferguson can't prove his whereabouts that night and blackmail is a powerful motive, but he comes across as frightened of women rather than angry.

Then there's the family. Becca Washburn went to work that Saturday, leaving the baby with Francis and her mother. Elliot Crowe is the only gap in my research. Nobody answered my knock at his bedsit in Bristol and he hasn't replied to the message I pushed under the door.

Perhaps the killer was a random stranger who watched Elizabeth having sex in public or arranged to meet her through an online chat room or dating service. He could have followed her home, talked his way inside and managed to kill mother and daughter before they could raise the alarm.

Julianne appears in the doorway. I've been concentrating so hard I didn't hear her climb the stairs. I close a folder quickly, like a schoolboy caught looking at a centrefold.

'You missed a telephone call,' she says, holding my phone. I have a vague memory of ringing. I look at the screen. The caller doesn't have an ID. 'They'll call back if it's important,' I say.

Julianne is still in the doorway, regarding me solemnly. I notice the dark shadows beneath her eyes and the thin line of grey at the roots of her hair where she's pulled it back from her forehead. She hasn't had time to visit her hairdresser, or perhaps doesn't see the need.

'I thought you were in bed,' I say.

'I'm heading there now. What are you doing?'

'Packing up.'

'Have you finished?'

'I'm going to wrap this up tomorrow. DCS Cray can get by without me.'

'Really?'

'I thought I might take Emma to Longleat to see the animals.'

'She'd enjoy that.'

Our youngest is obsessed with Africa. She's been writing letters to David Attenborough since she was five, asking him very specific questions about meerkats and honey badgers, her favourite animals. The naturalist has written back to her twice, but is probably rather frightened by her intensity.

Julianne steps into the room and begins rearranging Emma's menagerie of stuffed animals – a panda, a patchwork elephant, a flop-eared rabbit and a whole family of teddy bears, who share Emma's bed as though it's a life-raft. The silence reminds me of the cold quiet of the past six years, when divorce always beckoned and Julianne's affections were parcelled up and doled out like donations to charity.

'Why didn't you remarry?' I ask.

'I don't think I had the energy,' she replies.

'Is it that hard?'

'Not the words, I guess. The compromises.'

'Was I a compromise?'

'Don't go fishing for compliments, Joe; you know the answer.'

Julianne shivers and I offer to fetch her dressing gown. I hold it open for her and she slips her arms into the sleeves. As I wrap the gown around her, I give her a hug. She settles against me and I smell her shampoo and see the lone freckle beneath her right ear.

I turn her slowly and cup her face and pull her towards me. I feel her heart beating and the soft swell of her stomach. She doesn't pull away. She doesn't kiss back. I harden against her.

'Don't,' she says, twisting sideways and leaving the room.

My hands are trembling but it has nothing to do with the Parkinson's.

The pillow beneath my head is vibrating. Maybe it's an earthquake. I slide my hand beneath the soft toys and search for the source. *When did I begin sleeping with my mobile phone?*

The digital clock next to my head says 03:52. Nothing good ever comes at this hour. Virtuous people are dreaming. Polite people call at a sociable time. I roll over and leave the call unanswered.

The phone vibrates again. This time I answer it. 'Who is it?'

'DCS Cray.'

'Who?'

'Ronnie Cray.'

'You can't be Ronnie Cray. She wouldn't call me at three in the morning.'

'It's almost four.'

'DCS Cray knows I'm a late riser. She knows I have to be medicated.'

'It's important, Joe.'

'I'm hanging up now.'

'There's been another murder!' she says suddenly, not trying to hide the urgency in her voice. 'A woman was reported missing in North Somerset at nine o'clock last night. She was found three hours ago. We think she was strangled, possibly raped. It's too early to tell.'

'I still don't understand.'

'It could be linked to the farmhouse murders. The victim had her fingers dipped in bleach – just like Harper Crowe.' Cray clears her throat. 'There's something else. She had a symbol carved into her forehead.'

'What do you mean by a symbol?'

'The letter "A".'

My mind begins flitting through the possibilities.

'It's the fourth attack in eight months,' says Cray, 'but none of the others were fatal.'

'The letter "A"?'

'Yes.'

I swing my legs out of bed. 'Send someone to pick me up.'

'Bennie is waiting outside.'

I move to the window and pull the curtains aside. An unmarked police car is parked opposite the cottage. Bennie raises a gloved hand. Behind her, across the darkened fields, I notice a lone light burning at a farmhouse. Someone is awake, a farmer getting ready for work. The intricate machinery of the countryside has always been a mystery to me – the ploughing, planting, harvesting and husbandry – to feed people hundreds of miles away, living in cities, still snuggled in their beds. They, too, will wake and join a machine, rattling to work on buses and trams, gliding to offices on escalators or in lifts, producing and consuming in patterns that are as predictable as the dawn. And then one of them will do something entirely unpredictable, something violent or antisocial, and another assembly line will begin whirring – the police, pathologists, lawyers and judges. We are all part of a machine.

Moving through the cottage, I try not to the wake the girls, but the old floorboards creak and groan under my weight. Teeth brushed and face washed, I'm still groggy and misaligned when Julianne appears at her bedroom door.

'What's wrong?'

'I have to go.'

'Who was on the phone?'

'Ronnie Cray.'

The air seems to grow colder. Sitting on the edge of the bed, she watches me dress. 'You said you were finished.'

'Something has happened.'

'I have my scan today.'

'I'll be back.'

I want to say something to reassure her but I'm still half asleep and I can't think of anything that would assuage her disappointment. People sometimes say the three most powerful words in the English language are 'I love you', but they're wrong. The three most powerful words are 'Please help me'.

25

A dozen police cars and emergency vehicles are parked in the turning circle of the Holy Trinity Church, whose steeple is etched starkly against the lightening sky. Nearby gravestones are beginning to reveal the names of their dead and I hear birdsong in the branches of the trees.

The gates to the churchyard have been sealed off with blue-and-white police tape. More tape has been threaded between fence posts of an adjacent field where a newly erected white tent, lit from within, seems to glow in the dark.

Seventy yards away, police and volunteers have gathered in the parking area for a briefing. Fuelled by thermos coffee and tea, they listen to Ronnie Cray tell them to stay focused and not to leave anything behind. At 6 a.m. they move off, crossing the fields in a straight line with their heads bent, searching the long summer grass and unkempt hedges where the tea-coloured branches and holly look almost black in the low sun.

Cray lifts a plastic cup to her lips. The tea has grown cold. She spits it out.

'Thank you for coming,' she says, wiping her mouth. 'The victim's name is Naomi Meredith, aged twenty-nine. Her husband reported her missing last night. She'd spent the day in Weston-super-Mare, shopping and having lunch with her friends. She planned to catch the four o'clock bus and should have been home by five. Her house is three hundred yards from here, past that line of trees.'

'Who found her?'

'The husband. He arrived home around seven and expected Naomi to be there. He spent the evening phoning her friends and family. He talked to the bus driver, who remembered Naomi. Then he decided to retrace her steps. He discovered her just after 2 a.m. Her body was on the far side of the fence, partially covered with branches and an old sheet of corrugated iron.'

'How did he know where to look?'

'He found her handbag next to one of the gravestones.'

Cray ducks under the police tape and we walk to a splintered fence. On the opposite side I see flattened grass and nettles and the bent stems of thistles. Climbing over, we cross duckboards until we reach the white tent. Arc lights are throwing shadows against the canvas and a portable generator provides a throbbing backing beat.

The flap opens as a camera flashes. Twin white dots of light are left dancing behind my eyelids. My sight recovers. Amid the boxes of equipment and tripods, I see the body of a woman, who is no longer young or old. Wearing a skirt and blouse, she is lying on her side, with one leg bent beneath her and her head resting on her lower arm as though she's curled up and gone to sleep.

The blood that covers her face resembles a mask. Something sharp – a scalpel or razor – must have opened up her forehead while her heart was still beating. Three lines – two longer than the other – intersecting to form the 'A'. The cuts were not meant to be neat or precise, simply legible.

An image comes back to me – a young woman called Catherine Mary McBride lying in a shallow grave on the banks of the Grand Union Canal. It was ten years ago, opposite Kensal Green Cemetery in London, a Sunday morning, when I watched police recover her body. Ruiz was in charge of the investigation. He asked for my help and I said, 'What do I know about predators and psychopaths?'

A decade later and I'm staring at another crime scene and asking myself the same questions. Who was this woman? What did she mean to the man who killed her? Where did he confront her? How quickly did he strike? Did they interact? The answers are important because they influence the much larger question of motivation.

A SOCO speaks to Cray. They're ready to move the body. We're in the way. Cray motions for me to follow and we retrace our steps across the duckboards.

Walking past the church and through the gates, I come to the main road. There are houses on either side with gaps in between. Somebody might have seen him following Naomi, but more likely he waited for her. Was it opportunistic or did he target her because she meant something to him, or represented someone else?

DCS Cray has followed me.

'Was she raped?' I ask.

'Not according to the initial examination.'

'What about the bleach?'

'The paramedics could smell it on her fingers. It could be a coincidence.'

I don't answer immediately. Walking into the churchyard, I stop at one of the newer graves — a husband and wife buried next to each other. He died in 1942, shot down over Germany. She lived for another fifty years.

Cray is itching to ask me about the symbol and its significance. First I want to know about the other attacks.

'We know of three,' she says. 'The victims were choked unconscious and scarred with the same symbol — always on the forehead. Police didn't link the crimes because they took place in different counties and were investigated independently.'

'Did any of the victims know each other?'

193

'No.'

'You said there was an attack on the day of the murders.'

'A thirty-one-year-old bookkeeper, walking on the coastal path between Portishead and Clevedon, was grabbed from behind in a chokehold and lost consciousness. When she came to she had blood in her eyes. She didn't realise what he'd done until the paramedics gave her a mirror.'

'How far is the footpath from the farmhouse?'

'Less than two miles.'

'Any sign of bleach?'

'None.'

'What about the other attacks?'

Cray rattles off the basic facts. The previous October, a radiologist working at a private hospital in Bristol was on her way home. Someone broke into her car and was hiding in the back seat.

'Was she married?' I ask.

'Separated, but she was dating a married doctor at the hospital.'

The second attack was two months later in Newport, Wales, on the eastern side of the Newport City Footbridge. 'The victim was married, aged forty, with two kids. He was trussed up like a Christmas turkey. If a security guard hadn't found him he would have frozen to death.'

'You said "he"?'

'Male, a sales consultant, he wouldn't give us a statement.'

I'm standing at the highest point of the churchyard, looking across the valley to where sheep are dotted on the distant pastures and a tractor moves in slow motion, pulling a trailer along a track.

Cray has spent enough time admiring the view. She wants my thoughts. I clear my throat.

'Nathaniel Hawthorne wrote a famous novel called *The Scarlet Letter*.'

'I've heard of it.'

'It's about a woman called Hester Prynne who is found guilty of adultery and is made to wear a scarlet "A" sewn on to her dress as a sign of shame.'

'You think this is about adultery?'

'All the victims were married or separated.'

'As a matter of routine we considered the possibility of infidelity as a motive, but apart from the radiologist the rest of them claimed to be happily married.'

'Maybe they lied,' I say.

'OK, so let's say you're right – what has this guy got against adultery?'

'Perhaps his wife left him or had an affair.'

'Well, that narrows it down,' says Cray, not hiding her sarcasm.

'Where is her husband?' I ask.

'With Naomi's parents.'

'You should keep an eye on him.'

The DCS signals to Monk, pulling him aside for a quiet word. 'I want you to bring Theo Meredith to the station. Keep it quiet. No fuss. Tell him it's routine.'

Monk nods.

'See if he'll give us permission to search the house,' says Cray.

'You want me to apply for a warrant?'

'We don't have enough.'

Cray comes back to me with another question. 'OK, let's say you're right and we're dealing with some religious nutter or moral vigilante – the other attacks weren't fatal. Why did he kill Naomi?'

'It could have been accidental or part of an escalation.'

'And the bleach?'

'Shows forensic awareness and possibly a link to the farm-house murders, but it's not a strong connection. You need to look at the other cases and re-interview the victims.'

Cray puffs out her cheeks and exhales slowly. 'The first two victims refused to make a statement and the bookkeeper withdrew hers a week later.'

'But you'll try again.'

'Of course,' she says sceptically. 'I'm sure they'll put the kettle on and open the Hobnobs.'

26

Built like a bunker beneath the coroner's court, the mortuary at Flax Bourton has twelve pathologists doing fifteen hundred post-mortems a year. I know this fact because of the chart on the office wall.

A young lab assistant comes to collect me and I follow her along brightly lit corridors that reek of floor polish, disinfectant and a strange mixture of stomach acid, gall and faeces. It's thirty years since I was in medical school, but I still recognise the smell.

'If you'll just wait here,' she says.

The man I've come to see, Dr Louis Preston, has a down-turned mouth, slumped shoulders and a Brummie accent that makes him seem eternally miserable. If Preston won the National Lottery he'd make it sound as if his dog had just died. Right now I can see him through an open door, surrounded by interns who have gathered around a cadaver on the slab.

'This is Mr Norman Griggs,' says Preston. 'He spent sixty-two years on this earth and I want you to treat him with the same care and decency as you'd show your own grandfather. Am I understood?'

The interns nod.

'Dr Earley will perform the autopsy. Watch and learn, people.'

Still peeling off his surgical gloves, Preston meets me in the corridor. 'Do you have an appointment?'

'I need five minutes.'

'If I had five minutes I'd be taking my morning shit.'

'Please, Louis.'

He grumbles and starts walking. 'You want to know about Naomi Meredith?'

'Was it a blood choke?'

'Yes.'

'Could he have miscalculated?'

The pathologist stops and turns, intrigued by the question. I tell him about the earlier attacks – none of which were fatal.

'How much do you know about blood chokes?' he asks.

'I know the effect.'

'Force is applied to both sides of the neck, constricting the carotid artery, decreasing blood flow to the brain. A short compression is relatively harmless, but if you deprive the brain of blood for four minutes we're talking brain damage. Six minutes, it's death.'

'So in this case?'

Preston shrugs. 'He didn't let her go.' He starts walking again.

'What did he use on her forehead?' I ask.

'Best guess – a box-cutter with a retractable blade. Cut her skin to the bone.'

We've reached his office. He sits behind his desk and pulls a sandwich and a carton of juice from the bottom drawer of a filing cabinet. 'If I can't shit, I'm going to eat,' he says, tearing off a mouthful of sandwich and forcing the corners into his mouth.

'You also did the autopsy on Harper Crowe.'

He nods, his mouth full.

'Was that a blood choke?'

His jaw stops moving, recognising where I'm going with this.

'Harper Crowe showed limited evidence of neck trauma.'

'What do you mean by limited evidence?'

The pathologist is thinking out loud now. 'She had some minor perimortem bruising on her jaw, which could have been caused by the small silver crucifix she wore around her neck . . . if it was pressed hard into her skin.'

'By a forearm choking her?'

'Possibly.'

Preston puts down his sandwich, more interested now. He quizzes me on the other attacks, wanting to know how long the victims were unconscious and how they were gripped. I don't have all the answers.

'What about the bleach on Naomi Meredith's fingers?' I ask.

'Sodium hydroxide – your basic household cleaner. He tried to destroy his DNA. We managed to get one sample, but it's highly degraded.'

'Was it the same bleach used on Harper Crowe?'

'It had the same chemical combination, but so do most household bleaches.' Preston wraps his half-eaten sandwich, dropping it into the bin beside his desk. 'So tell me, Professor, what's this guy's motive – power, jealousy, sexual gratification?'

'Revenge and perhaps control,' I reply.

'You don't sound very sure.'

'I don't know him yet.'

The pathologist shakes his head. 'That's the difference between you and me – you want to *know* your subjects. I prefer them dead.'

I am always scared in the days that follow. What if I was seen? What if the police come knocking? What if I left something behind – some trace of me that will lead them here? I have tried to imagine such a scenario, but cannot hold the picture in my mind.

I know I should stop now. But each time I think of pulling back or stepping away, the world becomes dull and vague and pedestrian; so bleached of colour, so boring, so full of cheats and liars.

This one barely struggled. Some people react like that, incapable of comprehending their situation, let alone planning a way out. She didn't kick or squirm or claw at my forearm when I wrapped it around her neck and began to squeeze. When she regained consciousness she couldn't remember being asleep.

'Who are you?' she asked. She noticed the tape on her feet and hands. 'No, no, no. Please let me go. I can pay you. Take my purse.'

'I don't want your money.'

She threatened to scream. I held my hand over her mouth and nose, letting her understand how easy it would be for me to suffocate her.

'You really shouldn't walk home alone,' I said. 'Not through a lonely churchyard.'

'Why me?'

'You betrayed your husband.'

'No.'

'You're still fucking your boss.'

She hesitated, trying to fathom how I could possibly know this.

'You think you're so clever – sneaking around behind your husband's back . . . cheating on him. You think nobody knows. You're wrong! I know!'

'Why do you care?'

'Think of what happens to the children when their parents lie and cheat and sneak around behind each other's backs.'

'I don't have children.'

199

'Your boss does.'

She began to cry and say she was sorry, repeating the word over and over, thinking her tears could melt my heart. The shock was subsiding. Her mind was waking up.

'Where is your husband now?' I asked.

'Waiting for me.'

'He should be here. He should be the one to punish you.'

'Please don't tell him!'

'Oh, it's too late for that. I'm going to write him a letter.'

'What?'

'A letter. Shhhhh. I'm just going to put my arm across your throat again. You'll go to sleep for a while.'

'Please don't hurt me.'

'You won't feel a thing.'

I squeezed. She twisted. Twitched. Time suspended . . .

Something happened as I wrapped my forearm around her neck. I didn't want to stop. I wanted to rock her in my arms forever, serenading her into the longest sleep. A clock is a clock. A knife is a knife. A life is a life.

27

Ruiz paces back and forth between the sink and the fridge. Three paces, turn, three more, turn . . . it's like watching a guardsman on a battlement. He's surprisingly light on his feet for a big man, but I can't concentrate unless he stops moving.

'So he didn't suffocate her.'

'It was a chokehold,' I explain.

'Like they use in cage fighting?'

'Exactly. Instead of closing the windpipe, you deprive the brain of blood.'

I make Ruiz sit down and then move behind him, wrapping my right arm around his neck, so that my elbow is beneath his chin. Then I put my left hand on the back of his head and use it as leverage as I slowly squeeze his neck.

'You'll find it a little more difficult to breathe, but I'm not trying to close off your windpipe. Blood flows to the brain along two pathways – the carotid and vertebral arteries. The carotid artery is where the back of the jaw meets the neck, which makes it quite easy to compress.'

I squeeze. I feel Ruiz struggle. His legs twitch and he reaches for my arm, but within seconds his muscles relax and he wants to flop sideways, his eyes still wide open. I release my forearm and brace myself against him until he regains consciousness.

'Was I out?'

'Yes.'

'How long?'

'Seven, eight seconds.'

'I don't remember.'

He touches his neck and regards me sceptically, as though I might have hypnotised him and made him forget the whole episode.

'Six pounds of pressure is all it takes. By cutting off the blood supply I tricked your brain into thinking your blood pressure had plummeted and it closed your body down.'

Ruiz rolls his head from side to side, checking that nothing is damaged. 'What sort of person carves a symbol on a woman's forehead?'

'A is for adultery.'

Ruiz looks at me questioningly. 'Cheating on your spouse might be immoral and selfish, but it's not against the law.'

'Not since 1857.'

'OK, how do you know shit like that?'

'I just do.'

Getting to his feet, Ruiz rocks forward as though testing the firmness of the floor. He begins pacing again. 'So we're looking for a cuckolded husband or a jilted lover.'

'Or a jealous wife, or her family.'

'Could it be religious?'

'Feels more like a vendetta. He doesn't just punish, he wants to shame.'

I begin telling Ruiz a story from my clinical work when I was summoned to Broadmoor, the secure psychiatric hospital, to interview a seemingly mild-mannered plumber from the Midlands who had beaten a man to death outside a secondary school. He was in his forties, average height, but hugely powerful, having bulked up in weight rooms and fuelled himself with protein shakes and possibly steroids.

The plumber told me he was hearing voices, but I couldn't find any evidence of psychosis. Instead I discovered a man who was kind and considerate and even-tempered, until I mentioned his wife. The change in him was physical as well as emotional. It was almost like watching David Banner turning into the Hulk.

The plumber was convinced that his wife was having an affair. And it didn't matter how often she denied it or professed her love for him, he could not shake the belief that she was unfaithful and the world was laughing at him.

Unpacking more of his past, I learned that his father had run off with another man's wife, scandalising two families. He came back six months later. Forgiven. Impervious. Undeterred. The cycle began again. Another affair. More tears. Recriminations. Humiliations.

The son grew up watching his mother suffer these indignities and vowed it would never happen to him. He'd thought he'd found the perfect woman. She was bright, beautiful and adoring. They were married for fifteen years and had three daughters, but the plumber still suffered from low self-esteem. He took up bodybuilding, punishing himself with heavier and heavier weights. At the same time he grew increasingly critical of how so many young women dressed and acted, spilling out of the pubs on Friday and Saturday nights, going home with strange men. He vowed that his own daughters would turn out differently.

Around this time he became aware that someone connected with his wife's work was spending more time with her. She was a drama teacher and directed a few amateur plays for a local theatre group. He asked her to stop. She couldn't understand why. Slowly the demons entered his mind – the dark thoughts of his wife touching another man – the memories of his father's faithlessness and his mother's tears. He confronted her. She denied it. They stopped having intercourse. He found himself doing all the things his mother used to do – going through pockets, checking receipts, reading emails and text messages.

Then one day he saw his wife talking to a father outside the school gates. She laughed at something the man said and that was enough. The plumber beat him to death in front of a dozen witnesses, most of them children.

'Jealousy,' says Ruiz, filling the kettle. 'Love is either equal or a tragedy.'

'That's very poetic,' I say.

'I must have read it in a fortune cookie.'

Teabags dance at the end of their strings. He takes the milk from the fridge, sniffing the carton before pouring. 'Elizabeth Crowe didn't have anything carved on her forehead.'

'I know.'

'So the only link between the farmhouse murders and Naomi Meredith is the bleach?'

'You think I'm overreaching?'

'It could be a coincidence.'

He's right, but I can see other similarities – less tangible or easy to put into words.

Ruiz gives a heave as though shifting his weight from one shoulder to the other. 'So let's assume you're right and he's targeting unfaithful spouses. How is he finding his victims?'

'Elizabeth Crowe had sex with strangers in public places.'

'She also used an online dating service.'

'DCS Cray is trying to get access to the company's database to check if any of the other victims are registered users.'

There is a muffled cataclysm outside. Raised voices. An argument. Ruiz goes to investigate, calling out from the front door. 'You might want to see this.'

A new-model Jaguar with personalised plates is parked outside the farmhouse. The driver, dressed in a well-cut suit, has a clipboard and seems to be ticking off boxes and scribbling notes. Hovering in the background, Elliot Crowe is dressed in an overcoat that's too heavy for the weather with an upturned collar and his hands deep in the pockets.

'What do you mean, I can't get any money?' he says.

'That's not how it works,' replies the estate agent.

'Just a few thousand up front – this place is worth a shitload.'

'We don't give advances or loans.'

'I'll go to another agent.'

'That's your prerogative, Mr Crowe. Can I look inside?'

Elliot hesitates. 'I need to get the place cleaned up.'

He doesn't see me until the last moment and reacts as though I've jumped out from behind a tree. 'Who the fuck are you?' he demands, scratching at a patchy rash on his neck.

'This is a crime scene, Elliot,' I say. 'Nobody is allowed here without permission.'

'It's my fucking house.'

'Not yet.'

'Do I fucking know you?' he says, trying to shirtfront me. The whites of his eyes look jaundiced and streaked with blood. 'You're trespassing on my property.'

The agent suggests they should leave but Elliot is too busy screaming at me, sending white flecks of spit peppering the air. Ruiz suggests he take a step back and tone down his language.

'You can't tell me what to do! I own this fucking place.'

A woman emerges from the Jaguar. Barefoot and in her late twenties or a decade older, she's wearing a discoloured dress that hangs from her bony frame. The neckline loops low enough to reveal ribs shining through her skin and shoulder blades as sharp as knives.

'Calm down, babe,' she says, putting her arms around Elliot.

'He won't give us the money,' he whines.

She hushes him like a mother placating a sulking child, stroking his hair.

'It's my house,' he says petulantly.

'We'll get it soon.'

I introduce myself. She doesn't give her name.

'I'm sorry for your loss,' I tell Elliot. He shrugs and looks again at the farmhouse.

'I need to get a few things.'

'That won't be possible.'

He looks puzzled then petulant and finally angry. 'You can't stop me.'

'I can,' says Ruiz.

Elliot tries to step around him. Ruiz matches his movements. It's a strange dance, right and left. Elliot threatens to call the police before realising how stupid that sounds.

His girlfriend tugs at his hand. Elliot pushes her away and sees the Jaguar bouncing down the drive. 'Hey! Arsehole! What about us?'

The brake lights flare as the car reaches the road. Elliot looks deflated. 'That's our ride.'

'We can drop you in town,' I offer, glancing at Ruiz, who doesn't seem impressed by the idea. Elliot wants to refuse, but his girlfriend accepts. 'You can call me Ant,' she says. 'It's short for Antoinette.'

I watch her climb into the back seat of Ruiz's car, almost mechanical in her movements, as though her limbs are battery-operated. Her knees, pale as candle-wax, are pressed together and I see the outlines of her bones beneath her skin.

I try to make conversation.

'You were adopted,' I say.

'So?' snaps Elliot.

'How old were you?'

'Nine.'

'That's quite late.'

'I had to wait for my parents to die.' He smiles and fist-bumps with Ant before scratching at his neck again.

'Where were you on the night your mother and sister died?'

'Why do you care?'

'You can tell them, babe,' says Ant. 'I'm not angry any more.'

Elliot fidgets and drums his fingers on his thigh. 'I hooked up with a dancer in Bristol that night.'

'Where did this dancer live?'

'I can't remember. I was wasted. She lived upstairs. Kept cats. The place stank of cat piss.'

'The police haven't managed to find her.'

'Yeah, well, if they do I want her address. The bitch stole my phone.'

'Did you report the theft?'

He shrugs and mumbles, 'Maybe I left it on the bus.'

We're driving through the outskirts of Clevedon, getting closer to the sea. The sky is streaked from edge to edge with pale trails where jets have passed at high altitude.

'Did you get on with your mother?' I ask.

'Which one?'

'Elizabeth.'

Elliot sighs as though exhausted. 'I'm not going to sprinkle sugar on dog-shit. She was a tight-arse who knew where every penny went – and none of it came to me. Look at what she did to my dad. She screwed his best friend and then she screwed him.'

'You knew about the affair?'

'Oh, I knew. I saw them together – kissing in the front seat of her car. She said I was imagining things, but I know what I saw.'

'Did Harper know?' I ask.

Elliot shrugs. 'I didn't tell her. Wish I had now. Then again, it made no difference. She couldn't wait to leave that house. That's why she planned to run away.'

'Harper?'

'Yeah. She and her boyfriend were going to take off and ride a motorbike across the States.'

'When did she tell you this?'

He waves me away dismissively, as though the details are

207

unimportant, but it's something else that Blake Lehmann failed to mention.

'I thought Harper wanted to go to Falmouth University,' I say.

'That was my mother's grand plan. Harper had her sights set on travelling for a year.'

'Who else knew this?'

He bends forward, clutching his stomach, as though his internal organs are persecuting him. His tremors are different from mine. Self-inflicted. Drug-related. Withdrawal symptoms.

'Are you using?' I ask.

'I'm clean.'

'What's wrong, babe?' asks Ant.

'I haven't eaten today.'

The cramps hit him again. He's coming down off something, huffing, puffing. His face is slick with sweat and a fleshy animal stink rises from his overcoat.

'You should see a doctor,' I tell him.

'I don't need a fucking doctor.'

We're near the centre of town, opposite a pub called the Harp.

'You can drop us here,' says Ant.

She opens the door before the car has stopped moving. Elliot trips over the gutter and falls; Ant lets out a squeak and helps him to stand. He looks at his grazed hands as though he's forgotten what they're for. Pedestrians have to step around him.

'I can help you,' I say.

'Good,' says Ant. 'Get out of his house.'

Ruiz pulls away. Turning to watch them through the rear window, I see Elliot and Ant heading for the pub, searching through his pockets for money.

28

Julianne's arm slips through mine as we walk up the steps of
St Michael's Hospital in Bristol and follow the signs to the
pathology screening rooms. She has a particular lightness to her
step, as though feeling positive about today. A young man with
an Abe Lincoln beard is sitting behind a glass partition. He
gives Julianne a form to fill out and we're told to wait in a
small room with chairs and a low table covered in magazines
and medical leaflets.

'Do you want something to read?' I ask.

'No, thank you,' she replies.

'A drink of water?'

'I'm fine.'

'It's going to be all right.'

'I know.'

'What's the oncologist's name?'

'Alex Percival.'

'A man or woman?'

'Woman.'

Outside I can hear a jackhammer thudding into concrete
and vibrating the air. I stand at the window. Men in hard hats,

protective boots and high-visibility vests are digging up the footpath. Some toil, others watch. A bus disgorges passengers. A mother crosses the road holding tightly to a child's hand. Resting my forehead against the glass, I can see the hospital entrance. A middle-aged man and woman are sitting on the steps having a cigarette. Two nurses wave to them as they pass. The world is carrying on. Nature is neither cruel nor capricious. It is indifferent. It doesn't care that my wife has cancer and is waiting for a medical test and contemplating surgery.

The door opens. A West Indian nurse with a lovely lilting accent takes us through to a changing room where Julianne is given a gown and thick socks to keep her feet warm. She begins to undress, slipping out of her summer dress and unhooking her bra. When was the last time I saw her naked? Two years ago.

'You can look away now,' she says, holding her bra against her chest. I turn my back.

'You can look now.'

Standing pigeon-toed in a green gown and socks, she looks like an orphan. I have to wait outside the MRI room, watching as she lies on a narrow bed that slides her into the space-age sarcophagus, which will fire magnetic pulses through her body, examining her inner workings.

Left alone, I begin to daydream. I picture sitting in the doctor's office and getting the news that the tumour has miraculously disappeared. Julianne's ovaries are clear. They are the pinkest, healthiest, most perfect reproductive organs the doctor has ever seen. Other staff members are called in to marvel at the results. Papers are published. Dr Percival is asked to tour. Julianne becomes famous.

An hour later the first part of the daydream is made solid as we wait for the oncologist. Her office walls are decorated with diplomas and photographs. Some of the pictures show a field hospital in Iraq or Afghanistan, or somewhere else with deserts and mountains.

The door opens. Dr Percival peels off a pair of latex gloves and drops them into a HAZARD bin before leaning over her desk. A tiny bird-boned woman with pepper-and-salt hair and veiny white arms, she takes a large white envelope from radiology and reads the report. Glancing up, she cocks her head to one side. 'Joe?'

'Yes.'

'You don't remember me?'

I rack my brain. She prompts me. 'London. Medical school. It must have been . . .'

' . . . 1980,' I say.

'Close enough.'

Her whole face lights up. She shakes my hand and tells me how well I'm looking, which we both know isn't true.

'We were at university together,' I say to Julianne, who has gathered this much. 'But your name wasn't Percival.'

'I married,' says Dr Percival. 'I took my husband's name, which is rather old-fashioned, but I was desperate not to be called Grimes for the rest of my life.'

'Alex Grimes, of course.'

She grimaces and takes a seat. Her hands are resting on the open file. 'How is your father?'

'Semi-retired.'

'I was one of his interns for a while. That was a tough three months.'

'I'm sorry.'

'Not your fault.'

Dr Percival looks at Julianne, who is feeling a little left out. The jackhammer has fallen silent for a moment.

'Right, let's get down to business. We've done all we can to identify and map the tumour. The mass is about seven centimetres, which is what we expected.'

Julianne nods. She's holding my hand.

'I wish to schedule an exploratory laparotomy. I'll make an incision through the abdomen to the ovaries and then, with

211

your permission, I'll try to remove all the visible tumour and see if it has spread any further.'

'What stage?' asks Julianne, struggling to get the words out.

'I can't be certain until I get inside.'

'And my ovaries?'

'I'll remove both ovaries, the uterus and some of the surrounding tissue.'

Julianne's fist tightens around my fingers. Nothing shows on her face.

Dr Percival is still talking. 'After the surgery we'll decide on a programme of chemotherapy.' She looks at me. 'Do you have any questions, Joe?'

I have several hundred but I'm not going to upset Julianne by asking about survival rates and the risk of recurrence.

'Right then,' says the doctor. 'We'll bring you in to hospital on Friday night and operate first thing Saturday morning.'

'So soon,' says Julianne.

'The sooner the better. You'll be in hospital for four to seven days. Initially you'll have an intravenous drip in your arm and a catheter in your bladder and possibly a tube down your nose into your stomach, but these will be removed gradually over a few days. Some women also have calf-compression devices or elastic stockings to keep the blood in their legs circulating. Once you're mobile, we'll take the compression devices off, but you'll still wear the stockings to avoid blood clots.'

There are more instructions, but the words jumble, collapse and wash over me. I cannot believe that something so insidious has taken root inside my beautiful wife and that now they're going to cut her open.

Julianne nudges me. I look up. I've been asked a question.

'I'm sorry.'

'I was talking about her recuperation,' says Dr Percival, 'which normally takes about six weeks. She'll have to take things easy. Avoid heavy lifting. Only gentle exercise. No driving for a month.'

Julianne looks at me. 'Is that OK?'

'Of course.'

'Penetrative sexual intercourse should be avoided for about six weeks. I'm quite strict about that,' says the doctor.

'That's OK, we're not—'

'I'll make sure he keeps his hands off me,' interrupts Julianne.

'Good,' says the doctor, making a note on the file. 'So I'll see you Friday evening. Judy will get you to fill out an admissions form and give you an information pack. If you have any questions, please call the nursing sister. And if you want to talk to a clinical psychologist – someone other than your husband, I mean – we have one on staff.'

'I'll be fine,' says Julianne, sounding more confident.

Dr Percival closes the file and walks us to the door. 'We should catch up,' she says, and I agree, but both of us know it's not going to happen. Too much time has passed and the circumstances aren't right.

Forms are signed and brochures collected before we take the echoing walk and descend in the lift and cross the foyer. I sneak a glance at Julianne. Side by side, we're an odd couple. I resemble a broken-down film director next to his newest leading lady.

'I don't want to go home yet,' she says. 'Let's get a coffee.'

We walk up St Michael's Hill and find a café on the next corner with tables on the footpath beneath an awning. Nurses and hospital workers queue at a hissing machine being operated by a dreadlocked barista who keeps up a constant patter, flirting with the women and winking conspiratorially at the men.

Julianne finds a table while I order at the counter. Waiting my turn and watching the barista's floorshow, I notice Becca Washburn seated in the corner. She's dressed in her nurse's uniform, beige slacks and a blue-and-white-striped blouse with epaulettes on the shoulders. The chair opposite her is empty. Ahead of me in the queue Dominic Crowe is sugaring a coffee and carrying two cups back to the table.

Becca looks up. She sees me and frowns. Dominic follows her gaze and walks over to me.

'Are you following me?' he asks accusingly.

'No.'

'Are you following Becca?'

'I'm here with my wife.' I point to Julianne.

Momentarily lost for words, he eventually mumbles an apology and turns away.

'I thought the family hated you,' I say.

'Mrs Washburn called me this morning. She and Francis had a visitor last night. Elliot came looking for money. Things got a little heated and Francis threatened to call the police. Elliot broke a window and woke the baby. He frightened a family who have been through enough.' Dominic has delivered this explanation with his head down as though unable to look at me. He adds, 'I love my son, but he has a sickness. He's been in rehab twice. Twice. I've been trying to get him a place at a high-dependency unit in Bristol, but there's a waiting list and he needs a court referral.'

'I'm sorry to hear that,' I say. 'Where is Elliot now?'

'I don't know.'

'He came to Windy Hill Farm yesterday looking for money.'

Dominic doesn't reply. He's waiting for me to say something more and looks embarrassed when I don't continue.

'Well, I just thought . . . I didn't want . . . ' Unable to finish, he turns away and crosses the café, looking like the lone survivor of a plane crash, picking his way through the wreckage.

'Who was that?' asks Julianne.

'Someone I met the other day,' I reply.

She cups her hands around the coffee, sipping at the edge. Out of the corner of my eye I see Becca leaving. She doesn't make eye contact. Elsewhere in the café, a young mother navigates an over-sized pram between tables and parks it close to ours. The baby girl is sitting up, chewing on a rusk, her huge brown eyes framed by llama lashes. I glance at Julianne, expecting her to be smiling. Instead I see a single tear wobble free and roll down her cheek. She wipes it away with the side of her hand.

'What's wrong?' I ask.

She shakes her head, not knowing where to begin. 'They're going to take out my uterus.'

'They're cutting out the cancer.'

'A part of me is going to be missing – something that makes me a woman.'

'You don't want any more children.'

'That's not the point.'

She pulls a tissue from her sleeve and blows her nose, balling the soggy paper in her fist. I tell her that being a woman is about more than having babies – she's done that bit. Now she's a parent, which is more important. 'Nothing is going to change. You'll still be the same woman, your mind, your personality, your soul.'

'You don't believe we have a soul.'

'You're the exception.'

29

It rains that night. Water soughs and gurgles down the drainpipes and tumbles over gutters that need cleaning – one of many odd jobs that need doing around the cottage. Hinges need oiling and taps need washers and the vegetable garden is over-grown. I should make a list.

Julianne has gone out this evening. She's telling her closest friends about the surgery, no doubt spinning the news to make herself sound undaunted and upbeat. I know that's not true, but I can understand her motives. Fear is mostly a transient thing – it flashes out of the dark like a car swerving on to the wrong side of the road – and then re-corrects before passing.

Emma is avoiding bedtime. She wants to show me something 'really, really, important'. Dragged into her room, I am made to sit on her bed while she pulls various dresses from her wardrobe as well as her school project – a poster about cloud formations.

'I know why it rains,' she says.

'Good.'

'And I know how babies are made. We had a lesson at school, but I knew already because Samantha Padenstowe told me that boys put their willies inside girls and it makes babies.'

'What did they teach you in class?'

'The lot.'

'So now you know everything?'

'Yep.' She flops on to her bed and stares at the ceiling. 'They told us about puberty and how we get hair down there.' She motions with her head. 'And when you have a baby it's attached by a sort of hose that goes from the belly button and they have to cut it off and tie a knot otherwise the baby's insides will fall out.'

She looks up at me to make sure she's being believed. 'And I know about periods, which are sort of like the cycles of the moon. You once told me the moon was made of cheese and an old man lived there. I guess you lied about that . . . and Santa Claus and the Easter Bunny. I never believed in the Tooth Fairy, so that didn't matter so much.'

'I'm sorry for lying.'

'That's OK. I guess there are good lies and bad lies.'

Emma has always been the worrier in the family. Depending upon what news headline she overhears she will fixate on global warming or planes disappearing or terrorist attacks. She was a late child, longed for and then arriving just when we'd almost given up hope of having a second.

'Is Mummy going to die?' she asks, giving me a clinical stare.

'No.'

'Is that one of your good lies?'

'It's the truth.'

'So what about this operation?'

'She's going to need lots of help for a while. We'll all have to pitch in and do the chores.'

'OK, but I can't go in the garden shed.'

'Why not?'

'Spiders.'

I leave her tidying up her clothes and rearranging her stuffed toys.

Charlie's bedroom door is open. She's sitting on her bed,

knees up, typing on her laptop, texting on her phone and watching TV – multitasking in the modern age. She mutes the TV when I knock. I glance at the flickering screen and see images from Syria, Iraq or Ukraine. They seem to be recycling the news these days, repeating wars like old episodes of *The Simpsons*.

'So what really happened at the hospital?' she asks.

'Mum told you.'

'I want to hear it from you.'

I sit on the edge of the bed and look at her feet. Her toenails are painted black and look diseased but I won't comment because I know nothing about fashion trends or make-up.

'She goes into hospital on Friday evening and they'll operate first thing Saturday.'

'They're going to take the cancer out.'

'That's the plan.'

Charlie raises her chin and gives me her serious look. 'Has Mummy been crying?'

'She's sad about leaving you and Emma.'

'But it's only for a few days, right?'

'Right.'

Her gaze wavers and she fiddles with a loose thread on the hem of her track pants. 'I don't know what I'm supposed to be doing,' she whispers.

'Doing?'

'What's my job? What do I say?'

'You don't have to *do* or say anything.'

'This is serious shit.'

'I know.'

For a moment we're becalmed. In the wastepaper basket beside the bed I notice a broken china figurine of a horse rider who no longer sits astride her horse. I wonder if it was broken by accident or out of frustration. When I ask Charlie, she changes the subject. 'Why do you think Mummy asked you to come back?'

'I guess she wants me here.'

'Why?'

'To look after things, Emma, you . . . '

'I don't need looking after.'

'I know.'

'What about afterwards – when she's well again?'

'I'm trying not to think too far ahead.'

'It must be hard.'

'What?'

'Marrying someone who decides they don't need you any more, but then they decide they do. I don't think I'll ever understand.'

'You'll fall in love one day.'

Charlie dismisses the notion. Hair falls across her face. 'I can't imagine getting married – telling someone I belong to them and they belong to me.' Unexpectedly, she changes direction. 'Are you taking Mummy out to dinner?'

'Yes. Tomorrow.'

'That's good. You have to woo her. Try to be romantic.'

'I think we're past the wooing stage.'

Charlie gets cross. 'Do you *want* to be alone forever? Do you? Huh? Mummy must still love you. It's not like she's found anyone else. Not lately.'

'Lately?'

'You know what I mean. And it's not like you're dating.'

'How would you know?'

'I've seen your wardrobe. This is your chance to win her back.'

My daughter is giving me dating advice – can it get any worse?

'Maybe we shouldn't be having this conversation,' I say.

Charlie sits up straighter. 'I'm not doing this for you. I'm doing it for Emma and me. Someone has to sort out this family.'

I laugh but Charlie doesn't get cross. Instead she leans against me and I put my chin on the top of her head.

'Can I come with you tomorrow?' she asks.

'I'm working.'

'I thought maybe I could help you. I could be your driver. I could run errands.'

'It's a murder investigation.'

'I know, but I'm going to university in October. You don't have to shield me from things.'

Yes, I do, I want to say, but hold my tongue.

'You should be hanging out with your friends.'

'They're busy,' she replies.

'Weren't you and Bridget planning a trip to Paris?'

'She found a boyfriend.'

'You could find a boyfriend.'

'Good idea – I'll order one online from ASOS.'

'What about Nina or Jade?'

'They're working.'

'Matilda?'

'Away.'

Charlie sits up and brushes hair from her face, so she can fix me with both eyes. 'This is really important to me.'

'Why?'

'We haven't spent enough time together, you know. You've been in London and I've been at school.'

Is she trying to guilt me into this?

'We're spending time together now.'

She pauses as though marshalling her arguments, biting her bottom lip and leaving pale teeth marks in the pinkness. 'You wanted to know what I'm going to study at university.' Another hesitation. 'I've accepted an offer to study experimental psychology at Oxford.'

'You want to be a psychologist?'

She nods.

'Why?'

'It interests me. I want to get a doctorate and then study forensic psychology.'

My first reaction is to say no. I want to argue. I want to

stop her. She's making a mistake. Forensic psychology is brutal. It's about delving into the worst of human behaviour – socio-paths, psychopaths, rapists, paedophiles, abused children, victims of violence . . . it takes a toll. It diminishes.

'Do you understand what a forensic psychologist does?'

'Yes.'

'When you say you're "interested" . . . ?'

'I want to understand why people do things – the good and bad. It's like you and Great-Aunt Gracie.'

She's referring to my maternal grandmother's youngest sister, who died at the age of eighty, having not set foot outside her house in nearly sixty years. A classic agoraphobic, she burned to death in a house fire rather than risk going outside. Gracie is the reason I became a psychologist.

Charlie is still talking. 'I also want to understand why someone would hurt another human being . . . would kidnap them . . . hold them in the dark. Why they would fantasise about doing horrible things.'

My heart flips over. When Charlie was twelve she was abducted and kept chained to a radiator with masking tape wrapped around her head. Blind, trapped, breathing through a hosepipe, she spent two days in that hell before I could find her. That was six years ago – a third of a lifetime for Charlie and I had always hoped, no prayed, that these events had been locked away in a safe place where they couldn't hurt her. I wanted Gideon Tyler to become like a fairytale villain from a bedtime story – the big bad wolf or the wicked witch – but Charlie must have gone over and over those events, trying to decide whether she was to blame, wondering if there was something written on her skin, some sign or mark that had singled her out. Nothing traumatic is ever truly forgotten. *Beware the Jabberwock . . . the jaws that bite, the claws that catch!*

I should have seen this coming. Picked up the signals. Spent more time with Charlie. Instead I failed her. What sort of

221

psychologist doesn't recognise post-traumatic stress in his own daughter?'

'Let's talk about this tomorrow,' I say softly.

Charlie's eyes cloud and she reacts as though I've shoved her in the chest.

'Please don't get upset,' I say. 'I don't want you delving into terrible crimes. I don't want you *thinking* about them. You're eighteen. The world shouldn't be a dark and dangerous place for you.'

'The world is what it is,' she says.

'You're right, but I'm frightened by what I do. I rage against it. My guts churn. I have nightmares. You've made a mistake, Charlie. Reconsider. Choose something else. Please.'

Her arms are braced and shaking from the strain. She tilts her head and sways infinitesimally from side to side. 'Am I allowed to speak?'

I nod.

'So you're telling me that I can't study psychology?'

Her tone is one of indignation, without any ranting, stamping theatrics.

'I don't think you appreciate or understand—'

'Oh, I understand,' she says. 'You think I'm some silly teenager who can't make a decision without Daddy. Or maybe you think I'm not strong enough because I'm a girl.'

'That's got nothing—'

'You had your turn,' she says, cutting me off. 'How dare you tell me what I can or cannot do! You haven't been here for the past six years. In case you haven't realised – I grew up. I can do what I damn well please.'

'Maybe when you're older—'

'Oh, good, play that card! How's that going for you – being so old and wise? From where I'm sitting, I see someone who lives alone in a shitty flat and is still in love with a woman who booted him out six years ago and who only wants him back because she's terrified.' Charlie's whole body is trembling. 'So

I have a frightened mother and a frightened father. What sort of children will they produce, I wonder. You're the psychologist – you tell me.'

She pauses, but I'm not sure if I'm supposed to answer.

'Well, I refuse to be scared,' says Charlie, her voice so thick with fluid I know she's about to cry. 'I haven't forgotten what happened to me – I think of it every day – and that doesn't bother me. *You're* the one with the problem – not me.'

I feel paralysed with dismay, not daring to move for fear of bringing more of Charlie's distress crashing down around my unwilling ears. When did fatherhood take on such an ugly, distorted shape?

'Get out of my room,' she whispers, unable to look at me.

I close the door behind me, breathless at how far I've fallen in my daughter's eyes.

There is a passage in the Bible – Ecclesiastes 3:1–15 – about there being a time for everything. 'A time to be born, a time to die, a time to weep and a time to laugh, a time to kill, a time to heal . . . '

Everybody knows that passage, even if it's just from the Byrds song, which protested against the Vietnam War. The real passage was never about peace. People do that all the time – hijack slogans and twist history.

Life is a matter of timing. A good joke is a matter of timing. Pregnancy is a matter of timing. Take right now. Across the street, a waitress is setting tables at a restaurant. Pale-skinned and green-eyed, she has peroxided hair, dark brows and a shiny forehead. A different evening, another hour, a minute earlier or later, and I might not have noticed her. But now I have. Timing is everything.

The name on her blouse says Kamila and she's from Warsaw, via Munich. She's married, but she's sleeping with her foreign language teacher – the man who taught her English at a college in Bristol. He has a wife and three children, but it hasn't stopped him giving his students private tuition.

I wait to be seated and watch as she moves between customers, pushing a strand of hair from her forehead and tucking it behind her ear.

'Table for one?' she asks, her accent still thick, her mouth not eager to smile, her face not quite finished, as though God had decided to down tools for the evening and forgotten to come back and complete the task.

'Can I get you something to drink?' she asks, after showing me to a table.

I open my mouth but nothing comes out. She waits, eyebrows raised.

'Water,' I say.

'OK, that narrows it down. Still or sparkling?'

'Tap is fine.'

'That wasn't so hard now, was it?'

She's making fun of me. I silently seethe.

Kamila looks different from when I saw her last. Her hair is longer and she's wearing less make-up. She doesn't remember me, but that's understandable. We were never formally introduced. I didn't shake her hand or make small talk. I could see she was nervous — most of them are when they're fucking someone in secret.

That was five months ago. I don't know if Kamila is still sleeping with her language teacher. It doesn't matter to me if it was a one-night stand or a weekly date. She made her bed and she can die in it.

When I finish the meal, I go to the register. Handing over twenty pounds, I scoop coins from my pocket and begin counting them out on my palm. She waits, making me feel like a pensioner paying with coppers at a supermarket checkout. I give her the coins and watch her re-count them. My cheeks are glowing.

'Have a nice evening,' she says glibly.

Fuck, no! *I want to scream.* I've decided to have a shitty evening. I want to wipe that smirk off your face. I want to teach you a lesson.

That word 'want' seems to goad me. I want so much. My share. More. I want to punish those who lie and cheat. My wants have become needs and then necessities and finally a matter of life or death, as my vision clouds and my heart races and I must put my forearm around someone's throat and begin to squeeze.

Kamila reminds me of a girl I used to know at school. Rachel Belinsky was three years below me and only thirteen, but looked much older. She was up for it, you know, hot to trot. We were behind the grandstand at the Creek during a football game between Bristol Manor Farm and Bishop Sutton. Rachel offered to blow me for a tenner. She unzipped my fly and opened her mouth, but I kept thinking of my mum and Mr Shearer and the accident. Nothing happened. Rachel laughed at me. Next thing I had my hands around her neck and she blacked out. I spent the next two weeks waiting for the police to knock on my door, but nobody came. Either she didn't complain or nobody believed her or she was too busy spending my tenner. After a month I began to relax. I'd been stupid. It wouldn't happen again.

Standing in a doorway across the road, I wait in the shadows until Kamila finishes her shift. I see her collecting her money, questioning her share of tips, saying goodbye to the others. She pulls on a cardigan and walks to the bus stop.

What shall I do?

– Follow her home.

No, it's too soon.

– When?

Tomorrow.

30

I can hear Charlie crying. The noise seems to flow down the throat of the chimney and through the wall, every sob unzipping a part of me until I feel excoriated and exposed.

Julianne arrives home just after eleven. I hear her key in the lock and her weight on the stairs. I meet her on the landing.

'Is everything all right?' she asks.

'Charlie is upset.'

'What happened?'

'I screwed up!'

Julianne hesitates. She motions me to her room and closes the door. I sit on the bed while she removes her make-up. I feel as though I'm striking a match at the opening of a cave, uncertain what lies inside.

'Charlie has applied to study psychology,' I say. 'It's because of what happened – the kidnapping. I tried to talk her out of it. I messed it up.'

Julianne doesn't react. She splashes water on her cheeks and buries her face in a towel. The slightest nod of sympathy or understanding will bring me grovelling to my knees.

'I'm sorry,' I say. 'This is my fault.'

'You really have to stop blaming yourself for everything,' she says, matter-of-factly.

'What?'

'Charlie made this decision – not you.'

'When did you know?'

'I didn't – not for certain – but she's been borrowing books from the library and sneaking them into the house.'

'What sort of books?'

'Criminology. Psychology.'

'Why didn't you tell me?'

She shrugs. 'I thought Charlie might satisfy her curiosity and move on.'

'Are you disappointed?'

'There are worse reasons to study a subject,' she says, squeezing a splodge of toothpaste on to her electric brush. 'I don't care if she's a firefighter or a schoolteacher or a penniless poet – as long as she's happy.'

I contemplate this as she brushes her teeth, wondering why I'm so upset. Was I worried what Julianne would say, or is this *my* problem? Am I frightened for Charlie or for me?

Julianne rinses, spits and rinses again. 'Have you noticed how Charlie dresses quite modestly, compared to her friends?'

'She's always been body-conscious.'

'No, I think it's more than that. She rarely goes to dances or parties. She likes old romantic movies and Hollywood musicals.'

'What's your point?'

'Charlie hasn't had a boyfriend since she was fifteen – and even then it was that deadbeat Jacob, who abandoned her in London. He was the "test" – all girls bring at least one bad boyfriend home.'

'Did you?'

'Absolutely.' She nudges the bathroom door, which half closes. 'I think Charlie was more affected by what happened than either of us realise. She's still looking for answers.'

228

I hear the toilet flush. Julianne comes into the bedroom.

'Charlie wants to come with me tomorrow – as my driver,' I say.

'Will she be safe?'

'Of course.'

'Maybe she needs to spend more time with you.'

'Should I try to talk her out of studying psychology?'

'Don't talk. Listen.'

31

Ronnie Cray calls me early next morning. I can hear phones ringing in the background and the clacking of keyboards.

'Theo Meredith has been cleared,' she says, eating breakfast as she talks. 'He trains greyhounds and was picking up a new dog in Dorset on Tuesday afternoon. We've confirmed that he didn't get home until seven, expecting Naomi to be there. He assumed she had gone out on an errand and didn't start to worry until nine o'clock, when she wasn't home or answering her mobile. He began calling her friends and family.'

Cray pauses, takes another mouthful . . . 'And you might be right about the adultery angle. Naomi started an affair with her boss more than a year ago.'

'The veterinarian?'

'He's married with three kids. His eldest girl is only two years younger than Naomi – randy bugger!'

'Who told you?'

'Naomi's best friend.'

'Where was this vet on Tuesday evening?'

'Nestling in the loving bosom of his wife.'

'Did he meet Naomi online?'

'She answered a job advertisement in the local paper.'

'What about having sex in public?'

'The office sofa was more his speed.'

Cray crumples greased paper next to the phone and belches softly. She gives me a progress report on the other victims – different towns, different jobs, no links between them.

'Turns out adultery isn't a popular topic of conversation,' she says. 'We do have one new lead. Remember Dominic Crowe's former business partner?'

'Jeremy Egan.'

'His wife changed her statement last night. She says Egan wasn't at home on the night Elizabeth and Harper Crowe were killed.'

'Why did she give him an alibi?'

'He promised to stop sleeping around.'

'And what does Egan have to say?'

'Lawyered up the moment we came knocking and declined to give us a DNA sample.'

'Did you ask him about Tuesday?'

'Says he was working late.'

'With his secretary?'

'How did you know?'

'Lucky guess.'

Cray has to go. We agree to talk later. I knock gently on Charlie's door. She's awake.

'You're not dressed,' I say.

'Why?'

'I need a driver.'

Wearing her best jeans, a long-sleeved T-shirt and a short leather jacket, Charlie sits forward in the seat with her back straight and both hands on the wheel. She drives with assured movements, one hand touching the other as she corners the Volvo. I wonder what happened to the gangly adolescent whose limbs were like rogue knights rebelling against the Crown.

I know she wants to ask me about the case, but she won't because she's worried that I might change my mind. Instead she talks generally about criminal behaviour. She asks me my opinions on Eysenck's 'Trait Theory' – the view that criminality is the product of biological and psychological traits rather than rational choice. It is the age-old nature versus nurture debate that's been played out for two centuries.

'I've read about phrenology,' she says, 'but that seems a bit primitive – reading bumps on people's heads doesn't sound very scientific.'

'Not when we can map the human genome.'

'Exactly.'

'Most trait theorists don't suggest that a single biological or psychological feature can explain criminality,' I say. 'Each of us has a unique set of characteristics that explain behaviour. Some people might inherit criminal tendencies, some have neuro-logical problems, some have blood chemistry disorders and some have shitty childhoods.'

'But it's not predetermined?'

'A few people think so, but it's not the mainstream belief.'

Just after nine o'clock we pull up outside a ramshackle group of buildings and pole sheds on the eastern approach to Bristol Airport. The sign on the gate says *Vale Boarding Kennels and Cattery*. As the engine dies, the dogs start barking – one setting off the other.

'You should wait in the car,' I say to Charlie.

'How long will you be?'

'That depends on whether they talk to me.'

Opening a painted iron gate, I walk through a neat garden to the door of the house. A young woman constable answers my knock. She's been appointed as the family's liaison officer, assigned to keep them briefed on the investigation and keep the media at bay.

'The guv said you might come,' she says, glancing past me. 'We had reporters outside until midnight. I expect they'll be back.'

A gruff male voice calls from inside. 'Who is it?'

'It's not a reporter,' the constable replies, looking at me apologetically.

I step fully into the small cluttered sitting room. Introductions are made. Naomi's father is a big square-headed man with hair shorn down to stubble and farmer's hands, calloused and scarred by machines. His name is Tony and he scrutinises me with jittering, hopeful eyes, as though wishing I might bring him news that a mistake has been made and his daughter is still alive. His wife, Lorraine, is smaller, diminished, with brittle grey hair and a beak-like nose.

'A psychologist – what good are you?' she says, before raising her hand, embarrassed by the harshness of her own question.

'I'll make a pot of tea,' suggests the constable, disappearing into the kitchen.

Lowering myself into an armchair, I sink into the worn cushion until my bum feels as if it's touching the floor. There are family photographs on the mantelpiece and side table – and someone has pulled several albums from the bookshelf and opened them on the coffee table.

'I'm hoping you might tell me about Naomi,' I say. 'It can help me understand what happened.'

'Understand?'

'By knowing Naomi, I move a step closer to knowing the man who did this to her,' I explain.

Tony raises his eyebrows. 'You think she knew him?'

'I think he followed her. I think he knew where she lived.'

'Our Naomi doesn't mix with people like that,' says Lorraine.

'People like what?'

'Perverts. Rapists.'

'Naomi wasn't raped,' says Tony, as though wanting it made clear.

I begin gently, asking if they'll show me the albums. Lorraine lets me sit beside her on the sofa. She turns the pages, pointing to pictures and telling me the stories behind them. Naomi is their youngest. Her two brothers are both married and have children. One lives in Scotland and the other in New York.

'They're due to arrive today,' says Lorraine, pointing to a picture of her three children together.

I hear about Naomi's childhood. How she lost her milk teeth early but had zero cavities. How she once met the Queen and won a short-story competition and was bridesmaid at two weddings on the same day. Naomi had asthma as a child but the attacks reduced in her teens. She went to a local Catholic primary school but followed her friends to the nearest comprehensive. After finishing her A-levels she spent a year as a house-mother at a boarding school in Scotland. Later she did a secretarial course and got a job as a receptionist at an animal hospital in Weston-super-Mare.

Bright. Funny. Shy. Self-conscious. She thought she was over-weight, but none of the diets ever seemed to work. She loved vintage clothes and spent a lot of time scouring second-hand shops and online sellers, looking for dresses and jackets.

Lorraine has some more photographs on her phone. They show Naomi dressed up in some of her buys, smiling at the camera. Until now, I haven't appreciated how much joy existed in this young woman. She had a different personality from Elizabeth or Harper. Elizabeth was blessed with natural poise and charm – aware of how her physical looks and personality could captivate someone. Naomi was always surprised when boys showed an interest in her.

She met her husband, Theo, at a church social when they were both in their early twenties. He was her first proper boyfriend. They married in 2009 and rented a cottage in Cleeve.

I ask if Naomi was streetwise and perceptive? Would she make eye contact with a stranger, or look away? Would she struggle or fight back?

'My girl would have fought,' says Tony. 'We didn't teach her to be pushed around.'

'Would she have talked to him?'

'She was a friendly girl.'

'Flirtatious?'

His voice hardens. 'Friendly.'

My mind goes back to the churchyard. Why did he choose that place? Most predators trawl busy footpaths or well-used shortcuts. This man didn't watch a dozen women walk past and wait for the one that matched his fantasy. He followed Naomi. Either that or he knew she was coming. If he caught the bus, someone must have noticed him. If he waited in the graveyard he risked being seen.

'I have to ask you a difficult question, but it's important otherwise I wouldn't be here. Was Naomi seeing anyone else?'

Tony bristles. 'She was a good girl.'

'She loved Theo,' says his wife. 'They were trying for a baby.'

'You see, I'm trying to understand why her attacker carved the letter "A" into her forehead.'

The couple don't answer. They *can't* answer. A daughter isn't likely to tell her parents about an illicit love affair. She will let them think she's the same sweet girl they raised to be polite, proper and to make them proud. Every parent makes excuses for their children. We mitigate. We forgive. We change the narrative. All because their blood is our blood. Hope springs eternal in the human breast. Tomorrow is another day. Next year will be better. We will save money, lose weight, quit smoking, exercise more, fall in love and be fulfilled.

These are my thoughts as I leave the house and walk through the garden. Charlie has been at the kennels, putting her fingers through the wire mesh, accepting licks from the dogs. I wave and she acknowledges me, walking across the damp grass. In the meantime, a vehicle pulls up and parks beside the Volvo. Father Abermain is dressed in his usual attire, neatly pressed black trousers and a white open-necked shirt with small gold crosses pinned upon each collar.

I say good morning and he smiles – an automatic response from someone who must meet so many people in his job.

'Professor Joe O'Loughlin. We met briefly on Tuesday – at the Crowe funerals,' I say.

'Of course, of course,' he says, shaking my hand. I can see him making a conscious effort to memorise my name for next time.

'I didn't realise that you knew Naomi's family,' I say.

'Yes, for many years. Naomi used to help run my Sunday scripture classes.'

'When was that?'

'Before she married.'

Extremely precise in his movements and speech, Father Abermain is, I suspect, the sort of person who revels in being needed, but once the miracle has been worked he loses interest and moves on. Maybe that's my natural scepticism at work, rather than any prejudice against organised religion.

'When did you see Naomi last?' I ask.

He contemplates the question, drumming his fingers on his chin. 'Oh, let's see, a month ago. My cat was sick. I took him to my vet. I had no idea Naomi was working there. I barely recognised her. So grown-up.'

'You didn't officiate at her wedding?'

'No, I wasn't asked.' He looks up at the house, keen to get inside.

'There's a question I wanted to ask, Father. As a priest, have you ever been asked to perform an exorcism?'

'Pardon?'

'Drive out a demon . . . clear a haunted house.'

His face has a chiselled quality and his eyes seem to stare straight through me as though my skull were made of glass.

'Are you making fun of me, Professor?'

'No.'

He glances towards the house again. 'I have a grieving family to comfort, so if you'll excuse me—'

'No.'

'What?'

236

'I won't excuse you.'

He opens his mouth to protest, but I speak first. 'You see, Father, I've been reviewing the investigation into the farmhouse murders. I was talking to Becca Washburn the other day and she mentioned that Elizabeth thought her house was haunted. Then I got to wondering why a Bible would be open on the coffee table and candles arranged around the room.'

The priest doesn't answer. Sensing the situation, Charlie has changed direction and veered towards a nearby fence, where two horses are grazing. Father Abermain hasn't spoken, but his mouth moves silently as though I'm watching a film with the sound turned down.

'The police pulled fingerprints from the Bible,' I say. 'They haven't matched them to anyone yet, but I doubt if they have *your* prints on file. You could always offer to give them a set – just to eliminate yourself from the investigation.'

His eyes look scorched. 'I don't know what you're talking about. I don't need to be eliminated.'

'You're right. I'm sure the police will understand why you haven't come forward.' I pause, studying him. 'Why is that exactly?'

He sighs raggedly. 'This is highly embarrassing. I've been awfully foolish. Elizabeth thought the farmhouse had a ghost. I told her she was imagining things, but she wasn't a woman to be trifled with. She kept badgering me, insisting I help. I was passing that evening. I dropped by and said a prayer, sprinkled holy water through the rooms and blessed some candles.'

'What time was that?'

'Nine-thirty.'

'What time did you leave?'

'Ten-fifteen.'

'You seem very sure of the times.'

'I was home by ten-thirty.'

'Can anyone vouch for that?'

'I live alone. My housekeeper only comes in during the day.'

The priest runs his tongue over his teeth as though polishing his smile.

'Did you find any ghosts at the farmhouse?'

Abermain stiffens. 'By all means make fun of me, Professor, but don't demean my faith.'

'You conducted an exorcism.'

'I blessed a house.'

'And then lied to the police.'

'I wasn't asked. I know that sounds like a feeble excuse . . . '

'Yes, it does – a coward's excuse. You cared more about your reputation than helping solve this case.'

He lowers his eyes as though accepting his penance.

'Were you sleeping with Elizabeth?'

'What?' His nostrils swell.

'I'm sorry if I've offended you, Father, but the police will ask you the same question.'

'That's an outrageous slur!' His eyes are fixed on mine. 'I took a vow of celibacy when I became a priest. I have honoured that vow.'

'What is your attitude towards adultery?'

'It's a sin against God and a betrayal of someone you have sworn to love and honour.'

'Elizabeth Crowe was unfaithful to her husband.'

'I will not speak ill of the dead, Professor.'

'She will answer to God.'

'Just as you and I will.'

'Do you counsel adulterers to repent?'

'Of course.'

'But you forgive them.'

'Our Lord absolves sinners who are truly sorry.'

'The get-out-of-Hell-free card.'

'I didn't come here to have my faith questioned by you or anyone else. A family needs comforting.'

Turning quickly, he walks up the path and opens the painted gate. At the front door he knocks and waits, glancing back at me. He no longer bears the serene smile of a man who has banished from his life all doubt or uncertainty. Instead I can almost hear something rattling inside him, shaken loose by his fall from grace.

He calls out: 'Are you going to tell the police?'

'Yes.'

'Will you let me talk to them first?'

'You have until midday.'

32

Perched on a promontory overlooking the Severn Estuary, the Walton Park Hotel resembles the setting for an Agatha Christie story where a body will be found washed up on the rocks or poisoned in the pantry.

Bennie is standing beside the unmarked police car like a soldier on sentry duty. Although in uniform, she's hasn't had time to pin up her hair. I suddenly remember where I first saw her – at the public meeting in Clevedon. She had been dressed in civvies with her hair down, standing near the back of the hall, filming Milo Coleman with her mobile phone.

I look for DCS Cray. She's talking on her phone in the shade, crushing chestnut husks beneath her shoes as she paces up and down.

'Yes, sir, I understand . . . if I just had more resources . . . we believe they are linked, sir . . . bleach, that's right . . . Yes . . . with more time and personnel we could find more links . . . Yes, sir, I appreciate the constraints . . . I understand . . . I'll keep you appraised.'

Bennie pretends not to listen.

'I don't even know your proper name,' I say.

'PC Benjamin, sir,' she replies.

'Your first name.'

'Emily, but everyone calls me Bennie.'

'How long have you known Milo Coleman?'

Her whole face seems to spasm. She glances at DCS Cray. 'We've met.'

'Does the DCS know that you're seeing him socially?'

Bennie is breathing hard, her throat aflame. 'We're just friends . . . I mean . . . I've only been out with him a few times.'

I don't answer. She wants to explain. 'I know the guv hates Milo, but he isn't so bad — a bit full of himself, but he's not trying to sabotage the investigation.'

'He's scaring people.'

'Milo thinks the investigation should be more proactive. He says we should be challenging the killer. Rattling his cage.'

'And what do you think?'

She shrugs hesitantly, her eyes shining. 'Please don't tell the guv. I don't want to lose my job.'

Cray has finished her phone call. She jams the phone into the pocket of her jacket.

'Trouble?' I ask.

'Bannerman did a radio editorial this morning calling for me to be replaced, which prompted the Chief Constable to issue a statement saying he has every confidence in me.'

'Oh.'

'Yeah.'

We both know the subtext. In football parlance, whenever a club chairman expresses full confidence in a football manager, that manager's days tend to be numbered.

A sigh inflates and deflates her lungs. 'There's something else. The Chief Constable doesn't want us linking the farmhouse murders and these attacks. He says the bleach isn't a strong enough connection.'

'What about Harper Crowe being choked?'

241

'He doesn't think it's relevant. He wants a separate team to take over the Naomi Meredith investigation and the choking attacks. I'm to concentrate on the farmhouse killings.'

'So why are we here?' I ask.

'Personal curiosity,' replies Cray. She glances across the parking area. 'Is that your Charlie?'

'She's my chauffeur for the day.'

'Is she old enough?'

'Eighteen.'

'Must make you feel old.'

'Just one more thing.'

Leaving the parking area, we walk through a grove of trees and emerge on to Walton Green, which slopes steeply towards the sea. Early summer flowers are growing in sunnier corners, yellow-tipped daisies and bloated dandelions. Two council gardeners are mowing the grass, turning in their seats to check the line of the previous cut. Moths and other insects fly up as the mower passes.

Cray unfurls a satellite map on a park bench, showing me this stretch of coastline. 'You asked about the attack on June sixth. The victim was Maggie Dutton, aged thirty-one, married, one child. Her husband is working in Saudi Arabia. Short-term contract. Big money. No tax. Maggie is a bookkeeper. She lives in Clevedon and walks most weekends, often with other ramblers but sometimes on her own. Portishead to Clevedon is one of her favourite walks. It's about six miles. On Saturday the sixth of June she had lunch at a café in Portishead and started along the coastal path just after two o'clock.'

The map bulges in the breeze and I help hold it down. Cray runs her finger along the line of the footpath. 'Four other walkers have come forward to say they saw her along the way – two passed her at the lighthouse, and others at the Redcliff Bay Caravan site and Charlcombe Wood. A woman at the caravan park saw Maggie filling up her water canteen from a tap. That was at three-thirty, so she was making good time. We don't know exactly what time she reached Ladye Bay, but we estimate about five o'clock.

'We don't know if the attacker waited for Maggie or followed her from Portishead,' says Cray. 'None of the witnesses reported seeing anyone loitering on the footpath that afternoon.'

Folding the map, she leads me along the path where sunlight filters through the hawthorn bushes on either side that form a green gorge, sculptured in places by the weather. The footpath opens out into a view over a pretty bay with craggy cliffs, shallow caves and boulders. Beneath us the outgoing tide has laid bare a widening strip of shingle.

We've reached an old toilet block, shaped like a turret and built from the same grey stone as most of Clevedon's historic buildings. Now abandoned, the windows are bricked up and the gutters rusting. Continuing along the footpath, we come to an intersecting track. A right turn takes us up steps to the nearest road. A left turn leads to the beach. The main footpath continues straight on and begins to climb higher up the cliff, entering a dense grove of trees.

'We think she was attacked here,' says Cray, pausing near the summit. 'She was choked unconscious and dragged off the path into those trees. He bound her wrists and ankles with masking tape and carved the letter into her forehead.'

Sections of the undergrowth open up beneath the trees where the ground is pitted with old animal burrows. I crouch down beneath the lowest branches, discovering a pocket of isolation, invisible from every side except the water. I try to picture what happened. There was no initial exchange, no greeting or conversation. He struck quickly from behind, before she could raise the alarm.

Below us on the beach two teenage boys are throwing a Frisbee and a rock fisherman has set up a tripod to hold his rod. A small boat, fat-bellied and brightly painted, is bobbing on the swell.

DCS Cray is still talking. 'There were three people on the

beach when it happened. Two of them were rock climbers practising on the traverse. The other was a woman walking her dog. None of them saw Maggie, but the woman thought she heard someone shouting from the direction of the path.'

'Did forensics come up with anything?'

'A few shoeprints and scuff marks.'

'DNA?'

'No.'

'And you've interviewed her?'

'Twice. She's become less and less cooperative. Wants to forget.'

'Who found her?'

'Two fisherman were heading down to the bay. They found Maggie curled up and crying in the undergrowth. She had managed to remove the masking tape from her mouth, but couldn't see where to go because of the blood in her eyes.'

Retracing our steps, we reach the intersecting path and climb the steps to the road.

'Was Maggie Dutton having an affair with anyone?' I ask.

'She denies it, but her husband is away for months at a time.'

'You think she got lonely.'

'It happens.'

'What about the other victims?'

'Unswervingly uncooperative.'

Somewhere high in the firmament, a hawk cries out and a Union Jack flutters and snaps on a flagpole.

'There are likely to be others,' I say. 'People who haven't come forward.'

'We're making enquiries,' says Cray. 'Looking at the obvious places – hospitals, medical clinics, women's shelters, marriage counsellors . . . '

'What about the online dating service Elizabeth used?'

'The company is based offshore. The registered address is a post office box in Bermuda, but we've tracked down one of the directors. He told us to talk to his lawyers, so I'm trying a different approach. I've told him that the media might appreciate a story linking an online dating service with a double murder and a series of mutilations.'

'How did he react?'

'A change of heart is imminent.'

Cray has been glancing around casually, but her eyes now meet mine. 'I had another thought last night,' she says. 'I was trying to think outside the box – to look at things from another angle.'

'And?'

'What if Elizabeth Crowe killed Harper?'

'Why?'

'Hear me out. We know she hated her ex-husband. It was like the Wars of the Roses between them. What if she wanted to punish Dominic Crowe by killing their daughter? Look at how carefully Harper was left – with the teddy bear tucked under her arm and her hands folded. A mother would know her favourite childhood toy.'

'And then what?'

'Dominic Crowe turned up. He saw what Elizabeth had done and went berserk, stabbing her to death in a rage.'

'There's no proof that Elizabeth called Dominic that night.'

'They talked earlier. Fought.'

'I can't see it,' I say. 'There's no evidence of depression or a mental disorder. They weren't involved in a bitter custody battle. Harper was about to leave home and go to university.'

The DCS accepts the logic of this with a shrug as though it was worth a try. Dandelion seeds swirl around her like summer snow.

'I bumped into Dominic Crowe yesterday,' I say. 'He and Becca Washburn were having coffee at a café near St Michael's Hospital. They looked rather cosy.'

Cray raises her eyebrows. 'You think they're seeing each other?'

'I think they're closer than we imagine.'

Her limestone-blue eyes linger on mine, trying to reach inside my mind. 'I'll get someone to pull Becca's phone records.'

I glance at my watch. It's just gone midday. 'You might also want to check out Father Abermain.'

'The priest!'

'He was at the farmhouse on the night of the murders. Elizabeth thought the place was haunted. She asked him to exorcise her demons – literally not figuratively.'

'So the candles and the Bible . . . '

'Some form of blessing.'

'Why didn't he come forward?'

'I'm sure you'll ask him.'

Cray turns away from me, moving as ponderously as a knight walking in a full suit of armour. On the edge of the horizon, a container ship barely seems to be moving, as though pinned between the sea and the sky like a drop of moisture trapped between two panes of glass.

Having done a circuit, we arrive back at the cars where Bennie and Charlie are chatting as though old friends. My shirt is damp with perspiration and clinging to my back.

Cray has walked under the tree again, tucking one thumb into her belt as she talks on her mobile. She's reporting Father Abermain, spinning another thread in an investigation that has spread her resources so thinly there is no strength left in the web.

The farmhouse is empty today. The psychologist must be busy elsewhere. He has some sort of shaking disorder or strange palsy, Parkinson's perhaps — not a death sentence, but he'll die sooner than he expects. He'll lose his balance and fall under a car or a train. Either that or he'll aspirate food into his lungs and die of pneumonia or another pulmonary condition.

I have watched the house for the past hour, making sure nobody is home. Moving towards it now, I skirt the edge of the stables and follow the stone boundary wall until I reach the western corner. I cannot see the road but I will hear any vehicle approaching.

It wasn't like this on the night they died. I didn't wait an hour, weighing up my options or debating what to do. Internal monologues are repetitive and annoying.

Elizabeth opened the door and asked what I was doing here.

'I have a present for Harper.'

'Her birthday is tomorrow.'

'I want her to have it when she wakes.'

I thought she was going to argue, but she saw I wasn't alone and became distracted. Although outwardly calm, inside my mind was screaming, 'She knows, she knows, she knows. She'll tell the police. I'll be interviewed. They'll poke around . . . try to dig up dirt.'

Elizabeth waited in the sitting room while I climbed the stairs to Harper's room, just as I'm doing now. Quietly, I opened her door without knocking. She was asleep. The curtains were closed. Today they're open, yet I half expect to see Harper still lying on her bed beneath the window, curled up under her duvet in her nightdress.

I knelt beside her bed. I listened to her soft breathing. I leaned my face close, inhaling and exhaling in the same rhythm, slowing my heartbeat. Her eyes opened.

247

'What's wrong?' she asked sleepily.

'Nothing.'

She pulled the cover up beneath her chin.

'Why are you here?'

'I brought you a present, but don't open it now.'

I ask her about the bag she was carrying when I saw her that day.

'Where do you keep it?'

'Bag?'

'It was blue and grey.'

'Somewhere,' she said sleepily.

'I need you to find it.'

She thought. Frowned. Shrugged. 'Can't it wait? I'm tired. I'll find it tomorrow.'

Then she remembered something else and asked, 'Did you see the news? A woman was attacked on the footpath.'

'When?'

'This afternoon. Did you see anything?'

'No. What did you see?'

She shrugged and yawned, turning towards the digital clock. 'It's nearly midnight. I'm almost eighteen.'

'Yes, you are – happy birthday for tomorrow.'

I hugged her from behind, slipping my arm around her neck. She laughed and pushed against me. I remember how her hair smelled of coconut shampoo and was still damp from the shower. I applied pressure. She fought. Her body bucked and heaved. Her legs thrashed at the bedding. Her fingers clawed at my arms.

If only she hadn't been there. If only she hadn't seen.

– She saw nothing.

She saw me.

– Nobody will believe her.

She can place me there.

When it was over, I opened the bottle of bleach and dipped each of her fingers inside. I could hear Elizabeth talking downstairs. Waiting for me.

'I'm sorry – I woke her,' I said, when I reached the ground floor.

Elizabeth had poured herself a glass of wine. 'Did she see her present?'

'Yes.'

'What did you get her?'

'It doesn't matter.'

She offered me wine. I told her no. She topped up her glass and said it helped her sleep.

'Did Harper mention that she saw me today?' I asked.

'On the footpath.'

'What else did she say?'

'She said a woman was attacked. Did you see anything?'

'No.'

'I told her to call the police – just to make sure. Are you sure you won't have a drink?'

She waved the glass in front of my face.

'No.'

'You really have to learn to relax around me. I won't bite . . . not unless you want me to.'

Her dressing gown drifted open. She stepped closer, pressing her body against mine. I tried to shove her away, but she clung on.

'Nobody has to know,' she whispered into my mouth. 'I won't tell.'

I held her hands above her head as we kissed. Her pelvic bone was grinding against me and I could hear the soft sandpaper sound of her pubic hair on the front of my jeans. Her tongue wormed into my mouth. I wanted to gag.

I swung the knife, metal on air, and heard the gurgling noise, as her flesh gave way to the blade. She staggered. I lay her down. 'See what you made me do,' I said as certainty faded from her eyes.

A bubble of snot popped in my nostrils and I moaned in self-pity as the knife rose and fell. When it was over, I knelt beside her body, rocking back and forth, shaking uncontrollably. The rest was theatre. The rest was show.

Everybody thinks they are important. Unique. Special. They imagine their life to be like a journey and talk about finding themselves and gaining closure, when there is nothing to find and the only closure

– the one that matters – is the ultimate one. Death. Deliverance. The end.

I hear a sound outside. My heart quickens. There is a vehicle coming. I stand for a moment on the landing with an ear cocked. The car has stopped outside. Keys jangle. One of them slides into the barrel of the lock. Turns.

A door opens and closes. I feel the tiny tremor of footsteps in the hallway.

33

Charlie stands by the car and studies the farmhouse as though trying to decide if a building takes on the particular character or ambience of the events that occur inside. Does it become soaked in blood or tainted by tragedy? Having reached the front door, I begin unhooking the padlock.

'Why won't you let me come in?' she asks.

'You know the reason.'

'I don't have to look in that room.'

'Just stay by the car.'

'But I have to pee.'

I look at her sceptically.

'I have a small bladder,' she says defensively. 'And I'm not squatting in the field.'

We walk around the house and I take her through the kitchen door.

'There's a toilet under the stairs,' I say. 'Down that hallway is off-limits.'

'I know, I know,' she replies.

I open my laptop on the kitchen table and boot up the hard drive, looking for Jeremy Egan's statement to police and copies of his phone records.

The toilet flushes and Charlie reappears, shaking her wet hands. She walks around the table, glancing at the crime scene albums that are stacked on the bench.

'You can't look at those either,' I say.

'I know.' She runs her fingers over the lid of a half-opened box. Inside there are hundreds of Polaroid photographs with distinctive white frames. 'What are these?'

I glance at the label. 'They came from Harper's room. The police must have finished with them.'

'Can I look?'

'OK.'

She reaches into the box and grabs a handful of photographs. Most of them seem to be random shots of pouting girls and punkish boys, pulling faces at the camera or striking silly poses. Some are selfies of Harper, sitting on her boyfriend's lap, kissing his cheek or putting her tongue in his ear.

After a while Charlie gets bored and wanders through the other rooms on the ground floor – studiously avoiding the sitting room. She calls to me from the stairs. 'Did Harper do the paintings?'

'I think so.'

'They're really good.'

'Some of her sketchbooks are upstairs.'

'Can I see them?'

'You're supposed to stay in the kitchen.'

'Why? Is there something scary up there like, I don't know, *a bedroom*?'

She's teasing me. Maybe I'm being too cautious. There are no bloodstains or symbols painted on the walls of Harper's room. I take Charlie upstairs and she moves slowly from room to room. I notice how she occasionally touches things, brushing her fingertips over the face as if trying to pick up some vibration or hidden energy.

'Everything OK?' I ask.

'It's a bit weird,' she replies.

'What is?'

'Harper and I were the same age. She was going off to university. I'm going off to university. Makes you wonder if anyone should bother making plans when life can be so transient. You're here one day, gone the next.'

'I used to feel the same way,' I tell her. 'When I was your age we were still dealing with the Cold War and the possibility of nuclear attack. There was something called the "four-minute warning" – an alarm that was going to sound if the Soviets launched a missile.'

'Why four minutes?'

'That's how long it was going to take for the warheads to reach us. We made all sorts of plans about what we'd do in the four minutes.'

'Four minutes isn't long.'

'Yeah, well, I had a great imagination.'

Charlie laughs. 'Did it change the way you behaved?'

'I don't know, maybe . . . I think I learned not to dwell on what *might* happen and save my energy for the real stuff.'

I retrieve a pile of sketchbooks from beneath Harper's bed. They're covered in a fine dusting of fingerprint powder and labelled with a police evidence sticker. Detectives must have looked through the sketches and decided they had no investigative value.

Charlie sits on a chair and begins leafing through the pages. I look over her shoulder. Most of the portraits are done in charcoal or pencil. I recognise Harper's boyfriend and her father.

'Why don't you study art?' I suggest.

'I can't draw,' replies Charlie.

'I thought you wanted to be a fashion designer.'

'When I was twelve.'

'You could be a lawyer.'

'You're kidding!'

'How about medicine?'

'I don't have the right A-levels.'

253

'You could do a bridging course.'

'Please don't do this again,' she says, flashing me her mother's look. She goes back to the sketchbooks, opening a new one. 'What day did it happen?'

'Saturday June sixth.'

'Harper must have been drawing. Look –'

Charlie holds up the page. The unfinished sketch is of a large Victorian house with steeply sloping roofs, asymmetrical chimneys, a vertical façade and a generous garden. Through the trees, I can just make out the coastline.

'I don't understand.' I say, leaning closer to the sketch.

Charlie points to the bottom right-hand corner. Tucked away, written in tiny handwriting, I notice four digits: 6615.

'It could be the date,' says Charlie. 'The sixth of June.'

She turns the page. 'Here's another one.'

The second drawing is also unfinished. It's a portrait of an old man with a craggy face and wisps of hair clinging to his scalp. The crosshatching shows his deep wrinkles and weathered skin. The number in the right-hand corner is the same: 6615.

I turn back through the pages – confirming Charlie's discovery, the numbers appear to be dates.

'The missing hours,' I whisper.

'Huh?'

'There is a gap in Harper's timeline. The police couldn't fill in her movements that Saturday afternoon. We knew she was sketching but didn't know where.'

'So this is important?'

'Maybe. It's a good pick-up. An excellent one.'

Charlie studies the sketch, looking pleased with herself.

Out of the corner of my eye, I notice the door sway and feel a change in the air pressure – as though someone has opened a door or window somewhere else in the house. Cool air kisses the back of my neck and I feel a tiny tremor beneath my feet. I go to the landing and look over the banister.

'Ruiz?'

Silence.

Returning to Charlie, I scan the room. Two drawers on the dresser are slightly open. The contents are pushed forward, as though someone might have searched them.

'Wait here,' I tell her.

I move from room to room, looking for more evidence of an intruder. I cautiously descend the stairs, wincing as a floorboard creaks. I look along the hallway. The front door is closed. We came in through the kitchen. I glance into the dining room but don't go inside. The mahogany table and matching chair are so dark they look like silhouettes. Small brass animals line the mantelpiece next to a porcelain horse and scented candles. I can see the room reflected in a mirror on the wall. There's nobody hiding behind the door, but still I sense a flaw in the ambience, a lingering ripple where someone has passed through.

Moving along the hallway to the kitchen, I try to remember how I left the house yesterday. Has anything been moved? Disturbed?

Charlie shouts from upstairs. 'Is everything all right?'

'Just stay there.'

I have reached the laundry. The door is open. I'm sure I locked it yesterday. Perhaps Ruiz has been back.

I take out my mobile and call him. He's on the road.

'Have you been to the farmhouse today?'

'No.'

'The laundry door is open. I think someone has been in the house.'

At that moment I hear the creak of floorboards.

'It's only me,' says Charlie. 'Can I come downstairs?'

'Not yet.'

Ruiz hears the conversation. 'You should get her outside. Don't touch anything. I'm ten minutes away.'

Charlie is full of questions. I distract her by mentioning the kittens. Walking across the flagged yard, I glance over my

255

shoulder at the farmhouse, half expecting to see a face peering from an upstairs window.

Inside the stable, we navigate between the empty drums and reels of fencing wire. The kittens have started to wander. Two are wrestling with each other, tumbling in the dusty straw. Charlie almost steps on one of them and admonishes herself, picking it up and holding it against her cheek.

Gathering the other kittens into the crevice of her lap, she scratches their ears and beneath their chins. 'They're adorable. Can we have one?'

'You're going off to university.'

'What if Mummy says yes? Can we take one home and show her? Emma hasn't had a kitten before. It can be her birthday present.'

Within two sentences Charlie has it all planned.

Ruiz pulls up and I meet him halfway across the yard.

'You're sure?' he asks.

'I'm sure I locked it. It was yesterday afternoon. You were here. We drove Elliot and his girlfriend into town.'

'Did you check every room?'

'No.'

'OK, let's do it now.'

Leaving Charlie with the kittens, I follow Ruiz into the house, still trying to recall how things looked yesterday, wondering if particular picture frames are angled the same way or whether the clothes were hanging in that order. Every shadow and corner has become a hiding place.

We're standing on the first-floor landing. 'You should call Ronnie Cray,' says Ruiz. 'She'll want to know.'

'Will they send a scene of crime team?'

'Not unless something is missing.'

I remember Elliot Crowe's visit to the farmhouse. He had wanted to come inside and got angry when I told him to leave. They say a junkie will steal from the dead and still cry at the funeral.

Outside the wind has picked up and a loose section of corrugated iron clangs against the joists of the chicken coop. I am crouched below a windowsill, squeezed between the diesel tank and the rear wall of the stables.

The psychologist has a daughter. She's playing with the kittens, which are tumbling and squirming in her lap or clawing at the front of her long-sleeved cotton top. One of them climbs on to her shoulder.

'Where are you going?' she laughs, pulling the kitten back into her lap.

My knees hurt. I shift my weight. The diesel tank makes a hollow ringing sound as my heel hits the metal cradle. The girl's head snaps up, staring at the window. I duck below the sill.

The girl is moving. I hear her put down the kittens and pick up a torch. She's searching the horse stalls and storage areas, bouncing light off tools and dust-covered tack. Now she's standing at the window. If she leans closer to the glass and looks down she will see my knees.

Almost without thought, my fingers have found the box-cutter in my pocket. Can I catch her before she screams?

Another sound. She's at the side entrance, sliding the bolt. I scramble up and reach the door, hiding behind it as it opens. Through the narrow crack between the hinges, I see the fine downy hairs on her neck. Her hand is only inches from mine. I could reach out and touch her. I could run the blade across her throat.

The tin roof is clanging. She takes a step, looking right and left. I raise the blade. If she turns her head a little more . . .

'Charlie, where are you?'

She looks over her shoulder. 'Out here.'

'The police are coming.'

'Why?'

'I think someone has been in the house.'

257

She turns back into the stables and closes the door, sliding the bolt into place.

'We should wait outside,' says the psychologist.

'But I haven't fed the mother yet.'

'Hurry up, then.'

I edge along the wall until I reach the corner of the building and take cover in a little wilderness at the edge of the kitchen garden. Still hidden, I raise my head and take one last look at the farmhouse before taking off, running across the field, leaping thistles and cowpats.

Eighty yards seems longer. Reaching the copse of trees, I throw myself behind a fallen log and catch my breath as more vehicles begin arriving.

After crawling through a bramble hedge, I climb over the barbed wire fence and fall into the leaf litter. Lying on my back, I stare up at the branches and the clouds moving behind the leaves.

You nearly killed her.

— I would have killed her.

She did nothing wrong.

— She almost saw me.

One day you'll make a mistake. What then?

— Closure.

34

Ronnie Cray squints into the brightness of the afternoon. 'I'm not doubting you, Professor, but nothing seems to be missing and there's no sign of a break-in.'

'The laundry door was open.'

'Maybe you didn't close it properly.'

'I locked it yesterday. We came in through the kitchen.'

She holds up her hands, accepting my word. Behind her Monk appears out of the trees, striding across the field. He looks normal-sized from a distance, but keeps growing as he gets nearer.

'There are fresh footprints near the fence,' he says, scraping cowshit off his shoes.

'Did you check on Tommy Garrett?' asks Cray.

'His grandmother hasn't seen him since breakfast.'

'What about Elliot Crowe?' I ask. 'He was here yesterday.'

'I'll send someone to his last-known address, but that kid is slipperier than a Teflon-coated turd.'

The DCS rocks impatiently from foot to foot, keen to leave. She has more important things to do than investigate a possible break-in. I tell her about the sketches that Charlie discovered in Harper's room. She doesn't seem interested.

'They fill in Harper's timeline,' I say.

Cray ignores me and walks towards her car. I chase after her, blocking her path.

'Have I done something to upset you?'

'What?'

'I get the impression that I'm wasting your time.'

'Right now – yes, you are.'

'So I should go home.'

'Suit yourself,' she mutters. 'I've had a gutful of psychologists.'

I step back, but Cray doesn't pass. Her jaw flexes. 'When did you last talk to Milo Coleman?'

'After the funerals.'

'Not since then?'

'No.'

'An hour ago he went on radio and linked Naomi Meredith's murder to the farmhouse killings. He knew about the bleach and the symbol carved on her forehead.'

'I don't understand.'

'None of those things were made public. How did Coleman find out?'

'You think I told him?'

'Did you?'

'No, and I'm offended that you think so little of me.'

'You're pissed off – join the fucking queue,' she says bitterly. 'The Chief Constable has gone nuclear. He expressly told us not to link the cases.'

I contemplate telling her about Bennie and Milo, but I have no evidence that she leaked details.

Cray is still talking. 'Milo Coleman is all over the radio and TV, calling the killer a sad sadistic pervert fixated on adultery. How in fuck's name did he find out?'

I don't answer. 'What are you going to do?'

'My job,' she replies. 'Mr Coleman is in possession of infor- mation only the killer could have known, which makes him a

260

suspect. That being the case, I'm going to crawl up his rectum and set up camp until I find out what he was doing on the night of the murders.'

When the detectives have gone, Ruiz joins me at the gate, offering me a boiled sweet from a tin that he keeps in his pocket.

'The Fat Controller doesn't look happy – did someone set fire to her nipple tassels?'

'The Chief Constable has expressed every confidence in her.'

'Oh, shit!'

'Yeah.'

Ruiz almost looks sorry for her. He returns the tin to his pocket. 'The big detective told me something interesting. They've found two other choking victims – one in Torquay and the other in Weymouth. The reports came from two A&E departments at local hospitals. Same deal – the attacker carved a letter into their foreheads.'

'What else did he say?'

'One male, one female, both married.'

'Were they having an affair?'

'Someone has gone to interview them.'

I try to picture the scene. A detective turning up on the doorsteps of two different spouses, asking if they were sleeping with each other and who might have discovered their infidelities. Doors are going to be slammed. Toes bruised.

'So we have six people with the letter "A" carved into their foreheads – four women and two men. Naomi was definitely having an affair. Most of the others have denied it.'

'They're probably lying,' says Ruiz.

'Agreed.'

'All of which begs the question – where do Elizabeth and Harper Crowe fit into this?'

'Elizabeth slept with her husband's best friend and had sex in public with a married man.'

261

'There was nothing carved on her forehead.'

'Harper died from a blood choke.'

'And then there's the bleach . . . '

Charlie is inside, sorting through Polaroids on the kitchen table. Ruiz breaks into a huge grin. 'Hello, princess, do I get a hug?'

'Not if you call me princess.'

He hugs her anyway and Charlie responds awkwardly, hands at her sides. 'When did you get so tall?' asks Ruiz.

'I'm not twelve any more.'

'Do you have a boyfriend?'

'Why would I want one of those?'

'A girlfriend then.'

'Dream on.'

Charlie picks up one of the Polaroids to show me – a photograph of an old man whose face is so pitted and creased that his cheeks resemble moonscapes. He has an absent-minded smile and seems to be staring into space, as though he's reminiscing about the past.

'It's the man in the sketch,' she says. 'The one Harper was drawing on the sixth of June.'

I study the photograph and the sketch. She's right. It's the same man. His eyes have more warmth in the drawing and he seems more grounded in the present.

'And I also found this one,' says Charlie, holding up a photograph of the house in the sketchbook. 'Maybe I can find it.'

'Now you want to play detective?'

'Keeps me out of trouble.'

'I don't want you knocking on any strange doors.'

'I'll stick to the high street.'

'Or taking sweets from dirty old men.'

Ruiz looks up. 'Who's a dirty old man?'

'Talk of the devil,' says Charlie.

35

The large detached Edwardian house is in a fashionable part of Clevedon, overlooking Fir Wood where the trees are hanging heavily in the heat. I ring the bell. Bare feet come thundering towards the door, which quakes as locks and bolts are keyed and slid. It opens and reveals a sandy-headed boy, his face below the lock, peering up at me sceptically. He is bare-chested, wearing swimming trunks. A TV is playing somewhere within – applause followed by an English voice: *'Advantage, Miss Sharapova.'*

'Is your mummy home?' I ask.

He looks at Ruiz. 'Are you policemen?'

'No.'

He closes the door and I hear the same bare feet retreating down the hallway. Softer footsteps follow. A woman appears, opening the door a crack. I can only see one half of her face.

'Maggie Dutton?'

'What do you want?'

'I was hoping we could ask you a few questions about an incident that occurred a month ago.'

'Are you the police?'

'No, I'm a psychologist.'

Her eyes flick to Ruiz and back to me. 'I withdrew my statement. You shouldn't be here.'

'I understand that you—'

'Did the police give out my address? That's not allowed. What about my privacy?'

'Another woman has been attacked.'

Something changes in her eyes, but she regains her composure. 'I have nothing to say.'

The door is closing.

'Her name was Naomi Meredith. She was twenty-nine.'

'Nothing to do with me.'

'She's dead, Mrs Dutton.'

The door stops moving and opens a little wider, revealing her face. A large square bandage covers much of her forehead. Lowering her eyes, she stares at her right hand braced on the door, debating what to do. She could close it so easily. Lock us out.

'Just you,' she whispers.

'I'm not police either,' says Ruiz.

'I don't care – you look like one.'

Ruiz nods and says he'll wait for me. I follow Maggie into the front room, which has oak panelling, oversized sofas and fittings from another age. I imagine a bell beneath the rug to summon servants. Perhaps she has family money.

The TV has been turned down, but I can still hear the gentle *thwock* of tennis balls and the harsh grunts of the players, punctuated by applause. Maggie takes a seat. Thin and fair-haired, with high cheekbones and a short upturned nose, she's wearing trousers and a white blouse, loose around her neck. She sits bolt upright with her knees pressed together, hands on her lap, looking slightly dazed and disbelieving, like a refugee applying for asylum. Her rather prominent eyes are fixed on the floor and periodically she tugs at the collar of her blouse where it touches her neck.

Crayons are scattered on the low table next to a child's drawing of a knight who appears to be slaying a dragon, although the dragon resembles a dog and the knight looks like a robot.

'How old is your son?' I ask.

'Six.'

'Your husband works abroad.'

Something changes in her voice. 'We're separated.'

'I'm sorry to hear that. Why did you withdraw your statement?'

'It can't change what happened.'

'You could help catch the man who attacked you.'

'How? I could pass him in the street and not recognise him.'

'So you'd rather just forget?'

'Yes.'

'How is that working out for you?'

Her eyes flash to mine, trying to decide if I'm being sarcastic or cruel.

'Your questions won't work on me, Professor. I have some knowledge of psychology. I studied it for a while.'

'Where?'

'Exeter.'

'I know some of the lecturers there.'

I mention a few names, but Maggie isn't interested in making small talk. The silence stretches out, getting long and thinner like a rubber band that will eventually snap back. She tugs again at the collar of her blouse.

'How is your neck?' I ask.

'Fine.'

'Is it bruised?'

'No.'

'I once had a patient – her name was Nancy – who couldn't bear to have anything touch her throat. She couldn't wear necklaces or turtleneck sweaters. She couldn't stand her boyfriend touching her there. They were engaged. At the wedding she wanted to wear a necklace her grandmother had left her, but was afraid it would trigger a panic attack in the church.'

Maggie blinks at me. 'What happened?'

'I went through her entire history. Nothing. It was a complete mystery. Then I talked to her sister and discovered the trigger. When Nancy was about your son's age she was playing with a group of neighbourhood boys on an abandoned plot behind their house. One of them had wrapped a homemade noose around her neck and together they pulled her up into a tree. Left her dangling. A woman motorist saw it happen and managed to cut her down.

'You're probably wondering why Nancy didn't remember something that traumatic, but her sister was older and supposed to be looking after her. She made Nancy promise not to tell anyone. She made her swear on their mother's life – to cross her heart and hope to die. Nancy was young enough to believe such promises could come true, so she blocked out the hanging, but somewhere deep inside, she remembered. That's why she couldn't bear to have anything touch her neck.'

Maggie raises her hand to her throat and lowers it again.

'You're a strong, intelligent, independent, well-educated woman, Maggie. I can see that. You think that any sign of weakness is going to be punished or be used against you. If you break down and cry or admit to being frightened, you'll be proving that women are emotionally weak and fragile. But whatever you're feeling is a response to trauma.'

A single tear slips down her cheek, running into the corner of her mouth.

'You can try to forget the attack, but it won't go away,' I say. 'Unless you confront the truth and come to terms with it – this man will haunt you while he's hunting others.'

We sit for a long while listening to the sounds of Wimbledon. Maggie's shoulders stop shaking and she blows her nose.

'How tall was he?' I ask.

'Taller than me,' she whispers.

266

'You didn't see his face?'

'No.'

'What about his voice?'

She shrugs.

'Did you smell anything?'

'Seaweed.'

'Do you know how long you were unconscious?'

'Not long.'

'Did he say anything to you?'

She shakes her head a little too adamantly.

'What did he say?'

'Nothing.'

Again I let the silence stretch out, expanding in her mind, filling her chest, fraying her nerves. Everybody has three hearts – one they show to strangers, one they show to the people they love, and the last one that isn't shown to anyone. It's the last heart that I look for in people – the one that's normally most damaged.

When Maggie speaks it comes in a rush. 'He called me an adulterer. He said he'd seen me with a married man, but that couldn't be true. I've always been faithful.' Her eyes narrow to slits. 'I know what you're thinking. You don't believe me! I don't care. I know that I was a good and faithful wife.' Her voice is breaking. 'My husband didn't believe me. That's why he left.' She makes eye contact, holding my gaze. 'Do you know the worst part? Every time I look in the mirror I still see that horrible letter written on my forehead. One night I tried to scrub it off with steel wool. My little boy found me and asked me what I was doing. "Is it gone?" I asked him.' She lowers her eyes again. 'You said there were other victims.'

'We know of four others.'

Maggie gazes at me, wanting to believe I'm wrong. A small vein pulses on her jawline.

'I have to ask you some very personal questions,' I say, trying to tread carefully. 'Whatever you tell me will stay between us. I will not reveal the details to the police or anyone else.'

She nods.

'Have you ever joined an online dating agency?'

'No.'

'Did you ever swap partners or introduce anyone else into your sexual life?'

'No.'

'Have you had sex in public?'

'Never.'

'What about your husband?'

She shakes her head, less certain than before.

'Why do you think this man thought you were having an affair?'

'I don't know. I kept denying it. I said I had a little boy at home. He asked me if I liked oral sex. I didn't answer and it made him angry.'

'Why?'

'He said I was disgusting. He asked, how could I take another man's penis in my mouth, when I had a child at home? He asked if I went home and kissed my boy with my filthy mouth. He was screaming at me. He said he was going to put me to sleep. He asked me if I wanted to wake up. I didn't know what he meant. I begged him. "Please don't kill me. Please, please . . . "'

She sobs and rocks forward over her knees.

'What did he do, Maggie?'

'He cut me.'

'Show me.'

She shakes her head.

'Please.'

Reaching up, she pinches one corner of the surgical bandage and slowly peels it back. The wound on her forehead has healed, but the scar is puckered and pink. Three intersecting lines form the letter 'A'.

'I'll never forget,' she whispers. 'I'll never forgive him.'

36

Ruiz is waiting for me in the car, sitting with the door open, listening to cricket on the radio. England is playing Australia in Cardiff in the First Test. Tennis and cricket – the twin sounds of an English summer. He turns down the volume and I tell him what I've learned.

Maggie Dutton's pain had been so raw and uncompromising I can almost taste it coating my tongue. I didn't blame her for wanting to draw the curtains and crawl into bed, hiding away from the world. I have climbed into that hole and out again.

'Was she having an affair?' asks Ruiz.

'No, I don't think she was.'

'So we're wrong about his motivation.'

'Or he made a mistake.'

My mobile is vibrating next to my heart. I recognise Charlie's number. I'm about to speak but she cuts over me. Frightened. Out of breath.

'Daddy! He's trying to get in the car.'

'Who?'

'Some random. You've got to come.'

Her fear is real, I can tell from the rising inflection and her barely suppressed panic.

'Drive away,' I tell her.

'I can't! I dropped the keys. They're on the ground outside. I've locked the doors . . . but what if he finds the keys?'

Someone is yelling in the background, hammering on the glass. Charlie screams. Ruiz has heard half the conversation and puts his foot down, weaving through traffic.

'Where are you, Charlie?'

'I don't know,' she sobs.

'I need a street . . . an intersection.'

'I can't see one.'

'What can you see?'

'Houses. Cars.' And then, 'I walked past a pub. It was on the corner.'

I put her on speakerphone. 'What was it called?'

'I can't remember. Wait! Three words. The something . . . '

'The Little Harp?' says Ruiz.

'That's it!'

Ruiz swerves on to the opposite side of the road and cuts across a garage forecourt before throwing the car around another corner. I grab hold of the dashboard and sway back and forth, either bashing shoulders with him or thumping against the passenger door. Ruiz pulls out his phone and calls the police, giving the location.

'How far?' I ask.

'Two minutes.'

Charlie is still on the phone. 'I think he's gone,' she says. 'I can't see him. I'll get the keys.'

'No!'

In the same breath she screams and I hear a *whump* noise and the sound of breaking glass. Ruiz brakes hard and takes the next corner, swerving around a furniture truck. He runs a red light and forces an oncoming car off the road.

'We're here,' he says, turning hard into a new road. I see the

Volvo. A figure looks up and turns away, beginning to run. Ruiz flings open the driver's door and gives chase on foot, his heavy shoes echoing on the pavement. I go to Charlie. She's sitting behind the wheel, covered in broken glass. Pale. Shocked. She unlocks the door and I hug her, feeling her whole body shake.

'Did he touch you?'

'No.'

'Are you dizzy? Nauseous?'

'No.'

'Numbness. Disorientation. Shallow, rapid breathing.'

'I'm fine, Daddy. Really.'

Along the street, doors are opening. I want to yell at people, *Where were you! Why didn't help her! She could have been hurt. She could have been taken.*

Ruiz has returned. He shakes his head. He looks at Charlie and then at me, asking us what happened.

'I was showing people the sketchbook,' explains Charlie, 'and this one guy demanded to know where I got it. He said it didn't belong to me.'

'Did he say why?'

'No.'

'OK, where did it happen?'

'On the street, I think it's called the Triangle. I was on the corner and he came up to me.'

'What did he look like?'

'Young, I guess — older than me. Dark hair. Thin. He had on this heavy coat.'

Elliot Crowe was wearing a winter coat.

'Tell me again exactly what he said.'

'He said I shouldn't have the sketchbook.'

'Did he mention Harper's name?'

'Maybe.' She takes several deep breaths. 'He tried to take the book off me. That's when I ran.'

A police panda car pulls up in the middle of the road. Two

uniformed officers, one male, one female, step out and give their call sign over their shoulder radios. The female officer interviews Charlie, asking the same questions that I did, while her colleague talks to some of the neighbours, scribbling in his police-issue notebook.

I tell Ruiz he should go. I'll catch up with him tomorrow. Half an hour later the police have finished and I'm given a case number and told that someone will be in touch. I feel angry rather than reassured. I know that in the grand scheme of things a broken car window and tearful teenager are not high on the list of police priorities.

Charlie is waiting in the passenger seat, nursing the bottle of water. Brushing glass from the driver's seat, I get behind the wheel and drive us home. Air rushes through the broken window. It will have to be fixed. Insurance will pay.

The adrenalin has dissipated and Charlie looks scarily calm. I want her to be chastened, to be having second thoughts about studying psychology. Surely this will change her mind.

'Are we good?' I ask.

She nods. 'I don't think I'll make a very good psychologist.'

'What makes you say that?'

'The guy looked creepy, but I didn't recognise the danger. I should have known.'

'Don't be so hard on yourself.'

'But surely that's part of the job – being able to read people's body language, deciding if they're hiding something or blocking it out. Looking for the clues, you know, whether they stutter or start sweating or keep glancing up to the left.'

'Sometimes a stutter is just a stutter,' I say. 'We all have foibles and tics.'

'Do I have foibles?'

'Of course.'

'What are they?'

'They don't matter.'

'I want to know.'

She has turned in her seat, fixing me with her gaze.

'Well, let's see. You dress quite more modestly than a lot of your friends. You don't like tight tops or low-cut blouses or short skirts.'

'OK.'

'When you're worried about something the twin frown marks between your eyes get deeper. And you climb the stairs one step at a time instead of two. You're also impatient with Emma.'

'She's annoying.'

'She loves you.'

'What else?'

'When you drive you always check the mirrors in a certain order and tap your right leg three times before putting the key in the ignition. It's a small ritual you have – I don't know why. I also think you quite fancy Nina's brother Jake.'

'No, I don't.'

'You act differently when he's around. You tease him and twirl your hair. You're blushing now.'

She touches her cheek and says, 'That's enough.'

'Are you sure?'

'Yes.'

Nothing much is said on the rest of the journey. Charlie rests her head against the side window, staring at the passing fields.

Eventually, she speaks. 'Those people living in that street – some of them were looking out of their windows; they could see what was happening, but nobody came to help me.'

'They were scared.'

'When does someone stop being scared? What if I'd been drowning, or the car was on fire? Would they have done something then?'

'Yes, most likely. Often it's a split-second decision. If we spend too long thinking about it, we talk ourselves out of it, or reach a kind of paralysis that stops us making a decision. We think someone else will step forward.'

'But you always step forward,' says Charlie. 'That's why Mummy gets angry. She says you try to be a hero, when you're not meant to be one.'

'I don't try to be a hero,' I say.

'You know what I mean. Would you die for a stranger?'

'I don't know.'

'What about for me or Emma or Mummy?'

'Yes.'

Charlie seems to ponder this. 'I don't know if I could do that.'

'You won't ever have to,' I say.

Another thought occurs to her. 'Mummy can't know about this. You know what she's like. She'll say it's your fault. She'll kick you out of the house again. We have to keep it a secret.'

'What do I say about the broken window?' I ask.

'Tell her someone tried to break into the car.'

'To steal what?'

'I don't know. What do thieves normally steal? Radios. Mobile phones. I'll say I left my phone in the car.'

'You shouldn't have to lie,' I say, knowing that my daughter is right. Julianne doesn't need to know about this. She has enough on her plate.

37

Watching a woman dress is far sexier than seeing her undress. It's akin to a dance without music, a silent ballet where every movement is so practised and easy. Julianne lays a skirt on the bed and begins looking for a matching top. She decides and then changes her mind. Looking on, I revel in the familiarity of the scene.

'Sorry it's taking so long,' she says, going back to the wardrobe.

Having decided, she sits on the bed and rolls her tights over her legs, leaning back to pull the opaque black fabric over her thighs and her buttocks. (Less sexy, but still watchable.) Then she stands and shimmies into the dress, letting the fabric fall to just below her knees. Turning left and right, she checks out her reflection in the mirror.

'You look beautiful,' I say.

'It takes a lot of work.'

'You've always been beautiful.'

She rolls her eyes, dismissing the compliment, but I know that secretly she's pleased. It's not pretence or false modesty. A woman such as Julianne favours self-deprecation over self-assertion. It makes her feel more comfortable and less objectified, although sometimes I wish she could simply accept an accolade and say thank you.

I have booked a window table at her favourite restaurant along with champagne and flowers. Too much, I think, but I'm not very good at this. When I proposed to Julianne I sounded like Hugh Grant in *Four Weddings and a Funeral* (and every other film), umming and ahing, stopping and starting, mumbling and apologising.

She's ready. I follow her downstairs. Charlie and Emma look over the banister as though they're watching all their well-laid plans come to fruition.

When did tonight become such a big 'thing'?

We take Julianne's car. I don't want her seeing the Volvo. I let her drive. In profile I see an eyelash brush against her cheek and the pink shell of her ear poking through her hair.

'How did Charlie get on?' she asks.

'Great,' I say. 'She picked up something that we'd all missed.'

'What was that?'

'There are three hours missing from one of the timelines. Charlie found a sketchbook with a date. It might tell us what the girl was doing in the unaccounted hours.'

'Is that important?'

'Could be.'

Twilight has descended on the landscape as the angled sun creates a soft aura of light around the trees. I see a family picking strawberries in a field, stencilled like cardboard cut-outs against the light.

'Do you wish I had chosen to be something else?' I ask. 'Not a psychologist, I mean.'

'I would have fallen in love with you regardless.'

'Why did you choose me?'

'You had kind eyes.'

'Is that it?'

'You were clever, but you didn't show off. You had a nice

smile. I had gone out with boys who were handsome, but a lot of them were pretentious, vain or just stupid.'

'Not all of them.'

'No.'

I want to ask her if she's still in love with me, but I've learned not to lead with my chin.

'It's weird to think we have an eighteen-year-old daughter,' she says.

'You were nineteen when you met me.'

'I can't imagine Charlie falling in love.'

'It happens.'

'Should we hope that it doesn't happen too soon?'

'No.'

We park the car and she slips her arm into mine, leaning against my shoulder as we walk. 'Do you remember when we met?' she asks.

'That pub just off Trafalgar Square.'

She smiles. 'It was actually before then – at the Student Health Service Clinic.'

'Are you sure?'

'Oh, I'm certain. Rowena was with me. She thought she'd caught some terrible STD after a one-night stand with the drummer in a pub band called Chernobyl – which says a lot about Rowena's taste in men and music. I went with her to the clinic. It was on the ground floor of the Geography building at the Mile End campus. You were a medical student doing a clinical rotation. It was only your second day. You were dressed in a white coat with the stethoscope around your neck and looked absolutely terrified. The doctor in charge asked you to draw blood. You told Rowena, "It's just a little prick," and I said, "That's not what the drummer said," and Rowena glared at me and said ouch every time you stuck the needle in her.'

'I couldn't find a vein.'

'I know. You asked Rowena if she drank a lot of coffee and she thought you were asking her out.'

'She was dehydrated.'

'She was hung over.'

'I did manage to find a vein.'

'Eventually.'

'I'm sorry I didn't notice you.'

'Rowena had bigger tits.'

'I didn't look at her tits.'

'She said afterwards you were gay.'

'Gay?'

'Uh-huh. Do you remember what she said to you?'

'Something about not specialising.'

'She told you not to become a gynaecologist because no girl would want her boyfriend to spend all day looking at other women's bits.'

'There wasn't much mystery about Rowena.'

'True.'

I can't believe that Julianne has never told me this story before. I thought all our biographies had been written and rewritten and there were no surprises left; all questions posed, all anecdotes recalled. In my mind we first met at a pub near Trafalgar Square after an anti-apartheid rally in front of the South African Embassy. I'd given a soapbox speech from the back of a truck. Julianne introduced herself. My best mate, Jock, tried to chat her up, telling her he'd grow to be a better man around her. Julianne told him that a hard-on didn't count as personal growth.

'What are you smiling about?' she asks now.

'Jock.'

'He was such a rogue.'

'He and Rowena would have made a good pair.'

We've reached the restaurant. It is one of those incredibly trendy places done out in polished concrete and chrome, where you can look through to the kitchen and see eruptions of flame bursting from a wok or frying pan. The menu is almost completely indecipherable. I have never heard of caramelised *witlof*, *katsuobushi*, or *bagna càuda*. Our waiter reminds me of a greyhound and his French accent is so thick that I avoid the 'specials'.

We order and eat. The reminiscing hasn't finished. Julianne talks about our wedding at a little church in Chiswick, our two families separated by a central aisle. My side was full of doctors, surgeons, university buddies and family. Julianne's side had painters, sculptors, poets, nude models, actors and designers. She was barely twenty-two. Not yet finished her degree. I was a trainee psychologist – having abandoned medicine.

We danced to Lyle Lovett's 'She's No Lady, She's My Wife'. We cut the cake. We mingled. We grinned at each other. I made a speech poking fun at myself and she scolded me afterwards.

'You made yourself sound hopeless.'

'I am hopeless around you.'

I think every couple embellishes how they met, romanticising the moment, polishing the details into a shiny creation myth. I was older, but Julianne was worldlier. She had spent a year in Paris and Florence – a gap-year odyssey that involved lots of red wine, dope-smoking and riding on the back of motorcycles with boys called Marco and Paolo. She had experienced Europe, while I had only observed it on family holidays that corresponded with the medical conferences where my father was speaking.

I don't know why Julianne chose me. Perhaps I was reliable and stable – the entry-level requirements – or maybe it was something to do with her losing her father when she was barely in her teens. Perhaps she valued my rational mind after spending so long with an irrational one.

We keep chatting over coffee and herbal tea. By then we've talked about Charlie's birth and how long we waited for Emma. It's strange reminiscing like this. When we split up I told Julianne that she was throwing away twenty years and she said, 'You don't throw away the past. It will always be there.'

I still can't explain exactly why we separated six years ago.

279

It was easy to blame the Parkinson's. She could see the writing on the wall, growing spidery and small as my tremors grew worse. But it was never the disease, and it wasn't boredom or the desire for something new. I let my work get too close. I put Julianne and the girls in danger.

Would we have lasted anyway? Who knows? Even the best of marriages can become like a Pinter play, with long pauses, or characters finishing each other's sentences or having no dialogue at all.

When I was thirteen I used to go looking for bodies washed up on the beach. In my imagination I found dozens of them. Not bloated or decomposing — they looked untouched and almost alive, rolling in the shallows, or washed up on the shingle, skin pale, eyes open.

I don't look for bodies any more. That was childish. I'm a grown man now with responsibilities, but it still occurs to me whenever I read stories of fishermen going missing at sea or swimmers getting caught in treacherous currents. I wonder where their bodies might show up and who might find them.

They say that adolescence is when every child becomes an orphan. I was alone long before then, but something did wake in me. It stirred and it roared and it would not be put to sleep. I discovered girls and nothing was ever the same. Some were so beautiful my heart would ache. I would sit behind them in class or at the cinema, memorising every inch of their tanned legs or the soft, almost translucent hair on the nape of their necks, the swell of their breasts, the curve of their eyelashes. I could tell them from the way they walked, or laughed, or tossed their hair.

A girl called Daniela was the first to steal my heart. I saw her in a cinema queue in Bristol. She was with a girlfriend and gave the smallest of glances in my direction. Our eyes didn't meet, but I saw her clearly and in that instant I appreciated true beauty. I wanted to sit next to her. I wanted to smell her hair and hold her hand and hear her voice.

When the movie was over I followed her. Not in a creepy way. I wanted to know her name and where she lived and went to school. I caught her bus and sat behind her. She didn't notice. I didn't turn her head or lift her chin or raise her pretty plucked eyebrows. I was ordinary, nondescript . . . invisible.

A week later I was behind her again in the cinema queue. An older boy made this fphwawwww sound and shook his right hand as though scalded. 'Get a look at that,' he said, nudging his mate. 'She could sit on my face any time.'

His mate laughed. The boy's name was Adam Landrey. I knew that because he played league football and had trialled for Manchester United when he was only fourteen. He started chatting to Daniela. She laughed.

'Sit next to me,' he said. 'I won't bite, but I can't promise I won't eat you.' He poked out his tongue and wiggled it up and down.

I wanted him dead. I wanted him burned or crippled or deformed. I wanted to cut out his wriggling pink tongue.

Daniela should have slapped him. She should have belittled him or ignored him. Instead she sat next to him and I watched them whispering during the movie. I saw him put his arm around her shoulders and his hand slip down and squeeze her breast. She didn't push it away. I will never understand that. Why do women rail against sexism and chauvinism, yet they let someone like Adam Landrey paw their tits?

People say it's a man's world, but women let us be that way. They could chase off the cavemen or demand they change, but instead they pander to the jocks and alpha males and brutes. Maybe they imagine they can tame the savage beasts, but instead they perpetuate the cycle of chauvinism and misogny.

I wonder whether the psychologist would agree. He's on a date tonight – eating out with someone who might be his wife. She's not wearing a wedding ring so they might not be married, yet there's something very practised about their body language, as though they've had these conversations before.

I'm sitting at a bus shelter across the road, looking at them through the front plate-glass window of the restaurant. Buses come and go. I wave them on. A woman watches me from the near corner. A while ago she came and asked me for a light. I thought she might be a prostitute, but she didn't ask for anything else.

My stomach is gurgling hungrily. There's a fish and chip shop up the road and the smell of fried food is sticking to my nostrils. I did contemplate getting cod and chips, but was too anxious about missing my chance.

Three women, drunk, arms locked together, are staggering towards me, cackling with laughter. They're in their mid-forties, wearing uniforms from the local supermarket. One of them is quite pretty. Her name is Felicity – I can see her nametag. The others are heftier. One of them is a bleached blonde with a yellowing front tooth.

'All right, love?' she says as she passes. 'Like what you see?'

The others shriek with laughter. My neck goes hot.

I look back at the restaurant. The psychologist and his lady are leaving. Arguing. I can't hear what the fight is about, but she's in tears. She steps on to the road and waves down a cab. He tries to pull her back. She pushes him away.

The cab drives off. The psychologist yells something, but she can't hear him. She's gone. He's alone.

I follow him along Princes Street to the NCP car park. He takes the lift. I take the stairs two at a time. I watch his shadow moving between vehicles. He unlocks his car from twenty paces away. I take one last look around us, checking that we're alone.

He opens the door as I slip my arm around his neck and kick hard at the back of his legs so that his own body weight adds pressure to the choke. He is on his knees. I fall with him. We are hidden between vehicles.

He slumps against me. Unconscious. I lay him on the concrete – shame about that nice shirt, did she wash it for you . . . do the ironing? I wrap tape around his hands and over his mouth, counting down the seconds. He stirs. Jerks. Disorientated. I am behind him again with my arm around his neck.

'Can you hear me?'

He fights. I tighten my grip.

'Shhhhhhh.'

He mumbles into the gag. The psychologist wants to talk in his own defence, to plead his case, or beg forgiveness.

'Shhhhh. Now it's my turn to speak,' I say. 'Do you know who I am?'

He shakes his head.

'But you keep telling people that you know me. You call me names. You make up stories.'

He mumbles again, no doubt offering me money; telling me to take his wallet or his car or both.

'Would you like to die?' I ask.

He shakes his head.

My forearm forces his chin back and my other arm provides leverage. I watch the mystery of his limbs twitching and his eyes rolling before he sags like a puppet with cut strings. I rock him in my arms, holding the choke, denying blood to his brain.

'You think you're so clever, don't you — you and your fancy education and your big words. Don't worry. I'm going to hold you just long enough to ruin that big brain of yours. You won't be so clever then.

'Shhhhh. Relax. Close your eyes.'

38

Outside the long twilight has given way to night. Both girls are asleep when we get home. Charlie must be exhausted. I follow Julianne upstairs and prepare to go my separate way, but she takes my hand and pulls me towards her bedroom. The door is hardly closed before she kisses me, murmuring something I can't understand, but I don't ask her to repeat it. Her mouth is soft and she smells of wine and garlic and peppermint tea. Shushing and giggling like teenagers, we stumble to the bed and crash on to the mattress. I'm sure I hear Charlie's door open and close thirty seconds later.

'She'll be scarred for life now,' I say.

'One more thing to blame us for,' replies Julianne.

'She can sort it out in therapy.'

'Self-diagnose.'

'Didn't help me.'

'No.'

I am unzipping her skirt, pulling it down over her hips. I kiss her bare shoulders, her arms, the swell of her stomach, her hips. My hand slides up her thigh, passing through zones of deepening heat to the lace-enclosed swelling that makes her a woman. And when she's naked, lying beneath me, I hold myself back, but she lets me know there's no need and my breath quickens and a small cry escapes her lips and I wish I could hold on to this moment for another thirty years.

Afterwards, she falls asleep beside me. It's a strange feeling to be this happy and this terrified, to know that I'm gambling everything to gain everything. I will give this one last throw of the dice, but if I lose – if Julianne is indeed lost to me – I will walk away for good. I will not linger on the edges of her life as I have been doing for the past six years. This is not about giving up. It's about choosing to stay afloat when the easiest option is to drown.

Hours later when light edges the curtains and birds celebrate another morning, I stare at Julianne's sleeping form, her lips barely apart and hair loose upon the pillow. She wakes, stirs, straightening her legs. Her eyes open. Her vision seems to cloud. 'Was this a mistake?'

'You said yourself we cannot change history,' I reply.

'This feels like we're having an affair.'

'I couldn't possibly have an affair – I'm married.'

'So am I,' she choruses.

'You don't speak of your husband very much.'

'True, but he's very dear to me.'

She rolls away from my kiss. 'Just going to the loo.'

'Can you draw me a bath.'

'That's very decadent.'

'I think I deserve one.'

'You were good, but not that good.'

I lie in the steaming water, replaying last night's greatest hits. Julianne comes into the bathroom to brush her hair. 'There's something I need you to do today. I visited our solicitor and arranged to have our wills updated.'

'Why?'

'Charlie is eighteen now. If something happens to us, she can look after Emma.'

'Nothing is going to happen to us.'

'That's not the point.' She pulls back her hair and holds it in a clasp. 'I'm about to have major surgery. It's rule number one. I need you to sign off on the changes.'

I know she's right, but I want to argue. I don't want to update our wills. We can do it next month or next year.

There's a knock on the bedroom door. 'Where is everyone?' calls Emma.

'In the bathroom,' replies Julianne.

'Where's Daddy?'

'Having a bath.'

Her eyes ogle through the steam. 'Are you in there with him?'

'Not in the tub, no.'

'Good.'

Charlie yells up the stairs from the kitchen.

'Daddy, you should turn on the radio.'

'What is it?' asks Julianne.

'They're saying Milo Coleman is in a coma.'

39

Ronnie Cray isn't answering her mobile. I try to reach her at the incident room and at police headquarters in Portishead, but am fobbed off, transferred and stonewalled until I get through to DI Abbott.

'She's taking some time off,' Monk says cautiously.

'Since when?'

'Yesterday.'

'What happened?'

'Officially she took long service leave.'

'And unofficially?'

'The Chief Constable removed her. Bannerman got his way.'

'Who's in charge?'

He hesitates. 'Right now – I am.'

'I just heard the news about Milo Coleman.'

'I can't comment.'

'Come on, Monk, this is me.'

'Exactly. You'll be contacted by detectives in due course, Professor, and asked about your whereabouts last night.'

'You can't be serious.'

'Do I sound like I'm joking?'

'I went to dinner with my wife and then we came home.'

'Were you anywhere near the Princes Street car park in Bristol?'

'Not even in the same city.'

'Good to know.'

He hangs up. The phone has grown damp in my white fist. Julianne has been listening. 'What happened?'

'I don't know.'

I start getting dressed.

'Where are you going?'

'To see Ronnie Cray.'

Medicated and moving freely, I unlock the garden shed and find an empty cardboard box. Tearing it roughly into the shape of the Volvo's missing window, I wedge it hard into the gap left by the shattered glass and wrap masking tape around the frame of the door.

Charlie is watching me from the front steps. 'Where are you going?'

'To see DCS Cray.'

'What about me?'

'You're not coming.'

'Why?'

'Do I *really* have to explain?'

'That wasn't my fault yesterday. You said it yourself.'

'You're staying here, Charlie.'

'Hold on – that's not fair! I did nothing wrong. I won't go out on my own again. I'll stay with you.'

Julianne has come outside. Charlie stops talking in mid-sentence. Julianne looks from face to face. 'What's wrong?'

'Not a thing,' I say.

She sees the broken window and wants an explanation.

'Somebody smashed it,' says Charlie.

'I can see that. Why?'

'I left my phone on the seat,' says Charlie.

'Someone stole your phone?'

I jump in. 'No, I scared them off.'

'You saw them?'

'No, what I mean is, someone else must have scared them off. I didn't see them. Nothing was taken.'

Julianne looks at Charlie and back to me. 'What aren't you telling me?'

'Nothing,' says Charlie. 'We're just leaving, aren't we, Daddy?'

'You're not going anywhere,' says Julianne.

It's Charlie's turn to look from face to face. 'Why?'

'I need your help,' says Julianne, but what she really means is 'you're staying at home because I'm worried'.

Charlie glances at me, hoping I'll support her cause, but instead I look away.

'That broken window,' she says, spinning back to her mother, 'shall I tell you what *really* happened?'

'It was *my* phone!' I blurt. 'I left it on the dashboard. It was stupid.'

Charlie raises an eyebrow, waiting for me to say more.

'Listen, I'm not feeling very coordinated today. Would you mind if Charlie drove me? We won't be long.'

Charlie grabs the keys from my hand before her mother can counter.

I kiss Julianne on the cheek and whisper, 'I think I'm making progress on this whole psychology idea.'

The car pulls out. Julianne yells after me. 'Remember to look at the wills.'

Ronnie Cray lives in a farmhouse on the outskirts of Bristol in the green-belted hinterland beyond the council houses, barricaded shops and fight-prone pubs. She once bred horses, but now looks after animals that have been abandoned or mistreated. I've never seen her ride. I can't even imagine it.

She doesn't answer the door, so I walk towards the barn,

dodging the muddy puddles. I can hear her talking to someone on the phone.

'Listen, princess, I got horses to feed. You got nails to paint. Why don't you call your delivery guy and ask him when he's going to be here. Then we'll both have a nice day.'

The sight of me doesn't improve her mood. She's dressed for work in baggy jeans, an oversized shirt and wellingtons. Her right hand is bandaged.

She ends the call. 'What are you doing here?'

'I heard the news.'

'And what – misery needs company, I suppose?'

She turns away, moving deeper into the barn. The place smells of straw, dung, leather and saddle soap.

'Why aren't you at work?' I ask.

'The Chief Constable felt I'd lost focus and wanted a fresh set of eyes on the case.'

'And the real reason?'

'The hounds were baying.'

'Bannerman?'

'I never thought I'd see the day when a talkback radio host ran a murder investigation.'

'What happened to your hand?'

'What hand?'

'The bandaged one.'

'It's fine.'

'Show me.'

She lets me unwrap the soiled strapping, revealing discoloured flesh and swollen knuckles.

'What did you hit?'

'A wall.'

'Clever.'

'You should see the wall.'

'Can you flex your fingers?'

She makes a fist, grimacing slightly.

'Did you get this X-rayed?'

'I'm keeping it iced.'

She looks past me out the large double doors. 'Is that your Charlie?'

I nod.

'I heard about yesterday afternoon. They're looking for Elliot Crowe.'

'I'm more interested in what happened to Milo Coleman.'

Cray sucks in a breath. 'He was found just after midnight in a stairwell at the Princes Street car park in Bristol. No signs of violence except for abrasions on his knees and a bruise on his neck.'

'A blood choke?'

'He's in a coma, on life support.'

'Was anything carved on his forehead?'

'No.'

'Why, then?'

Cray tilts her chin down and flexes her fingers. 'If I were a betting woman – which I'm not – I'd say it's because he went on radio and called a sad sadistic prick "a sad sadistic prick". Then again – it's not my case. I'm not paid to have an opinion any more.'

I motion for her to give me her hand and begin rewrapping the bandage. When I'm finished she picks up a bag of horse-feed and slings it over her shoulder. A cloud of chaff dust floats around her head. She carries the bag to a scarred wooden bench and slices it open with a penknife before filling the feeding troughs.

'So that's it – you're giving up?' I say. 'This guy is killing at will and that doesn't bother you.'

'*Bother* me? My career is hanging by a thread, Professor. They're pushing me out.'

'Milo Coleman is in a coma. What if this guy comes looking for me?'

'You haven't pissed him off.'

'How do you know?'

Cray doesn't answer. I follow her to a different corner of the barn, feeling exhausted yet fired up by something other than the ceaseless introspection and pointless internal dialogue relating to my marriage and my sick wife.

'You dragged me into this. You asked for my help. Now you're telling me to walk away?'

The DCS sighs and turns. Her eyes are just as bright, but the lines under them are more pronounced. 'I will never understand you, Professor. You're not getting paid. You won't get any credit. If things go wrong, they'll look for someone to blame. Yet knowing all of that — you're still here, tearing strips off me. Go home. This is not our responsibility any more.'

She leaves the barn and walks across a field, hunched forward as though she's fighting against a headwind. Two dogs come bounding to meet her, their tails happily wagging in anticipation. She cups their heads in her hands, rubbing behind their ears, while they gaze at her loyally.

'You know why I love dogs more than people?' she shouts, everything about her softer. 'Feed them and pet them and they'll love you when no one else will.'

40

My makeshift cardboard 'window' is somewhere behind us on the motorway, having been sucked out by the rushing air. I've never been good at DIY. Charlie is driving and shouting questions, wanting to know about Milo. I have no answers.

My mobile is ringing. Ruiz gets straight to the point. 'I've been asking myself what I'd do if someone carved an initial in my forehead.'

'And?'

'I'd find him and beat the shit out of him.'

'Understandable.'

'Then I'd visit a plastic surgeon to see what could be done.'

'Wise move.'

'So I called a few specialists in Bristol and came up with another victim. A surgeon remembered a woman coming in with knife wounds on her forehead. She wanted him to patch her up so it wouldn't leave a scar.'

'When?'

'August. She was early forties. Married. The surgeon couldn't give me her name because of the whole doctor–patient privilege thing, but he suggested I visit the Rape Crisis Centre in Bristol. I figure they're more likely to talk to you.'

'What's the address?'

'I'll text it to you now.'

The Avon and Somerset Rape Crisis Centre has no sign above the door or any other hint of its function apart from metal bars on the lower windows and a CCTV camera at each corner, tilted to cover the entrance.

I press an intercom and hear three tones echoing through distant rooms.

'Can I help you?' asks a woman's voice.

'I'm looking for Patricia Collier.'

'Who are you?'

'Joe O'Loughlin. I'm a clinical psychologist.'

'Do you have an appointment?'

'No.'

I slip my business card through the mailbox and wait, glancing at the camera, sure that I'm being watched. After five minutes, I press the intercom again.

'Are your pants on fire?' asks the woman.

'I thought you'd forgotten me.'

'Oh, yeah, I'm that stupid.'

I wait for another few minutes until twin deadlocks turn and the door swings open, giving a little *eek!* on stiff hinges. The large woman is attractive in the fullness of her figure and roundness of her face. 'You can call me Ros,' she says, 'we use first names here. The boss is in her office.'

Following her up a set of narrow stairs, we pass through a large lounge area with an indoor climbing frame and boxes of toys. Several women are kneeling on the floor playing with toddlers. Along one wall there are shelves with clothing bins organised into ages and sizes.

I'm shown into a small room crammed with a desk, filing cabinets and boxes. There are posters on the wall showing battered women and crying children. One of them reads: *Don't be silenced — say no to domestic violence.*

Patricia Collier is standing by the window. The white streak in her dark hair looks almost luminous. She's wearing jeans, a sweatshirt and heavy boots. 'Thank you, Ros,' she lisps, not acknowledging me. Then she sits and swivels her chair. My business card is on the desk in front of her.

'How can I help you, Professor?'

I glance at the empty chair, but she's not going to offer me a seat. Clearly, I'm expected to say my piece and get out.

'At the request of Avon and Somerset Constabulary I have been reviewing the investigation into the murders of Elizabeth and Harper Crowe. On the same day a woman was choked unconscious on a footpath in Clevedon and had the letter "A" carved into her forehead. There have been other similar attacks.'

Barely a flicker registers on Ms Collier's face.

'Do you know of any similar incidents?' I ask.

'We don't discuss the details of women who come to us for help.'

'I understand that, but this is important.'

'Every attack is important. A third of women in Britain are victims of domestic violence.'

'These people weren't attacked by a spouse.'

'Partner, boyfriend, father, son, brother — makes no difference. A fist is a fist.'

Ms Collier begins rattling off domestic violence figures as though hitting me with a combination of punches. I wait until she runs out of statistics and then try again.

'There have been other attacks. On Tuesday night a young woman was murdered. She had the same symbol cut into her forehead.'

This information causes a tremor in her eyes, but only for a moment.

'Well, Professor, you'd best run along and catch him before he does it again.'

Her animosity has sucked the warmth from the air.

'I'm sorry to have wasted your time,' I say, turning to leave.

Ms Collier seems surprised that I've given up so easily. 'Are you married?' she asks.

'Separated.'

'Have you ever raised a hand to a woman?'

'No. Have you ever hit a man?'

'Plenty.'

'I hope they deserved it.'

'Every one of them,' she says defiantly. 'You probably think that makes me a hypocrite. I don't care. I stopped giving men the benefit of the doubt a long time ago. Too many women are dead because male judges refused to give them protection, or some bullshit evidence from a psychologist set their violent boyfriend or husband free.'

I'm almost at the door, but cannot let the accusation go unanswered.

'You're right, Ms Collier. What would I know? I've only spent twenty years treating battered women, rape victims, paedophiles, baby-shakers and children so traumatised by abuse they wet themselves at the sound of a male voice. You might keep some women safe, but I pick up the pieces. I make them whole again. But thanks for the gender appraisal and the advice.'

I'm on the stairs when she calls me back. There's no sign of an apology or any warmth in her voice, but her attitude has softened and she offers me tea or coffee. I decline.

'Please sit down.'

I take a seat.

She sighs and begins. 'At the end of last summer we had a woman turn up at the shelter. She had a bandage on her forehead. It must have been fresh because blood was leaking through the gauze. I thought her husband had beaten her, but she denied that he'd touched her. Then I wondered if she might have done it to herself. We get some cutters here, but they don't usually touch their faces. Eventually, she told me that she'd been attacked in a park while walking her dog. She was choked until she blacked out. When she came to she had blood streaming down her face. She thought she'd been scalped until she looked in the mirror.'

'Was she having an affair?'

'We don't ask questions like that. Makes no difference.'

'Did she go to the police?'

'I encouraged her to make an official complaint, but she had no idea who attacked her. She was embarrassed. Ashamed. Distraught. She'd left her kids behind – that's how bad she felt.'

Miss Collier opens a filing cabinet and retrieves a manila folder. 'I met her husband. I had him pegged as the controlling sort, but he was very calm and measured when he came here. He'd gone to a lot of trouble to find his wife. With her agreement, I put them in a room together. They talked for hours. Hugged. Cried. She left the shelter that night.'

'To go home?'

'I assume so.'

'I'm very keen to talk to her.'

'I can't give you her name.'

'Whoever attacked her is still out there – he'll keep going unless he's stopped.'

There is a moment when we stare at each other and I know she's caught between her loyalty to a victim and her desire to punish the man responsible.

'I'll call her,' she says. 'She can decide.'

41

A shadow passes behind the leaded glass panels of the door.

'Who is it?' asks a voice from within.

'Joe O'Loughlin. Patricia Collier called you.'

Two beats of silence and the deadlock releases. The woman is dressed in a white shirt with a round collar and tailored trousers. Her face looks almost bloodless until I recognise the heavy layer of powder that makes her look like a Japanese Kabuki actress. Applied most thickly to her forehead, the foundation conceals her scar.

She turns immediately and I'm expected to follow – along the hallway and down a set of flagstone steps into a modern kitchen with polished stone benches and brushed steel appliances. Someone has written a poem in magnetic words on the American-style double fridge.

> music is the sound of feelings
> the beating of wings and chant of the wind
> of rain and waves and babies crying
> play your crying fiddle don't beat an angry drum.

'I don't know what to call you,' I say.

'Gabrielle.' She looks at the wall clock. 'My husband will be home at one. I don't want him to . . . I mean . . . if we could be finished by then . . . '

In her early forties, she has dyed hair and fine-boned features that make her look unearthly and ethereal, as though if I reached out and touched her I would grasp only shadowed air.

'I love my husband,' she announces, as though wanting to make that clear before we start. 'I know that sounds insincere when I tell you what I did, but it's no less true now than it was when it happened. I made a mistake. My husband has forgiven me. I will not take this any further.'

'I understand.'

She perches on a stool at the kitchen bench and takes a sip of water from a tall glass.

'Have you heard of a website called Friends Reunited?' she asks.

'Yes.'

'I signed up a year ago. I thought I might track down some old school friends and find out how they'd fared over the years. Instead I found Simon. It's almost a cliché, isn't it – old flames reunited, childhood sweethearts.'

'You used to date?'

'We grew up only a few streets apart in Sheffield. His dad and my dad worked together at the brewery. The school did a play that year – *A Midsummer Night's Dream* – I was Titania and Simon played Puck. After our last performance there was a cast party. I lost my virginity to Simon that night. It was nothing to write home about – but I guess everyone says that.'

The statement hangs in the air. An overly loud cuckoo clock sounds from somewhere upstairs.

'You probably think I'm foolish, at my age. I have two children and this lovely house and a husband who loves me . . . '

'I'm not here to judge you.'

She closes her eyes and continues. 'About six weeks after I joined the website I received a message from Simon. He didn't believe that I was really me until I mentioned the cast party and what my father had wanted to do to him. Soon we were sending each other a dozen emails a day. Teasing. Laughing. Reminiscing. We swapped phone numbers. He called me. We talked for hours. That's the thing about meeting someone for the second time. Flirting with them. Falling for them. Wanting them. It happens so quickly because they already have a connection, a common history.'

'Where does he live now?'

'Sheffield. He never left.'

'When did you get together?'

'We arranged to meet up in Bristol and have lunch. It was as though the years just fell away. He looked the same. I felt embarrassed. We talked for more than four hours. It was just wonderful. Afterwards, he gave me a peck on the cheek and said he was happy to have found me again.

'We were both married, both had children, we knew where the boundaries were, but things changed after that. Simon arranged a business trip to Somerset. I told my husband I was meeting a friend for lunch. Afterwards, we went for a walk on a beach and couldn't stop kissing. It was better than teenage fumblings. It was tender. Exciting. I felt young again. Breathless. One thing led to another . . . ' She looks up at me, searching for understanding. 'Are you married?'

'Yes.'

'Have you ever been unfaithful?'

'Yes.'

'Did your wife punish you?'

'I punished myself.'

'Did she forgive you?'

It's a good question.

'I hope so,' I say, thinking about last night with Julianne.

Gabrielle can't sit still. She waters an indoor plant and wipes the spilled droplets that have beaded on the bench-top.

'My husband says a marriage should be like a strong tree with its roots deep in the ground. It can be buffeted by storms, but will not fall. He is a good man. Secure. Safe.'

301

'How long did the affair last?'

'A few months – we only slept together twice.'

'Your husband found out?'

'No, it was Simon's wife. She found a receipt. Not for the accommodation – we were always very careful – but for a bottle of champagne that Simon ordered. She thought that was odd and phoned the restaurant. The manager remembered us. Simon denied everything but his wife began watching him. She tried to access his email account. She looked at his text messages. Finally she hired a private detective and had Simon followed. He took photographs of us leaving a hotel together. Simon begged her for another chance. We stopped seeing each other. That should have been the end of it, but then this . . . '

She points to her forehead.

'Who else knew about the affair?'

'I told nobody.'

'What about Simon?'

'His wife knew. I don't know about anyone else.'

'Do you remember the name of the private detective?'

'No.'

'Did you ever meet him?'

She shakes her head.

Moving her forward, I ask her to describe the day of the attack in detail – a rainy afternoon in August. She took the dog for a walk between the showers, her usual route – through the park, past the tennis courts and around the cricket field. Early evening, she crested a gentle rise and the path turned through a glade of trees, a shadowed dell, a muddy bend, uneven ground . . .

'Close your eyes and concentrate on every detail,' I say, breaking down each moment. I want her to feel the breeze on her cheeks and see the patches of damp watery light. What was she wearing? Did she pass anyone on the path, or notice any cars?

Her whole body has started to shake.

'Did you see his face?'

'No.'

'Did he say anything?'

'He asked me if I wanted to die.'

'Did you recognise his voice?'

'No.'

'Did he have an accent?'

'No.'

Cracks are forming in the powder on her forehead.

'Do you have any idea who would do this to you?'

Her head rocks from side to side unconvincingly.

'You must have asked yourself that question,' I say.

She falters. 'Yes, but I have no proof. Simon's wife is Sicilian. She comes from a big family. Four brothers. You probably think I'm stereotyping her as the hot-headed Italian, but she could have sent one of her brothers to warn me off.'

'Did she ever threaten you?'

'No.

'Have you heard from Simon since the attack?'

She avoids my gaze. Her mobile is ringing. She glances at the screen and her pupils dilate slightly. She ignores the call, covering the phone with her hands.

'Do you know anyone called Maggie Dutton?' I ask.

'No.'

'What about Naomi Meredith?'

She shakes her head. 'Who are they?'

'Two other women who were choked unconscious.'

I can see Gabrielle wanting to ask the obvious question. Did he cut them?

I run through a list of names: Dominic Crowe, Jeremy Egan, Dion Ferguson. None of them triggers any response.

'What about Elliot Crowe?'

She frowns. 'I might have heard that name.'

'His mother and sister were murdered at a farmhouse outside of Clevedon.'

She inhales sharply and a hand flutters to her mouth. 'Was it the same person – the one who attacked me?'

'I believe so. Listen to me, Gabrielle. I need to ask you some questions that you may find embarrassing, but it's important you tell me the truth.'

She nods.

'Have you ever had sex in public with random strangers or let others watch you?'

'Never!'

'Have you swapped partners or gone on dating websites?'

'No.' She is growing more and more distressed.

'Somebody else discovered your affair. Could anyone have read your emails? Or followed you?'

'No.'

'Were you seen together?'

'No, please, I think you should leave. My husband is due home. I'm lucky he forgave me.'

I could always spot them. They'd arrive in separate cars or at different times, or would sometimes book an extra room to hide their subterfuge. Others pretended to be married, telling me stories about leaving the kids at home, or having a second honeymoon.

Fake names and false addresses were pretty standard, along with paying cash and travelling at least twenty miles from home, so they wouldn't bump into someone they knew.

Some arrived with overnight bags, others without even a toothbrush, while a few would act out Pretty Woman *fantasies, pretending to be high-class hookers in long overcoats with precious little else underneath.*

The men usually took charge, while the women hung back. I would ask for a credit card swipe 'for incidentals' and this would prompt offers of a cash deposit or a handshake with twenty quid pressed into my palm. Some men were very specific about the room they wanted. The floor had to have at least two exits – the stairs and a lift – with no CCTV cameras. They didn't sign for room service bills or buy porn on the in-house movie channels.

Many didn't bother staying the whole night. They ordered champagne, shagged and showered and were away by midnight, home to their 'other halves'. The gym bags and tennis racquets were a nice touch – providing an excuse for their freshly perfumed selves.

'I hope you enjoyed your stay, Mr Foster or Mr Smith or Mr Howard,' I'd say, and then watch that moment of indecision before the penny dropped and they remembered which fake name they'd used.

'Yes, of course, absolutely,' they'd reply.

'Perhaps you'd consider signing up to our loyalty programme?'

'No, thank you.'

'We give you fifty per cent off your next stay with us.'

'No, not this time.'

'Does Mrs Foster need help with her bags?'

'No, she'll be down shortly.'

'You forgot your receipt.'

'Throw it away.'

'I can post it to you.'

'No, that won't be necessary.'

Finding their real names and addresses wasn't particularly difficult. DVLA employees are very helpful. I'd call and say that someone had scraped a car in the hotel car park and driven away without leaving details. 'The driver looked young. I think she panicked. I wouldn't want to get her into trouble. That's why I didn't call the police.'

I filled out a form, paid a small fee and the name and address were supplied.

In the beginning I sent anonymous letters to their wives and husbands, but the same men (and women) kept coming back; repeat offenders, so to speak, forgiven but unrepentant, schooled in deceit. Most of them got better at hiding their activities, using secret email accounts and separate mobiles, keeping spare clothes and checking their pockets for receipts.

That's why I had to teach them a lesson. I had to ask them a question with only one answer.

'A'.

42

A passing shower has freshened the air, leaving behind a light mist and droplets that cling to leaves and blades of grass. Ruiz seems to want to feel it on his cheeks, raising his face to the sky. Despite his gruff exterior he is not a pessimist by nature. In a long career as a detective he witnessed countless acts of violence and cruelty, but these have not shaken his faith in people. Human beings might be unreliable, stupid, self-serving and prone to disappointing him, but most were still fundamentally well meaning.

'So all of them were having affairs or lying about it,' he says, without sounding judgemental.

'Except for Milo Coleman,' I say.

'Who pissed the killer off.'

'Or got too close.'

'And we still don't know how this guy is finding his victims. What about Friends Reunited?'

'Apart from Gabrielle Sallis, none of the others were registered.'

Ruiz digs into his pocket and takes out his tin of sweets. 'So we're looking for a common thread between at least seven victims from different areas, different jobs, different ages. Maybe this guy dangled lots of hooks in the water by signing up to various websites.'

'Which would make him almost impossible to find.'

Charlie is nursing a soft drink at a pavement table. She wanted to go into town with the sketchbook, but I won't let her walk the streets alone. Ronnie Cray was right – this isn't my problem. I should let the police handle the case and take Charlie home. We could spend the afternoon with Julianne before she goes into hospital. Yet I cannot rid myself of a disquieting ache in my lower belly, an agitation connected to a thought that I cannot put into words. Some people kill impulsively, in the heat of the moment. Their brain snaps or they are overcome by extreme rage or jealousy or another primary emotion. Afterwards they are horrified by what they have done, haunted by the sheer amount of blood. They panic. They flee. They make mistakes.

The farmhouse killer would have been shocked by the blood and frightened by his actions, but his mind stayed focused and sharp. He didn't bring the weapon. He made the decision when he arrived at the farmhouse, committing two murders that seemed contradictory and paradoxical – one savage and the other almost reverential. F. Scott Fitzgerald once said that the test of a first-rate intelligence is the ability to hold two opposing ideas in mind at the same time and still be able to function. This man could do that.

If acting alone, he must have killed Harper first. Either she let him inside or she was asleep when he entered her bedroom and he choked her before she could react. By comparison, the scene downstairs resembled an abattoir. Aroused and unforgiving, he exploded in rage and corrupt lust, stabbing Elizabeth thirty-six times. Afterwards, out of breath, his adrenalin still surging, he knelt beside her body. He looked at his bloody hands. He saw what he'd done. The truth expanded in his chest.

Many killers would have panicked. Some would have vomited at the smell and sight of a disembowelled body. Not this man.

He calmly took off his clothes, bundled them up and carried them to the laundry.

I try to imagine myself in his mind. I am covered in blood, walking through the house. Harper is lying upstairs in her bed, arranged to look like a storybook princess. Something made him stop in the hallway. Blood dripped from his fingertips on to the wooden boards.

I close my eyes and feel my heart begin racing. Someone is coming. They're going to find me. A motorbike approaches the house. I cannot turn off the lights in time. Instead I stand behind the door and wait.

Someone knocks. I don't answer.

'I know you're in there,' says a voice. 'Let me talk to Harper. Is that you, Mrs Crowe? Please let me in. I want to tell her I'm sorry.'

A second voice, female: 'I'm here, too, Mrs Crowe. We're sorry it's so late.'

I wait. I hear them walk away. Not away . . . they go to the side of the farmhouse. I hear gravel rattling against Harper's bedroom window. They're calling her name. Arguing.

I hear the motorbike rumble down the drive and I breathe again. Clean up. Change my clothes. I notice the Bible and the candles in the sitting room. I need to lay a false trail – more than one. I paint the bloody pentagram on the wall and light the candles. I break open the front door and trigger the alarm. On the doorstep I discover a birthday present for Harper – a peace offering from her boyfriend. I take it with me, along with the knife.

Who am I? I know about loving relationships, fidelity and family, but something has warped my sexuality. I'm angered and frustrated by acts of betrayal. Perhaps I come from a family torn apart by divorce or infidelity. Either that or I've been scorned by a girlfriend, or cuckolded by a wife.

I am not an adolescent. My sophistication and forensic aware-ness have come with age and experience. I have done this before, which is why I deserve respect, not insults and scorn. I am watching the media coverage. I know what they're saying about me.

Most of my victims have never come forward. They're too embarrassed or won't risk the public shaming, but the murders of Elizabeth and Harper were different. I crossed a line. Initially, this terrified me. I was frightened of what I'd become . . . what I was capable of . . . but now I relish those memories, which colour my world – the smell of her hair, the beating of her heart.

'I need a piece of paper,' I say to Ruiz.

He takes out the battered notebook that he carries everywhere. The pages are dog-eared and buckled by sweat, held together by a rubber band. He tears one out and I begin writing.

> – mid-twenties to mid-forties, most likely at the higher end of the range, with a high sex drive and burning sense of betrayal.
>
> – known to Elizabeth or Harper.
>
> – confident of his surroundings. He has good working knowledge of local footpaths and bus time-tables, which is why he could attack and disappear quickly without being noticed or attracting suspicion.
>
> – he'll most likely work in a service job or something that takes him away from home, but brings him into contact with people.
>
> – good verbal and social skills – enough to avoid suspicion.
>
> – physically strong.
>
> – forensically aware.
>
> – highly intelligent, but with a poor academic record.
>
> – his family and friends may not even consider the possibility that he could be responsible.

– he will not be abnormal.
– he will not look guilty.
– he is escalating.
– this will happen again.

When I finish writing, I read the page again. Four of the primary suspects match elements of the profile – Dominic Crowe, Jeremy Egan, Dion Ferguson and Elliot Crowe. But nothing that I've written explains how Elizabeth and Harper fitted into the killer's picture. Elizabeth had a history of infidelities, but no symbol was carved into her forehead. Harper was single, eighteen, unsullied by life. She is the anomaly.

I look up at Ruiz. 'I think we've been looking at this the wrong way around.'

'How so?'

'We've been focusing on Elizabeth because she bore the brunt of his anger, but what if Harper was the real target?'

'He barely touched her.'

'That's my point – it was an act of contrition, maybe of love.'

Ruiz leans over the table, propping on his elbows. 'So we're back to the father or the boyfriend.'

'Or some other admirer.'

'Tommy Garrett?'

'No. Jeremy Egan talked to Harper at the pub that night.'

'You think he wanted to add Harper to his list of conquests?'

'Maybe.'

'Unless Elliot had a thing for his sister,' says Ruiz. 'They weren't biological siblings. It's happened before.'

'Harper wasn't sexually assaulted. She represented something to the killer that Elizabeth didn't. She was pure. She was blameless. She didn't deserve to die – but had to.'

'Perhaps she saw something or knew something,' says Ruiz.

Instinctively, I know he's right. The answer lies somewhere in the timelines. Folding the sheet of paper, I put it into my pocket and tell Charlie to collect her things.

'Where are we going?' she asks.

'I have to take your mum to the hospital.'

'I wanted to keep looking for the house – the one in the sketch.'

'No, not on your own.'

She's about to argue, but Ruiz interrupts, 'I'll look after her. Just tell me when you want her home.'

43

A shaft of sunlight, teeming with dust motes, spills through the window and paints a square of light across the queen-sized bed. Julianne's small suitcase has been packed and repacked. She doesn't know whether to take pyjamas or a nightgown.

'A nightgown makes more sense, don't you think?'

'Absolutely,' I say.

'Dr Percival said I might need a catheter.'

'True.'

'I should maybe take two nightgowns – just in case.'

'Good idea.'

'Are you going to agree with everything I say?'

'Probably.'

I'm trying to be supportive and positive, but my heart is knocking against my chest. Julianne picks up a photograph of the girls and puts it on top of the folded clothes. Her mother is waiting downstairs with Emma.

There are hugs and forced smiles and instructions repeated about meals and separating 'the whites' and a birthday party that Emma has been invited to on Sunday.

'We'll be fine,' says her mother. 'You'll only be gone a week.'

'We promise not to fall apart,' I add.

'And you'll miss me.'

'Oh, we will.'

'I thought Charlie would be here,' says Julianne, looking outside. 'Did you call Vincent?'

'They're fine. Charlie will call you later,' I tell her, wishing I could make our elder daughter suddenly appear.

On the drive to the hospital I keep making small talk, yet I feel strangely detached from things around me. The radio is playing in the background – news at the top of the hour.

Police have issued an arrest warrant for a twenty-six-year-old man wanted for the murders of Somerset mother and daughter Elizabeth and Harper Crowe.

I turn up the volume.

The suspect has been named as Elliot Crowe, the adopted son and stepbrother of the victims. The warrant follows a police raid at first light this morning when two SWAT teams broke into a bedsit in Eastleigh, Bristol. Forensic teams have since used earth-moving equipment to dig up the rear garden.

A spokesman for Avon and Somerset Police would not comment on whether anything was found during the search, but said the investigation was ongoing.

I glance at Julianne, who hasn't reacted. Zen-like in her calm, she has bundled up her hair and pinned it high on her head with a tortoiseshell clasp.

'Why would he kill his mother and sister?' she asks quietly.

'He's a drug addict,' I say, as if no other explanation were needed.

'Well, I'm glad its over.'

At the hospital there are stairs, and more stairs and swinging double doors. Julianne has a private room. She puts her suitcase next to a locker and hangs her dressing gown on a hook behind the door. I watch as she unpacks, putting her bedsocks, underwear and a loose-fitting dress on separate shelves. Her cup with a flexible straw goes on the bedside table, next to the photograph and a twin pack of Polo mints.

314

'I can't find my phone charger.'

'I'll bring one tomorrow.'

'That's not the point – I know I packed it. What if my battery runs out?'

'It won't.'

'I should have brought my little radio.'

'You've got the TV.'

'I'm going to miss *The Archers*.'

'You'll catch up.'

Sitting on the mattress, she bounces a little as though testing the springs.

'You don't have to stay.'

'I don't have anywhere I'd rather be.'

She leans back against the bedhead. A clock ticks on the wall, louder than before.

'What time is the surgery?' I ask.

'First thing in the morning.'

'Can I call you beforehand?'

'It might be very early.'

'What happens then?'

'After the operation I go to the recovery room.'

'I'll come in the morning.'

'No, don't come until I'm awake. Stay with the girls.'

'Should I bring them?'

She thinks about this. 'No, leave them at home until you've seen me. I might be groggy. I want to look my best.'

'They won't care.'

'It's not for *them*.'

Further along the corridor comes the sound of 'Happy Birthday'. There is also a beeping sound like an alarm, which halts after a few moments. A nurse puts her head around the door and stops in mid-sentence, surprised to see me.

'I'm sorry about the noise,' says Becca Washburn, recovering her composure. 'One of the patients is having a birthday. There's plenty of cake to go around. Would you like a piece?'

We shake our heads.

'Can I get you anything else?' asks Becca, stepping into the room. 'The TV is dodgy, I'm afraid. It can only get two channels: Sky News and UK Gold.'

'I'm not bothered,' says Julianne.

'Well, I'm off home, but I'll be working tomorrow,' says Becca. 'If you need anything, just press the buzzer. There are nurses on duty all night.'

After she's gone, Julianne turns to me. 'That's the woman we saw in the café.'

'Yes.'

'Did you know she worked on this ward?'

'No.'

Visiting hours are almost over. I hug Julianne tightly and almost lift her off the ground. Half a head shorter, she looks up at me. 'I'll see you tomorrow.'

'Call me if you want to talk.'

'I'll be fine. I have my book to read and friends have been calling me ever since I broke the news. They all want to come and visit, but I've told them to wait until I get home.'

'It's nice they care.'

'They're all asking about you.'

'Me?'

'They want to know if we're back together.'

'What do you tell them?'

'I tell them it's a work in progress.'

44

Leaving the hospital, I drive through Bristol to Eastleigh, turning off Fishponds Road into a bleak-looking street full of cheap terraces, bedsits and council flats. Police cars are parked outside one particular house, flanking a forensic service van.

After driving past the address, I pull over and walk to the next corner. Climbing on to a brick wall, I can see across the rear gardens of a dozen terraces to where arc lights are blazing. Police have used a small mechanical digger to scrape aside weeds and carve out a trench in the dark brown soil. Now they're erecting a tent to protect the area.

Dogs are barking. Curtains move. I can feel myself being watched. I jump down and retrace my steps until I reach the front of the building. Two uniformed police officers are standing outside on the footpath, while another – PC Benjamin – guards the front door. Ducking under the crime scene tape, I reach her before the other officers can react. She signals them that it's OK.

'I didn't expect to see you here,' I say.

'It's my job, sir,' she says resolutely, standing a little straighter. Her eyes are puffy and red.

'I was sorry to hear about Milo,' I say. 'How is he?'

Fear momentarily clouds her face and she cannot hide the tremor in her voice. 'I don't know, sir.'

'Have you been to see him?'

'No.'

'Why not?'

She lowers her voice. 'I broke up with Milo.'

'When?'

She hesitates. 'We had an argument last night. I stormed out of a restaurant.' Her voice grows more desperate. 'I took a cab home. I wouldn't let him drive me. Perhaps if I'd . . . if I hadn't . . . '

'You are not to blame for what happened.'

'Don't you see – Elliot Crowe must have been watching us. He must have followed Milo to the car park.'

'Did you see Elliot?'

'No, but they found Milo's wallet dumped in a rubbish bin in the back lane.' She motions over her shoulder.

'Why would Elliot Crowe attack Milo?'

'Because of what Milo said on the radio,' says Bennie. 'He got too close to the truth. Milo said it was Elliot who killed his mother and sister, and he was right. They found the murder weapon buried in the garden.'

'How did they find it?' I ask.

'Metal detector.'

'How did they know where to look?'

Bennie ignores the question. She glances at her colleagues. 'You have to leave, sir.'

'Listen, Bennie, I've kept your secret. I haven't told anyone about you and Milo, but you were probably the last person to see him before the attack. They're going to find out. You should make a statement.'

Bennie doesn't answer.

'I want to look inside,' I say.

'Absolutely not.'

'Five minutes.'

'No.'

I take out my mobile. 'I make one call and everybody knows the truth about you and Milo.'

If looks could kill . . .

PC Benjamin opens the door and steps to one side. 'You have two minutes.'

The smell inside the bedsit is indescribable. It's a junkie's nest, ravaged by neglect. Discarded bottles of vodka, whisky, gin and schnapps are lying amid overflowing ashtrays, burger wrappers and dirty clothes. Stepping over discarded shoes, unopened letters, dry bread rolls and bags of rubbish, I reach the kitchen. Something that might be vomit has dried in a yellow-red patch on the floor and food is congealed on every plate, saucepan and available surface. As hard as I try, I cannot equate such squalor and self-loathing with the sense of calm and afterthought that characterised the farmhouse murders.

I'm often accused of giving people too much credit and ignoring the worst in their natures because I'm sympathetic towards the underprivileged and exploited. But I don't accept the label that I'm soft on criminals or a bleeding heart. I simply understand the contradictions and paradoxes, the layers of personality within each of us.

Why do good people do bad things? There are lots of reasons – denial, peer pressure, tunnel vision, low self-esteem, ignorance, arrogance, disorder, competition, time pressure, cognitive dissonance, addiction, settling old scores or recovering losses. I could keep going, but the point is that nothing is black and white except for mathematics and pandas.

Elliot Crowe's life tumbled out of control owing to some combination of the above. His biological parents are either dead or they abandoned him. His adoptive mother was unfaithful and brutally efficient at getting everything she could from her divorce. Like all addicts, Elliot is skilled in deception. He deceived himself that first moment he slid a needle into his vein or inhaled from a crack pipe. He told himself it wouldn't become an issue. And later he justified every action because he was hooked, taken, spoken for; or the dragon was in charge.

The result is an angry, bitter and addicted man; greedy, selfish, self-loathing and calculating, but I'm not convinced that he's a killer. To begin with, he's not stupid enough to have kept the murder weapon and he's not clever enough to have staged the crime scene – not without help. The killer wasn't a trophy-taker and the knife isn't some treasured artefact.

Right now he's running or holed up somewhere with his girlfriend, most likely in a squat or derelict building. He won't stay hidden for long. Scum always floats to the top.

'Where have you been?'

'I had errands to run.'

'Did you remember the bread?'

'No.'

'That's all I asked you to do.'

'I'll go now.'

'Supper is ready. I picked up fish and chips from our favourite place.'

'Put mine in the oven.'

'You're hopeless. You'd forget your head if it wasn't screwed on.' She taps my head with her knuckles. 'Knock, knock, is there anyone home in there?'

'Don't do that.'

'What?'

'That.'

'I'm only teasing.'

'Don't treat me as if I'm an idiot.'

'Well, stop acting like one. Eat your supper.'

'I'm not hungry.'

'Fine, then.'

She pulls the plate away and carries it into the kitchen where she opens the pedal bin and dumps my supper inside. Then she comes back and sits down, grinning at me smugly. It's that same self-satisfied, condescending smile that she always uses when I've disappointed her. I've never been good enough. I don't spend enough time with her. I'm not sensitive to her needs. I'm not smart enough. I don't earn enough money. I'm not ambitious. I fail on every count, yet I love her and I defend her.

When I complain about her taunts and bullying she says that I'm exaggerating, or imagining things or whining. If I spend too long at work I'm a workaholic. If I take a day off I'm lazy. She preys on my fears and weaknesses, my compassion and my imperfections. She pushes me away and then tries to be affectionate. If I rebuff her or I don't respond immediately, she says I'm being cruel and uses that as an excuse to push me away again, showing me that I'm undesired, unwanted, unloved, unlovable.

'Where are you going?' she asks.

'Out.'

'Why?'

'The nursing home called,' I lie.

'What's wrong?'

'I don't know — that's why I'm going there.'

She says something else but I don't hear the words. Instead I imagine them. She makes me so angry that I want to lash out and hurt someone; I want to punish them, I want to purge myself of the poison that build up inside me.

It's still light outside when I reach the nursing home. It is the smell I can never get used to — a combination of a male urinal and an RSPCA shelter. I once worked at an animal shelter. I was sixteen. Mostly I had to hose out the cages from the night before, but once I saw them putting down the dogs that couldn't be rehomed. They fired a bolt gun into their brains and burned the bodies, but no amount of carbolic acid and air freshener could take away the smell of piss and shit and fear.

My father is in the lounge watching a TV infomercial for a food processor. He cocks his head to one side, birdlike, and sneaks glances at his reflection in the concave security mirror bolted high on one wall.

'That's only you,' I say, waving at our reflections. He looks baffled at a level beyond anything rational. I sit next to him on the sofa and pick up the TV remote.

'Don't change it,' he says.

'Why not?'

He points to the screen. 'It can chop as well.'

A nurse arrives. My father smiles but it's not a real smile. It's as if someone has asked a child to say 'cheese' for a photograph.

'Are you all right, Arthur?' she asks.

He doesn't reply.

'It must be nice to have your son come to visit. You should be sitting outside. It's a lovely evening.'

'Not today,' he says, turning back to the TV.

The nurse gives me a sympathetic shrug and asks if I'd fancy a cup of tea. I tell her no. She bends to straighten a pile of magazines on the low table.

'Are you engaged?' I ask.

'Pardon?'

'I noticed your engagement ring. It's lovely.'

'Thank you.' She examines her hand proudly.

'When is the big day?' I ask.

'Not until October.'

'Well, I hope you live happily ever after.'

'That's a very sweet thing to say.'

After she's gone I spend another half-hour trying to have a conversation with my father, who is unavailable, out to lunch, missing in action, AWOL. Then I walk through the dining room and on to a patio where rose bushes have created a thorny perimeter stopping patients from wandering off. One of the orderlies, a skinny Jamaican, is sneaking a cigarette. He flicks it away and grabs the handles of empty wheelchair. Then he recognises me.

'Shit, mon, you scared me!' He retrieves the cigarette. 'Thought you were the boss lady.'

'She's a ballbreaker.'

'Tell me about it. Hey, mon, your daddy makes me laugh. He's hilarious. You should put him on TV.'

Yeah, terrific, I want to say — a comedian who shits his pants — he'd be funnier than Jimmy Carr.

The orderly opens the side gate and tells me to take it easy. I'm almost at my car when I catch sight of someone standing in the garden. The psychologist's daughter is holding something open in her hands . . . a sketchbook. I remember where I've seen it before.

Further down the slope, beyond the wall, a man leans against a

Range Rover, watching her. It's not the psychologist. This one looks like a copper, a detective maybe. At that moment a car alarm shatters the evening quiet in a nearby street. My sphincter tightens instinctively.

The girl is moving up the path. I cut across the lawn. She doesn't see me until the last moment.

'Can I help you?' I ask.

She jumps. Startled. 'I've been looking for this house.'

'Hoping to buy, are you?'

She half laughs. 'No, I've been trying to find the house in this sketch. I definitely think this is the place. It has the same roofline and look at that weathervane — it's shaped like a hedgehog.'

I look at the open page.

'Did you draw this?'

'Me? No, I'm hopeless at drawing.'

'It looks more like a dog than a hedgehog,' I say.

'No, this is definitely the place,' she replies, reaching into her pocket and pulling out two Polaroid photographs. 'See?'

'Mmmm, you might be right.'

'What is this place?' she asks.

'A nursing home.'

'Do you work here?'

I contemplate lying, but the truth works better. 'I'm visiting someone. Why is the sketch so important?'

She shrugs.

'You're not going to tell me.'

'I'm not supposed to.'

I glance at the man watching her from the road. 'Is he following you?'

'No, he's my minder.'

'Are you someone important?'

I get a proper laugh this time. 'No.' She looks up at the house and a thought seems to occur to her. She turns the page of the sketchbook and comes to another half-finished drawing. 'Maybe this is someone who lives at the nursing home.'

I look at the drawing. My father's eyes are staring out at me. Harper managed to capture the blankness of them.

'He could be any old man,' I say.

'I think he looks quite unique,' she says. 'Maybe I should ask.'

'Visiting hours have finished. And I don't think you're allowed to visit residents here unless you're friends or family.'

She frowns.

'What's your name?' I ask.

'Charlie.'

'Well, I'd love to help you, Charlie, but the sketch isn't very clear. Do you have any other photographs of the old man?'

'I don't know. Maybe. I have a whole bag of Polaroids.'

'Maybe I could look at them.'

She hesitates, her eyes lowered, looking at the spot where I'm standing. 'They're not here.'

'Shame.'

45

I once asked Emma what she'd do if she had one wish. She said she'd buy a house that we could all live in. 'What would you do?' she asked me in return. I couldn't answer. My mind went blank. I could have told her I would banish my Parkinson's or repair my marriage or asked for world peace, but instead I made some lame joke about not needing a wish because my life was perfect.

That's my problem — I never ask myself the questions I ask of others. I never say, 'Joe, how are you feeling today? What do you fear? What have you been dreaming about?' I refuse to analyse myself because I'm frightened of what I might find.

I have tossed and turned for most of the night, falling asleep at three and waking at six. In my dream Mr Parkinson is a bent, crippled, skulking figure, the Gollum of my nightmares, scuttling after me, pulling at my body, trying to make me play with him. His arms and legs jerk in symmetry and he turns his eyes upon me, cocking his head in curiosity. 'It won't be long,' he says, 'you'll be here soon.'

That's how I wake, arms and legs moving, doing a strangely energetic dance, as though someone is torturing me with a cattle prod. I take my pills and close my eyes, picturing Julianne being wheeled into surgery.

Maybe I fall back to sleep because I dream that a cab pulls up outside the cottage and Julianne is paying the driver.

'What are you doing here?' I say in the dream.

'It was a false alarm,' she says. 'There's nothing wrong with me. I'm famished, let's have bagels for breakfast.'

I wake at seven, tremors gone, and piss like a horse on steroids. Then I shower and dress. Downstairs I make a cup of woody-tasting tea and sit on the back step in a patch of sunshine. It's going to be a hot day. On the radio they're discussing a heatwave and possible storms.

After a while I hear Charlie in the kitchen pouring cereal. She joins me. I slide along the step. We sit side-by-side as she spoons muesli into her mouth, holding the bowl beneath her chin. Her knobbly knees stick out of her denim shorts.

'Will she be in surgery by now?'

'Yep.'

'When can we see her?'

'Maybe this afternoon – or this evening.'

Charlie puts down the empty cereal bowl and picks up the bag of Polaroid photographs that she borrowed from the farmhouse. 'I found that place that Harper was sketching. It's a nursing home.'

'Did anyone remember her?'

'I didn't get a chance to ask.'

'Good job, but those pictures have to go back.'

'I know.'

My phone is ringing. I fumble for the receiver, dropping and catching it again.

'I'm sorry to trouble you so early, Professor,' says Monk.

'That's all right.'

'You sound anxious – is everything all right.'

'My wife is in hospital. I thought . . . it doesn't matter . . . how can I help you?'

327

'I need to collect the case files.'

'They're at the farmhouse.'

'I'll send someone to pick them up – along with the keys.'

Monk isn't in the mood to talk, but I ask him if there's any word on Elliot Crowe.

'We arrested him last night on a train to London. He was driven back and will appear in court this morning.'

'Has he confessed?'

'He hasn't entered a plea.'

'What about the attack on Naomi Meredith?'

'It's still being investigated,' says Monk, growing tetchy.

'Just one more thing,' I say. 'How did you get a warrant to search his bedsit?'

'We had a call from a jeweller in town. Elliot had been trying to flog a pair of earrings that belonged to his mother.'

'Why did you dig up the garden?'

'A tip-off.'

'From whom?'

'It was anonymous.'

'Don't you think that's strange – an anonymous caller knowing exactly where to look?'

Monk loses patience. 'Maybe Elliot mouthed off in the pub, or bragged to a hooker, or he was so high he thought he was King Zog from the planet Untouchable. It doesn't matter, Professor. We found the knife and Milo Coleman's wallet. I think that's enough, don't you?' He doesn't give me time to answer. 'I wish your wife a speedy recovery. Be at the farmhouse at nine.'

Charlie has been eavesdropping. 'Where are you going?'

'I have to give back some keys.'

'When will you be home?'

'Later.'

She follows me into the kitchen and rinses her bowl. 'Do you think Elliot Crowe killed those people?' she asks.

'It looks that way.'

'But you're not sure.'

'He's a junkie.'

'I thought that made him dangerous.'

'Addicts can lie, cheat, steal and sometimes kill, but they tend not to be very good at what comes next.'

'What comes next?'

'Getting away with it.'

'But he hasn't got away with it,' says Charlie. 'They caught him.'

I could explain it to her – the difference between an organised and a disorganised offender – the planning and preparation, or the chaos and disorder – but I'd rather convince my daughter to study something else at university.

She is grinding her toe into the linoleum floor as though trying to dig an imaginary hole. She can be disconcerting when she's like this, unfathomable and truth-seeking, akin to a diamond-cutter examining a rough gem, deciding how to make the first cut.

'Can I come with you?' she asks.

'Someone has to look after Emma. It's going to be hot today. You should take her for a swim.'

As if on cue, princess number two arrives downstairs, still dressed in her polar bear pyjamas. Her hair is mussed up and she has toothpaste smeared on her cheek. 'I thought we were going to see Mummy.'

'That won't be until later.'

Emma shakes a box of cereal. Satisfied, she sets out her bowl and spoon, making sure they're centred perfectly on the table. Slowly she begins pouring the puffed rice as though counting each grain.

Charlie pulls a face. 'She's such a freak.'

'I heard that,' says Emma.

Already the roads are starting to shimmer and pools of heat look like puddles on the tarmac. It's a picture-perfect summer's day, but the beauty is wasted on me. I cannot think of anything except Julianne and Elliot Crowe and Naomi Meredith and Milo Coleman.

By nature I'm a problem-solver – someone who likes specific answers to specific questions. I can accept uncertainty but every loose end becomes a flapping shoelace, nagging for my attention.

Bennie is waiting at the farmhouse when I arrive. She's in uniform, her trousers creased, boots polished, hands tucked into her pockets. I unlock the front door, where crime scene tape is frayed and torn.

'Have you talked to DCS Cray?' I ask.

'Yes, sir.'

'You don't have to call me sir.'

'I know, sir.'

She's treating me very formally, pretending that yesterday didn't happen. I remove the memory stick from my laptop and pack the crime scene albums into boxes, helping Bennie carry them to the police car.

'Does Elliot Crowe have an alibi for the night Naomi Meredith was attacked?' I ask.

'I'm not supposed to discuss the case, sir.'

'You don't have an opinion?'

'I'm here to collect the materials.'

'Were his prints on the murder weapon?'

She doesn't answer.

'Has anyone talked to Blake Lehmann or Dion Ferguson or Dominic Crowe or Jeremy Egan? These other attacks are linked to the murders.'

Bennie puts her hands on her hips. 'I'm not going to talk to you, Professor, and you're not blackmailing me again. I've given a statement to the task force. They know about Milo and me, but it doesn't matter any more. Elliot Crowe has been charged. He had motive, opportunity, means and the murder weapon. His goose is cooked.' She gets behind the wheel, tossing her hat on the passenger seat. 'Nice meeting you, Professor.'

She doesn't wave or look in the rear-view mirror as she leaves.

I glance at the stables and remember the kittens. Someone will have to look after them. Walking across the field, dodging cowpats and thistles, I enter a copse of trees where fallen leaves rustle beneath my feet. Pulling apart the strands of barbed wire, I climb through the fence and skirt the milking shed, approaching the farmhouse, which is little more than a shack.

Doreen Garrett answers the door. The parchment lines around her mouth suddenly deepen. 'What do you want?'

'Is Tommy here?'

'He's not s'posed to talk to you. Our solicitor said you put words in his mouth.'

'I need someone to look after the kittens.'

'Drown 'em for all I care.'

She is about to close the door when Tommy yells from deeper in the house. 'I'll talk to him, Nan.'

'He'll only try to trick you.'

'It's OK.'

Tommy appears, standing awkwardly in the hallway, keeping his hands in the back pockets of his jeans.

'You want to sit down?' he asks, pointing to a small sitting room with a pot-bellied fireplace. The walls and mantelpiece are decorated with family photographs of christenings, weddings and births, many of them in sepia tones or yellowed with age. The men are stern, the women solid, the babies dressed in lace.

'I need someone to look after the kittens.'

'I thought you were going to help rehome them.'

'I will. When they're ready.'

He stands at the centre of the room, making it feel smaller.

'I never asked you about your mum and dad,' I say.

'What about 'em?'

331

'You live here with your grandmother. What happened to your parents?'

'What do you care?'

'I'm interested.'

Tommy rolls his red tongue around the pink cavern of his mouth. 'I don't give a shit about my parents.'

'Are they alive?'

'My dad still lives in town. My mother ran off when I was just a boy. Said she were going to Australia. Promised to send for me. Never did.'

My eyes slowly scan the room and settle upon an object in the centre of the mantelpiece – a small oil burner carved from soft stone. What did Blake Lehmann say he bought Harper for her birthday?

'Where did you get that?' I ask.

Tommy has followed my gaze. His mouth opens and closes but no sound emerges.

Doreen has been standing in the hallway, eavesdropping on the conversation. 'Tommy gave me that as a present,' she announces.

'When?'

'Ages ago . . . Christmas.'

'It hasn't been used.'

'Haven't got around to it.'

I haven't taken my eyes off Tommy.

'I think you better leave,' says Doreen.

'I know you were there, Tommy. Did you go inside?'

Doreen steps in front of me, poking me in the chest. 'Get out of my house.'

'Did you see someone, Tommy?'

'It was a present,' she says again, louder this time. 'You tell him, Tommy.'

He doesn't answer.

'Just tell me what you saw. Who was there?'

46

TV cameras and photographers are milling outside North Somerset Magistrate's Court, waiting for the prison van to arrive. A handful of uniformed police officers are keeping watch over the crowd. Some stories capture the public's imagination more than others – missing children, murdered teenagers, serial killers, love triangles, matricide and fratricide . . . I don't know who makes those choices, but I wonder if the media will be as interested when it discovers that Elliot Crowe is a drug addict. Junkies don't sell papers. They don't rate.

In 1946 George Orwell wrote that for a murder to be newsworthy it required dramatic and tragic elements, such as spectacle, graphic imagery and moral outrage. He could have added 'the ideal victim' – someone vulnerable and worthy of our sympathy.

A prison van swings into view. TV cameras find shoulders and cameras begin clicking. Photographers surge forward, surrounding the van, shooting blindly through the heavily tinted windows on either side. The roller-door opens and the van pulls down a ramp and disappears.

Ruiz has saved me a seat in the public gallery, which is already full with the overspill from the press benches. The presiding judge is wearing spectacles that become bright orbs when they catch the overhead lights. He has some minor matters to deal with first. Submissions are made. Agreement reached. Solicitors swap over. Reporters lean forward to catch a glimpse of Elliot Crowe as he emerges through a side door, handcuffed and head bowed. He stands in the dock, unshaven, hollow-eyed, with a damp sheen of sweat plastering his fringe to his forehead.

Dominic Crowe is two rows ahead of me, sitting next to Francis Washburn. He cranes forward, trying to make eye contact with Elliot, who doesn't respond.

The case number is called. Elliot is asked to confirm his name and address. He is charged with two counts of murder, assaulting police, resisting arrest, breaking and entering, theft and perverting the course of justice.

'Do you understand the charges?' asks Judge Mitchell.

'He does, Your Honour,' says his lawyer.

'I wish to hear from the defendant. Do you understand the charges, Mr Crowe?'

'I didn't do it,' whispers Elliot.

'You don't have to say anything,' says his lawyer, holding a finger to his lips.

'I didn't *fucking* do it!'

'The defendant will refrain from uttering profanities in my courtroom,' says the judge.

'Fuck you!' Elliot yells, turning to the public gallery. 'I DIDN'T DO IT!'

As he recognises his father, his shoulders slump and tears form. He stops shouting. Whispers, 'I didn't do it.'

The judge remands him in custody. Court security officers are summoned. Elliot fights at their arms, his wet mouth gaping pinkly in his distress. 'You're hurting me! You're hurting me!'

The door closes. Out of sight, I hear a baton fall.

The courtroom empties quickly. Stories must be filed. Online editions updated.

Francis Washburn puts his arm around Dominic Crowe, trying to console him. He's looking for a taxi. People are watching – a young mother with a pram, a jogger in Lycra tights, two long-haired boys with skateboards. I find myself beside them, unsure of what to say.

'You have to help us,' says Francis. 'They're making a mistake. Elliot won't survive in prison.'

'There's nothing I can do.'

'I've talked to Becca. We're going to take out a second mortgage on the house. We'll get Elliot a good lawyer . . . post bail.'

'He won't be granted bail,' I say.

'We have to do something,' says Francis.

A couple of reporters have spied Dominic and broken from the rest of the pack, signalling their photographers to follow. A taxi pulls up and Francis bundles Dominic into the back seat, where he turns his face to the window, too stunned or shocked to hide from the cameras.

The taxi pulls away and slowly the crowd separates, breaking into pieces. I stare at the sky and glimpse a skydiving plane whose jumpers have leapt free and look like tiny dots falling through the infinite. I'm always amazed at the lengths people will go to when seeking to feel alive – swan-diving into empty air, falling towards the earth with only a rucksack of woven cloth to save them from disaster. I guess one could say that about almost everything in life – crossing a bridge, catching a flight, driving a car – most things are predicated upon our faith in mechanics, designers, engineers and technicians.

Ruiz has joined me. Fumbling in his pocket, he opens his tin of sweets and pops one on his tongue, saying, 'I guess it's over.'

I don't answer.

'Your silence seems to suggest that you're not convinced,' he says.

'Have you ever heard the term "the lion's gaze"?'

'No.'

'When you throw a stick to a dog, the dog will chase the stick. When you throw a stick to a lion, the lion will chase you.'

'I must be missing something.'

'The dog will follow the object – the lion will follow the person, which makes the lion the true predator. I think someone has been throwing sticks and we're chasing after them.'

Ruiz smiles wistfully. 'You're not going to stop, are you?'

'I don't know how to.'

Already the underarms of his shirt are damp with sweat and his face is starting to shine.

'I heard something interesting this morning,' he says. 'Remember the two victims from Weymouth and Torquay? Turns out they knew each other. One of them owns a private gym in Weymouth and the other is a personal trainer from Torquay. Both married. They had a one-night stand at a fitness convention in Clevedon last September.'

The detail snags in my mind just as the parachutes begin to blossom above our heads and the faith of the falling is repaid. Dion Ferguson sells fitness equipment. Naomi Meredith went to a gym on the morning she was attacked. When do coincidences become a pattern, and a pattern become a trend?

Dion Ferguson's wife answers the door. She's a big woman dressed in roomy pleated khaki shorts and a blouse that can hide a lot of calories. I can hear children fighting. Something falls. Breaks. She ignores the sound.

'We're looking for Dion,' I say.

'He's running a few errands.'

'When is he due back?'

'Shouldn't be long.'

Mrs Ferguson has short curly hair contained by bobby pins and clips, but already strands are pulling loose and sticking to the back of her neck. She has a round, pleasant face, a little flushed and tired around the eyes, but she seems comfortable in her own skin and something tells me her self-esteem has been hard won.

'Would you prefer to wait inside?' she asks. 'It's cooler, but full of children.'

I look past her into the cluttered hallway littered with toys, clothes and a half-drunk bottle of orange juice. 'We're fine waiting here.'

'You're not from the council, are you?'

'No.'

'What's Dion done now?'

I want to ask what he did *before* but I let it pass.

'It's a private matter,' I explain, but she's not going to be fobbed off.

'Is this about that woman who got killed?'

'What do you know about her?' asks Ruiz.

'Just what I heard on the news.'

A child appears next to her.

'Go inside, Marcie.'

'I wanna make bubbles.'

'You'll have to wait.'

The girl pouts and flounces off.

Mrs Ferguson looks back at us. 'I know my husband better than he knows himself and you're barking up the wrong tree if you think he had anything to do with them murders.'

'He told you he met Elizabeth Crowe?'

'No.'

'You found out anyway,' says Ruiz.

'Men can be so stupid. Dion thinks I don't know about him looking at computer porn or getting hard for other women. Then he goes and joins a dating agency – which is fine – but he used his only credit card and who do you think does the accounts? Yeah, me.'

'Why didn't you stop him?' I ask.

She laughs, her mouth gaping, fillings on show. 'My husband

has to look at me twice and I get pregnant. I got four kids under five and I'm the size of a bus. I don't want him touching me.' She scratches her armpit. 'If he wants to get his rocks off talking dirty on the phone or pretending to be a lonely heart, I can live with that, but I put a stop to it when I saw that money was missing.'

'Dion paid her money?'

'I caught him taking cash from our joint account. He gave me some bullshit excuse about the car needing a new automatic transmission. I told him I'd get a second opinion.'

'How much?'

'A thousand quid.'

'Did he give it to Elizabeth Crowe?'

'No! That bitch didn't get a penny from us.'

'You do realise that she's dead,' I say.

Mrs Ferguson apologises. 'I'm sorry, but she didn't get her money. I made sure of that.'

Ruiz shakes his head in admiration. 'And Dion still doesn't suspect that you know about his date with Elizabeth?'

'My husband's not the sharpest knife in the drawer.'

'Are you going to tell him?'

'I'm saving it up for a rainy day.'

A car pulls into the driveway – a seven-seater Hyundai with sticky finger marks on the passenger windows and colourful booster seats strapped in the back. Dion hurries up the steps carrying bags of groceries, anxiously looking from face to face. 'Is everything all right?'

'These two men from the council have come back to talk to you,' says his wife.

'Right. Yes. Good. I'll just give you these.'

His wife smiles at me knowingly as she takes the groceries.

'You said you wouldn't come back,' mutters Dion, once she's out of earshot.

'You sell fitness equipment,' I say. 'Did you go to a fitness convention in Clevedon last September?'

'No.'

'You seem pretty certain,' says Ruiz.

'I don't do the conventions,' explains Dion. 'That's someone else's job. I visit the gyms and fitness centres, but the company has a special team for the expos and trade shows. They choose the younger reps.'

'You arranged to meet Elizabeth Crowe on the night she died. You *were* going to pay her money.'

'I gave her nothing.'

'You withdrew the money, but your wife found out.'

'No, no.'

'Don't lie to us, Dion.'

'OK, OK, Elizabeth wanted money, but I didn't pay her, I swear. My missus got suspicious. I couldn't risk it. That's the truth. Scout's honour.'

'You were in the Scouts?' asks Ruiz.

'Yeah.'

'That figures.'

Dion glances behind him at the house. 'How did you find out about the cash?'

'Your wife told us.'

His mouth opens. 'What?'

'She knows everything about you, Dion,' says Ruiz. 'The dating agency, the late-night porn-watching, your date with Mrs Crowe . . . '

The realisation sinks in and I can almost see Dion's mind working through the consequences. 'So all this time . . . '

'Don't beat yourself up,' says Ruiz. 'She hasn't bin-bagged your sorry arse, so maybe she still loves you.'

I drag the discussion back to the point. 'Did you meet up with Elizabeth Crowe on the evening she died?'

Dion nods.

'Where?'

'Clevedon Court Woods on Tickenham Road.'

'Who chose the location?'

'She did.'

'And then?'

'I told her I wasn't going to be blackmailed.'

'What did she do?'

'Laughed at me and told me to go home to my wife. I don't think she cared about the money – it was just some power trip for her.'

'So you followed her home and killed her,' says Ruiz.

'Noooo! Never! You got to believe me. I'm not a killer. I'm a coward. Ask my wife.'

We leave Dion standing in the garden, looking like a condemned prisoner about to be executed slowly over the next twenty years. He's wondering why his wife said nothing to him, why she cared so little.

'I know I shouldn't feel sorry for him,' says Ruiz, 'but that guy couldn't get laid if he was dipped in chocolate and shitting Italian shoes.'

Midday. Julianne will be out of surgery by now. I want to be there when she wakes. I picture myself quizzing the doctors, answering calls and bringing Julianne her make-up when she's ready to receive visitors. And, when they're gone, I'll sit beside her on the bed and we'll watch afternoon game shows and old movies.

Ruiz drives me back to Clevedon so I can pick up my car. Travelling in silence on baking roads, we pass through the outskirts of town where doors and windows have been thrown open, trying to catch the breeze.

'What are you thinking?' he asks.

'I keep wondering what I've missed.'

'Maybe there's nothing. You talked about the lion's gaze, but what if there's nobody throwing sticks?'

This has something to do with the timelines. Father Abermain visited the farmhouse at 9.35 p.m., by which time Harper was at the Salthouse pub with Sophie Baxter and Blake Lehmann.

Harper argued with Blake and was home by eleven. Later Blake and Sophie rode a motorbike to Windy Hill, but nobody answered the door. Blake left a present on the doorstep, which Tommy Garrett picked up and took home.

There are too many names, too many possibilities. Maybe Ruiz is right – I'm ignoring the obvious. Elliot killed his family.

I change the subject. 'Charlie said she found the house in Harper's drawing.'

'She did well,' says Ruiz. 'It was a nursing home. She thinks Harper might have been sketching one of the residents.'

'Where was it?'

'Above Ladye Bay.'

'That's near where Maggie Dutton was attacked.'

Ruiz takes his eyes from the road. 'You didn't tell me that.'

'Which puts both Harper and Maggie Dutton in the same proximity on that Saturday afternoon.'

'You think maybe Harper saw something?'

'Did Charlie talk to anyone at the nursing home?'

'Visiting hours were over. She wanted to go back today.'

I look at my watch. We don't have time to do it now.

When my father was diagnosed with dementia, I would make him lists and print them in capital letters on five-by-seven cards using coloured felt-tip pens. It was like programming a computer, reducing everything to a binary code. I hung one card over the sink: Wash face. Pull stopper from sink. Wring out flannel. Brush teeth. *Another went next to his bed:* Put on underwear. Pants. Shirt. Socks. Slippers. Go to breakfast.

I gave up trying to teach him some things – such as how to post a letter or withdraw his pension from the Post Office. Sometimes he'd look at me as though I was the moron, but then he'd smile and do what I asked. Mostly he likes to walk, which is why I take him out when I can. I let him loose and he always come back. He's like a homing pigeon or a bird dog.

The nursing home receptionist, Mrs Hamilton, is an overly cheerful woman who is addicted to watching TV soaps. She talks about the characters as though they're real people and has been in mourning ever since Pauline died in EastEnders *in 2006. She stops me as I lead my father across the entrance foyer.*

'There was someone looking for you,' *she says.*

'When?'

'Just now – maybe ten minutes ago – she had some photographs of your father.'

'What did you tell her?'

'I said you'd taken him for a walk.'

'You're sure she had photographs?'

'And a sketch.'

'Where is she now?'

'I saw her heading towards the beach. You might still catch them.'

'Them?'

'She was with her sister. I think they were going for a swim.' *She*

342

glances through the large bay window. 'I hope they hurry. Looks like we're in for a storm.'

My father has already gone back to his room. He'll be unlacing shoes and sitting on the bed, waiting for someone to tell him what to do next. Mrs Hamilton is still talking about the weather, but my mind is elsewhere. Calmly I walk out of the main doors, and down the front steps and across the sloping lawn. This is what I feared – the photographs can expose me. Somehow I have to get them back and keep the girl quiet. She's brought her sister along. That complicates things. What will I tell her? What excuse can I use?

Harper didn't stay quiet. She didn't believe my story. I saw her that afternoon on the coastal path. I still had the box-cutter in my pocket and blood on my hands. Maggie Dutton lay bound and gagged and bleeding in the undergrowth.

'Did you hear a woman scream?' Harper asked.

'No. It must have been a seagull.'

She looked along the footpath, unsure what to do. She had a large sketchbook beneath her arm and a zipped case of pencils and charcoals.

'Where are you off to?' I asked.

'I'm going to sketch the cliffs.'

'I'm just going to see my dad,' I told her, motioning back along the path in the same direction that she'd come. 'You should come and sketch him. You always said he had a great face.'

'Would he mind?'

'He won't care. He doesn't know what day it is.'

And so she came with me to the nursing home and sketched my father in a corner of the garden and took photographs with her Polaroid camera. I washed my hands under a tap and hid the box-cutter amid the rose bushes. I didn't think about the sketches or the photographs until later when Harper called and said she'd seen a story on the TV about a woman being attacked on the footpath.

'Did you see anything?' she asked me.

'No.'

'But you must have walked right past her.'

343

'Who?'

'The woman who was attacked.'

'I didn't see anything.'

'The police are asking witnesses to come forward – anyone who was on the footpath. We should call them . . .'

Jogging across the narrow lane, I reach the entrance to the footpath and take the steps to a viewing platform overlooking the bay. The clouds are churning overhead and thunder rumbles in the distance.

I scan the shoreline. Families are packing up, folding umbrellas and collecting toys. Small sunburnt children are being washed off, squealing at the cold, but not wanting to leave the water.

Charlie is sitting on a rock watching a younger girl paddling. Her sister looks about eight or nine, dressed in denim shorts and a T-shirt, carrying her sandals.

Swinging between boulders, I move closer. A group of teenage boys is also looking at Charlie. They've been drinking. Smoking a little weed. One of them asks Charlie if she wants to join them. She shakes her head.

'You promised I could go for a swim,' says the little girl, gazing down at her toes. The nails are painted bright pink.

'Later,' replies Charlie.

'When?'

'Soon.'

47

Julianne's eyes open and she gives me a dreamy smile, as though I'm drifting in and out of focus. Her dry lips are stuck together. They separate slowly like a zipper opening.

'Did they cut off my legs?' she asks.

'No.'

'You hear stories, don't you – of people going into hospital and they amputate the wrong limb or cut off the wrong breast.'

'Your legs look great.'

'What about my breasts?'

'Very perky.'

'Perky?'

'That's the left one. Pinky also looks good.'

'You have names for my breasts.'

'Is that wrong?'

'I think they call it sexual objectification.'

'But that assumes that I treat them merely as sex objects, which I don't. I love every part of you equally.'

She tries to smile and squeezes my hand. I'm lying awkwardly half on the bed, half off.

'How are you feeling?' I ask.

'Sore.'

'Shall I get off?'

'No, don't move. Stay. How are the girls?'

'Charlie has taken Emma swimming.'

'Did you have to bribe her?'

'No.'

I can't take my eyes from her – the way her mouth moves when she speaks, the slight careless arching of her brows, her scent. She has always been like another language that I've never quite managed to master.

'They want to see you.'

'Maybe later,' she says, sleepily. 'They should drug me all the time. Feels wonderful.'

Her eyes shut and her breathing becomes shallow and steady. I climb off the bed and walk along the corridor. I try to call Charlie, but she isn't answering her phone.

Becca Washburn is at the nurses' station, talking to one of her colleagues.

'Has your wife woken up?' she asks.

'She's sleeping again.'

'That's pretty normal. There's a cafeteria downstairs. The coffee isn't as good as up the road, but you could always have tea.'

I tell her that I'm fine and just stretching my legs. I go back to Julianne's room. Sitting by the window, I look across rooftops that are dotted with chimney pots and aerials. Picking up the TV remote, I turn on Sky News, muting the sound. Banner headlines roll along the bottom of the screen. Bombings. Beheadings. Threats. Refugees. A new story: *Attack Victim Wakes* is the headline. A photograph of Milo Coleman flashes on screen. I turn up the sound.

'. . . *psychologist found unconscious in the stairwell of a Bristol car park yesterday has woken from a coma. However, neurologists at the Royal Infirmary hold grave fears that Milo Coleman has suffered severe brain damage and may never recover his mental or physical faculties . . .*'

A deep sadness swells in my chest and rises to my throat. I didn't admire or respect Milo, but of all the fools in the world – and there are many – I feel as though he is my responsibility. I would rather be dead than live like a vegetable, but I could never ask others to make that choice for me.

'The lion's gaze,' I whisper to myself.

Elliot Crowe didn't kill his mother and sister. I don't think he attacked Milo Coleman, yet someone wants to make him responsible. There are seven other known victims – different ages, genders, locations and demographics. Most have admitted to having extramarital affairs and the others might be lying, but I want to believe Maggie Dutton is telling the truth.

The same man is responsible for all these crimes – someone who feels betrayed, marginalised or cheated, who sees the world in black and white. How did he find his victims? Internet chat rooms. Online dating services. Dogging sites. Maybe he's a cab driver or a marriage guidance counsellor or a divorce lawyer. What do people buy their mistresses? Flowers. Lingerie. Where do they take them? Restaurants. Hotels.

All at once I feel a surge of realisation like ice water running down my back. Every door and window in my mind seems to open and wind blows through lifting papers from desks and dust from corners and causes that tiny figure madly pedalling inside my head to stop for a moment and slap his forehead, saying, *Of course, a hotel!*

He sees them come and go. He has their names or addresses or number plates. In the same breath, another detail catches and holds. When I visited Jeremy Egan's office in Portishead he had a scale model of the Regency Hotel in Clevedon. His company is redeveloping the site – turning it into luxury apartments.

Punching my mobile, I call Maggie Dutton. Her answering machine picks up.

Hello, this is Maggie. Sorry I can't come to the phone just now, but leave a message and I'll get back to you soon . . . wait for the beep.

'If you're there, Maggie, pick up. It's Joe O'Loughlin. I have a question. It's very important. Did you and your husband ever stay at the Regency Hotel in Clevedon?'

I wait, listening, muttering, 'Pick up! Pick up! Pick up!'

The receiver lifts. I hear Maggie's voice.

'Did you ever stay at the Regency?' I ask.

'Yes.'

'When?'

'I'm trying to remember . . . it must have been about seven or eight months ago.'

'Did you pretend to be strangers? I mean, did you and your husband act as though you were having an affair?'

She hesitates. 'Brendan thought it might be fun. He got me to wear a wig and short skirt. I chatted him up in the bar. Told him I was married.' The penny drops, her voice changes. 'Is that why I was attacked?'

I don't answer her question. I'm running now, down the stairs and across the foyer. I call Ronnie Cray. She can stop this. She can take the credit. They've charged the wrong man.

48

The temporary incident room is being dismantled and packed way, whiteboards wiped clean and case files put in boxes. Most of the task force has been reassigned and only half a dozen detectives remain, inputting the backlog of statements and preparing a report for the Crown Prosecution Service. The case now belongs to the lawyers who will take it to trial.

I make an entrance, veering sideways and colliding with the furniture. People look up as I pick up a fallen chair and straighten a stack of files that have almost toppled from a desk. I nod apologetically and rattle pills into the palm of my hand, swallowing them dry.

DI Abbott emerges from an office. Not happy. 'What's this about?'

'Where's DCS Cray?'

'On her way.'

As if on cue she arrives, throwing open doors and pushing aside chairs, acting as though she's the one who's been kept waiting. Bennie is behind her, hanging back because she's unsure of her role.

'What's this about, guv?' asks Monk.

'The Professor has a theory,' replies Cray, taking a seat and summoning the other detectives, who pull up chairs or prop buttocks on the corners of desks.

I waste no time laying it out, putting the pieces together as they came to me, avoiding a desire to skip ahead or to let details tumble out without context. If I cannot remember a particular time or date, I don't attempt to fill in the blanks or force the facts to fit my conclusions.

'Leaving aside Milo Coleman, seven people were attacked and mutilated. Almost all admit to having an affair – but we haven't managed to establish how they were targeted. What if they were guests at the same hotel? They arrive separately and check in, possibly using fake names and bogus addresses. It doesn't matter when or why – it's how he found them.'

'Who?' Monk asks.

'Jeremy Egan. His company is redeveloping the old Regency Hotel in Clevedon. Last September it hosted a fitness convention where two of our victims had a one-night stand. It's also where Maggie Dutton stayed with her husband. This links Egan to at least three victims. He was also having an affair with Elizabeth Crowe, which links him to the farmhouse murders.'

'Hold on,' says Monk. 'Maggie Dutton denied having an affair.'

'She and her husband stayed at the Regency pretending they'd never met.'

'Why would they do that?'

Bennie punches him on the shoulder. 'It's called role-playing.'

One of the other detectives pipes up: 'Naomi Meredith's boss took her to the Regency on their first weekend together.'

'That's another one,' I say. 'And Egan's wife changed her statement. He doesn't have an alibi for the night Elizabeth and Harper Crowe were murdered.'

Monk reacts belligerently. 'Elliot Crowe killed his mother and sister. We found the murder weapon buried in his garden.'

350

'Jeremy Egan could have planted it there. We also know he talked to Harper at the Salthouse pub a few hours before she died.'

I look at Ronnie Cray, hoping for support. 'I'm not even supposed to be here,' she says, deferring to DI Abbott.

Monk gets to his feet, giving nothing away. He walks to his desk, opens a drawer and takes out his badge. Then he picks up his coat from a chair.

'All right, let's take another swing at Jeremy Egan . . . see if he blinks.'

Late afternoon and dark clouds, humped and bruised, are moving across the sky with surprising speed, giving the impression that the Earth is spinning at a faster rate. The wind has picked up. First come little gusts and then stronger ones that sing in the rigging of yachts moored in the marina and make the trees sway like drunken dancers.

Charlie still isn't answering her phone. Maybe she's cross at me for making her look after Emma. Two police cars pull up in front of the building site, beneath a billboard displaying an artist's impression of the finished development: *Regency Apartments*. High plywood fences, dotted with posters and stained by graffiti, surround the construction area.

Nobody answers our knock at the site office, but high on the scaffolding we hear nail-guns firing and tiles being cut. Ladders lead between the floors of the old hotel, which is now draped in plastic sheets to prevent debris from falling on the road.

'Looks as though we're climbing,' says Monk.

'I'm not good with heights,' I say.

'Tough.'

We pass a workplace safety sign that says all visitors must have hard hats and high-visibility vests. Monk goes up first and I follow. There are no windows on the first level, just empty wooden frames, waiting for the glaziers. Inside I can see kitchens being fitted out, the appliances still wrapped in plastic and resting on wooden pallets.

A workman looks up from a circular saw. He lets the machine idle and takes off his mask.

'We're looking for Mr Egan,' yells Monk.

The workman points upstairs. We climb. The saw starts up again. I glance down and see the workman flip open his phone.

On the next level the apartments are nearer to completion. One of them has been decorated and furnished, perhaps for display purposes. There are sheets on the unmade bed and dirty clothes on the floor. I notice a half-empty glass of milk and a ham and lettuce sandwich on the kitchen bench.

A gust of wind makes the scaffolding shudder. It's not the wind. There's someone outside. Monk crosses the open-plan living area and opens the sliding door. He discovers Jeremy Egan hanging from the lower edge of the balcony, trying to shimmy sideways so he can drop to the apartment below.

Monk is quicker. He leans over the framed glass screen and snaps one handcuff around Egan's right wrist, attaching it to the lowest railing, trapping him between floors.

'I can't hang on,' yells Egan.

'Then let go,' answers Monk.

'I'll break my bloody wrist.'

'Possibly,' says Monk, 'but at least you're wearing a hard hat.'

Egan's fingers slip a little further off the edge. He tries to readjust and only makes it worse.

'Help me.'

'First tell me why you were trying to run from the police.'

'I thought you were someone else.'

'Who?'

'This build is six months behind because of bad weather. I took out bridging finance, but I stopped making the payments.'

'And that's the only reason?' asks Monk.

'Yes.'

Egan falls and swings on one cuffed wrist, screaming in pain.

Monk bends over the glass and unlocks the cuffs, grabbing the architect and hauling him on to the balcony, where he collapses, breathing hard.

Lightning streaks through the sky and pushes a bony finger into the sea. One. Two. Three. Thunder.

Egan rubs at this wrist, sulking, 'I'm not talking to you without my lawyer.'

'You don't have to talk. You can listen,' says Monk, who turns to me. 'It's your show, Professor.'

I pull up a chair. Egan is still sitting on the ground with his back to the glass.

'You bought the Regency Hotel three years ago and kept it running,' I say.'

'Yeah, so?' he replies.

'It took you two years to get planning permission to do the conversion, which is why money became an issue.'

'What's that got to do with you?' asks Egan, taking off his hard hat and smoothing his fringe.

'Do you know someone called Maggie Dutton?' I ask.

'No.'

'What about Naomi Meredith, or Gabrielle Sallis or Matthew Blair?'

'I don't know any of them.'

'They all stayed at the Regency when it was still a hotel. Some time afterwards they were attacked and choked unconscious, bound with masking tape and had the letter "A" carved into their foreheads by someone who accused them of committing adultery.'

Egan lets out a ragged groan. He rises and walks slowly to the sofa, putting his hard hat on his knees.

'You think I'm a sadist?' he asks quietly.

'I think you're the link between all the victims – you and this hotel.'

'You're right. I am a link, but not because I own this place.' He pauses rubbing at his wrist. 'At least you solved one mystery.'

353

'What do you mean?' asks Monk.

Egan lifts his chin and pushes back his fringe, revealing the scar on his forehead. Pink. Puckered. Unmistakable.

Lightning flashes and thunder seems to peel away from the earth and rise into the clouds.

'When?' I ask.

'A year ago.'

'Is that why you and Elizabeth Crowe stopped seeing each other?'

'One of the reasons.' He pats down his fringe, covering his forehead again.

I have more questions, wanting to know when and where, but Monk has already found his feet and is walking towards the door. 'We're sorry to trouble you, Mr Egan.'

'But I have more questions,' I say.

'No, we're done here.'

Every sound is heightened, every emotion magnified. I hear feathery laughter, car doors slamming, sandals being slapped together and the hiss of water washing over shingle. The girls are leaving the beach, walking along the path. They're twenty yards ahead of me. Alone. Arguing.

Until now the air had been so still that it barely registered against my skin, but now stronger gusts are whipping through the trees, dotting the sea with whitecaps and sending waves thudding against the rocks. Strands of Charlie's hair flatten and then stand, drawn by the electricity in the air.

The younger girl has run ahead. Charlie is carrying two beach towels and a cloth shoulder bag. The sketchbook peeks from inside.

She turns. 'Are you following me?'

'No, I'm looking for you.'

Some girls her age avoid eye contact, but she looks directly at me, confident, yet wary. Perspiration gleams on her top lip.

'I've just come from the nursing home. They said you had some photographs.'

'I found the old man in the drawing,' she says. 'The lady at reception recognised him.'

'Are you sure?'

'She remembered a girl coming to sketch him.'

She reaches into the pocket of her denim shorts and produces two photographs. 'Do you know him?'

'No,' I say, without bothering to look.

'But the lady at the nursing home said he'd gone for a walk.'

'She made a mistake. He doesn't live at the nursing home.'

My tone of voice makes her flinch. Her sister has turned back and joined us. She scratches at an insect bite on her leg and eyes me suspiciously.

'And who might you be?' I ask, trying to smile.

'This is Emma,' answers Charlie.

The light has changed. To the west I have lost sight of the pier, cloaked by the coming storm. Fat drops are beginning to rattle the leaves and dot the dusty path.

'You're not going to get back in time,' I say. 'I know a place we can shelter.'

'We'll be OK,' says Charlie. 'I like storms.'

'You'll get drenched.'

'Can I have the photographs back?' she asks.

'I think you should leave them with me. Are there any others?'

'No.'

'You should also give me Harper's sketchbook and forget about the old man.'

She's backing away from me now, holding her sister by the shoulder. 'You know her name.'

'What?'

'You said Harper's name.'

'You must have mentioned it.'

'No.'

'You shouldn't have come here. You should have let bygones be bygones.'

'What is a bygone?' asks Emma.

'Something that should be left in the past,' I say, tearing the Polaroid photographs into pieces and tossing them into the wind like confetti.

Lightning rips opens the sky in a jagged tear and the crack of thunder is almost simultaneous, rattling bones, branches and rocks. Emma screams. Charlie steps in front of her, shielding her from me. She glances from side to side, looking for an escape. I'm blocking the path.

A strange feeling fills me now, excitement rather than fear. This girl could be the architect of my undoing. She could bring my two worlds crashing together and I will be trapped in between.

'Who are you?' she asks again.

'I'm nobody important.'

'How do you know about Harper?'

'You're being foolish. Give me the sketchbook.'

'No.'

Emma is looking from face to face, rubbing her bare arms as though suddenly cold. She doesn't understand. If they run I will not be able to hold them both. I'll take Charlie. No, the younger one! Charlie won't leave her sister behind.

I take a step towards them. Charlie pushes Emma behind her.

'Run!' she cries. 'Get help!'

Charlie launches her body at me, her fists clenched, but I'm too quick and strong. I knock her aside and reach Emma within a few paces, hoisting her off the ground, carrying her towards the top of the cliff.

I turn to Charlie. 'Come with me or she dies.'

49

Monk hasn't said a word. He walks ahead of me, his large frame seeming to shake with anger.

'I was wrong about Jeremy Egan, but we found another victim,' I say.

'Congratulations,' he says sarcastically.

'It helps us fill in the pieces.'

'Shut up and go home, Professor.'

'The hotel theory is the right one.'

'The only correct word in that statement is "theory". You had a theory, which proved to be wrong, and now Jeremy Egan is likely to sue me for assault and wrongful arrest.'

'I don't think he will.'

'Oh, good, I'm relieved. You've been bang on the money so far.'

The temperature has plunged and big drops of rain are beginning to dot the road. Monk pulls up his collar and crosses to the waiting police cars. I pause for an old man pushing a bicycle along the footpath with shopping bags draped on the handlebars.

'It's going to blow,' he says, showing me his brown teeth. His eyes look like watery eggs. 'Best you find some shelter.'

I'm about to cross, but he grabs my arm, telling me about another storm in which four fishermen died off the coast. I listen to him because it strikes me that nobody else will.

Dragging myself away, I try to call Charlie again. This time she answers, but I can't hear her voice. Instead there are muffled sounds, as though the phone is still in her pocket. She must have answered it accidentally, unaware that I'm on the line.

I shout, hoping she might hear me.

'Charlie – pick up your phone.'

Nothing. I listen again. There are faint voices, words, broken sentences, snatches of conversation . . .

'Stop pulling her hair! She's going to cry if you pull her hair.'

'If you don't make her shut up . . .'

'Please don't hurt her . . . We've done nothing to you.'

'Just let us go. Can't you see she's frightened . . . we won't tell anyone . . .'

A sinkhole opens up inside me and I struggle to breathe. At the same time I feel a teetering sensation, as if my head were half full of water, sloshing from side to side. A clap of thunder detonates above me and I hear the same sound echoing through the phone. They're close! Where?

People talk about time speeding up, but it does what it does at moments like these – expanding slowly, creating a space in which every sense pops and fizzes with energy. I can feel my clothes brushing against my skin and the cool air on the edge of my nostrils. I can see the fat drops exploding like miniature atom bombs on the hot asphalt, creating an almost invisible vapour.

One look and Ronnie Cray knows something is wrong. I don't recognise my own voice. I am someone else. A stranger. A madman.

'Someone has taken my daughters!'

Lightning arrows against the dark clouds and trees thrash at the air as though furious at being rooted to the ground. I look over my shoulder and see how the distance has vanished in sheets of rain, along with the village and the pier and the rolling hills.

The child is getting heavy. I make them both walk, wrapping a fist around their hair, dragging them across the muddy ground. Whenever they slip, I pull them up and they cry out in pain. Nobody is going to hear them.

We come to an outcrop of rocks and clamber over, buffeted by the wind. Leaving the footpath behind, I push Charlie ahead of me, making her crawl through bushes and brambles, while I drag Emma behind. The sea, wild and woolly, is somewhere to our left and a steep bank to the right.

'You're hurting us,' says Charlie.

I scream at her to shut up. Wind snatches the words away. Emma falls. She has blood on her knees, smeared by the rain. I drag her upright. Charlie beats at my chest with her fists, telling me to stop. I lift her off her feet by her ponytail. She has to grip my forearm to stop her hair being ripped from her scalp.

There is a signal station above Pigeon House Bay. It looks like a truncated lighthouse, painted white, squatting on the cliffs. My father showed me the station years ago. He told me that in the early days it sent messages to the ships at anchor, telling them when to sail onwards to the docks at Avonmouth and Bristol. They communicated using flags and later radios before newer technology made the station obsolete. Unmanned. Abandoned.

It's half a mile from here . . . too far. I need to find somewhere closer. Sheltered. I need time to think. Plan.

Clawing our way up the slope, using trees to help us climb, we come to a thick hawthorn bush. It's growing around the base of a large oak, creating a natural den with a canopy of leaves and walls of green. The bare ground is still relatively dry. Pulling the branches aside, I push the girls through the narrow opening.

Another blast of thunder shakes the world. Charlie is holding her sister in her arms, whispering words of encouragement.

'Tell her not to be frightened?' I say, shouting above the noise.

Charlie doesn't answer. The little one examines her bloody knee.

'Give me the sketchbook,' I say.

Charlie tosses me her bag. The pencil and charcoal drawings are starting to buckle and smudge, the faces melting like Munch paintings or leaching into oily stains. I tear the pages into sodden strips and screw them into balls before tossing them outside.

Emma has her head tucked under Charlie's chin, but her eyes are watching me. There is something unnerving about her stare, as though she's a caged beast who wants to pounce on me and rip out my throat.

'Didn't your parents ever tell you it's rude to stare?' I say.

She doesn't look away.

More thunder. A small stream of water has started to run through the middle of our shelter, carrying dead leaves and trapped insects. Ants are scurrying to escape a flooded nest, crawling over each other as though trying to build a bridge to safety.

'Are you going to kill us?' asks Charlie.

I don't answer.

'If you let us go, I won't tell anyone. I can keep a secret.'

Still I don't reply.

'Emma doesn't know anything. Let her go and I'll stay. You don't need two hostages.'

'Maybe you're not hostages.'

Charlie's sodden blouse is clinging to her chest and shoulders. I can see the outline of her bra and the shape of her breasts beneath the thin fabric.

She's the sort of girl I used to fall in love with at school – the ones I grew to hate because they would never look at me or talk to me. She's a girl just like all the others, greedy and dissatisfied, scheming and resentful.

— I could do what I want to her now. Right here.

No, you can't.

— Why not? She's just like all the others.

But that would make you no better than them.

50

In my worst nightmares – the recurring ones – I relive the moment when a man called Gideon Tyler entered my life and destroyed my marriage. Every detail of that silent, sunlit afternoon remains. I remember looking for Charlie, running down Mill Hill Lane, across the bridge, up the next rise. I knew what had happened. I tried to tell myself I was wrong, but I knew.

I found her bicycle in a ditch, half-hidden by weeds, the frame buckled by the force of the impact. I waded into the nettles and thorns and dragged the bike free. Crows exploded from the trees above my head, caw-cawing as though mocking me. I bellowed in pain and anguish. I cried out to a God who I didn't believe in, calling for a miracle that I didn't deserve.

We all make promises at a time like that. I promised Julianne that I would get Charlie back. I promised her it would never happen again. How much are my words worth now? Nothing! Abject, meaningless, empty promises. I don't care if Julianne kicks me out again. I don't care if I never lie beside her or make her smile. I want my girls back. I want them safe.

The phone has become the centre of my world. The line is still open. Four of us are huddled around a desk in the incident room, leaning over the handset, trying to pick out words from the background noise, but all I can hear is wind, thunder, waves and occasional snatches of unintelligible sentences.

Cray encourages me to keep listening and tells me not to lose hope. I know my daughters' voices better than anyone. I will pick up details that others miss.

Meanwhile, Monk has taken charge of the incident room. He wants a SWAT team on standby and every available officer ready to mount a search. Patrols are looking for Charlie's car and detectives are contacting the phone server hoping her mobile signal can be tracked using the nearest towers.

'I can hear a bell,' says Bennie. 'It could be a navigation buoy.'

I'm staring at the phone, which is old and out of date. The girls laugh at me because I don't have a smartphone, but I tell them that my mobile is going to be hip one day when people start buying distressed phones with cracked screens because they're retro and cool.

For the first time I hear Emma's voice. She wants to go home. Charlie tells her not to cry. My heart is breaking. I want to scream down the phone. *Come on Charlie. Give us a clue – a landmark, a direction.*

Then I hear a sentence clearly. *'Did you kill Harper?'*

Cray has heard it too. There's no reply. Charlie speaks again: *'What are you going to do with us?'*

I lean closer, but the storm drowns everything out. Cray shakes her head.

'Don't touch me! Leave us alone!'

Suddenly the screen goes blank. We've lost the call. My chest goes hollow. I reach for the phone.

'Wait!' says Cray.

I look at her as though she's crazy. 'We have to call her back.'

'No. Think about it. What if your Charlie ended the call?

As far as we know she's in charge of the phone. She's keeping it secret. If we phone her back it could alert him – you see what I'm saying?'

I know she's right. I'm trying to think rationally but emotion trumps reason every time.

'Let's give her a few minutes,' says Monk. 'See if she calls us.' He yells across the incident room. 'How are we going with the trace?'

'Still waiting, guv,' comes the reply.

Breathe, I tell myself. *Think*. My daughters need me. Whoever took them must have killed Elizabeth and Harper. If Charlie worked that out, surely I can. What have I missed? This has something to do with the Regency Hotel . . .

A memory catches and tears at my consciousness. I picture a bathroom. I see a tiny square of wrapped soap on the edge of the sink. Above it, a shelf contains dozens of miniature bottles of shampoo and conditioner, all with the same logo. Where? I was in the Washburn house . . . it was after the funerals.

'Get me Becca Washburn on the phone,' I say. Ronnie Cray doesn't question why. The number is found. Called. I listen to it ringing. She answers. I try to sound calm.

'On the night that Elizabeth and Harper died, you had a phone call from Harper. Why?'

Perhaps sensing my urgency, Becca doesn't hesitate. 'I wanted her to babysit. I'd left her a message that morning but she didn't get back to me until evening.'

'How did she sound?'

'Fine. Normal. She was out with friends.'

'Who answered the phone?'

'What?'

'Who answered the phone when she called?'

'Me, I suppose,' she hesitates. 'No, it was Francis. My mobile was downstairs. I was getting ready for work.'

'Francis talked to Harper?'

'I guess. What's this about?'

'You told me Francis had a new job working for a property management company. What was his old job?'

'He was night manager at the Regency Hotel, but they closed it down.'

'Where is he now?'

'At work, I suppose.'

Thunder and lightning detonate simultaneously as though overlaid in a massive display of fireworks that shreds the air and turns the sea to foam. The girls no longer flinch at the noise unless it's directly overhead.

I have been crouching. My knees are sore. I lower myself down and sit with my back to the trunk of the tree. I've been trying to think, but the noise is driving every thought from my head.

'Why are you doing this?' asks Charlie, pushing wet hair from her eyes and smearing mud across her forehead.

'You should have left me alone.'

'We've done nothing to you.'

'You kept asking questions – kept looking for me.'

'I don't even know who you are.'

'Shut up! I need to think.'

'I gave you the photograph and sketchbook. Let us go.'

'I told you to shut up!' I lean towards her, cocking my fist. She ducks and wraps her arms around her sister.

How has it come to this? My mind gropes backwards searching for an answer. The last few days are tumbling in my slipstream, the mistakes and missteps. The photographs were like a landmine waiting to be stepped upon. I worried about the police finding them. Instead it was this girl.

– I fucked it up.

You fucked it up.

– What now?

Make it right.

What have I achieved? Nothing. I am what I always was – locked in the same prison, the black vacuum, hearing the same ceaseless laughter. I was doing the world a service. I was punishing the unworthy. I was safeguarding something that other people take for granted.

367

The younger one is shivering. I wish she'd stop staring at me. I should cut out her eyes. Two jabs — a quick one-two. She wouldn't look at me then.

— She's done nothing wrong.

She can identify me.

— It's your own fault.

What's done is done.

I can still get out of this. I have to be smart and think ahead clearly. Plan ahead. The police can't place me at the farmhouse that night. Maggie Dutton didn't see my face. None of the others can identify me. It could still be all right. I just have to work out what to do with these two.

They could drown. A young girl is seen paddling by the shore. She goes out too far. Her older sister tries to rescue her, a double tragedy — all too common. By the time their bodies are found I'll be miles away. I can drop into one of the holiday lets. Shower. Dry my clothes. Later I can help with the search.

Mrs Hamilton at the nursing home will recognise Charlie and Emma. She'll tell the police about the sketches and the photographs. So what? They're gone. Destroyed. I haven't been seen with the girls . . . unless someone on the beach . . . ? No, they were too busy packing up.

The young one is still staring at me. I've forgotten her name. I tell her to stop. Charlie puts a hand on her sister's head and pulls it to her shoulder, whispering something.

'What did you say?'

'I told her to look away. See?'

'That's better.'

I lean back against the tree and close my eyes, trying to press reset. I can still get out of this.

'What's your name?' Charlie asks.

'It doesn't matter.'

'Are you married? Do you have a girlfriend?'

'Be quiet.'

'I haven't had a boyfriend since I was fifteen. People make a big deal about sex and think people my age are doing it all the time, but we're not.' She has moved away from her sister, edging closer to me. 'I didn't have sex with him.'

'Who?'

'My last boyfriend.'

'Why are you telling me this?'

She shrugs. She's next to me now. Pale. Young. Pretty. Her mouth down-hooked at the corners.

'I'm cold. Will you hold me?'

'Hold your sister.'

'I'd prefer to hold you.'

She puts her arms around my neck, resting her head against my chest.

'I can hear your heart,' she says. 'Are you cold? I'm freezing. We should get out of these wet clothes.'

'I'm fine.'

'I normally love storms,' she says, 'the thunder and lightning.'

'What?'

'Storms. All that power and noise . . . the ground shaking . . . doesn't it make you feel alive?'

She starts unbuttoning her blouse, peeling it off her shoulders. Her sister has peeked. 'Turn away, Emma. Don't look back until I tell you,' says Charlie.

Emma does as she's told.

Charlie rocks forward on to her knees and moves a little closer to me. 'I'm just saying that storms are exciting.'

'You shouldn't be saying things like that. Put your blouse back on,' I say.

She reaches out and touches my knee, sliding her hand along the inside of my thigh.

'Please don't do that.'

'I saw you looking at me. We don't have to do it in front of Emma. You could let her go. We could keep each other warm.'

She reaches for my belt buckle and pulls it loose. I grab her wrist. 'I told you to stop.'

She slides her hand over my stomach and down into my trousers. I push her backwards, but she doesn't go away. Instead she reaches behind her and undoes her bra. Her nipples are sticking out in the cold.

'Don't do that! Put it back on.'

I see her tears. Who is she crying for? She's just like all the others. She'll spread her legs when she wants something, but withhold love and affection when it suits her.

Emma is still sitting with her back to us, but I can feel her eyes upon me. She's accusing me. She thinks I'm a pervert.

I grab at Charlie's shoulders and try to shove her away. She grips my head in both her hands and rocks back, before whipping forward, driving her forehead into my nose. A flash of white pain explodes in my skull and seem to rocket down my spine. I almost black out, falling sideways. Dizzy. Disorientated.

The bitch! I thrust my arm out blindly, touching a foot. My fingers close. I pull at the leg. She kicks me in the stomach. I lunge again.

She's gone. I touch my face. I'm bleeding. The bitch has broken my nose. I get to my knees, swaying, groaning, the pain turning from fire to ice. I can hear her shouting. She's telling her sister to run.

Run, Rabbit, Run.

51

Five detectives are squeezed into Cray's office. My phone is still on the desk, silent yet calling to me.

'There's no proof that Francis Washburn was anywhere near the farmhouse that night,' says Monk. 'He comes across as the only sane member of the family – happily married with a new baby. Why would he kill his niece and sister-in-law?'

'I think Harper saw him on the footpath when Maggie Dutton was attacked,' I say.

'There's no evidence—'

'Harper signed and dated every drawing. That day she was sketching a nursing home only a few hundred yards from the footpath. That night Harper saw a TV news report about a woman being attacked. According to Sophie Baxter, Harper became agitated. She phoned her aunt soon afterwards.'

'About babysitting,' says Monk.

'Yes, but first she talked to Francis. He brought the phone upstairs to Becca, who was getting ready for work.'

Cray interrupts. 'Washburn was looking after the baby that night.'

'That's not an alibi,' I reply.

'His mother-in-law was in the house.'

'She lives in a self-contained wing.'

Monk scoffs. 'So you think Washburn left his baby at home, drove to the farmhouse, murdered his niece and sister-in-law, cleaned up and went home again without anybody noticing his car or his bloody clothing.'

'No, he took the baby with him.'

This triggers laughter from the group. Even Cray looks sceptical.

'I'm serious. We're all agreed that Elizabeth let the killer into the house some time around midnight, so it must have been someone she knew and trusted – like her brother-in-law. I think he arrived carrying baby George.'

My mind is picturing the scene – the knock on the door, Elizabeth coming downstairs, surprised by such a late visitor, but pleased to see her nephew. Francis left George with Elizabeth and went upstairs to Harper's room, knowing he had to silence her. He choked her quietly and then returned, taking a knife from the kitchen and killing Elizabeth in the sitting room. Everything that followed was theatre – the pentagram, the candles, the Bible and the break-in.

'Do you still have the crime scene photographs?' I ask.

Cray boots up a nearby computer and calls up the images. I scroll through them quickly, ignoring Elizabeth's defiled body. I concentrate on the rest of the room, particularly the floor. I remember the unexplained pattern on the rug – the bloodstains forming two axis of a right angle.

'See that? Right there!' I point to the screen. 'Something was covering the rug when Elizabeth was stabbed. If I'm right, it was a baby seat.'

My mobile begins ringing. My heart leaps. I don't recognise the number. Monk grabs my arm. 'It could be Washburn.'

'What should I do?'

'Put it on speakerphone.'

I press green. 'Professor O'Loughlin,' says a female voice.

'Yes.'

'This is St Michael's Hospital. There has been a complication with your wife's surgery.'

'Why? What's wrong?'

'She's been moved to the ICU. You should come to the hospital.'

'But I only just saw her . . . '

'She's suffered an embolism. They're operating now. Can someone drive you?'

'I can't come now.'

'Take a taxi—'

'No, you don't understand. I can't come.'

I hang up and stare at the phone. Nobody speaks or moves in the room. It's as if someone has hit the pause button on a recording and the actors are frozen in place.

'You should go to the hospital,' says Cray. 'We can handle this.'

'No.'

'We have this under control.'

'I'm not leaving without my children.'

She argues with me, but I can't hear the words. I try to concentrate on watching her lips move but all I can hear is a long continuous *eeeeeeeeeeeeeeeeee* noise like a car alarm going off in my head. I cannot think. When I last talked to Ruiz he planned to check out of his hotel and drive back to London. I need him now. He'll know what to do. I call his mobile. He answers and I swallow a sob, my voice a half-octave too high. 'I need you to get to St Michael's Hospital in Bristol.'

'Why? What's happened?'

'Julianne has gone back into surgery.'

'But you said—'

'It's an embolism. Somebody should be there.'

'Where are you?'

Again I have to swallow. 'Charlie and Emma are missing.'

'What?'

'Francis Washburn has taken them. I think he's the killer.'

In the background I hear tyres screech and horns blare. Ruiz has done some sort of U-turn or radical manoeuvre in traffic. 'I'm coming.'

'I need you at the hospital. Someone has to be there when Julianne wakes up.'

'I'll be there.' He hammers on the horn. 'How did he get the girls?'

'I don't know. They're somewhere near the sea.'

'The nursing home,' says Ruiz.

'What?'

'Charlie wanted to go back to the nursing home. She was looking for the old man in the sketch.'

Almost in the same breath, Bennie yells from across the far side of the incident room. 'Francis Washburn's father is at a high-dependency nursing home in Clevedon.'

52

There are no sirens. Police cars pull through the stone gates and block both entrances of the curved driveway. Heavy boots splash through puddles and pound up stairs. Raincoats drip on the floor. The woman behind the reception desk barely has time to get to her feet.

'Do you know a man called Francis Washburn?' asks DCS Cray.

'He was here earlier,' the woman stammers, forgetting to close her mouth.

'When?'

'Um . . . ah . . . before the storm.'

'You talked to him.'

'He came to see his father.' She thinks of something else. 'There was someone looking for him – a teenager – she was with her little sister.'

'Where did they go?' I ask.

'I think they went to the beach.'

I don't hear the rest. I'm already outside, leaping off the steps, sprinting crossing the lawn, down the slope, out of control, over the lane on to the footpath. The world is being lit by flashes of lightning – branches, buds, leaves, rain, rocks and water. I'm running but nothing feels as though it is happening quickly enough, except for the throb of my heart, which batters at its walls. Who is this man – born with winter in his heart – who would take my children? How dare he touch what's mine.

Clumps of spume are floating through the air, splattering against trees or clinging vainly to leaves. More night than day, there is no horizon. The sea and air seem joined and the entire land has disappeared. I wish for more light. I wish I could hear Charlie's voice or Emma's voice.

My phone is ringing. I fumble with the receiver and almost drop it.

It's Charlie. Breathless. Running.

'Help me!' she cries.

'Where are you?'

'We got away. He's behind me.'

'Emma?'

'I told her to run.'

'What can you see?'

She doesn't answer. I hear her panting.

'Charlie, what can you see?'

'Nothing . . . it's raining . . . we were on the beach . . . He's coming!'

Monk catches up with me, shouting above the rain. I tell him to shut up and press the phone to my ear. A gust of wind almost knocks me over. Monk stops me falling.

'We should wait for the others,' he yells.

I shake my head, flicking water. He tries to say something else, but his words are stolen by the wind. Charlie isn't talking any more. I can hear her breathing. Running. I shout into the phone. Nothing.

Waves are exploding against the rock shelf, sending clouds of spray into the air, where the wind turns each droplet into a needle stabbing at my exposed skin. I keep wiping my eyes, but nothing comes into focus.

I set off again, making a choice, heading east along the path, which begins rising sharply. I seem to be slowing down, as though I'm being sucked into the mud, taking root in the earth. My legs are aching and I struggle to stay upright, but each time Monk catches me before I fall.

A small figure appears on the path ahead of us. Emma. Her legs and arms are pumping and she runs with her head down, slipping and sliding, trying to stay upright. Leaves and twigs on her clothes. Mud. Blood.

She looks up and sees Monk. The sheer of size of him makes her mouth open in a scream. In the next instant I seize her and bury my face into her neck, holding the back of her head as she sobs.

'I'm here . . . I'm here . . . I'm here . . . Are you hurt? Shhhhh . . . I'm here . . . Where's Charlie?'

I'm dimly aware of people shouting behind me. Bennie and Cray and the others are coming.

'Here, take Emma,' I say to Monk.

'Wait!'

'No.'

Emma clings to my neck, not wanting to let go. 'I have to get Charlie,' I shout. She releases her hold.

I run ahead again, holding the phone. I have only desperate minutes. That's how Charlie's life is measured now, minute by minute: Charlie time.

'Talk to me,' I say. 'Talk to me.'

The bitch! The bitch! The bitch!

She broke my nose. Now I can't breathe properly. How am I going to explain that? I was a fool. She tricked me. I will deal with her first. No, I'll make her watch her sister die and then make her beg.

She's thirty yards ahead of me, pulling on her blouse, trying to climb and do up the buttons. Slipping. Falling. Blinded by the rain, and she doesn't know the path as well as I do. Only fifteen yards away now. I'm closing the gap. How stupid to think she can outrun me.

She's close now – almost within touching distance. I reach out for her neck. Fingertips swipe her blouse. Suddenly, she stops and drops. I trip over her, throwing my hands out for the fall, palms stinging as I hit the ground. Grunting. Hissing. Fuck!

I look around. Where did she go? She's hiding in the trees. Smart thing. Foolish thing.

'Come here, you little shit.'

I dance to the side, looking behind the trunks and under bushes. Where are you? I know you're there. I can hear your little heart beating.

A branch snaps. I look up. There! I can see you now.

She shoots out from her hiding place, the slope pitching her downwards. If she's not careful she'll run straight off the cliff. Good! Save me the trouble. Bitch! Cunt!

I hurl myself down the slope, branches stinging my face, roots turning my ankles, the wind and rain forgotten. Any second. Any second. She crawls through a wall of brambles. I have to follow. Thorns tear at my skin and tug at my clothes.

We're out again, open space at the top of the cliff. She stops at the edge. Spins. Wide-eyed. Oh, rabbit, where are you going to run to now? There's nowhere to go.

Boom! The sky splits again.

She looks over her shoulder at the waves. I move closer. She kneels. Defeated. On her stomach, forcing herself to move, slipping away. She's trying to climb down the cliff. I've got to give her credit. She's a game little thing.

When I try to grab her wrist, she lets go and slides down the rock wall. For a moment she drops from sight. I think she's gone. I can't see her in the water. I lean out further and see a rock shelf only inches wide. She's balancing on her toes and clinging to two handholds.

A wave surges and smashes into the rock wall, creating a cloud of mist that engulfs her. She emerges, still clinging on. Foolishly brave. I feel sorry for her and almost proud.

She takes one hand off the cliff face and reaches into her pocket. What's that she's holding?

My legs fold under me and I try to stand. Nothing happens. I try again. *Up. Back. Stop. Engage. Forward.* It's like trying to stand in a canoe. Mr Parkinson is laughing at me. What good am I when I cannot keep my family safe? Julianne was right all along – this is my fault. I've brought this upon my family.

Visibility is so poor that I stumble from the path and almost run headlong off the cliff. Swaying on the edge, I glance down at the roiling sea, which buckles and bulges as though a sea monster is trying to breaking out of a white womb.

Brrrrrp-brrrrrp! Brrrrrrp-brrrrrrr!

I grip the mobile with both hands.

'*Daddy!*'

'Where are you?'

'*The waves are going to knock me off.*'

'I'm coming.'

'*I can't hold on. It's OK. I can swim.*'

'Don't go in the water!'

'*Did you find Emma?*'

'Yes.'

'*I'm going to fall . . .*'

'No.'

'Look for me!'
'Charlie? . . . Charlie? . . . CHARLIE!'

I draw my head back, open my throat and bellow her name, demanding to be heard by some higher power. I will *howl* Him into being. I will demand He help me.

Sucking in another breath, I charge forward. Time has slowed again. I see my daughter born, slick with amniotic fluid, her face scrunched up and her eyes open, full of wisdom and wonder. I see her at age two dancing to Van Morrison's 'Brown-Eyed Girl'. At four she's pulling a red wagon full of toys. At six she's going to school in an oversized tartan tunic that reaches below her knees. I see her picking blueberries, catching tadpoles, running under a sprinkler, chasing a Labrador across a field, riding a horse, blowing out birthday candles, playing Miss Dorothy Brown in a school play and holding my left hand when it trembles. A thousand such images blur together as though a giant pack of cards is being peeled back at the corner and released.

The rain is starting to ease. I can make out the shapes of trees and the edges of the path and the ridge above me, where fresh waterfalls are sweeping down and cascading from the cliffs.

A figure leaps from hiding to my left, smashing his fist into the side of my face. I hear my jaw crack and my knees buckle. Arms churn at nothing. He is younger, stronger. He is armed with a blade. I'm aware of him lifting my head, tilting it back, exposing my throat. He raises the box-cutter.

This is death. This is my death.

A bubble of time seems to expand and slow, heightening every sense. I must fight. I must call upon every memory of every failure. One chance. I drive my fist into his groin and he doubles over. The blade falls and skitters into a puddle.

He has his arm around my neck, tightening his elbow around my throat. I kick out, trying to get purchase on the muddy earth, clawing at his skin, grabbing at his clothes. My field of vision is darkening at the edges. My fingers are weakening. My legs shake. He grunts and squeezes harder, flexing his bicep.

My hand searches the puddle, opening and closing emptily. I'm being pulled by the blackness, drawn into the heaviest sleep, while behind my closed lids I see a spectacular explosion of cinders burning and fading. Darkness descends like a velvet curtain falling upon a stage. No applause. No encores. My fingers close around the box-cutter. I raise it with my left hand and bring it down along his thigh, severing his artery. He clutches at his leg. He mumbles, urging himself to do something, but his trousers are already turning red. I roll away as he rages, his head lashing from side to side, his shoe filling with blood, his breathing shallow . . .

'Where is she?' I yell. 'What have you done to her?'

He gets up. Falls. Half sits. Robbed. Desolate. He looks at the blood pumping from his leg.

'Where? Please?'

He points to the sea. Monk has reached us. He kneels beside Francis, pressing his fist into the wound, trying to stem the bleeding, but it's too late.

I'm standing on the edge of the cliff. A wave explodes against the rock shelf, creating a cloud of fine mist. I can't see anything. Monk is on his mobile. He's calling the coastguard and Royal Lifeboat crews.

I'm on my knees, my stomach.

'You can't go down there,' says Monk, grabbing my belt to stop me sliding forward.

'Hold me.'

I lean out further, looking into the maelstrom of white water. I scream her name. The sound hits a wall of wind. I try again, blinking into the spray.

'Did you hear that?' I glance at Monk. He's heard it too. We both listen. It's a hoarse baby-cry like a gull, startlingly close.

'She's down there?'

'You can't go – it's too dangerous.'

The waves suck back and I see Charlie's head bobbing in the swell. She's trying to swim away from the rocks, but is being swept back and hammered against the cliff-face. She won't survive.

I look at Monk. 'I have to go.'

'You'll kill yourself.'

'Let me do this.'

He doesn't hesitate. A man with a wife and three sons at home doesn't pause to reconsider. 'We go together,' he says. 'Wait for the next wave.'

Side by side we contemplate the jump as rain runs down our faces and the sky and sea are one.

'Now,' he screams, and we're running, falling. We hit the water feet first, plunging into the cold. *Kick. Surface. Breathe.* Salt stings my eyes. I can't see Monk or Charlie.

The water sucks away. I'm at the bottom of a trough, between the swells, and can feel rock beneath my feet and the cliff ahead. I see some sort of cave. Then I'm hit from behind by the next wave and carried forward, slamming into rocks. Curling into a ball, I try not to fight the current or lose my bearings. The water seems to be holding me under. I need to breathe. The wave sucks back. Air. Light.

I see Charlie. She's on the rocks, trying to climb. Monk is guiding her. He turns and yells for me to swim. I try to stand between the waves, but I can't feel my feet and the rocks are so slick with weed that I cannot get a footing. Water surges over me, sweeping me across the ledge towards the cliff. It tries to suck me back, but I cling on and crawl forward. I'm at the rock-face, reaching blindly for a handhold. Another wave smashes me from behind. It recedes. I drag myself higher.

The cave is twenty feet above me. Charlie is almost there. She can make it. Monk will keep her safe.

I've stopped moving. My body won't respond. *No! Not now! Not like this!* The following wave explodes over me and I feel as though I'm shattering into a million pieces, being scoured off the surface and washed away. I cling on. Climb. *Right hand. Pull. Left hand. Pull.*

Impossibly, I feel someone next to me. An arm slips around my waist.

'You can let go,' says Monk. 'You're here now.'

The cave isn't really a cave, but it's above the water and out of the wind. I've never been so pleased to be somewhere so wet and cold. Charlie is holding me or I'm holding her, both of us shaking.

I don't know how long we stay wrapped in each other's arms. Until there are lights and voices and men on ropes are coming down the cliff. They have thermal blankets and head torches. They lower a coffin-shaped cage and buckle Charlie inside. I'm next. They strap my arms and legs inside. Someone tugs on the rope. The cage lifts and swings out.

Monk puts his hand on my shoulder. 'You're a madman,' he says.

'I'm a father,' I want to answer, but the cage carries me away.

53

The paramedics let me ride with Charlie and Emma in the ambulance. The girls are talking, which is good, recounting what happened as though we've all been on a big adventure, but every so often I catch Charlie staring into space. Emma hasn't let go of my hand. She's still full of questions and observations.

'I wasn't scared of the thunder, but why did that man pull my hair? He made us hide in a bush. Look at my knee. Will I need stitches? Will it hurt? Grace Adema fell out of a tree and needed twelve stitches in her arm.'

We're taken to Weston General Hospital. My jaw is swollen, not broken, and Charlie has deep cuts in her hands and feet. The doctors poke and prod and bend limbs, shining torches into ears and eyes. I want to call Ruiz, but my mobile is somewhere at the bottom of the Severn Estuary.

Ronnie Cray stays with us at the hospital, which I appreciate. I keep asking about Julianne until she comes back with an update.

'She's critical but stable.'

'Ruiz?'

'He's with her.'

Cray talks about Francis Washburn, telling me how he changed his name in his teens after a string of convictions for assault and a stint in a psychiatric hospital in Leicester. He spent two years at a seminary, training to be a priest, but was dismissed following complaints from other students, who accused him of spying on them.

'You were right about the baby seat,' says Cray. 'Forensic services found traces of blood and the same household bleach.'

I ask whether Washburn survived, but know the answer already.

'You saved us the trouble of a trial,' says Cray.

That's twice I've taken a life, but I will not regret this one – not for a minute. I will not lose sleep or have nightmares over Francis Washburn. All I care about is my family and right now I want to see Julianne.

'Bennie is going to drive you,' says the DCS. 'She's waiting downstairs.'

It is almost ten o'clock by the time we leave one hospital and reach the other. The storm has passed, leaving air so clear that every star resembles a pinprick of light in a moth-eaten curtain.

Emma and Charlie are with me. We cross the foyer and take the stairs. The corridor seems to get longer as our feet echo down its length. Each time I think we're getting to the end there's further to go. A nurse suddenly appears. She asks me if I'm looking for someone. I can't get the words out.

'My wife . . . I want to see her.'

She looks at my swollen face and bandaged hands. 'Are you Mr O'Loughlin?'

'Yes.'

'Dr Percival wants to talk to you.'

'Where's Julianne?'

'If you'll just come with me.'

There are nurses in the background. Hovering. Not making

a contribution. I look for Ruiz. He should be here. Emma takes hold of my hand. I look at Charlie and see my own fears reflected back at me.

'Can we see Mummy now?' asks Emma.

'Soon,' I say, trying to sound upbeat. 'Are you hungry? Charlie can take you to the cafeteria.'

'It's closed,' says the nurse. 'There are vending machines.'

'I'm not leaving,' says Charlie.

'I'll look after the little one,' offers the nurse.

Emma complains and starts to cry. 'I want to see Mummy.'

'In a little while,' I say. 'Just do this for me.'

The nurse takes her hand. Emma looks put-upon, but she's too exhausted to fight.

A door opens and Dr Percival motions us inside. She doesn't seem surprised by the state of us – the borrowed clothes, bruises and bandages.

'Can I get you something? Coffee? Tea?'

'I want to see Julianne.'

'Of course, I understand, but first I want to explain the situation. There was a complication with your wife's surgery. It's quite rare, but not unknown. The operation itself was uneventful. She had normal vital signs throughout. I removed the tumour as well as her uterus. The cancer was at stage one, which is what we'd hoped. Everything was pretty textbook. We moved Julianne into postoperative recovery. She seemed perfectly OK. I'm told you talked to her.'

'Yes. What happened?'

'At 4.53 p.m. this afternoon she suffered a massive pulmonary embolism. We believe the clot originated in her lower extremities after the surgery. Fragments detached and travelled through the venous system, passing through the right side of the heart and lodging in the main branches of the pulmonary artery. The right ventricle was unable to maintain adequate forward blood flow and her heart failed. We started resuscitation with intubation and administered epinephrine, but it took nearly fifteen minutes to restore her spontaneous cardiac output. A chest radiograph confirmed the embolism. Thrombolytic therapy was started immediately. Having increased the doses with little effect, we operated, inserting a catheter into her upper thigh and threading it to the clot.'

'You found it?'

'Yes.'

'It's gone?'

'Dissolved.'

'And Julianne?'

She looks at Charlie and then me, her eyes over-bright and her voice wavering. 'As I said, it took us fifteen minutes to restore her heart. She had suffered a catastrophic haemodynamic collapse. Head CT scans are suggestive of hypoxic cerebral damage. We won't know for sure until she wakes, but at the moment she's stable. Comfortable. Not in pain.'

The room seems to tilt and I feel a fluttering sensation as though every time I blink I'm closing the shutter of a camera, taking another image. I hear laughter from the corridor outside. The world is carrying on. It doesn't care. Charlie is holding my hand. I can feel her fingers around mine.

'Can we see her?' I whisper.

'Of course.' Dr Percival gets to her feet. 'I'm very sorry, Joe. This couldn't have been foreseen.'

I don't answer. I have no words. I follow her down the waxed white-tiled floor, aware that muzak is playing as though we're in a Holiday Inn. She nods to the nursing station and a security door opens. Charlie whispers to me, 'What did she mean by cerebral damage?'

'Nothing. It's going to be fine. If you're going to have an embolism a hospital is a good place for it.'

'But she's in a coma.'

I can't answer her. As we walk along the corridor, I see Ruiz emerge from the ICU. He has withered since I saw him last, his big frame buckling under the weight of events or the sadness

387

pressing down upon him. How brittle he suddenly seems: how easily breakable.

My innards do a slow heave as he raises his eyes to mine. He pulls me into his arms, where I muffle a sob against his shoulder. He reaches out and grabs Charlie, bringing her into the hug.

'She's going to be OK,' he says. 'You can see her fighting. There's colour in her cheeks and she's breathing better just in the last hour.'

Ruiz notices our bandaged hands and the bruises on Charlie's forehead. He brushes back her hair. 'Are you all right, princess?'

She's gnawing at her bottom lip. 'It's my fault.'

'Don't say that,' says Ruiz.

'I shouldn't have gone to the nursing home.'

'You weren't to know he was there,' says Ruiz.

Charlie sneaks at a glance at me, wanting to know if I blame her.

'You're here and you saved Emma. Nothing else matters,' I say.

Dr Percival signals to us. We can see Julianne.

'I'm going to get some fresh air,' says Ruiz. 'Where's the little one?'

'A nurse is looking after her,' I reply.

'Maybe I'll catch up with them.'

He walks down the corridor, shuffling his feet like a little boy kicking at a empty can.

Charlie is ahead of me as we enter the ICU, moving past cubicles where desperately ill patients are being monitored by machines – wired, plugged in, taped up and ventilated.

I have been in places like this before, but never in circumstances that mirror this. I haven't seen my wife in a hospital bed since she told me our marriage was over and I had to move out. That was six years ago. Before that it was when Emma was born and before that Charlie. Now I see her, lying on a white sheet, the bed tilted, an oxygen tube up her nose, an IV, catheter and cardiograph wires and pads. She is at the mercy of machines, looking greenish white in the diffused light – like an astronaut shot into space on her way to Mars.

I take a seat in a chair beside the bed and stare at her face, willing her eyes to open. Charlie is holding her other hand, looking at the monitors, trying to make sense of the numbers.

'We have to talk to her,' I say. 'Tell her everything – old stories, new ones, but don't tell her about today.'

Charlie nods. She leans forward and puts her head on the bed next to her mother. We talk and talk and talk. When Charlie falls asleep, I keep going, talking as though my voice alone will keep Julianne alive. 'I am here,' I whisper, tracing the words on her skin, letter by letter on her open palm.

'I am here. I am here. I am here . . . '

54

In the days and weeks that follow I try to be all things to all people. I want to be a good father to Emma and Charlie, and to allay the grief of others. I accept their condolences. I make the arrangements. I decide on the service. I reply to the cards. And when it all gets too much for me, I lie on the floor of Julianne's walk-in wardrobe, surrounded by her clothes.

I comfort myself with the knowledge that she didn't feel a thing. She slipped into blackness, which is a nice way to go, much nicer than creaking and leaking into old age. That's the good thing about dying young. You don't have to lament too many mistakes or carry too great a burden of regret about the people you wronged or the dreams that were unfulfilled. It's much better to die in your prime, before the damage is done to your body or other people.

Through the rest of the summer and the autumn, Emma sleeps in Charlie's bed or mine. She's not frightened of the dark. She's afraid that the whole world will fall asleep and she'll be the only person left awake, fighting the night on her own.

Asleep or awake, Emma lives in constant readiness to save us from unhealthy foods, passive cigarette smoke, dangerous drivers, and men who would drag children from footpaths. She has no problem with the concept of death. She knows her mother isn't coming back, but believes she *will* see her again in Heaven. She also believes that evil comes in many guises – and that doctors and hospitals are to blame for what happened.

Charlie has been my rock. She has dealt with the day-to-day running of the cottage, making the meals and looking after Emma. She even cobbled me together from broken pieces so we could walk in front of the hearse, side-by-side, the three of us together. It was only a few hundred yards up Mill Hill Lane. Emma didn't want us walking in the middle of the road because she was scared someone might knock us over.

On the morning of the funeral Ruiz had found me lying on the floor between the sofa and a table, having consumed the best part of a bottle of Scotch. My arms shook. My legs shook. My head shook.

Emma saw me. 'What's wrong with Daddy?'

'He fell out of bed,' Ruiz told her.

'That's not his bed.'

'He's not feeling very well.'

Charlie got my medication and Ruiz stood me under a cold shower until I thought I was going to drown. Then he gave me the talk about how Julianne had loved me very much and would hate to see me falling apart when I had the girls to look after. To be honest, he said that I didn't deserve Julianne but then neither did anyone else. She had always been the smartest, funniest, kindest, most loyal person in the room.

They could have filled the church four times over with friends and family and people whose lives Julianne had touched. I cried for many reasons, mostly various forms of self-pity. I cried because I missed her. I cried for Charlie and for Emma. I cried because I was scared of death.

I measure time differently now. There is *before* Julianne and *after* her. Days have turned to weeks and then months. Friends keep telling me to 'keep busy' and to 'keep moving' and not to become morbid or stop to think. Well, maybe I want to become morbid. Maybe I want to wallow and to remember.

On my sad days, which are most days, I walk miles through familiar neighbourhoods and frayed knots of woodland and along rivers that twist slowly towards the sea. Julianne is with me. I talk to her. She listens. I tell her stories about the girls and try to make sense of what's befallen them . . . me . . . us.

I bear no ill will towards anyone. Having witnessed so much hurt from so many sources, I have begun to wonder if that's my function – to soak up pain, so that others are given sweeter, happier lives to lead. I know that's ridiculous and stupidly self-indulgent, but a grieving husband, running on fumes, will tell himself almost anything if it helps. He will sleep and forget, wake and remember – and be shocked by the news all over again.

He will drown and swim, suffocate and breathe. And sometimes, late at night, when he kicks off all the sheets, he will feel a finger trace a message on the palm of his hand.

I . . . AM . . . HERE . . .